Valley of **Spies**

VALLEY
of SPIES

KEITH YOCUM

Book cover design and typesetting by Stewart A. Williams

As always, for Denise

CHAPTER 1

He opened his eyes, but the glare was blinding, and he shut them.

"I think he just opened his eyes," someone said.

"Sir, can you hear me?" a man's voice floated from far away. "Hello? Sir, can you open your eyes?"

He opened his eyes again, closed them, and finally squinted through thin, watery slits. A man's face was only a foot away.

"Sir, can you hear me? Just nod if you can hear me."

He nodded.

"That's great. Can you open your eyes? Can you look at me? Yes, I'm right here. Can you see my hand? I'm waving it."

He nodded.

"Great. How are you feeling?"

He stared up at the face of a young man with dark hair and a white coat.

"Can you talk, sir? Can you tell us your name?"

He felt immense confusion as if he were locked inside a white room with white walls, a white table, and a white light. He tried to speak, but his lips felt leathery and cracked. He tried to raise his right hand to his face, but his hands would not move.

He craned his neck up from the pillow and looked at his hands. They were bound to the sides of his bed. He dropped his head back onto the pillow. He coughed.

"Sally, can you give me the water?" the man said.

He felt something on his lips and saw the man was pressing a straw from a container against his lips. He sucked and his mouth filled with cold water. He gulped huge amounts of the liquid until the overflow streamed down his chin and onto his chest.

"There you go," the man said.

He coughed, cleared his throat, and tried to speak, but only managed to gargle. He heard a motor humming and felt his head being raised.

"That should be better for you," the man said. "Now, can you speak? Can you tell us your name?"

He tried again to speak, but his tongue felt like it was fighting a mouthful of steel wool. He managed a word.

"What was that? What did you say?" the man said.

"Hand," he said.

"Hand? Did you say 'hand'?"

He nodded.

"I see. Your hands? Your hands are being kept in restraints. You're in a hospital. I'm afraid we were required to use restraints before you hurt yourself or someone else. Do you understand? You were brought into the hospital last night by the police. You were naked and had no identification. We'd like to know what your name is. Can you tell us? It would help us a great deal if we know who you are."

He closed his eyes. *Naked. No name. Hospital. Police.* He shook his head.

"You don't know your name?" the man asked. "Did you fall and hit your head? Did someone hit you? Were you taking any drugs, or were you drinking heavily, sir? Is there anything you can tell us about what happened last night?"

☉

Sixteen days earlier

It was a typical round of golf for Dennis. Relatively new to the sport, he had a few good holes, some bad holes, and some really, really bad holes. Even though it was winter in Western Australia, the day temperatures in July were often pleasant.

His playing partners were non-judgmental and friendly. Amateur golf, he discovered, is really an excuse to chase a small, dimpled white ball around a beautiful landscape just so you could gossip, grumble, and share stories for several hours. Afterward, you could sit around the clubhouse and rehash the intricacies of chasing the white ball through the landscape, all the while drinking alcohol.

Dennis played regularly with three men at golf courses around Perth. The best golfer of the group was Joe Parsons, an American executive working for a South African mining company. A small, compact man in his fifties, he was an excellent golfer with a low handicap and a laugh that broke the sound barrier.

Fergus McMaster – or Fergy – a tall, red-headed Aussie corporate lawyer in his late forties, was a solid golfer with a dry sense of humor and a penchant for profound self-abasement after a bad shot. "You bloody, bloody idiot," was his favorite phrase after launching one of the white balls into the bush.

And then there was Norman Cower, a diminutive Aussie retiree in his late sixties who played an indifferent game of golf but was charming, funny, and a genuinely nice fellow.

The four golfers sat around a small table in the clubhouse of the public golf course in Melville, nursing their second beers. Ordinarily, there would have been a spirited recap of the preceding round, with accompanying guffaws at lame putts or magnificent hooked or sliced drives into the surrounding landscape.

But today Dennis was not engaged in the conversation; instead, he was tense. He gripped the frosty beer glass with two hands as if he was steadying himself. The cause of his discomfort was the presence of two strangers sitting nearby.

The strangers sat at a table on the other side of the clubhouse sipping soft drinks and watching golfers finish up on the eighteenth hole.

The presence of the two men was rattling Dennis.

Ten months into early retirement from the CIA's Office of the Inspector General—OIG—he had constructed a new life in faraway Perth. He had followed Judy, his Australian girlfriend, to the quaint city on the west coast and settled down to golf, beaches, Aussie Rules Football – but not cricket, especially not cricket, the single most boring sport invented by mankind.

The stress of being one of the agency's internal policemen had receded nicely. He was near equilibrium in his new life; he no longer fidgeted and acted distracted in mixed company. The agency's bizarre, unorthodox employees and byzantine political forces were no longer his concern.

But those two men sitting at the table were agency people, and he could feel their presence. His felt his right foot tapping the floor nervously.

He recognized the classic agency procedure of agents announcing their presence; show yourself from a distance to alert the subject. Afterward, at another time and place, make a formal introduction. Most importantly avoid surprises. Surprises always create trouble.

"You with us today?" Fergy McMaster said to Dennis.

"Oh, yeah. Sorry. Just thinking."

"Was it the seventeenth hole you were thinking of?" Parsons said. "Thought for sure you were going to birdie that thing."

"Not to be," Dennis said. "One day I'll learn how to putt."

"Maybe we all will," Cower said. The group laughed.

"Excuse me for a second, guys," Dennis said.

He pushed back his chair, stood, and strode quickly across the room. He loomed over the two men.

"What the hell do you want?" he said.

"Nothing," said the older of the two, a man in his forties with thick, wavy gray hair.

"Why are you here?" Dennis said.

"We're watching golf," he said, with a Midwest American accent.

"I could smell you from way over there," Dennis said. "Sort of like rotten eggs, but worse. More like horse shit."

"Mmm," the older man said.

"So get lost," Dennis said.

"Sure," the man said. "We're almost done."

Dennis returned to the table, sat down, and took a huge gulp of beer.

"Friends?" Fergy asked, looking at the two men as they left the clubhouse.

"Hardly," Dennis said, his eyes tracking the men as they left.

⊙

The drive southeast toward Mandurah was pleasant enough, though Judy was distracted.

"What's on your mind, Jude?" Daniel, her Australian Federal Police partner asked. "Not that Yank boyfriend of yours is it?"

She smiled. "No, it's not Dennis. Well, not directly him. Just every-thing. And nothing."

"Why are women so mysterious," Daniel asked. "They have these secret lives that men just can't understand. I swear sometimes that Monica is not really paying attention when I talk to her. We've been married fourteen years, and have two children, but I sometimes feel she's not really there, you know?"

"Oh, Monica is there," Judy said. "Perhaps you need to ask what she's thinking about."

"I have, and she just says, 'Oh, nothing really.'"

"Well then, I would let it go," Judy said.

They drove in silence until Judy said, "Who are we meeting with again?"

"The senior sergeant down there. Fellow named Murphy."

"And why are we meeting with him?"

"He says that there's a young fella that we should talk to. I guess the fella lives at home in Golden Bay with his parents. The parents have gone to the police several times complaining of their son's odd behavior and his unsavory friends. They think he might be into drugs. The sergeant suspects the son might be involved in the distribution of methylamphetamine, and he requested help from the AFP to visit the parents."

"What can we possibly get from talking to the parents?" Judy said.

"Now don't start, Jude. The sergeant down there doesn't quite know what do with this meth problem. And it's a nice day for a drive."

"Mmm," Judy said, staring at the flat landscape. "Righto then."

⊙

Senior Sergeant Murphy was remarkably rotund, and Judy wondered what the physical standards were for police in Western Australia.

"It's just that his parents keep calling me," Murphy said. "I've talked to the fella once when I saw him in town here at the chemist. He looked sick. I mean, I'm not an expert in this drug situation. I can't say that he is dealing drugs, or not dealing drugs. And, well, you're the experts. Being with the Task Force and all."

Judy looked at Daniel.

"I guess we'll go out and talk to the parents then," Daniel said. "Is the son home now?"

"Don't know about that," Murphy said. "Should I ring his parents?"

"No need for that," Daniel said. "We'll take care of it."

The house was thirty minutes from the police station. A neighborhood grid of traditional, one-story homes with small yards and red tile roofs spread out east from the town's popular beaches.

Judy pulled her coat tight as she stepped outside. Winter in the southern hemisphere had moderated over the past decade, but there were still cold spells like this one. They walked up a chipped and cracked concrete path to a small flight of steps and onto the covered porch. Daniel knocked on the rock-solid jarrah wood door.

Judy could hear movement inside and she shivered a little in the cold. The door cracked open, and a man in his early fifties put his head out.

"Can I help you?" he said.

"Are you Steven Cappocia?"

"Yes. And who are you?"

"My name is Daniel Carson, from the Australian Federal Police in Perth. This is my colleague Judy White. We understand that you have been in contact with Senior Sergeant Murphy here about your son."

The father took a quick glance inside his house, then stepped outside and closed the door behind him.

"Yes, well, my wife and I have had some concerns about Nick for some time. We don't quite know what to do about it. My wife has MS and is in a wheelchair, and I need to be available to care for her."

Judy and Daniel nodded but waited for more.

"And well, our son Nick, he's changed over the last year or so. Doesn't work any longer, but he's not on the dole. He has a nice car, you can see over there."

The two officers panned to the driveway and noticed a new black Mini Cooper with red racing stripes.

"Is your son home now?" Judy asked.

"Yes, he is, but I think he's sleeping. He sleeps a lot during the day."

"Sergeant Murphy said you and your wife are concerned that he might be involved in drugs. Is that so?" Judy asked.

"Perhaps. Yes. But again, we don't know much about drugs. We were hoping that the sergeant could come and have a talk with Nick. You know, we reckon Nick would get the message that he needs to stop what he's doing. That's if he's doing anything. We're not sure of anything, really. These young people are difficult to understand."

The father shivered a bit in the cold and stared at Daniel, then Judy, then back at Daniel. No one spoke as a car drove by in the street.

"Would you like us to talk to Nick?" Daniel asked.

"He's still sleeping," the father said. "He's sometimes in a disagreeable mood if we wake him. He can be quite cross."

"Why don't you try to wake him?" Judy said.

The father frowned, he turned and as he put his hand on the door, it flew open.

Nick glared at Judy and Daniel.

"Who are these wankers?" Nick said to his father.

"Police, son. They just stopped by."

"What do they want? You," he said jutting his chin at Daniel, "what the fuck do you want?"

"Son, watch your language please."

"Shut the fuck up," Nick said stepping onto the porch toward Daniel.

"I assume you're Nick Cappocia," Daniel said.

"No, I'm Father fucking Christmas," he said.

Judy felt an electrical current of fear. Years of working with violent people had sharpened her instincts. She had seen this kind of behavior before from angry men: they would instantly ignore her and move to exert control over the male policeman.

This young man was gaunt and yellowish in pallor. Judy noticed a scab on his right cheek and the stubble of a beard. It was his eyes, though, that bothered Judy. They were wild and bulged like small ping pong balls. Daniel took a step back.

"What are you staring at?" Nick said to Daniel.

"Relax, mate. We're just talking to your father."

"He's an idiot. If you have something to say, say it to my face, copper."

"Nick, there's nothing to get upset about," Judy said.

"Who's talking to you, cunt."

"Nick, watch your language!" his father said.

In her years on the force, Judy had heard about every possible combination of curse words and invective in the English language. But the one word she could not tolerate was the four-letter word Nick had just uttered. She didn't know why it made her blood boil, but Judy felt a rage building as she stared at the spindly young man.

Daniel had seen Judy react to that curse many times before, and he hurried to head her off.

"Nick, there have been reports that you may be involved in drugs, and we're here to ask you about that."

The young man took a step back from Daniel, swiveled his head to look at his father, turned and re-entered the house slamming the door shut.

"Oh, that did not go well," the father said. "Perhaps you both should leave now."

"Are you sure you and your wife will be alright?" Judy said.

"Yes, he'll calm down I'm sure. He's agitated right now."

Daniel and Judy thanked Cappocia for talking to them and said they'd follow up with Murphy. The father nodded, shook their hands, and returned inside.

They walked to the street, both glancing at the new Mini Cooper. Reaching their car, Daniel opened the driver's side door, while Judy walked to the passenger side. The front door of the house suddenly flew open behind them, slamming against the outside wall. The two turned to see Nick standing on the porch steps. He held a large pistol in his extended right hand.

The first shot shattered the driver's side window and the second hit the driver's side door with a thud.

Daniel dove across the hood of the car landing in a heap on the other side of the car; Judy had fallen and moved to shelter behind the rear wheel. She fumbled for her gun, pulling it out of the holster.

Two more rounds hit the other side of the car as Judy glanced at Daniel. Nick screamed unintelligibly and walked toward the car. Daniel had his gun out and peered around the front bumper at the approaching shooter.

"Nick! Son, come here!" his father yelled from the porch. "Stop it, Nick!"

"Dad, they're trying to kill me!"

"No, they're not! Just come here now. Now!"

Judy and Daniel looked at each other behind the car. In the small, strange world of police work, the two officers knew they were milliseconds away from being forced to kill or be killed. In policedom, events sometimes unfold so quickly that officers are forced to make instantaneous decisions: either shoot or be shot or both.

Judy craned her neck and peered underneath the car and saw Nick walking back to the front door. Her palms were wet around the pistol grip. For the first time, she noticed her right wrist was bleeding from scraping the asphalt as she dropped behind the car.

"Here, give me the gun," the father said.

"They were going kill to me!"

"Well, it's all over now. Just hand me the gun. Why don't you go lie down for a while?"

The front door slammed, and Judy saw the sad, hunched figure of the father holding the warm pistol.

CHAPTER 2

She rested her head on his left shoulder as they lay in bed. Judy inspected his chest hairs, twisting and turning a few of them. She wore her pajamas, while Dennis sported his old gym shorts and was bare-chested.

"I think this is a gray hair," she said.

"I don't have gray hair on my chest," Dennis said.

"Right here," she said pulling at a strand.

"Must be someone else's."

"No, it's yours. Getting old, Mr. Cunningham."

Judy continued to fiddle with his chest hairs, cozying up to his left side as Dennis watched CNN with the sound muted.

"Are you OK?" he said.

"Yes."

"You don't seem to be OK."

"I don't?"

"No."

"How can you tell?"

"You seem pensive. And distracted. Or something."

"You're exaggerating."

"And it's not every day that you get shot at by a meth addict."

Judy sighed and rolled over onto her back and stared at the ceiling.

"No, it's not every day; just some days," she said.

"I'm not really crazy about this police job of yours. I know you've been doing it for a while and are good at it. But can't you get a desk job away from these crazies?"

"You should talk," she said, rolling again toward him and placing her left leg over his thigh. "You were almost killed several times at the agency."

"But I quit, remember?"

"Yes, that's true. Perhaps I'll quit."

"You'd do that? Really?"

"The way I feel today, yes. The part that's so difficult is how this job goes from complete boredom to a killing zone in seconds. You think you know what to expect, but it just shocks you. I mean, that little bastard could have killed Daniel."

"And you."

"Yes, I know."

"Why don't you ask for one of those cushy desk jobs?"

"They don't just give desk jobs to agents because you ask for it, Dennis. Besides, I'm one of the few women agents in the AFP here in the west, and how would it look if I begged to get off the street? Another weak female who can't handle the pressure and needs to be coddled?"

"I'm just thinking of all the stress you're under, and the stress that I'm under worrying about you at work."

"Let's not talk about me any longer. How about you? What was your day like? How was golf?"

"Golf was fun, but I had some visitors."

Judy pulled back from Dennis and sat up on her elbow.

"What visitors?"

"Two idiots."

"Can you *please* speak English? What do you mean 'two idiots'?"

"Two guys from the agency were at the clubhouse. They just want me to know they're here."

"What are they doing here?"

"They'll make contact soon enough."

"Dennis, you're retired, correct? They have no right to contact you."

"They can do whatever they want. I have no intention of talking to them. Don't worry."

Judy sat up in bed and turned toward Dennis, crossing her legs and looking down at him as he stared at the TV.

"Dennis, don't you think this is very strange."

"Yes, a little. But remember it's a strange organization."

"Can't they just leave you alone? Why can't you report them?"

"Report them to who?"

"I don't know, someone important."

"Calm down. After what you went through today, I was almost afraid to tell you. In fact, I shouldn't have."

Judy stared at him, then slid back next to him in bed, and remained silent for several minutes.

"It is a gray hair," she said twisting a coiled strand. "Definitely gray."

⊙

Dennis had settled into a rhythm, of sorts, in his new life. While Judy lived in a single-family house in the suburb of Bicton, they decided that they would officially live apart while her son Trevor attended university in Nedlands. They spent almost all their nights together, mostly at his apartment on Wellington Street.

They never talked directly about marriage, though there was an assumption that as Dennis became more comfortable in his new setting that they would tie the knot.

After Judy left for work most mornings, Dennis would shower and, weather permitting, take a walk down five blocks to Langley Park next to the Swan River. He would hike either toward Lake Vasto or down to the Bell Tower. The winter weather was colder in Perth than he anticipated, and walking was more bracing than enjoyable. But he liked getting out and moving about.

After his walk, he would stop at a sleek, modern coffee shop on Hill Street and have several flat white coffees and a pastry. He bought two newspapers and read them thoroughly, finally getting back to the apartment by 10:30 a.m.

He had just returned from one of his walks when he heard a knock at the front door. He opened the door and saw the two men he'd seen at the clubhouse.

Before the older of the two could speak, Dennis slammed the door shut and returned to his laptop in the small kitchen.

The visitors continued to knock, with little pauses in between. The knocks got louder, until Dennis flew out of his chair, raced to the door, flung it open, and yelled, "If you two don't stop that shit, I'm calling the police."

Again, he slammed the door before they could finish speaking, but not before he heard the words "your visa" yelled at him.

He stood motionless inside the door.

"Cunningham, you better listen," he heard through the door. "They're going to revoke your goddamn visa if you keep this shit up. We're just messengers. You need to calm your ass down and listen to what we have to say. Otherwise, they're going to make sure your visa is revoked. Got that? Serious shit if you keep acting like an asshole."

Dennis faced the closed door, his head pointed down as he stared at the floor tiles. In the ten months decompressing from his career in the agency, Dennis had relaxed to the point of boredom. But he liked being a little bored, and he thought it suited him nicely.

Now, with the two messengers just feet away from him on the other side of the door, he felt the old tension rise in his shoulders and neck. His jaw tightened, and he took shorter, shallower gulps of air.

Revoke your visa? What the hell were they talking about? he thought. *My travel visa is good for two more months.*

He opened the door again. The three men stared at each other as the cold air from outside poured into the apartment.

Dennis turned and walked into the apartment, leaving the door open behind him. The two men walked in, closed the door, and followed him into the living room.

"Can we sit down?" the older man asked.

Dennis shrugged. The men sat down on the couch, but Dennis remained standing.

"Be better if you just sat down and relaxed," the older man said.

Dennis sat down and tried his best to remain calm. He swallowed several times as if doing so would contain his anger.

"Listen, we know this is upsetting you, Cunningham. We don't like this any more than you do. We have a job and it's to deliver a message to you. Simple as that. Then we're out of here."

"What's this visa thing you mentioned?" Dennis barked.

"Well, given your reluctance to even hear us out, we were directed to tell you that unless you talked to us, they were going to get your visa revoked."

"My travel visa from Australia that's good for 12 months?"

"Yes, of course—that visa."

"Who's going to do the revoking?"

"Jesus, Cunningham, who do you think?"

"The agency would come all the way over here, to this remote little city, and threaten to revoke my travel visa? Give me a break."

"You know they can do that. But no one wants to do that. We were instructed to use the threat as a last resort to get you to talk."

Dennis sighed, swallowed again, feeling his Adam's apple bob viciously.

"The fact that I'm no longer an employee hasn't gotten through to anyone? Why are you folks playing heavy with me? I'm a nobody retiree playing golf or trying to play golf. Revoke my fucking visa? You assholes."

"Listen, Cunningham," the younger of the two finally spoke up, "all you have to do is listen to us. We'll make this quick. The director wants to talk to you about a sensitive matter. That's all. You just need to chat with him for a few minutes. That's all. Just chat. After that, we'll leave you alone. It's simple. No need to get worked up. Right, Bill?"

The older man nodded.

Dennis closed his eyes to keep from looking at the two men, and he took several long, measured breaths. He opened his eyes.

"You want me to talk to the director on the phone for a few minutes, and you've come all this way to threaten to pull my visa if I don't?"

"No, not on the phone," the younger man said. "Talk to him in person."

"OK. Let me do this again: You two have come all this way to ask me to fly back to Langley to talk to the director of the Central Intelligence Agency for a few minutes. Or else you'll yank my visa and force me out of the country? I've never met the director and have no idea who he or she is."

"No, that's not it," the younger man said. "Tell him, Bill."

"No," the older man said, "the director will be here tonight. All you have to do is meet with him. Maybe ten or fifteen minutes, max. All done. Game over."

"Wait. Did you say the director of the Central Intelligence Agency – the same guy who's in charge of 21,000 employees and has a budget of about $15 billion – is going to come to visit me in Perth to chat for ten minutes? Have either of you been drinking or using illegal substances?"

The young man chuckled. "The director is flying through to Singapore and is planning a stopover at the airport here. He's not going to leave the plane. We'll escort you there. You chat. You leave, he leaves. All done."

"You didn't answer my question?"

"What question?"

"What are you drinking, smoking, or injecting?"

⊙

"That's preposterous!" Judy said.

"I agree, but what the hell am I to do? I don't want my visa pulled. I like it here, not to mention what it would do for us being apart again."

She sat in her small office, mobile phone to her ear, scribbling a series of shapes on a pad of paper.

"I don't want you to leave Perth," she said.

"Well, I don't want to leave either. And I can tell these two guys are for real. They don't like it any more than I do."

"The director of the CIA is coming to Perth?"

"He's supposedly stopping over for a while. I'll just go along, listen to whatever he has to say, and then leave."

"That's not how it's going to go, and you know it."

"What do you mean?"

"Aren't you suspicious about the director just chatting with you? When you enter that plane, who's to say the director will even be in there? You're just walking onto a plane. You've trained me to be suspicious about anything your former employer does, and now you want to walk serenely onto an empty American plane?"

"Well, yes, that is a little odd. But I haven't done anything. They wouldn't just arrest me. I didn't do anything."

"Do you think they opened an old case or something?"

Dennis paced around the apartment with the phone to his ear.

"No, my instinct—to the extent I have any of that left—is that this isn't some kind of crazy rendition of a former employee. They wouldn't bother with a complicated ruse like the director and his plane to do that. They'd just grab me at a coffee shop."

Dennis stopped walking. "Or would they? Shit, there's no way I'm walking onto that damn plane."

"They must be bluffing about your visa," Judy said.

"Shit! I'm just minding my own goddamned business on the other side of the world. Why are they doing this? I haven't done anything."

Judy kept doodling in big circles and Dennis started pacing again. Neither spoke as each processed this strange request.

"If it's one thing you've taught me," she said, "it's that you can't trust anything they say. Any of them."

⊙

The knock was quiet, almost timid.

Dennis opened the door and the two men stared at him.

"Ready?" Bill, the older one, said.

"I'm not going."

"What?"

"I'm not going."

"You can't bail now, Cunningham."

"Why can't I? Go ahead and yank my visa. I don't give a shit. Do you think I'm dumb enough to walk onto a government airplane, probably a military flight, and expect to talk to the director of the Central Intelligence Agency? Just for a cozy chat? You two are the dumbest fucking bunch of idiots to think you could just talk me onto a plane by showing up and asking."

"I told you, Bill," the young one said.

"Yeah, Bill, he told you," Dennis said.

"Shut up," Bill said to Dennis. "You've just complicated a very simple effort to get you ten or fifteen minutes with the director." He looked at his watch. "Shit, the plane lands in an hour."

For the first time, Bill looked really, really pissed off, and Dennis felt his anger like the glow of a heat lamp. He also recognized the anger as that of a bureaucrat who would be forced to explain a plan gone awry. It was the de-personalized anger of all bureaucrats, but it was still anger.

"You realize the director diverted his flight to land at Perth International Airport, just to talk to you? Do you know how pissed he'll be?"

"He'll be pissed at you, or your boss, not at me. He doesn't know me from a hole in the wall. That's even if he's on the plane. And let me remind you two Einsteins that you haven't even shown me your IDs, and even if you did, there's no way I can verify they're real. Go cancel my visa, kids. Have a good night."

Dennis swung the door shut, but Bill had placed his foot in the doorway and the door bounced back open.

"Cunningham, please don't make us get crazy. We have very specific orders to get you to that plane to meet with the director. We have no reason to believe he's not on the plane, but as you probably already know, we're two goofballs that have orders, and we're determined to complete those orders. Your job is to come along."

"No, my job is to stay here and watch TV with my girlfriend, who, by the way, is an agent of the Australian Federal Police."

Judy stepped into view down the small hallway behind Dennis. Bill sighed heavily.

"We know who she is, Cunningham. We've read her file."

"Yeah, well, move your foot, Bill, so I can close the door."

"Can't do that."

"You'll have to, or it might end up broken."

"Hey, Judy," the young man said suddenly. "Why don't you come with us to the airport? You can keep Cunningham company in the car and wait for him on the tarmac. After he comes out of the plane, we'll drive both of you back here. With an agent of the AFP in attendance, you can't possibly think we're going to do anything crazy. We typically avoid international incidents with strategic partners."

CHAPTER 3

Judy had her arm snugly around Dennis's as the rental car sped through the early evening rush hour. None of the four people in the car uttered a word. Dennis and Judy sat in the back. Dennis stared morosely at the smear of lights flashing by in the darkness.

A part of him was nervous for precisely the reasons that Judy had raised: how could you ever trust the agency? He was painfully aware of the corrupting influences of power, money, and secrecy exerted on the country's intelligence services.

Yet, embarrassingly, there was another sliver of Dennis's brain that was excited as they drove through the darkness. His life since early retirement was empty of raw excitement. Dennis was reluctant to admit he missed the thrill of hunting down those miscreants that gave the agency endless amounts of trouble.

The reason his boring life in Australia had worked so far was the thrill of being near the woman he had fallen in love with. Still, although he kept it secret from her, he was bored.

The younger man drove the car past the departure lanes at the airport and around to a section for employee parking. Judy clutched Dennis's arm tightly.

They approached a chain-link gate that did not have a gatehouse. It looked innocuous enough, she thought, except for the black SUV on the other side of the gate. They stopped several feet from the gate, and Bill got out and walked to the gate. He spoke briefly to another man on the other side. He returned to the car as the gate slid open.

Judy craned her neck to look for a parked jet but there were only several huge aviation hangars illuminated with flood lights. Their car followed the black SUV as it navigated a well-marked driving lane past the hangars toward another set of hangars farther away. They eventually turned a corner and came upon a towering Boeing 747. A humming generator truck fed it from ground level. A walk-up gangway was connected to an open rear door that shined brightly from within.

A small white utility van was parked near the bottom of the gangway, where the SUV pulled up. The car stopped, and Bill turned to Dennis.

"Just so we're clear on what's going to happen, Cunningham, you're going to be searched and wanded. You'll need to leave every single piece of metal behind before you enter the plane. The aircraft is one of the most secure in the world, as you can imagine, and no one is allowed on it without being one hundred percent cleared of any potential eavesdropping devices. Got it?"

"Any anal probes?" Dennis said.

"Not unless you request it," Bill smirked.

"Just checking."

Judy shook her head and sighed. She could never understand Dennis's sense of humor at tense moments like this. She held his arm tightly.

"It's going to be alright, Judy," he said gently prying her arm from his.

Bill got out of the car and opened Dennis's door. As he did, the back of the van opened, and two men got out and surrounded Dennis. One held a hand scanner, and the other ran his hands repeatedly over Dennis's body. They removed his watch, his wallet, and a pair of reading glasses in his jacket pocket, his mobile phone, and his belt.

As they led him to the gangway, he turned and gave thumbs up to Judy. She waved.

Inside the running car, Judy stared up at the bulbous US Air Force jet. She bit the inside of her lip, sighed, and sat back in the seat.

"I know you don't trust us," the young man said looking in the rearview mirror at Judy, "but he's going to meet with the director, and he'll be back out before you know it. I'm sorry this is so distressing for you."

"Distressing is not the word I was thinking of," she said.

"What word were you thinking of?"

"Several words, actually. Like 'What the hell is wrong with you people?'"

"I see," he said.

⊙

Dennis was relieved to see the jet, which he recognized as the Air Force's E-4B, or National Airborne Operations Center. A modified Boeing 747, it was the designated secure airplane for the Director of the CIA when traveling overseas.

Dennis followed a strikingly tall, casually dressed agent up the steps, with Bill behind him. They entered the plane's rear door and were led through a small kitchen into a walled-off lounge area, with two couches in an L shape to his left, and several stuffed chairs to his right. All the furniture was bolted securely to the floor, and the comfy upholstery gave the room the feel of a Hilton business suite.

The lounge area was empty, and the tall agent directed Dennis to sit down on one of the small couches. Both the agent and Bill sat down on the couch facing him. While they sat, Dennis heard someone walk up the gangway, step into the plane, and pull the door shut.

He was not prepared for this lock down and reflexively stood up.

"Hey," Bill said. "Chill out. You can't leave a door open to the outside world. Anyone can train a parabolic disc on that door and listen to what's being said."

Dennis sat, but he was not content. He kept his eyes on the hands of the tall agent; the hands don't lie. He knew the tall, buff, and stonecold agent sitting across from him would be the heavy in an altercation.

After several awkward minutes of silence, a door to the small lounge opened, and the face of a thin-lipped, gray-haired man with blue-gray eyes scanned the room, and then disappeared. Almost immediately, the door opened again and in walked the diminutive, slightly rotund figure of CIA director Kenneth Franklin, or Kenny, as the media referred to him. He was followed by the gray-haired man.

Everyone stood, including Dennis.

"For god sakes, sit," Franklin said.

The director walked over and thrust his hand out to Dennis, who shook it.

"Pleased to meet you, Mr. Cunningham," he said smiling broadly. "Boy, you sure have one of the most interesting files I've read. Amazing stuff, albeit some of it is an embarrassment to the agency. You got the worst of it from several of our more wayward folks, and I'm sorry for that."

Franklin sat directly across from Dennis, while the gray-haired man sat on one of the open stuffed chairs to the side.

"Bet you're wondering what you're doing, sitting in an E4-B with the director in Perth, Western Australia?" he laughed.

Dennis tried to smile back, but his teeth were clenched, and his earlier caution had been replaced by paranoia. *Yes*, he thought, *what the hell am I doing here?*

"I don't blame you if it seems a little strange," Franklin said, leaning back. "But everything we do seems a little strange to the outside world." He laughed again, and this time Bill and the gray-haired man chuckled in the cynical, inside-baseball way Dennis had seen many times before.

"Hey, Phil," Franklin said to the gray-haired man, can you ask Stephanie if she could take an order?"

"Dennis—you don't mind if I call you Dennis, do you?—this is Phil Simpson, deputy director of operations. Simpson shook hands with Dennis and then left through the door into the belly of the giant airplane.

"I never know what time zone I'm in," Franklin said. "These international trips are not my favorite part of the job." He laughed, and Dennis tried and failed yet again to smile in return.

The door opened, and a young, short dark-haired woman wearing a white cotton blouse and dark-blue slacks entered. Dennis guessed she was Air Force from her short, military bob and modest earring studs.

"Sir, can I get you a Diet Coke?" she said to Franklin.

"Stephanie, that would be great. And you, Dennis, what can we get you? We have everything, including beer, wine, and the hard stuff."

"Nothing, thanks."

"Oh come on, Dennis. If I'm going to sit here and drink a Diet Coke, you need to have something. Coffee? Beer?"

"Water."

"Still or bubbly?" Stephanie asked.

"Still, thanks."

She left, though Phil had never returned after leaving to fetch her, and Franklin seemed to notice his absence. He reached for a small phone set on the wall beside him and picked it up, pushed a button, and said, "Is Phil up there? Can you send him back, please? Thanks."

He hung up and smiled at Dennis.

⊙

"Can I get outside for a minute?" Judy asked. "I need to stretch my legs."

"No, ma'am. You can't do that—" but Judy had already exited the car onto the tarmac.

The young man bolted out of the car and raced to Judy.

"Please get back in the car, miss."

"Oh, now it's 'miss.' Just a second ago it was 'ma'am.'"

"Please get back in the car, ma'am. Please. You're not supposed to be out of the car and I'll be reprimanded severely. Please?"

With the glare of flood lights from the plane illuminating only one side of his face, Judy guessed he was perhaps thirty-five years old. His bristly, short black hair stood straight up, as if in alarm. His dark eyes were pleading with her, and for a moment she felt sorry for him.

"What's your name?"

"My name? Ma'am, please. Just get in the car." He glanced wildly around the tarmac.

"Your name?"

"My name is Joe," he said. "Please!"

"Do your friends call you Joe, Joey, or Joseph?"

"Oh Christ, they call me Joe."

"OK, Joe, I'll get back in." He yanked open the door, she slid in, and he closed it behind her.

He raced back to the driver's seat and they sat in silence, while Joe kept looking at his mobile phone.

After several minutes, he said, "Actually, my friends call me Joey."

"Alright, Joey, can you answer one question?"

"I'll try."

"Am I going to see Dennis again?"

Joey twisted abruptly to face her. "I think you're a little too cynical, ma'am. Not everything we do is so diabolical."

"Says who?" she said.

He turned again to face the front. "You're a tough one," he said. "We didn't expect that."

⊙

Phil returned to the lounge area, and the small group of men stared at the director.

"So, I understand you quit the agency about ten months ago," Franklin said. "You were involved in a very complicated case involving a missing employee from the London station."

Dennis shrugged. Of course, all that was true, but it was a pitifully short summary to a painful case involving duplicitous employees of the great agency that Franklin ran.

"And I gather you were nearly killed by a foreign entity while pursuing the case, which is a high price to pay for anyone in service of the agency," Franklin said, pausing for another sip of Diet Coke.

"You mean 'in service of the inspector general,'" Dennis said. "I wasn't serving the agency, I was serving the internal department that investigates the agency."

"Ah yes, well, that office is an agency department," Franklin said. "We're all on the same team."

"No, actually they're not. The inspector general has three bosses: you and the two congressional intelligence committees. That was done to keep it an independent group."

"You might be splitting hairs very closely there," Franklin said, "but I grant you that your old department has a unique purview over the agency's business."

Franklin took another sip of soda, and the sound of a nearby airliner taking off shook the plane momentarily. Dennis found Franklin's demeanor friendly and not particularly intimidating. He seemed genuinely friendly toward Dennis, but Dennis was not lulled into a false sense of camaraderie. High achievers like Franklin get ahead in the world for precisely these kinds of people skills, not in spite of them.

"I'm sure you understand then how complicated the intelligence business is, with operations simultaneously unfolding throughout the world. My task is to make sense of all this and provide adult supervision."

Dennis kept his gaze on the director, but peripherally he noticed that all sets of eyes were on Dennis, as if he was the critical element in the day's drama, sitting in a jet on an isolated patch of the runway in an isolated city on an isolated continent.

"Sir, if you don't mind, can I ask why I'm here?" Dennis said. "I'm not an employee, and I'm not aware of any reason why we're having this conversation." He noticed that all eyes in the lounge now slid to the director as if they were a crowd in the bleachers at a tennis match.

"Well, they said you were quite direct, and I guess they were right," Franklin said. "I'm meeting with you because I have a problem."

Dennis expected Franklin to continue, but he didn't. Instead, Simpson suddenly asked Bill and the tall agent to give them some privacy, and he opened the door into the plane's interior. After they left, Simpson closed the door, sat, and said, "You understand of course that anything that is discussed today is still covered by your oath of secrecy."

Dennis did not like being cornered by this sudden legalistic imperative.

"Cunningham, did you hear me?" Simpson said leaning toward him. "Please acknowledge."

Dennis said nothing.

"Damnit, Cunningham, acknowledge!"

"It's OK," Franklin said raising his hand toward Simpson. "I'm sure we have his understanding on this."

"It's like this," Franklin said looking out the small window into the darkness, "there was an incident involving someone that is important to the agency. After a comprehensive investigation by Simpson's group in Operations, it was determined that a foreign country was involved in this incident. The incident was very serious, and typically, in cases like this, we'd authorize a counterstrike against the foreign service. But these things can quickly get out of hand, especially" – here he looked at Simpson – "if we had it wrong about who was involved. Do you get where I'm going with this?"

"No."

Franklin shifted in his seat, folded his hands together in his lap, and for the first time seemed frustrated.

"Simpson's group and several other very capable professionals recommend that the agency act aggressively toward another country's foreign intelligence service. I have the greatest respect, of course, for Operations"—he nodded to Simpson—"but I'm reluctant to approve the action without one more pass at due diligence. I'm not afraid to order the deaths of some foreign nationals, Cunningham, but those deaths will likely lead to the deaths of our agency personnel. It's a tit-for-tat world, and they'll come back after some of our people. I want to be certain it's the correct thing to start, or as certain as anyone can get in this business. Does that make sense?"

"I guess so."

"I'm under tremendous pressure to move ahead on this project. It's very sensitive and has people worried at the agency and elsewhere. The Director of National Intelligence is waiting for my recommendation."

Franklin fiddled with his fingers as they rested in his lap. He turned and peered out the small window again into the darkness.

"What do I have to do with any of this?" Dennis said. "I'm just a tad confused right now."

"Ah, the reason is that you might be part of the solution," he said, reaching for his Diet Coke. "One of my assistants suggested you were good at finding people, or at least finding out what happened to people.

I didn't know we had folks with that kind of special expertise, but we do. You're the expert I was looking for." He took a big gulp and smiled at Dennis.

Dennis laughed. "Me? Didn't we just agree that I am no longer in the agency? I'm retired."

"But you're perfect for this kind of thing," Franklin said. "You have no ax to grind, are suspicious about everyone's motives, I'm told, and come at this with a fresh set of eyes. I need someone just like you to give this investigation one more go. Either confirm or dispute the conclusions that I'm working with. I need more certainty than I have now."

Dennis took a small sip of water.

"Um, thank you for your consideration, but I can't help you. I'm done with this kind of work. Sorry." Dennis stood.

"Please sit down until the director is finished," Simpson said.

Dennis sat down.

"Aren't you just a bit curious about who recommended you for this job?" Franklin said.

"No, I could care less."

"Well, this person seemed to think you were a natural, especially since you knew the missing person quite well."

⊙

The drive back to the apartment was quiet except for the swooshing of cars passing by in the night. Judy held Dennis's arm tightly and except for a moment when he returned to the car, she avoided looking at him. Nevertheless, there was tension in his arm muscles, and she noticed his head pointed straight ahead and never swiveled.

My God, what did they do to him? she thought. *It's taken ten months for him to decompress, and now, in a matter of minutes, he has that look again.*

The car stopped in front of the apartment, and they got out without exchanging a word with their escorts. Dennis watched the rental car drive off into the night before moving from the sidewalk.

"What happened back there?" Judy asked.

"I don't really want to talk about it," Dennis said.

This was the first time that Dennis's voice was clipped, and Judy did not like it.

Inside the apartment, they hung up their coats and Dennis immediately went into the kitchen and grabbed the Macallan single malt from the cabinet, put in one ice cube, and poured the amber liquid slowly into the small glass.

"Dennis," Judy asked. "Are you going to talk to me? I don't like this. Can you please let me into your life? You haven't acted like this in a long time."

"I'm sorry," he said. "I was caught off guard. Guess I'm still processing everything."

"Can you process with me, instead of by yourself?"

"Technically I'm not supposed to be discussing it."

"Dennis!" she snapped. "Stop it. Talk to me."

He swirled the glass and watched the lone ice cube slowly circumnavigate its confined space.

"Do you remember I used to see a therapist?" he said. "I was trying to get over my wife's death and about a hundred other crappy things that orbited around me."

"Yes, but that was several years ago. You stopped seeing the therapist."

"Yes, her name was Dr. Forrester. Don't know if I even remember her first name. Anyway, she was one of the approved therapists that the agency uses. The approved therapists have to get clearance and then meet certain security requirements about storing notes, stuff like that."

"So?"

"Well, Dr. Forrester disappeared on a business trip. The agency is pretty sure they know who grabbed her and why, but the director's not so sure. Wants someone else to look at it before he authorizes an action plan."

Judy frowned and tried to get Dennis to look at her, but he was focused entirely on the amber liquid in the glass.

"Dennis, the first thing that comes to mind is why in heaven's name would someone want to nab a psychologist who's seeing some CIA employees? Doesn't that seem a little 'out there'?"

"Well, there are lots of reasons why some adversary would want to get their hands on her. She knows too much about her patients. She knows their weaknesses, their vulnerabilities, and even their dark secrets. Some of the information could be used to compromise an employee. I know it's a little strange, but this is a strange business."

"Alright, I grant you that she might have some information they'd want, but my other question is: why you? What in god's name is the director doing enlisting the help of a retired member of the inspector general's office? There's something very odd about this."

"Yes, that's a little more complicated," he said, taking a small sip of scotch. "The director appears not to trust the recommendation about who nabbed Forrester. I guess he's looking for a second opinion."

"He comes all the way here to ask you to help out? Something doesn't sound right, Dennis. I'm sorry but you're being very naïve about this."

"He said I was recommended as an independent evaluator, someone who could find out what happened to Forrester and who the bad people are."

"I know who the bad people are," Judy said, walking out of the kitchen. "They're the Central Intelligence Agency."

"He said I can turn this request down and just walk away. He made that very clear."

"Then we have no worries. Just decline. End of story."

CHAPTER 4

Calvin Miller's office was spacious, with an enormous window facing Murray Street. As director of the AFP's office in Perth, he was appropriately officious and self-important. Like many bureaucratic officials, he was respected by the rank and file, but not particularly liked.

Miller had scheduled a meeting with both Judy and Daniel for 9:30 a.m. That alone was unusual, since the director was notoriously slow moving in the mornings. Judy and Daniel had speculated on what was behind the meeting, but neither could come up with a plausible answer. Except for the unnerving incident with the meth addict in Golden Bay, there was nothing to talk about.

"As you know we have a new internal affairs director back east," Miller said, cradling his cup of tea in both hands like a chalice. "His name's Calhoun. A real stickler for details. He's questioning the protocol you used with that young man in Golden Bay."

"Protocol?" Daniel said. "Are you serious?"

"Yes, I am. Calhoun does not believe you two handled the situation properly."

"Calvin, I can't believe this is happening," Judy said. "We handled it exactly as we should have. No one was injured, and the young man was taken into custody later without incident. What do you mean about 'protocol'?"

"Judy, there were two shots fired, am I correct?"

"Yes, but—"

"Let me finish, please. You and Daniel had your backs to the front door when the young man returned and started firing, correct?"

"Calvin, the bastard had already gone inside the house," Daniel said. "As far as we were concerned, the conversation was over. There was no suspicion of him having a firearm."

"Yes, but he did return with a weapon, didn't he? And one of you could have been injured. Or worse."

"Is this fellow Calhoun the cause of all this?" Judy said.

"Well, he did request more information," Miller said, taking a quick sip of tea. "And an investigation."

"A what?" Judy shouted.

"Please, there is no need to overreact. I'm sure nothing will come of it."

"Calvin," Daniel said, "please tell me that you're not going to authorize an internal affairs investigation of what happened this week in Golden Bay. You can't be serious."

"He is the director of internal affairs, Daniel."

"He's an idiot," Judy said standing. "And I can't believe you didn't put your foot down and stand up for us."

"Judy!" Miller yelled as his two agents stalked out of the office.

⊙

"So, are you going to stay in Australia?"

"Heck, I don't know, Beth," Dennis said. "I feel like I just got here, but it's already been ten months. I like it here."

The phone calls with his adult daughter were always a little stilted, since the two were never very close when she was growing up. Dennis's work had taken him around the globe in search of those agency miscreants who sprouted like dandelions on freshly mowed lawns. Being on the road for so long had deprived Dennis and Beth of the typical father-daughter relationship during her school years. And now, with his wife deceased and Beth living in San Francisco with her lawyer husband, the two of them were still trying to solve the riddle of how to make the relationship work.

"Are you and Judy still, like, an item?"

He laughed. "Yes, we're still an item."

"Do you think you're going to get married?"

"I guess so."

"You guess so? Doesn't sound very definitive to me, Dad. You're not still thinking about Mom all the time, are you?"

"Mmm. I do sometimes. But that's not an issue. I'm just trying to get used to living here. And I'm not working any longer, and there's a lot of adjustment. But I have no intention of leaving Judy. Remember she has a son here in university, and her family is here too. I suppose at some point one of us is going to have to decide to move permanently."

"My guess is that you're going to have to decide, Dad. She's got a job and a family that is going to be hard to leave."

"That's a good call on your part," Dennis said. "You seem to have your mother's wisdom. I suppose I should try to make it easier on Judy and just settle down here."

"I'm sure she'd appreciate it, Dad. I've only met her once, and she seemed very cool. And she's quite pretty, you know. You shouldn't wait around forever."

"Yipes, you haven't been talking to her, have you?"

"No. But some things are just obvious."

⊙

He had never seen her like this. Judy called him in a rage, stopping half-way through sentences to curse, and then continuing. Dennis rushed over from his apartment to find her half undressed from work, gesturing wildly, and stalking around her house throwing couch pillows and small kitchen utensils.

"An investigation! Who in the bloody hell does this idiot back east think he is?"

"I'm sure it's going to be fine," Dennis said, following her from room to room. She had taken off her blouse, kicked off her shoes, but walked around wearing only her skirt and bra.

"It won't be fine!" she said. "Do you know what these internal affairs reports look like in your file? Forget a promotion. I'd be lucky to be able to carry a firearm! And Daniel, well, he's fit to be tied. God, the nerve of these people."

"Can we just sit down for a minute?" he said. "Come here. Sit down." He sat down on the bed and patted the area next to him. "Sit. Please."

Judy ignored him, ripping off her skirt and tossing it onto the bed. She pulled open a drawer in her dresser, grabbed a pair of denim jeans, and tugged them on. Then she pulled out a sweatshirt and tugged that over her head.

Judy continued to murmur to herself in the mirror as she removed her earrings and tossed them into her jewelry box. Then, as if a plug had been pulled from the socket, she stared into the large dresser mirror at herself, twisting her mouth in concentration.

Her eyes caught his in the mirror's reflection, and she turned. "Did you say something?"

"No, not much," he said. "Why don't you sit down here."

She sighed, walked over, and sat down. He patted her knee. *Just be there for her,* he thought. *And shut up. She's not listening anyway.*

"I'm thinking of taking a leave of absence," she said.

"Really?"

"Yes, absolutely. Bloody idiots."

"Whatever is best for you," he said. "Just give the situation a little time to settle, then do what you think is best."

⊙

Dennis looked down at the business card and nudged it with the tip of his right forefinger as if it were alive. He sat in the coffee shop and fussed with his frothy, flat white coffee.

How strange it was to be surrounded by chaos again, after dodging it for a while. In what seemed like a millisecond, he transitioned from suffering the trauma of bad golf shots to the angst of returning to the dark, thankless work that nearly killed him.

Earlier in his career, he had convinced himself of the righteousness of his cause: there were a handful of bad people in the agency who slipped through screening and caused profound problems. He was the policeman, they were the criminals. Good versus evil.

But that was before he retired to an oasis of sublime ennui, where languid days chasing a dimpled white ball around the landscape were the highlights. A modest amount of self-reflection had drawn the curtain back on the dark, dirty truth about Dennis. It was not the mission to rid the agency of bad people that drove him all those years; it was the chase itself. The truth was that the agency was the repository of every form of duplicitous individual known to mankind, and they were only good or bad employees depending on happenstance and whim. Every analyst or agent was ten seconds away from making an incompetent— or worse—a criminal decision. There really was no tiny cadre of sinners hiding among the saints. They were all sinners to some extent, just some were worse than others.

Now that he had reconciled himself to that truth, he also recognized what excited him about his work. It was simply the hunt. It gave him structure and momentum. He could forget the rest of the world and simply focus on the hunt. It enthralled and consumed him.

It also separated him.

Isn't that what Dr. Forrester had tried to show him? The psychologist had dutifully reminded him over and over that by taking refuge in the hunt, he cut himself off from the normal emotions extended to family and friends. It was "hunt and hide," not "hunt to rid the agency of bad people," she said.

How odd, Dennis wondered, that of all the people to go missing it was an obscure psychologist with a small contract to provide therapy to agency employees. He had stopped seeing her about a year and a half ago, yet here she was again making her presence known.

Siren call or call to noble action? Would the hunt take him away from Judy, or could he balance the two powerful forces—passion for a woman, and passion for hunting—so that he survived?

He nudged the business card again. In the airplane, Simpson had given him a cheesy business card for Fred's Painting Services. It sported an image of a paintbrush and the motto: "Interior/Exterior Painting at an affordable price." At the bottom was an 800 number.

"Within twenty-four hours you need to call this number and leave a message saying you'd like to have your house painted," Simpson said. "If you don't call, that means you're not interested in this project. Very simple. In or out. Your call."

Dennis looked at his watch, took a sip of coffee, and nudged the card one more time to see if it was alive.

⊙

"I'm thinking of asking for a leave of absence," Judy said.

"You can't do that, Jude," Daniel said. "It will look bad. Let this investigation play out. There was nothing else we could have done differently. You'll see."

"I'm tired of this work," she said, sitting on the corner of his desk. "I thought it was exciting and different for a woman, at least in the beginning. It's bad enough to get shot at, but then getting reprimanded afterward is bloody awful."

"It will pass, I promise you," he said. "Everyone says it's bullshit. This new internal affairs wanker is causing all the trouble."

"During the shooting, I looked at you while we were behind the car," she said.

"You did?"

"I saw a person who was petrified. Your face was twisted and distorted. I don't think this kind of stuff is good for human beings."

"But I *was* petrified! Thought the bastard was going to kill me. Or you. Or turn around and shoot his father."

"But is that a job worth having? Not knowing whether something ordinary will turn deadly in a split second? I don't think so. Not to me. Or at least not any longer."

Daniel spun around in his office chair and stared up at Judy.

"How are you getting along with your Yank?"

"Why do you ask?"

"Don't know. You seem preoccupied lately. Wondered if you two were still together."

"Yes, we're still together."

"Is he going to move here?"

"Yes. Or that's what I think."

"Last week you said you thought he was bored."

"Well, he is a bit bored."

"Is that a good thing or a bad thing?"

She sighed. "I'm not sure, actually. We'll see."

⊙

"I think I owe it to her," Dennis said.

She arched her eyebrows. "You 'owe it to her'? Are you serious?"

Dennis sat inside their favorite small restaurant in Subiaco. The temperature had dropped during the day and a stiff easterly breeze off the Indian Ocean brought a cold rain with it.

"Dr. Forrester did help me a lot, or at least it seemed that way."

"What you're saying is that you want to go back to work."

"No, not permanently. I can't do that. But this one job seems like it's the right thing to do."

"Do you realize what it might do to us? As a couple? You get consumed by investigations and strange things happen. Dangerous things. You've trained me not to trust anything they do. Now you want to go back to find a missing psychologist? Really?"

"As I said, that woman helped straighten out my life. I think it's worth trying to find out what happened to her. I'd be doing it for her and her family, not for the agency."

"It feels like you want to avoid dealing with us."

"What does that mean?"

"That you don't want to settle down with me. This way you can run off again and avoid making a decision." She had already put down her knife and fork and had pushed her plate away. She took a sip of wine and closed her eyes.

"Well, then it's settled," he said reaching across the table and covering her hand with his. "I'll pass on this thing. They can get someone else."

She pulled her hand away. "Don't be daft. If it's not this one, it will be another case. Go chase your Dr. Forrester, wherever she is. I'm tired and would like to go home now."

⊙

Judy insisted that Dennis drop her off at her house and that they sleep apart.

"Really?" Dennis said. "You're angry."

"No, just tired," she said. "Don't read too much into it, Dennis. We both need a little alone time every now and then."

Dennis continued to plead that she was overreacting, but she refused to engage him.

Why is it that I never see men's intentions clearly? she thought.

By the time Dennis entered his apartment, he was drained. He limited himself to a modest pour of single malt, hoping to avoid a long night of drinking, as he struggled to make sense of the apparent rupture of his relationship with Judy.

He sat down at his small kitchen table and pulled out his phone. Looking at his watch he texted Judy:

time expired; turned down job…r we ok?

After ten excruciating minutes came a return text:

u need to take this job. don't worry about me

am worried about us; job not important

take the job. u r bored

too late

His phone rang.

"Dennis, you need to take that job," Judy said. "Maybe I'm feeling a little fragile lately. Don't worry about me. I'm being selfish. Please take this job."

"I told you the time limit passed. It's over. Let's just forget I brought it up."

"Dennis, you're not hearing me: it's fine for you to get back to work. We'll be fine."

"And you're not hearing me, Judy, I'm not taking it. Now get some sleep."

"Damnit, Dennis, now I feel guilty!"

"Judy, you're wasting energy feeling guilty. Go to bed. I'm hanging up now. I'll call you tomorrow."

He pushed the disconnect button, sat back in the creaky metal chair and took a long sip.

It was Dr. Forrester, he remembered, who kept reminding him that life is only ten percent what happens to you, but ninety percent how you *react* to what happens to you. Two goons had shown up at a golf course and dragged him into an airplane and a job offer— that was the ten percent. And now he was struggling with his own self-esteem, boredom, and guilt for disrupting a perfectly solid relationship—this was the ninety percent. Dr. Forrester said he needed to work on the ninety percent; he had no control over the ten percent.

He slowly finished his drink, changed into his old gym shorts and faded gray George Mason University t-shirt, brushed his teeth, and turned off the light. He had just settled in and could smell Judy's shampoo from the pillow next to him.

The sound of a key unlocking the front door jolted him upright in bed.

The goons!? he thought.

The kitchen hallway light turned on, and he heard footsteps approach.

"Judy, you scared the shit out of me."

She walked over and sat next to him on the bed.

"You wouldn't listen to me, so I thought I'd come over and finish the conversation."

"What conversation?" he said, rubbing his eyes and clearing his throat.

"Stop it. Now you're being dense. The job. Take the job. It's all right with me. In fact, if you don't take the job, I'll be really angry. This is my issue, not yours."

Dennis flopped back into bed. "Why don't you come to bed? We'll talk about it in the morning. I can't do this anymore today."

She stood up. "Get up and make the call. Come on."

Judy walked into the kitchen.

"I have the business card in my hand right now," she yelled.

Dennis flew out of bed and raced into the kitchen.

She had poured herself a small juice glass of white wine from the refrigerator and was sitting at the table holding the card.

"Give it to me," he said.

She handed it to him. He tore it in half, then in half again, walked over to the trash bin, and the pieces fluttered down like confetti.

"Now, can we just get some sleep?" he said.

Judy picked up Dennis's cell phone that was being charged on the table. Without disconnecting it, she slowly punched in a series of numbers.

"Who are you calling?" he said.

"I'm calling a painting company."

He stepped forward and yanked the phone out of her hands, pulling it off the charge cord.

"Damnit, Judy, what's got into you? You can't just call that number. Jesus." He sat down and reconnected the phone charger.

"I don't mind saying you confuse me sometimes," he said. "But that's OK. It's good to be confused, I guess."

"You'll be making a very big mistake if you don't call that number," she said.

Dennis got up and poured himself a juice glass of white wine.

"Maybe we can talk about this in the morning," he said, rubbing his eyes again.

"As soon as you go to bed, I'm going to call the number and tell them that you want to hire them for a paint job. I memorized the number."

Dennis was halfway to his mouth with the small glass when he stopped and returned it with a bang to the table top.

"Please stop this, Judy! I do not want to take another job."

"You wouldn't be doing it for Dr. Forrester, you'd be doing for me. And us."

He threw the wine down as if it were a shot of tequila. "I think I'm going crazy or have a tumor. I keep hearing voices talking nonsense. I'm going to bed."

Back in bed he rearranged his head on the pillow and tried to sleep, but his eyes ripped open when he heard Judy speaking from the kitchen: "Yes, I'm calling for Dennis Cunningham. He'd like to have that paint job he was talking to you about. Cheers."

"Jesus Christ!" he yelled down the hallway. He pounded the pillow with his fist.

She crawled into bed after changing and snuggled up against him from behind, putting her arm around his stomach.

"You're my tumor," he said in a muffled voice.

"Not all tumors are bad," she said. "Some are pleasantly benign."

He made a noise she could not understand.

⊙

The next morning Judy got up early, dressed, and made a cup of tea. Dennis got up with her, and they acted like nothing happened the night before. He got ready for his daily bracing walk. A cold misty rain awaited him. Judy left to return home and change for work. She kissed him on the forehead before leaving. She seemed content and at ease as if something important had been settled inside her.

Dennis, on the other hand, felt nervous and agitated, like something strange had been unleashed.

He cut his walk short since his poncho wasn't long enough to protect his legs from the rain. The flat white coffee warmed him, and he had just put the porcelain cup down when his phone went off. The number was blocked, but he had an idea who it was.

"Cunningham, who the fuck was that calling in? Why would anyone else know that number and what to say? And besides that, your deadline was up."

"Calm your jets, Simpson," Dennis said. "I just asked my girlfriend to call that number and repeat what I said. Kind of a joke."

"Big goddamn joke, you jackass. I can't for the life of me understand why the director thinks you're going to do anything to help us. I've read your file ten times, and each time, you're still the same asshole who doesn't give a shit about rules and protocol. You think everything we do is just a joke."

It had not taken Dennis long to reacquaint himself with some of the bureaucratic truisms of the intelligence establishment. Dennis knew instinctively that Simpson hated having to deal with him, and was only following orders from the director, whom Simpson probably didn't like much anyway. So, while Simpson could bitch as much as he wanted about Dennis's breach of protocol, there was nothing he could really do about it. The last thing Simpson wanted to do was go back to the director and say that Cunningham was not following the precise rules of the trade and therefore was disqualified. No, Simpson was going to suck it up because he had to. Those were the only rules that mattered to Dennis. And he was already enjoying himself.

"When do we start?" Dennis said. "I've got some tee times to schedule this week."

"You'll be contacted, asshole."

"I think that's about the second time in this conversation you've used that term. You could be a little more creative."

"Fucking asshole."

"Brilliant," Dennis said, but Simpson had already hung up.

⊙

The questions were extraordinarily repetitive and asked by a middle-aged man wearing a tweed sports jacket, white polyester open-necked shirt, and black pleated slacks.

Judy felt calm and focused, and was careful not to contradict herself, even when the questions were open-ended, such as: "How would you and your partner Daniel normally prepare for interviewing a family about a potential drug problem with their adult child?"

She knew Daniel would be asked the same questions, and while they were told not to rehearse their answers, they had worked together for so long that there was no need.

After ninety minutes of polite but increasingly pointed questions, the interview ended. Judy had taken lunch at a nearby sandwich shop with Francis LeStang, another investigator she was fond of.

"I just can't believe they're putting you and Daniel through this," LeStang said. "We're all petrified. Is this what it's going to be like every time there's a shooting?"

"Daniel thinks it's because of what happened in Brisbane a couple of months ago," Judy said, nibbling at her curried egg-salad sandwich.

"The one where the copper was wounded?"

"Yes, that one. Daniel said the officer was shot when he turned his back. Something like that."

"Ridiculous," LeStang said. "They're going to investigate every single incident when an AFP officer turns their back? I'd just as well go back to uni and get a degree in forestry. Idiots."

Judy laughed. "It does seem that the system has nothing else to do but create more things for the system to do."

"Too right, Jude," LeStang said laughing. "Too bloody right."

⊙

At 2 p.m. Dennis's phone rang, and it was a local number.

"Hello?"

"Dennis Cunningham?" asked a man with an American accent.

"Yes."

"My name is Bill Lawson and I'm calling from the consulate here in Perth. I need you to come in and meet with me, preferably today. We've received a high-priority request."

"I could be there in about an hour, would that work?"

"Sure, ask for Bill Lawson."

"Will do, Bill."

⊙

The consulate was on St. George's Terrace, across the street from the Perth Concert Hall in a nondescript office building with a handful of foreign flags flying. Several consulates were in the building.

Dennis checked in on the fourth floor of the building. He waited no more than five minutes before a husky, fiftyish man showed up in the waiting room.

"Hey," he said holding out his hand, "I'm Bill Lawson. You're supposed to be Dennis Cunningham."

"Correct," Dennis said standing.

"Come along with me please." Lawson led him through another door that required a passcode, down a hallway into a small window-less room.

"You know the drill, so bear with me," Lawson said.

There were numerous drills Dennis encountered in his career, and he did not know which one Lawson was referring to specifically.

Lawson asked him to remove anything made of metal, and Dennis used his knuckles to rap his forehead. "Including this?" he said.

"Ha, you're one of the funny ones," Lawson said. "If it's made of metal, then let's have it."

After the belt, phone, coins, glasses, and watch were placed in a bin, Dennis stood up and was wanded. Then he was asked to stand in front of a device that was adjusted to his eye level, and a scan was made of his face. Another scan was made of his pupils. Lastly, he was asked to place both palms down onto a machine with a glass plate that emitted infrared light.

"Still doing this silly vein biometric stuff?" Dennis said.

"Yep," Lawson said. "Everyone's got a unique vein structure in their palms and it's more accurate than fingerprints, which, as you know, can be faked."

Lawson left the room and returned five minutes later. "Follow me, please."

They walked down another hallway and entered another room that was passcode protected. The room was spartan. A single CCTV camera pointed down from one corner near the ceiling. In the middle of the room was a white Formica table with metal legs and two small plastic chairs. On the table sat a black, ultra-thin laptop and charger, and a cell phone and a charger.

Lawson, the designated intelligence operative at the consulate, was of course not supposed to be an intelligence operative, according to international rules of diplomacy. But consulates are often important waypoints for moments just like these in faraway reaches of the globe. Lawson was likely a state department security official nearing retirement and was rotating through Perth with his wife to have some late-career fun.

Lawson explained how to use the encrypted cell phone. Then he showed him how to use the phone as a hot spot for accessing the internet and email. For a situation where there was no cellular signal, and it was important that Dennis use standard Wi-Fi for his computer, Lawson instructed Dennis how to ensure the encryption program was operating properly on the laptop.

There were no printed instructions, and Lawson made Dennis repeat all the steps for both devices.

"We're good to go, then," Lawson said, sliding the computer into a black carry case. "I've been instructed to tell you that you will be receiving a call today on the phone."

⊙

"I think I'm in some kind of crisis," Judy said.

Cilla, her best friend, listened carefully as they each sipped a glass of wine at the restaurant bar near Judy's office.

"What kind of crisis?" Cilla asked. "You don't seem to be in a crisis to me. How is it going with Dennis? Is that what you're talking about?"

Judy commenced a long monologue that detailed the shooting in Golden Bay, the follow-up investigation, her fears that Dennis was not happy in Perth, and maybe not happy with her. She finished with the conflict around Dennis being offered a job that would separate them again.

"Whew!" Cilla said. "I spoke to you a fortnight ago, and you were pleased as punch about your life, and today the sky's falling. Why didn't you tell me you were involved in the shooting in Golden Bay? I saw it on the telly."

"It was too upsetting to talk about," she said.

"And the investigation? What happened with that?"

"Nothing. They agreed that Daniel and I acted responsibly. Classic bureaucratic shit. I don't think I can do this any longer."

"Do what any longer?"

"Police work."

"Heavens, Judy, you *are* in a crisis. You love your work. And you're good at it."

"The shooting scared me, Cilla. I thought about Trevor and my parents. And Dennis. It's strange but given the other things that have happened to me, this single shooting has taken its toll."

"I can't imagine what being shot at feels like," Cilla said. "It's too gruesome to contemplate. But without switching subjects too quickly, how is it going with Dennis? What is going on? He's such a charming rascal, and you two go so well together."

"He's bored here, but I think he's just bored with me. Or that's what I thought. I told him to take that new contract job. In fact, I made him take it. I thought I was being selfish and insecure for stopping him. Maybe he does need to work. And maybe it will not affect our relationship. Maybe."

"Will this job take him away again? That's been the hard part for you two."

"Yes, I suppose he'll be traveling. I don't know where."

CHAPTER 5

I'm going to be your handler on this project, since it's very time sensitive, and frankly, I've been ordered to manage you," Simpson said. "So, you can imagine I'm about as excited as you are about this assignment."

Dennis sat in his apartment with a pad of paper and doodled.

"You have two weeks—that's fourteen work days—to make a recommendation on this case. Your recommendation with be confined to one of three options: one—you agree with the earlier conclusion that a particular foreign service is behind the abduction; two—you disagree with the earlier conclusion, and you offer reasons why; three—you are unable to make a choice between one or two and are unable to provide meaningful input."

"You can't be a handler," Dennis said. "You're a deputy director, for chrissakes. You're up to your ears in alligators, and you can't give this project the attention it needs. I'll be asking you for information, and you'll be in five simultaneous conference calls. I'll be lucky to hear from you next year."

"This is not starting well, as I anticipated," Simpson said. "You didn't hear me. I was *ordered* to manage you. That was from my boss—the director of operations—who was ordered by his boss, the director of the agency. Do you want to keep wasting time telling me what I'm capable of, or should you get off your ass and get to work?"

"I'm getting off my ass as we speak," Dennis said slowly, writing the word "ass" in capital letters on the pad.

"As a contractor, you are responsible for your own expenses, and you'll need to submit them at the end of the project. I'll be sending you a contract that you'll sign and return using the laptop you've been given. Do that immediately. Next, I'll be sending you a backgrounder file that you will need to read ASAP. After reading it, please call the following number and speak to Colin McCarthy. He will be your main contact with NZSIS. You will need to get there right away and dig into the details. Speed is required in this matter if we haven't made that clear already."

"NZSIS? That's the New Zealand Security Intelligence Service?"

"Yes."

"Why the Kiwis? What do they have to do with this?"

"Dr. Forrester disappeared in New Zealand while attending a psychology conference."

"No one mentioned that before."

"As you can imagine, this is another reason why the director agreed you would be the right person for this project since you're geographically close. And your benefactor said as much."

"The person who recommended me?"

"Yes, *that* benefactor."

"Franklin asked whether I wanted to know who recommended me, and I said 'no,'" Dennis said.

"Yes, the director asked you, and you declined."

"Well, I changed my mind. Who recommended me?"

"Are you certain you want to know?"

"Yes, I do."

"The name is Louise Nordland. She is a confidante of the director's, and one of the most influential people on his staff."

"Nordland!" Dennis said, tossing his pen onto the table top.

"I understand you've worked together before."

"That depends on how you define 'together.'"

"Well, however you define it, the director is giving you fourteen days from now to make a recommendation. Is that clear?"

"Clear as a goddamn bell."

⊙

Judy sat next to Dennis in the small apartment kitchen and could feel the drift in his personality. During his ten-month stay in Western Australia, Dennis had become a softer, more reflective person. He smiled more often and seemed vaguely relieved of something. His short-cropped, brown hair sported flecks of gray, and he looked like a man growing content with his life. His shoulders seemed less prominent, almost rounded, and he tended to slump slightly when sitting.

Now, sitting rigid in front of his new laptop, Dennis's jaw was more prominent, as his facial muscles stretched. His forehead sported several horizontal creases as he stared at the screen. His intense blue eyes, as always, were fathomless beacons.

"New Zealand?" Judy said.

"Yeah. Forrester attended a conference in New Zealand with a friend, another psychologist she's known for years named Phyllis Caldecott. I guess some medical professionals are required to have training every couple of years to get re-licensed. I gather you can attend a training program in an exotic location and write off some of the expenses for the trip on your taxes."

"She went to a conference with an old friend and then disappeared?

In New Zealand? North or South Island?"

"The conference was in Wellington on the North Island, but she traveled to the South Island with her friend to do some sightseeing. They were doing a wine tasting tour in the Marlborough area, and one night Forrester had a headache and ran out to a pharmacy near their hotel, and never came back."

"Is she married?"

"Yes, says here her husband is Nicholas Forrester. Works for the U.S. Department of Agriculture. Two grown children; one daughter married, one son single."

"When did she disappear?"

Dennis looked at the screen for a moment, scrolled, and said, "Caldecott calls the police that night when Forrester doesn't return. May 22, at 10:20 p.m. local time, she contacts police in Blenheim."

"Who does the agency think is responsible for the disappearance?" she asked.

"Where's your phone?"

"In my purse in the other room."

He grabbed his cell phone off the kitchen table, stood up and put it next to the milk inside the refrigerator, and closed the door.

"Haven't seen you do that in a while," she said.

"I haven't had to. This information is confidential. And it goes without saying that you will deny, even after five days of waterboarding, that I talked to you about this?"

"Please, Dennis, don't start with your super-secret silliness."

"Well, you've been warned."

"So?"

"So, they've fingered an Iranian cell operating in New Zealand. Husband and wife team by the name of Farhad and Astar Ghorbani. And another guy named Ramin Lajani. Operations says this group nabbed her off the street and tortured her for information on her

patients. When they were done, they killed her and buried or inciner-
ated the body."

"How would this Iranian team know an obscure therapist from the
US was even in New Zealand?"

"They think there's a leak in the agency," Dennis said. "They appear
to have some sigint to that effect."

"Sigint is 'signals intelligence'?"

"Correct."

"And the agency wants to exact some kind of revenge on the
Iranians?"

"Not revenge, actually; more like retribution."

"But the director is not buying the Iranian connection? Do I have
that right?"

"Looks that way."

"And he's asked you to take another look at it?"

"Yes."

"How long will the project take? Do you have a deadline?"

"Two weeks."

Judy laughed. "Are you serious?"

"I know, seems ludicrous," Dennis said, closing the laptop. He
leaned back and stretched his arms. "My guess is that the director is
trapped. His entire team is saying 'we know who did it and why, and
the Iranians needs to be punished.' He's either too wimpy to start a
small clandestine war, or he knows something else. Could be that he's
just stalling."

"So, you're on a wild goose chase?"

"Could be. Two weeks is silly. Can't really investigate this thing
properly in fourteen days. Still, I got the sense when we were talking in
the airplane, that he was bothered by something."

"Talk English, Dennis."

He stood up, stretched again, and opened the refrigerator. Judy had bought some take-out Chinese food, and the leftovers were sitting in their containers, the strong smells of garlic and hoisin sauce permeating the apartment.

"Dennis?"

He grabbed a bottle of sauvignon blanc and poured himself a glass. Holding the bottle up for Judy, she nodded, and he poured another glass for her.

"There are two narratives," he said sitting down. "I think I understand the first one, which is the disappearance of a woman in New Zealand. The second story is one that stumps me. Why isn't the director content with the staff's recommendation? And why me? In the realm of strange occurrences, the director sitting on the tarmac asking for my help is probably top of the list. Even Simpson thinks it's ridiculous. And I'm beginning to agree."

"But it can't be ridiculous," Judy said, taking a sip of wine. "The director—what's his name?"

"Franklin—Kenny Franklin they call him in the news media as if he's football player or something."

"OK, here's my two cent's worth: Kenny is at the top of this vast espionage service, with thousands of employees and billion-dollar budgets, and he doesn't trust the bureaucracy. And for the record, I don't trust bureaucracies either. So, he's worried that they're either being too lazy or reckless, but either way, he doesn't believe them. He has nowhere to turn. And Louise—you said that she is one of his top advisors—she remembers you're just the right investigator to get to the bottom of it."

He laughed. "Aren't you forgetting that Louise and I are not exactly best friends?"

"You're too hard on her."

"I am? Don't you remember her sordid role in sucking you into a dangerous set of events last year in London? And she was lying to you the whole time."

"I remember all too well, and I think she believed it wasn't dangerous. She's a professional, and she did what she thought was best at the time. I still think you were too hard on her. You always told me that you like to operate in the gray area; not black or white, but somewhere in between. I think that's where Louise works too, but you just don't like to have company there."

He turned, his eyes wide and his mouth open: "Where did *that* come from?"

"Just a reality check," she said, dropping her eyes. "I think it would be healthier for us to be honest."

CHAPTER 6

He was not happy, nor sad; he was some odd place in between. Dennis could not see the ochre landscape below as the passenger jet screamed through the night toward Auckland. Dennis bought a first-class ticket on the Air New Zealand direct flight. It provided more physical and emotional room to be anxious in the event they hit turbulence. A lifelong fear of airplane turbulence had solidified into something approaching a well-established phobia.

And besides, first class included free alcohol. Tonight, he needed something to help him hide from the avalanche of confusing feelings about saying goodbye to Judy at Perth International Airport.

"I feel like I'm saying goodbye forever," she said, clutching him tightly, her voice muffled as she pressed against his neck.

"Judy, stop that. How can a two-week assignment be forever?"

"It's just a feeling. Can't a person have feelings?"

"Well, I don't like the sound of it. I'm going to New Zealand, which is right around the corner here in the southern hemisphere."

She gave him a long, unsexy kiss; it felt more like a mother sending a child off to the first day of school.

"I love you," she said quietly.

"I love you too," he said uncomfortably. Dennis could not remember the last time he told anyone that he loved them.

Judy smiled at his awkwardness. "Just be safe," she said. "Lot of attractive Kiwi women I hear."

He laughed and did his best Cary Grant impersonation: "Judy, Judy, Judy."

"He never said that," she said, wiping a smudge of lipstick off his cheek.

"Yes, you keep reminding me that Grant never said that, but I like saying it anyway."

⊙

"Hello there, Dennis, my name is Colin McCarthy, from the NZSIS and this is my colleague Rangi Winchester, from GCSB. Sorry for all the acronyms. You know how governments work: string as many complicated nouns together as possible so that no one is left out."

Dennis shook their hands and tried to appear focused and alert. In fact, he was tired and a little hung over. The direct flight took six and a half hours, but it was overnight, and he had trouble sleeping even after several nips of single malt.

Simpson had told him to expect McCarthy as his contact, but never mentioned the other fellow. As Dennis pulled his roll-on suitcase behind him, the threesome made small talk about the flight, the time zone changes, and the weather.

A black Toyota sedan was waiting for them. The driver was a young blond-haired man introduced as Simon.

The three kept up innocuous chatter in the car as it slid through the busy highway toward the city's harbor area. Dennis tried to stay engaged, but he was anxious to get moving on what he knew was an impossibly short timeline.

"Colin, is there an agenda for today?" Dennis said. "I'm under a tight schedule and was hoping to get going."

"Of course, Dennis. Our offices are only about ten blocks away. We thought we'd meet here in our Auckland offices, then take a short flight to Blenheim on the South Island afterward."

"I'm sorry that I'm pressing, but, well, I'm being pressed."

"Understood," McCarthy said.

Winchester nodded in agreement.

⊙

The weekly meeting of the AFP investigators had been underway for at least thirty minutes when Judy's attention began to flag. It usually took her much longer to tune out, since Miller, the director, often asked agents, out of the blue, to comment on a particular case. For several years she remained on her toes and was able to answer any question suddenly thrust her way. But as of late, she found Miller's professorial style pedantic and condescending.

She looked out the window and watched the bullet-sized raindrops beat against the glass.

"And, Judy, what is your opinion on Frank's dilemma in Bunbury? You had a similar case last year with that informant in Fremantle."

She turned from the window and pursed her lips in feigned concentration. "I don't have an opinion on what to do with Frank's informant, I'm afraid. Frank is a competent agent. I'm sure he'll decide how best to proceed."

Her tone of gentle dismissal was not lost on the roomful of agents, and many turned to get a gander. Judy was normally mildly submissive in these meetings, so her change of demeanor was hard to miss.

Her partner Daniel, sitting to her right, gave her a what-the-hell-has-got-into-you look.

"We were discussing Frank's conundrum, Judy. Surely you were listening. I was wondering what you thought he should do."

"I'm sorry, I wasn't paying close attention. Perhaps you could summarize Frank's problem again?"

⊙

"Jude, you can't talk like that in the staff meeting!" Daniel said, sitting in her small office with the door partially closed. "What is happening to you? "Blowhard"—the team's nickname for the director—"is a stickler for paying attention. You know that."

"Don't you think after all these years on the force that Frank knows exactly what to do with his informant? Really, why do we have to sit there as a group and act like we're still at uni. It's demeaning."

"Maybe that shooting got to you, Jude."

"Not the shooting; that was bad enough. It was the humiliating investigation afterward."

"But they found we did nothing wrong."

"They shouldn't have put us through it to start with."

"It came from back east. The new bloke in internal affairs."

"I don't care if it came from the pope. Blowhard should have cut it off before it even came to us."

"He's just a political beast like the rest of us. Cut him a bit of slack, Jude."

"Not any longer."

Daniel took a sip of his bottled water, gulped it loudly and stared at Judy.

"Something going on with the Yank?"

"No, why do you think that?"

"Simply asking. You don't seem yourself."

"Maybe it's time for me to be someone else."

"I see."

⊙

McCarthy was an average looking man of middle age, with thinning brown hair cut short, and large, thick eyebrows and brown eyes. Dennis estimated he was about five feet nine inches, and a little paunchy around the waist. McCarthy sat across from Dennis in the small, windowless office inside the NZSIS building.

Winchester sat to McCarthy's right, and Dennis guessed he was of Maori heritage. He was broad-shouldered, stocky, and powerful looking. His broad forehead and short black hair were punctuated with piercing dark eyes. Winchester said nothing as his colleague explained New Zealand's government investigation into the disappearance of the American psychologist.

A country of fewer than five million residents, New Zealand was a member of the Five Eyes group, an alliance of countries that share sigint with each other. The members—the United States, United Kingdom, Canada, Australia, and New Zealand—were on good terms theoretically, but on an operational level, there was the normal bureaucratic squabbling and suspicions. And with the US being the grand member of the Five Eyes, it was not uncommon that resentments simmered just below the surface.

"Dr. Forrester disappeared when she left her hotel to purchase something from a chemist down the road. She appears to have talked briefly at the front desk to get directions to the chemist. The hotel CCTV shows a time stamp 8:12 p.m. when she left through the front door. The distance to the store was approximately three hundred yards. There are no CCTV cameras in the parking lot or sidewalk. The chemist CCTV fails to show an image of Dr. Forrester entering the store."

"There's no video evidence that she made it to the chemist, or that she re-entered the hotel?" Dennis said.

"Correct," McCarthy said.

"The presumption is that she was abducted between the hotel and the chemist?"

"Correct."

"No cameras in the street or parking lots, and there are no eyewitnesses to her walking on the sidewalk at night?"

"Correct."

"And her cellphone?"

Winchester spoke for the first time. "Her phone was left in her hotel room. She apparently had turned off roaming to keep her phone charges to a minimum, as many tourists do. If she had taken her phone with her, there would be geolocation tracking available."

"This question was asked many times before, but I have to ask again: there are no links to similar disappearances or serial murders?"

"Stranger abductions are extremely rare in New Zealand," McCarthy said. "Most cases of violence against women—including murder—are committed by men who know the victim. Dr. Forrester was not here long enough to establish relationships. She had her own hotel room, as the report shows, and her traveling partner, Dr. Caldecott, stayed in a separate room on the same floor. There is no video or electronic evidence that Dr. Caldecott left her room during the period that Dr. Forrester disappeared. Caldecott's room key was not used until after 10 p.m. that evening when she went to the front desk to ask about Dr. Forrester."

"Tell me something," Dennis said to Winchester, "I'm not familiar with the GCSB. What agency is that?"

"It's the Government Communications Security Bureau," Winchester said.

"And what do they do, exactly?"

"Signals intelligence. Our part of the Five Eyes."

"Yes, but what are you doing in this meeting?" Dennis said. "Why is sigint part of this investigation from the New Zealand side?"

"I assume you read the report?" McCarthy said.

"Yes, but there was no mention of GCSB or sigint in the report that I have."

The two New Zealanders looked at each other.

"We don't know what report you read, but this investigation from our side has always involved GCSB," McCarthy said. "It's the operating theory that your organization has developed regarding the disappearance of Dr. Forrester."

"Why don't you refresh my memory on what that theory is?" Dennis said.

McCarthy frowned and, Dennis thought, appeared genuinely confused.

"We can't do that," McCarthy said.

"Why not?"

"You're asking us to characterize a theory proposed by your organization, and that's not something we're comfortable with. Surely you can get that theory from your side."

"Yes, but I was wondering what you folks thought of that theory?"

"We're not authorized to give you our opinion; we're simply here to provide all of the facts surrounding the disappearance. Your side has made inferences based on those facts. We have nothing to do with inferences or theories."

"Yes, I know all that," Dennis said. "But what do you think of the theory?"

"Mr. Cunningham," Winchester said. "Perhaps you should discuss the theory with your team first, then we can share the details. Our marching orders are very clear in relation to your visit. We're to answer any factual questions regarding the disappearance, and to provide context. We're not authorized to provide opinions."

⊙

It was a short hour-and-a-half, early afternoon flight of three hundred miles from Auckland to Blenheim. Dennis stood at the intersection of two roads in Blenheim, a town at the northeastern end of New Zealand's South Island. About four miles inland from the sea, the town is the gateway to the Marlborough wine region that stretches southeast toward the west coast. It was a pleasant enough town, spread out in a gentle, English manner with tree-lined streets and very few buildings over two stories. He had walked around the small hotel Dr. Forrester stayed in, including the hallway to her room, the reception area, restaurant, and the parking lot. Standing next to Winchester and McCarthy, he said, "Let me get this right: the thinking is she might have cut across the park to get to the pharmacy?"

"Yes," McCarthy said. "The receptionist told her it was the fastest route."

Dennis started walking, his hands deep into the pockets of his raincoat. The sun felt warm on his face, but the cool winter wind chilled his hands. The three men walked up to the intersection, and then quickly hustled across the street to the entrance of a small park called Seymour Square.

"She walked this way?" Dennis said, pointing down the wide path that ran diagonally across the park. "Yes, that is how she was directed to get to the pharmacy," McCarthy said.

"Is it safe to walk in the park at night?"

"Yes, of course," Winchester said. "It's not New York City."

McCarthy shot his partner a sharp glance.

"Or Auckland," Winchester added.

Dennis took in the surrounding bushes, trees, and structures as they walked. The cement path was wide open at the entrance, but thirty feet farther down the path, a tall evergreen stood only five feet away from the path. Dennis left the path and walked around the tree, while his tour guides waited.

"Looks like a charming ambush site," Dennis said.

"Possibly," McCarthy said.

The path was bordered by several benches as it led toward a small clock tower. On the other side of the tower were a fountain and pool. Dennis stopped, turned around, and mentally retraced his steps.

"Hate to say it guys, but she could have been grabbed anywhere in here. She went out at 8:12 p.m., and I gather there are street lights that offer a lot of illumination," Dennis said. "I looked up the time for sunset on May 22 and it was 5:09 p.m."

"It was dark when she left," Winchester said. "The fountain there has colored lights that surround it in a continuing display. And the archway to the clock tower is well lit. It's certainly not completely pitch-black."

"No eyewitnesses?"

"None that have come forward."

"And that's the pharmacy over there?"

"Yes, but as we reported, they have no record of her purchasing anything. The CCTV confirms she did not enter."

"Somewhere between the hotel exit and the store over there, she disappeared?"

"Yes," McCarthy said.

Turning to Winchester, Dennis said, "If you were going to abduct someone from this park, where would you do it?"

He grimaced and looked to his partner. "That's really not our expertise," McCarthy interrupted.

"Come on," Dennis said, walking back through the park, "I'm not going to hold you to it, I'm just asking your opinion."

"We're not empowered to provide opinions," McCarthy said. "I think we already stated that."

"Winchester, where would you take her?"

"Mmm, probably at the entrance. Back there," he said pointing to the spot where they entered.

"Rangi!" his partner said.

"Oh, let him alone," Dennis said. "Come along, Rangi. Show me."

McCarthy groaned as they retraced their steps to the entrance.

"I suppose I would do it right here, and pull her into this area over there, behind those hedges," Winchester said.

Dennis left the path and walked twenty feet into a dense growth of short evergreens. He kicked the dirt at the base of the shrubs.

"Yeah, this is where she was taken. Good call, Rangi. The car was probably parked on the side street there."

McCarthy pouted, while the three men walked back to the hotel.

"Did you want to drive by the Ghorbani's home?" McCarthy said. "It's not far from here."

"No," Dennis said. "Not now. I'd like some time to myself, thanks. Can we meet again at around 4 p.m. this afternoon?"

"Certainly, but how will you get around? We drove you here."

"Oh, I'll just walk around until I find someplace for a cup of coffee."

"Fine," McCarthy said. The two New Zealanders walked back to their car and drove away.

Dennis was not trying to dump them; he was exhausted. Or worse.

There was a time several years ago when he was clinically depressed after his wife's death, and he had taken time off from work. With Dr. Forrester's help—albeit painful at times—Dennis had come away stabilized and mildly self-reflective. He tried antidepressants, but he did not like them and stopped.

His first case after returning to work took him to Australia, where he met Judy. Their romance had suffered through so many catastrophic disruptions, that it was a mystery to him how he ended up quitting the CIA and living in Perth.

Standing in a chilly parking lot in Blenheim, New Zealand, Dennis felt that brooding cloud of depression hovering. It worried him.

Walk, he told himself. *For god's sake just start walking. Do something. Anything! Don't let it get you.*

⊙

The phone rang three times before he answered it, just as Judy was about to leave a message.

"Dennis?"

"Gidday," Dennis said in his painful imitation accent.

"I see you've gone full Aussie," she said.

"Trying. It's hard. Can't stand Vegemite. And Aussie Rules Football, is, well, very strange. But the Sheilas are a bit of alright."

"Dennis, I have something to tell you."

He held the phone tightly to his ear since the coffee shop was loud. Judy's voice had been odd from the start of the silly exchange.

"I'm taking some time off work," she said. "Starting today."

"What? Leave of absence from work? Why would you do that?"

"Because I can't stand it any longer, that's why. It's not a leave of absence, just two weeks of vacation."

"Why now?"

"I can't stand my job any longer."

"Jeez, where did all this come from? I knew things were a little crazy with work. And perhaps I should have paid more attention to the shooting. I just didn't ... well, I wasn't paying attention."

"It's not just the shooting, but also the infuriating investigation afterward, and the trifling bureaucratic nonsense. Or maybe it was the shooting. Oh, I don't know. I just need a break, and I'm taking it. I feel bad for my partner Daniel, but he agrees that it's best that I do it now before I completely lose my temper."

Silence fell over the conversation.

"What are you going to do with your time off?" he asked.

"I'm not sure. My mum would like to visit Singapore, and dad isn't interested."

"You'll go stir crazy," he said. "You can't go from one hundred miles an hour to ten miles per hour. I tried it, and all I got was a really high handicap in golf."

"Ha, well, perhaps I'll take up golf."

Dennis ran the fingers of his free hand through his short hair, back to front several times.

"I have an idea," he said.

"Golf lessons?"

"No. Why don't you come to New Zealand?"

"Perhaps I'll do that after you finish your assignment. Might be a bit of fun."

"No, I mean now. Why don't you come now?"

"Dennis, you're on assignment. I've traveled with you before on assignment, and I'm a complete afterthought to you, which is understandable."

"Actually, I have a problem."

"What problem?"

"It's a police problem."

"Come again, Dennis?"

"The Dr. Forrester disappearance. It's a criminal investigation, not an intelligence investigation. I'm a little out of my element on this one, though I think I'm faking it pretty good. I feel like Inspector Clouseau in The Pink Panther or something."

"Have you been drinking?"

"No, well, not drinking a lot. Maybe I'm just rusty or something. But I can't figure out her disappearance. It really doesn't make sense, and I think someone with experience in criminal work could help. Like you."

"You do understand that you're privy to top secret information that is illegal for me to see?"

"You wouldn't see the information because I'd just talk to you about it."

"Dennis, you have been drinking. That's absurd. You're exposing yourself to serious repercussions, and I'm not going to be part of that. How many days do you have left on this thing? Twelve days or something?"

"Yes, exactly twelve days and that's why I need your help."

"First, stop drinking. Second, give it your best shot, and take the money and run. You said yourself that the entire case is nonsense."

Silence.

"Dennis?"

Silence.

"Dennis, speak to me."

"I think I'm a little messed up."

"I don't understand what you're saying."

"I thought I was fine until last night. Then I had a terrible dream. About my father and mother. All that family shit. I don't know why suddenly that came up. Maybe it's the Dr. Forrester thing. She opened the lid on that part of my life, and I thought I could put the lid back on. Feels strange that now she's missing."

"Are you depressed? Like you used to be?"

"I don't know."

"Oh, Dennis," Judy sighed. "Heavens, why did you take this assignment?"

"I thought it would occupy me, at least briefly. Remember, they came after me; I never sought it out."

"Why don't you quit and just come back to Perth?"

"I can't do that. I've never quit an assignment in my life."

"But you quit the agency, remember?"

"That was a job, not an assignment. Once I start, I never stop. I'm afraid to quit."

"Afraid of what?"

"I don't know."

"Dennis, you're worrying me, do you know that?"

Silence.

"Where are you staying?" she said.

He gave her the hotel in Blenheim.

"I'll call you after I make reservations."

⊙

Perhaps it was the knowledge that Judy would be joining him soon, or perhaps it was the walk around the pleasant little city of Blenheim, but Dennis felt buoyed somewhat when McCarthy and Winchester picked him up in the parking lot.

"Charming town," Dennis said.

"Yes, it is; we're quite lucky here in New Zealand. Away from most of the world's problems," McCarthy said. "Good climate, law-abiding citizens, and a great outdoor lifestyle."

"Well, not completely law-abiding," Dennis said. "Someone snatched our Dr. Forrester."

"Ah yes, well, there is that," McCarthy said. "I guess we can't escape all the world's evil. Luckily, we have nothing here for anyone to covet. Except for our rugby team, perhaps."

Winchester chuckled. "Hands off our All Blacks."

"That's the name of your national rugby team?" Dennis said.

Both men nodded from the front seat.

"You know, I thought Aussie Rules football was complicated, but when I watched a rugby match on TV, I had no idea what they were doing except beating the crap out of each other. And just when the game gets interesting, the ref blows a whistle, and they stop and gather in some kind of circle to push each other. And no helmets. Why no helmets?"

"Real men don't need helmets," Winchester said, sharing a sideways grin at McCarthy.

"Right," Dennis said.

They drove in silence as Dennis watched the town slide by. The call from Judy had revived him; he was now bantering, not brooding.

Keep focusing on the case, he thought. *Don't let that damn cloud overwhelm you. The hunt; focus on the hunt.*

◉

"In about a block, we'll be passing the Ghorbani house on the right," McCarthy said. "He's at work and she's out at a women's club meeting. You'll notice it's only twenty minutes from the park. That's how close they are to where Forrester was staying."

"Our folks suggest they brought her back here unconscious or disabled," Dennis said. "Took her inside and kept her until they got what they wanted, and then disposed of her body. Sound about right?"

"That's what we understand," McCarthy said.

"My report says our folks got into the house a month ago when the Ghorbanis were both out," Dennis said. "They found nothing of value inside the house; no DNA, no blood, no nothing. But the report says there *was* Forrester DNA found in the couple's car. Both on the back seat and on the right-hand interior door handle. If this were a court of law I'd say the case against the Ghorbanis rests on the DNA in the car. Otherwise, it's purely circumstantial. Would you say?"

The two men in the front both shrugged.

"Hello?" Dennis said.

"Yes?" McCarthy said.

"What do you think?"

"Think about what?"

"Christ!" Dennis said. "What do you think about the validity of the agency's report?"

"We told you already, Dennis; we don't have an opinion on the report."

Dennis suddenly felt angry; he was not sure why. The two men in the front seat were polite, though not terribly forthcoming. He knew their answers were vague, but he was sure they had been warned to stay neutral: keep out of the Yank's way, let those idiots do whatever they want.

Threads. Facts. Details, Dennis repeated to himself. *Follow the threads, not the bullshit.*

"You guys are useless," Dennis said, looking out the window.

"That's unfair," McCarthy said, his voice an octave higher than normal.

"You're telling me absolutely nothing. Zero. I can see why your bosses wanted me to huddle with you two bozos. Mutt and Jeff."

Dennis felt the car suddenly lurch left into a parking lot of a small strip of retail stores and come to a halt.

McCarthy swung around, his face pinched in anger, "You just hold on there, Cunningham. Unless you expect us to risk our careers dealing with you and your bloody agency, you should be more respectful. We have direct orders to refrain from offering up anything more than facts that have already been confirmed. Those are our direct orders, and for the record, even if we felt inclined to break those orders, you would be the last person we'd choose to do that with. You're boorish, unpredictable, and don't instill much confidence."

Dennis's mouth moved into an impish smile.

"Hey, Rangi," he said. "My guess is that you've been tracking the Iranians for a while, right?"

"Don't answer him," McCarthy said, staring at his partner.

"Yes, for some time," Winchester said.

"Rangi!" McCarthy said.

"And why exactly?" Dennis asked.

"We keep tabs on anyone suspicious that is located in the valley."

"Why?" Dennis said.

"Waihopai Station," Winchester said. "Electronic listening post at the end of the valley. Code name IRONSAND. We operate it, but you blokes use it too."

"Sorry, but isn't New Zealand pretty far off the grid for intelligence gathering?"

"Not really," Winchester said. "Radio waves travel quite far. And there's the Southern Cross Cable."

"Got me there. What's the Southern Cross Cable?"

"Do we really need to be talking about this?" McCarthy said.

"It's not classified," Winchester said. "The cable is part of the trans-Pacific network of communications cables. Runs in a big loop under the ocean including New Zealand, Australia and the United States."

"Ah, let me guess—some organization with a listening post might be tapping the cable," Dennis said. "And the listening post itself is of some interest to others. So, the Ghorbanis came under suspicion because they're Iranian expats and they're near the station."

"Yes," Winchester said.

"Are the Ghorbanis bad guys?" Dennis asked.

"Rangi, you should stop," McCarthy said.

"Yes, looks that way," Winchester said.

"How bad?" Dennis said.

"Medium bad."

"Does 'medium bad' mean they'd capture and torture a US psychologist for intel on her patients?" Dennis asked.

"Not in my definition," Winchester said.

"How about the Ghorbanis' friend Lajani? Bad guy?"

"He's an idiot," Winchester said.

"Bloody hell," McCarthy said, starting the car. "Would you please stop, Rangi?"

"Well, who do you think snatched Forrester then, if not the Iranians?"

"Who said she was snatched?" Winchester said.

"Damnit, stop it, Rangi!" McCarthy said. "I'm going to have to report you."

"McCarthy, you are such a pain in the ass," Dennis said. "Rangi's not harming anyone. At least he's trying to help. Whereas you're trying to impede. Do you realize those idiots in Washington are planning to take action against Iranian operatives somewhere in the world because they think they're behind the disappearance? I'm the guy who's going to save some poor Persians from being blown up in a car in Beirut or shot in the head while buying a baguette in Paris."

"That's not our responsibility. You Yanks can do whatever you want; you do anyway," McCarthy said.

"The report I have stated emphatically that an Iranian team of expats here in Blenheim abducted and tortured Dr. Forrester. They said there is DNA evidence and corroborating sigint that ties the expats to the disappearance. I read the sigint, and unless I'm a complete idiot—don't answer that McCarthy—the sigint intercept is innocuous and could mean anything."

"Right," Winchester said. "Glad someone else sees it that way."

"They were using code words," McCarthy said. "We all know that."

"Actually, can we back up? I'm trying to figure out what Rangi meant when he said, 'who said she was snatched?' Help me a little on that one, Rangi."

"What if she wanted to disappear?" he said. "It happens."

Dennis stared at the back of Rangi's head in the passenger seat.

"Shit," he said.

"You asked."

"Yes, I did," Dennis said slowly. "Yes, I did."

"You think she might have run off with someone? Maybe had an accomplice? Or she was depressed and killed herself?"

"No idea," Winchester said.

The car stopped suddenly in front of Dennis's hotel.

"Have a good day," McCarthy said drily.

⊙

Dennis read the intercepted text messages a dozen times and was impressed. While he had a very poor opinion of sigint in general, the current state of tracking was ingenious.

The text messages were between Farhad Ghorbani in Blenheim and Ramin Lajani in Wellington. The messages were in Farsi and translated by agency linguists. To Dennis, the messages were mundane and probably a code of some sort.

Ghorbani: *we are going to melbourne. can we stay with your friend?*

Lajani: *yes, I will tell him*

Ghorbani: *you are most kind*

The exchange took place eleven hours after Forrester disappeared. According to the GCSB, Lajani immediately sent an email after that exchange to an Iranian expat friend in Melbourne, Australia. According to the Australian Security Intelligence Organization, ASIO, the friend in Melbourne sent a text message to a Syrian expat friend of his in Brisbane, Australia. The Syrian sent an email to a friend in Lebanon.

In each exchange, the words "Ghorbanis" and "Melbourne" were repeated until they reached Lebanon. The recipient in Lebanon is, according to the CIA station there, a member of the Ministry of Intelligence, the Iranian spy agency.

The report further stated that the Ghorbanis made no obvious plans to visit Melbourne; they did not make airline reservations or rental car arrangements. Furthermore, the report mentions that the Ghorbanis have studiously befriended a young couple two doors away in their neighborhood; the husband of that couple works at the Waihopai eavesdropping station.

The DNA in the Ghorbani's car was pulled by an agency operations team, working without New Zealand assistance, during a nighttime operation. It was "touch DNA," that is typically a small flake of skin left behind by someone touching an object.

Dennis looked at the bottom right corner of his laptop and saw that it was nearly 6 p.m. He yawned, stretched his arms above his head, and took a sip of water from a glass next to the computer.

Judy had called earlier and said she'd be arriving early tomorrow morning in Auckland, would rent a car and drive to Wellington to take the inter-island ferry to Picton on the South Island. She would be in Blenheim by 2 p.m.

He was feeling better. Just the thought of her joining him in New Zealand lifted his spirits. And his immersion in the Forrester case kept his gloomy mind busy.

Forrester, he reminded himself. Of all people to go missing, it was Dr. Forrester. How strange. Was Rangi right? Did she plan her own disappearance?

And if he was wrong, who did take her?

The DNA evidence was startling; the lab showed it belonged to Forrester. No doubt there. But so much else was circumstantial. The text messages and digital bread crumbs to Lebanon were interesting and suggested a link between the Ghorbanis and Iranian intelligence services. Still, Dennis was not interested in whether the Ghorbanis were spies for Iran, but only whether they kidnapped Forrester.

The decision had been made in Langley, after consultation with their New Zealand counterparts, that it was better to leave the Ghorbanis alone and in place. It was easier to keep tabs on spies you knew, because they often lead to other spies. Hence, the Ghorbanis were not to be brought in for interrogation on the Forrester disappearance.

The agency would simply slap the Iranians somewhere else, covering their motives but not their thirst for revenge.

Dennis's phone rang.

"Cunningham, it's Simpson. I'm down in the lobby. Meet me in the hotel bar in ten minutes."

"Why didn't you tell me you were coming? And how did you know I was even here?"

"Jesus, Cunningham. You've grown rusty in retirement. You have an agency phone and a laptop. We know exactly where those devices are at any time. Assuming you haven't sold them yet on eBay. Ten minutes. I don't have much time here." Simpson hung up.

⊙

Simpson sat at a high-top table and barely acknowledged Dennis when he sat down. Two men sat nearby, staring directly at Dennis. They had the telltale twitchy nature of all bodyguards.

The waitress swung by and asked Dennis if he wanted a drink or menu.

"Sparkling water," he said, "with a lemon slice."

"You on the wagon, Cunningham?"

"No, just not interested right now. Why didn't you tell me you were coming?"

"Why would I?"

"As a courtesy, and to give me a chance to review some notes," Dennis said.

The waitress returned with Dennis's water and left.

"My countdown clock says you have twelve days including today to make a recommendation. I had a meeting in Honolulu and thought I'd detour here, though it was a long detour. I haven't heard a peep from you. The director is anxious for your report. I, on the other hand, know you aren't going to change the outcome. The report and its conclusions are solid. We have no idea why Franklin's dragging his heels on this one. Ridiculous. And you, of all people. That's how far we've fallen at Langley."

Surely Simpson knew of Dennis's reputation for surliness. This was waving a red flag at the bull.

And because it was obvious, Dennis paused.

"What do you want?" Dennis asked.

"An update that I can bring back to the director."

"You could have done that on the phone. You didn't need to fly thousands of miles out of your way to give me shit in person. The phone would have been fine."

"Cut the shit. What's your early take on this thing? Lots of folks are waiting in the wings to get things rolling. We have a rare opportunity to remove someone special from our list of Iranian adversaries. The window is tight. I just need you to give me a nod, and I can put things in motion."

"A nod?"

"Yes."

"A nod and a wink, or just a nod?"

"Asshole."

"That's neither a nod or a wink."

"Asshole."

"Have a nice flight," Dennis said, standing up. "Remember, sitting down for those long flights can aggravate hemorrhoids. Be sure to get up and stretch every now and then."

Back in his hotel room Dennis resumed his position in front of the laptop and tried to push the visit from Simpson out of his mind. Something was indeed wrong with this Forrester disappearance. What was he not getting?

Or was there *nothing* wrong with the Forrester case, and he was just depressed, angry, and full of self-doubt?

⊙

That night he had another dream about the death of his mother and father. He was a young boy again living in the Chicago's Irving Park neighborhood. In the dream, he was terrorized by someone trying to break into their home. He froze as the glass window broke and someone tried to enter the ground floor. He didn't know who was breaking in, but he could feel the presence of evil. It frightened the boy so profoundly that he could not move a muscle.

Dennis woke up confused, his brain still reeling from sleep chemicals and the emotional impact of the dream.

Lying in the dark, he stared at the illuminated hotel clock as if it held some power to fend off the doom that lingered like a bad hangover.

And dreams lie, as humans do.

In real life, the man coming into the house was Dennis's father. A drunkard and abusive husband, he was a Chicago cop who came home one afternoon from work, shot his mother dead while she was folding clothes, then shot himself while sitting in his favorite rocking chair. Dennis, an only child, found them that way after school.

It was Dr. Forrester's therapeutic skill that dragged him screaming and fighting into his past to revisit that event and review its effect on his life.

Staring at the glowing blue numbers on the clock radio, he knew it was Dr. Forrester's disappearance that was dragging him back down again.

How odd, he thought. *I'm not even sure I liked Dr. Forrester. But here she is kicking the living shit out of my insides again.*

⊙

At breakfast in the hotel, while stabbing at his scrambled eggs, Dennis had a thought that caused him to put down his fork. He stared at his coffee, took a sip, picked up his fork again, then dropped it.

He picked up his phone and dialed Simpson's number. As expected, it went to voice mail, and Dennis said, "Hey Simpson. I need the names of the agency personnel that Dr. Forrester was seeing in therapy.

Probably for the last two years. I need them immediately." He hung up.

Simpson was in an airplane, but probably had access to cell phone service. It was worth a shot. Why hadn't Dennis thought about this angle earlier? Rangi's suggestion that perhaps Forrester disappeared on purpose had opened other possibilities.

As outlandish as it seemed, could one of Forrester's CIA patients have planned this whole thing?

Dennis felt a tiny wave of anxiety ripple through his chest, like a low-voltage shock.

Was this idea a manifestation of his depression or the genuine question of an investigator?

Judy, where the hell are you? he thought.

CHAPTER 7

She called later that morning from Wellington after a brief layover in Sydney.

"How are you?" Judy asked.

"Great. Really looking forward to seeing you."

"I reckon I'll be in Blenheim around 2 p.m. Should I just go to the hotel?"

"Yeah. I'll be there. Just call me when you get off the ferry."

Right after he put down the phone, it rang again.

"Cunningham, you've got to be crazy," Simpson said. "Forrester's agency patients?"

"Yeah. Should be simple enough," Dennis said. "But quick, please. I'm running out of time."

"I'm not giving you those names. They would never allow it. And besides, it's a stupid idea. Let me guess: you think one of her patients followed her to New Zealand and kidnapped her?"

"I was directed to provide a judgment on the recommendation. That's what I'm doing."

"Not going to give you her agency patients," Simpson said. "Come up with some other lame idea."

"The director won't like it that you impeded the investigation."

"The director will never know about it, you jackass," Simpson said. "Remember? I'm your contact. You work through me. Do you think you can just call up the director of the CIA and talk to him? You have lost every single one of your marbles, Cunningham." Simpson hung up.

Dennis threw the phone onto his bed and stood up.

Shit, he's right, Dennis thought. *HR would never approve the release of their medical files, and even if they did, the bureaucratic machinery of getting authorization would take weeks. I don't have weeks, I've got eleven days!*

He grabbed the phone off the bed, put on his coat, and tugged on a baseball cap. He would go for a walk and let the environment wash over him. He'd had luck in the past walking around shopping malls or crowded city blocks seeking a moment of inspiration. But inspiration and depression don't mix well, and Dennis fought the impulse to get back into bed.

Get moving! Walk, you stupid son of a bitch!

Bolting out of the hotel he moved quickly to the sunny side of the street. Although it was winter in the southern hemisphere, the temperature was a pleasant sixty degrees. But a cool breeze sweeping inland from the ocean made the walk more challenging. He needed the warmth of the sun and vitamin D to combat his moodiness.

Dennis was lost in thought as he ran through a mental file cabinet of ideas on the Forrester disappearance.

Obviously, if the DNA sample from the Ghorbanis' car was accurate, the case was closed.

What was it about the Iranian connection that was odd? The sigint message intercepts were not definitive, he thought. *They were nothing more than Rorschach tests for analysts who interpret conspiracies out of the simplest conversations.*

He walked for an hour until he found a luncheonette and sat down to eat. The inspiration he hoped for never materialized. The only feeling he felt was hunger and a dull one at that.

Dennis was eating a sandwich at the small table when his phone vibrated. He pulled it out of his jacket pocket and saw that it was an agency number.

"Yes?" he answered.

"Cunningham?" a woman's voice asked.

"Yeah."

"It's Louise Nordland. How are you doing?"

He waited several seconds for that to bounce around his addled brain.

"What can I do for you, Louise?" he said, putting down his sandwich.

"How's the progress on your assignment?"

"Louise, I gather you're some mucky-muck at the agency now, and that you recommended me for this assignment. But you must also know that I've been directed to work through Simpson, not you. And I'm not an employee any longer, I'm a contractor. Getting fired or reprimanded has absolutely no effect on me."

"Yeah, got all that. How is the assignment going?"

"You know, even hearing your voice is throwing me off my lunch. Talk to Simpson if you want information on the assignment."

"I'm out on a bit of a limb with this one," she said. "Kenny is not convinced about the recommendation from operations. I share his concern. I thought that if anyone could shed some light on it, it would be you."

"Talk to Simpson, Louise."

"It's entirely appropriate for you to backchannel through me. The director asked me about it this morning."

"Tell the director to talk to Simpson."

"Simpson told the director that you're leaning toward agreeing with the analysis from operations."

"He said that?"

"Yes. He's already started preparations for the action plan based on your position."

"That's bullshit. I think you're making all this up just to pry out some feedback. I know your style, Louise, and this crap won't work. Talk to Simpson."

He hung up.

⊙

They kissed like long lost lovers, though they had been apart less than a week.

"I'm glad you're here," Dennis said. "It's been a tough couple of days."

"Not to worry. I'm here now." They kissed again. Then he took her roll-on suitcase from her, and they went to his room.

She unpacked and took two drawers for her clothes.

"Why do women pack so many shoes?" Dennis said. "How many pairs did you bring?"

"None of your business. Pay attention to your own clothes."

Later, they went for a brisk walk.

"What do you know about 'touch DNA'?" he said. "I've tried to read up on it, but I'm just not good with this stuff. You're a policewoman, you know about this stuff."

"Dennis, I'm not a crime lab technician, if that's what you mean. I can only tell you what I've had experience with."

"OK, 'touch DNA.' Tell me what you know about it."

"We've been using it for several years, and it's very useful for cases in which a crime scene offers up nothing. Also, it's useful for cold cases, but I'm not on the cold case team."

"How does this DNA test work?" Dennis said.

"It used to be that we needed blood or semen samples the size of a fifty-cent coin for DNA testing. Then the size of a five-cent coin was enough and even smaller. Now they can use skin cells."

"That's the 'touch' part?"

"Yes. We all shed skin cells, and they're left behind on things like a pistol grip, a door handle – items like that. If the tech swabs for those cells and gets a match, well, there you have it. And the tests are much faster than for standard DNA tests."

"Alright, here's the real question: How accurate are they?" Dennis said, pulling her over to a small bench inside an empty bus shelter.

"Mmm. Well, there are problems. I guess the big one is secondary contamination. You touch my hand, then I touch a door handle, and some of your skin cells are transferred to the door handle, but you never touched the door handle."

"Well, that's a problem," Dennis said.

"Of course, but in many investigations, there is no plausible scenario for secondary contamination. A lawyer would have to show that person A was in physical contact with person B, who then transferred skin cells to an object involved in the crime. But if person A was living a thousand miles away from person B, it's just not possible, if you see what I mean."

"Yes, I do. So, here's a scenario, and let me know what you think."

"Dennis, is this classified information you're going to tell me?"

"Maybe."

"Am I going to break any laws by hearing this?"

"Not if you don't know it's classified."

"But you just told me it was."

"I said it might be. And that means the breach—if there is one—is all on me, not you."

"I can't keep track of your convoluted thinking, Dennis," she said.

"You're very confusing."

"Just hear me out," he said. He described the broad case against the Ghorbanis, the sigint intercepts afterward, and the DNA evidence.

"So, what do you think?"

"About what?"

"The whole thing? The case against the Ghorbanis for abducting Forrester?"

"Heavens, I have no idea, Dennis. I'm not capable of commenting on your intelligence intercepts. Surely you understand that?"

"I don't care about that; how about the DNA?"

"I have no idea how sophisticated your teams are at capturing those samples, but I would assume they're pretty good, wouldn't you?"

"Yeah, I'd think they're pretty good. But what about the issue of cross-contamination?"

"Again, you'd have to consider who was in contact with Forrester and how they might have deposited the skin cells. I mean, from what you've said, it stands to reason that Dr. Forrester was in the back seat of that car, or one of the Ghorbanis was in contact with the doctor and then touched the back seat."

"The report I read doesn't say whether there were six skin cells in the back seat or five hundred. I don't know."

"Why are you questioning it?" she asked.

"I don't know, to be honest. It's too perfect, which, as you can imagine, is not a real reason."

"Well, you must have another theory then," she said, standing up. "Can we walk some? I'm getting cold."

"I have two opposing potential theories," Dennis said. "One, that Forrester disappeared on purpose. Either she ran away with someone, or she was depressed and killed herself. I know it's kind of lame, but one of the Kiwi investigators threw it out, and I realized it was at least worth thinking about."

"What's your second theory?" she said.

"The second theory is that perhaps one of the doctor's patients abducted her."

"In New Zealand?" she said. "Really?"

⊙

How far do you follow someone?

Judy walked hand in hand with Dennis down the windy streets of Blenheim and wondered. Growing up in Western Australia she'd had a vision of how her life would unfold, and initially, it had gone according to plan.

Until it didn't. There was her husband's affair, the divorce, his involvement in a criminal ring, and his imprisonment. Her own career in the AFP had gone well.

Until it didn't. She had been rocked by the internal affairs investigation of her police work, and she was now on a brief vacation.

Judy felt the warmth of the sun on her face as they sauntered like confused high schoolers past shop windows. What was going to happen to her and Dennis? Was he really going to return to Perth after his two-week contract, or was this the beginning of the end? She knew he was bored, but was he bored from lack of activity or bored of her? Was she not interesting enough?

"Sometimes I can almost feel you thinking," Dennis said.

"Don't be silly."

"No, really. It's almost like there's a small whirring sound, like a computer hard drive. And I feel you drifting away into thought."

"Not likely, Dennis. You're making things up again."

"And tell me, why do you raise your voice at the end of a sentence, even though it's not a question? I think it's an Aussie thing."

Judy laughed. "Yes, apparently it is an Aussie thing. It's called 'Australian question intonation.' Don't ask me where it came from. Maybe left over from the convicts first sent to Australia."

"Well, it's charming and a little confusing because I think you're asking a question, but you're just making a statement."

"Ha, that pretty much sums you up, Mr. Cunningham: you're endlessly confusing."

His phone rang.

"Yes, this is Dennis Cunningham. Oh, Dr. Caldicott. Yes, thanks for getting back to me. Is there any chance I could call you back in five minutes? This number? Great, I'll call you back right away."

"Who's Dr. Caldicott?" Judy asked.

"The last person to see Forrester alive. They were here in Blenheim on a side trip for a wine tour. Old colleagues."

Dennis looked around and noticed a coffee shop a half-block away.

"Do you mind if we stop in there for a few minutes while I call her back?"

"No," Judy said, as their hands separated.

He walked rapidly, and she struggled to keep up.

⊙

Judy watched Dennis take out his pen and a small notebook, open it to the first blank page, connect his earbuds to his phone, and call.

She sipped a flat white coffee and observed him closely. She was intrigued about how this abrasive investigator would coax critical information out of a highly educated and distressed woman 9,000 miles away.

Her answer came right away.

"Yes, I'm sure this is very distressing for you," he said, exuding empathy. "I can't imagine how awful this whole experience has been."

She watched him nod in apparent sympathy as Dr. Caldecott talked about the trauma caused by the sudden disappearance of her friend and travel companion. This was followed by a lengthy back and forth as

Dennis commiserated with her.

But, Judy noticed, he also began to gently prod the woman for details.

He would slip in questions like: Did Dr. Forrester have headaches often on the trip? Did she seem unhappy about anything in her life? Did she complain about any of her patients, her family, her health?

After fifteen minutes of this, Judy finished her coffee and got up to stretch.

Her phone pinged, and she saw that her son Trevor was texting her.

r u in kiwiland yet?

yes, blenheim. wish u were here. charming place. more british than aussie.

some blokes thinking of holiday there. could i go?

grades first

u r a tigermom

ggrrrrrrr

r u with dennis?

yes, he's on assignment. joining him for a spell

is he happy here?

in WA?

yes

think so. y u ask?

want u to be happy

am happy

really?

really

u seem stressed lately

work

why did u take vaca? grandma said u r unhappy there

u should pay attention to grades; grandma exaggerates

r u moving to US?

who told u that?!
wondering
back to studies; no worries about moving!

⊙

Later, Dennis sat at the bar in the hotel and leafed slowly through his notebook.

"So?" Judy asked.

"Caldecott is crushed with guilt. Seems depressed. Kept repeating that she should have walked with her friend to the drug store, but thought the town was safe."

"That's it?"

He shook his head. "Nothing momentous. She said Forrester seemed fine; was relaxed, funny, and they enjoyed the wine tours. Said she never complained about her husband, her career, and never mentioned her patients. Caldecott mentioned that it was unethical for psychologists to discuss patients with each other unless the patient's identity was hidden and there was some valid clinical reason to seek another opinion."

"Do you believe Caldecott was involved in her disappearance?'

"No. I mean that's what I think after a single long-distance phone call, but that's my instinct."

"Did she have anything to add to your investigation?"

"Not really."

"You're running out of time."

"I know."

⊙

They had dinner at a pub and then sauntered through the chilly evening.

"I think I've lost your attention," she said.

"What?"

"You seem lost in thought. I thought joining you here would be fun, but I should have remembered how intense you get when you're on the trail of something or someone."

"Do I seem preoccupied?"

"Ha, just a little!"

"I'm sorry. I should have been more careful about inviting you here. I knew you were having a tough time at work. And I missed you."

"Well, you could show it every now and then."

Dennis stopped on the sidewalk, pulled Judy into his body and kissed her.

"That helps a little," she said.

"Don't ever get confused about my feelings for you," Dennis said underneath the cone of white light from a street lamp. "I'm just a little off-kilter right now. But not with you. Never with you."

"Perhaps I'm feeling fragile these days. I don't know," she said, as they continued to walk.

At the hotel, they stopped off for a drink at the bar.

"You really are beautiful," Dennis said suddenly. "Stunning."

"I beg your pardon?" Judy laughed.

"Just stating the obvious."

"Remind me to complain more often about losing your attention," she said.

"I can't wait to show you some attention later," he said.

"My word," she said. "A man on a mission."

It might have been the drink at the bar, or just the moment, but there was an explosion of raw sexual passion when they got back to the hotel room. He kissed her neck the second the door closed behind them, and they could barely make it to the bed, undressing in awkward movements by tossing off clothing everywhere.

Afterward, Judy lay on her side pointing away from him. Dennis lay on his back. He ran his finger down her spine, to the deep curve at the base.

"You're tickling me."

"Just checking you out. You have a nice behind. Or arse, as you Aussies say. Very shapely."

"Oh, please."

"Just saying."

⊙

The phone sounded like a klaxon and Dennis knocked it off the bedside table trying to reach it. He cursed several times and used the charging cord like a fishing line, slowly pulling the phone up to the bed.

"Hello?"

"Louise here. Sorry to call you at this hour."

"What hour is it?" he asked.

"My math says it's 3 a.m. there; it's 9 a.m. here and you're seventeen hours ahead."

"OK, you win the math test. What's up?"

"Against all odds, I was able to get the list of agency employees seeing Forrester."

"How the hell did you know I wanted that list?"

"Simpson bitched about your request in another meeting, so I just ran behind him on it. HR caved when I told them of the director's impatience. They coughed up the list."

"Well, that's a welcome bit of initiative. Can you send it to me right now?"

"Yes, right away."

"Do you recognize anyone on the list? Anyone I know or should know?"

"Well, that's why I'm calling you."

"OK."

"My name is on the list."

Dennis concentrated on a thin sliver of light from outside the hotel room that crept through a crease in the curtains. It cut a bright line down the wall. He stared at the wall, blinking in the dark room. Judy stirred next to him.

"Cunningham."

"Yes."

"Did you hear what I said?"

"Yes."

"Why aren't you saying anything?"

"I'm thinking."

"About what?"

"About why you never told me from the beginning you were seeing Forrester. Seems like an important fact to leave out."

"I realize that, and that's why I'm calling. I made a mistake but wanted to come clean right away. I didn't think the fact that I was seeing her was relevant. But I'm telling you, aren't I?"

"How long had you been seeing her?"

"Less than a year. I liked talking to her. This is a stressful job."

"How many names are on the list?"

"Five, counting me. I also have some bad news about the list."

"Like what?"

"Only one of the names is interesting," she said.

"Besides you?"

"Stop it, Cunningham."

"I'm serious, Louise. I'd call it really, really strange that you never told me you were seeing her. I'll withhold judgment on that for now."

"Fine but hear me out. The other three are low-level employees. One is a new analyst, she's only twenty-seven years old. One is an administrative assistant, and another is an accountant in the finance department. Only one is a male, the interesting one. The name is Kyle Keating, a senior analyst for on the Middle East. His specialty is Iran."

Dennis refocused on the sliver of light on the wall. He could hear

Louise's breath rustling across her phone's mouthpiece.

"I'm sending the list to you now. Call me if you need anything else."

"One question," he said. "Why did you recommend me for this job?"

"I already told you: we needed a fresh set of eyes, and the director wanted my advice. I suggested you because you're good at finding people, or what happened to them anyway. And you're not afraid to step on toes."

"Can you make sure to send me the personnel files of all of the people on the list, not just the list of names?"

"Sure."

"Including your file."

"Is that necessary?"

"Yes."

"Then you'll have it right away. Goodnight."

"What the hell was that about?" Judy asked, her mouth pressed against the pillow.

"I'm not sure, to be honest. This case is curiouser and curiouser."

"What?" she said turning toward him the in dark.

"I think that's a quote from Alice in Wonderland," he said, "or maybe Louise in Wonderland."

"I think you're a stubbie short of a six-pack," she said turning back on her side.

"Is that a good thing?"

"No. Go to sleep."

CHAPTER 8

Judy tore another small piece from her croissant and ate it; Dennis sipped at his coffee, looking out the hotel window into the blustery daylight.

"You spent all morning reading those reports from Louise. Anything strike you?"

"Besides Louise's odd behavior?"

"Yes, besides that."

"This guy Keating is interesting. He's fifty-six years old, been at the agency for twenty-two years, and is the chief Iran guy. His personnel file is nothing but superlatives and promotions. It's hard to think why he was seeing Forrester. And his Iranian connection is obviously interesting."

"Did you have access to Forrester's notes on her sessions with him?"

"No. HR doesn't have that and wouldn't have it. They just have a notification that he was seeing an authorized therapist."

"Well, who has Forrester's therapy notes then?"

"They must be in her file cabinet."

"Can you get access to those notes?"

"I would hope so, though I don't know the legality of that. Medical files are pretty sacrosanct, even for the agency. Forrester kept a home office and I know she used notes with me. My guess is the notes are in her home office locked up."

"I'm sure her husband would allow you to look at them."

"Maybe."

"When are you going to talk to him?"

"According to my Mutt-and-Jeff team from kiwi intelligence, Forrester's husband flew to New Zealand immediately after being contacted by authorities about her disappearance. He came with one of his adult kids, they stayed for ten days, then went home when they couldn't find her. They were pretty upset, apparently, and created a fuss at the US Embassy in Wellington."

"Wonder who Mr. Forrester met with here in the police department?"

"I don't think he would have met with the police; probably met with the folks from kiwi intelligence."

"I'm sure he met with local police," Judy said. "It was most certainly a law enforcement issue initially."

"Are you sure of that?"

"Yes. Didn't you say that it took a while to pin the disappearance on the Iranians? In the meantime, it was a police investigation. I'm sure Mr. Forrester met with local police at some point."

"Damnit, of course he did. Colin and Rangi never brought that up. Hell, I'll just wander down to the police department in Blenheim here and have a chat."

"We're friendly with the Kiwis at the AFP. I'm sure I can find the person who initially handled the case."

⊙

Dennis kept re-reading Louise's personnel file, drawn to her meteoric rise in the agency. The tough, diminutive blonde had served a stint in

Afghanistan leading a team of SEALS as part of the kill-and-capture Omega Program. Later, on assignment in Beirut, she survived a devastating car bombing at a compromised safe house. She'd been buried in rubble for almost twelve hours; her left foot was so badly mangled that it was amputated.

By the time Dennis met Louise she had been unhappily detailed to the Inspector General's office, treating the transfer to the agency's watchdog as a demotion due to her disability. Dennis barely noticed her odd gait as a result of her prosthetic foot.

Their relationship was rocky given two strong personalities, but they eventually solved the bizarre disappearance of the missing London assistant chief of station.

Yet Dennis never felt comfortable working with Louise, and his suspicions were rewarded when he discovered her subterfuge. She had ingratiated herself with her former clandestine operations group by tipping them off to impending OIG investigations.

The OIG was barely tolerated by agency employees and contractors who were offended by the oversight. They also worried—not unfairly—about being scapegoated as a result of poorly planned and executed programs. The inspector general had the further complication of reporting to the House and Senate intelligence committees, as well as the CIA director. It was a messy and fraught department that investigated everything from misused funds and poorly managed contracts to criminal activity by off-the-reservation employees.

Dennis had a celebrated career within the OIG for his no-nonsense, abrasive investigatory style. But after several cases involving employee corruption and murder, he had grown too cynical and depressed; he slipped away to the other side of the world from Langley, following the woman he loved.

But now Louise had resurfaced in the CIA director's inner circle, pushing a retired, cranky, former OIG investigator as the antidote to an agency problem.

Was Louise to be trusted? he wondered. *Why me and why now?*

⊙

"Detective Michael Brown; that's your man," Judy said. "Blenheim Police. He was the initial investigator."

"That was fast," Dennis said, hunched over his notebook at the small desk in the hotel room. He searched Google for the number and dialed.

Judy sat on the bed with a cup of coffee from the hotel coffee shop and watched Dennis. She had no trouble finding out who the detective was; it had taken her three calls, and she was thrilled to be helpful.

But helpful for what cause? She knew that Dennis's assignment was preposterous. How silly to ask a retired investigator to solve a complicated disappearance in fourteen days. She had tried to get him to acknowledge the absurdity of it, but he seemed to latch onto the task with a fervor that reminded her of the other, more complicated Dennis.

After nearly twenty-five minutes of phone calls and voice messages to the police department, Dennis's phone rang.

"Detective Brown? Yes, this is Dennis Cunningham. I've been dispatched here at the behest of the US Government to investigate the disappearance of a US citizen, a Dr. Forrester. Do you know about the case?"

Judy watched Dennis scribble something into his notebook, then stop abruptly.

"Well, I can certainly show you some identification, if that's what you need," he said, and then listened for at least a minute, his eyes squinting in concentration. "Sure, I can do that. When? Today? You're at 8 Main Street? Great, see you then."

"Well, well," Dennis said to Judy. "He seemed very guarded. And he kept repeating that the jurisdiction for the case has been transferred to the intelligence service. This is a great lead, Miss AFP. You're nice to have around."

"Ha," she said, taking a sip of coffee. "I feel useless here. At least I can help a bit. And it takes my mind off returning to work."

"When do you have to go back?"

"I told Calvin I'd be back next week, earliest."

"Can't you stay longer?"

"Dennis, what would I do here?"

"Hang out with me? Keep helping on this case, like you are now."

"Don't be daft. I can't help you."

"You just did."

"That was nothing."

He stood up and sat next to her on the bed. He kissed her gently on the cheek.

"Careful, you'll spill my coffee, Yank."

"Please don't go," he said. "Stay here. I'm lonely without you."

"Well, you'll just have to come back to W.A. then, won't you?"

"Don't worry. I'll be there as soon as this thing is wrapped up."

"Mmm," she took another sip.

⊙

Detective Michael Brown was much older than Dennis expected, given his youthful telephone voice; he was perhaps sixty years old, tall, gaunt-looking with a thick, barely controlled mop of gray hair.

"I hope you're not offended," Brown said standing in front of Dennis in the public area of the police station, "but this is not my case any longer, and I need to see some kind of identification."

"Absolutely," Dennis said, handing over the official brown-colored government passport that had been fast-tracked to him.

"Do you have anything else? A badge perhaps? This passport is for official US government employees."

"No, we don't hand out business cards," Dennis said, smiling. "They can be faked easily. I'm sure you can understand that."

"Yes, but how do I know you're authorized to contact me about this case? Surely you can understand that? I called my contact Rangi in Auckland, but he was in a meeting. Even if you're on official business, I don't know why you want to talk to me."

"Oh good, you called Rangi Winchester then," Dennis said. "Great. I've already talked to him and Colin McCarthy. Good guys. They said I could talk to you."

"They did? Well, they bloody hell could have let me know," Brown said handing back the passport. "Follow me."

They went past the front desk and into a hallway, through another two doors to Brown's plain office. Family photos of his wife and three children through various stages of life were placed throughout the office; the newest one showed a huge family gathering with grandchildren.

"How can I help you?" Brown asked, settling into his very old and creaky chair.

"Do you have a police report for the disappearance of Dr. Forrester? I'd like to review it, if possible."

"I'll have to clear that with my boss," Brown said, leaning forward and writing on a pad of paper. "Anything else?"

"Yes, who was in charge of the investigation?"

"I was."

"Were you the first responder?"

"No, that was the officer on duty that night. I took it the following day. Strange case."

"Why so?"

"We don't have many stranger abductions. Drunken brawls, yes; domestic violence, yes; murder or abductions, not many."

"I hate to ask this, but was there anything about the case that jumped out at you? I presume you've been a detective for a while."

The desk phone rang, and Brown looked at the number. "Hang on a bit, mate. I need to grab this."

Dennis nodded and looked around the small office.

"Hello, Rangi, how are you?" Brown said.

Dennis's head swiveled sharply and watched Brown, who stared at his phone console as he listened intently.

"He's here now. I've got him in my office—"

Brown looked up and they locked eyes.

"I see. Yes," Brown returned his gaze down to the console. "Cheers." He hung up and leaned back, creating a variety of high-pitched squeaking sounds from the chair.

"Rangi says that you are not authorized to talk to me without either he or Colin in attendance. I'm afraid this conversation will need to end until one of them can arrange to join us. Would you mind if we continued tomorrow perhaps? Early afternoon? One of them could be here by 1 p.m."

"I like Rangi," Dennis said. "A good man. I'm not crazy about Colin, though. Seems very rigid."

They looked at each other.

"I think we'll need to continue tomorrow," Brown said, standing. "One o'clock?"

"No, I don't think so," Dennis said, still sitting.

"I'll have to ask you to leave."

"You can ask, but I won't leave."

Brown's face was animated, his eyebrows arched wildly.

"You must leave."

"What do you think happened to Forrester? You're a veteran detective. Been doing this for a long time. You met with Forrester's husband when he came here. It must have been difficult dealing with him."

"Yes, he was quite upset. But would you please leave now?"

"I just need you to answer my question before I go: was there anything especially unusual about this case? Something that just didn't add up? I'm just asking for your unofficial instinct on this."

"This is awkward, Mr. Cunningham. I've been ordered by Rangi not to talk to you without someone from his group in attendance. Please accommodate me on this request. I'm a simple policeman in a small town."

"Please," Dennis pleaded. "Just a moment longer. Rangi is a good man and is just following orders. But you know how silly some of these bureaucratic procedures can be. They have to fly someone down from the North Island just to sit in on a conversation that lasts five minutes."

"Well, you are welcome to sit in my office as long you like," the detective said. "But I'll be elsewhere."

"So, do you think Mr. Forrester had anything to do with his wife's disappearance? Did he seem like a normal concerned husband?"

"Why are you Yanks so impulsive and demanding? You can't go tromping around demanding answers instantly. Please have some respect for our laws, though we may be a small country with more sheep than people."

Dennis laughed. "How many people live in New Zealand?"

"About four and half million."

"How many sheep?"

"About thirty million or so."

"Well, you might want to start taking care of your visitors instead of your sheep," Dennis said standing. "Dr. Forrester was an important person in some quarters, and her disappearance has created a stir. I'm sorry to cause trouble for you, Detective Brown, but it seems your intelligence folks are keeping absolute control of everything I do here. And that makes me suspicious, as it would you."

Brown bit the inside of his lip. "That is unfortunate. The case was very perplexing. Very."

"Why?"

"As I said earlier, we don't experience many stranger abductions."

"How do you know it was a stranger?"

"She wasn't here long enough to have a relationship. She was only in Blenheim for two nights, and she disappeared on that second night."

"Did you think her friend Caldecott was involved somehow?"

"No."

"Why?"

"She was despondent; cried continually. Seemed very authentic. Just my guess. The hotel CCTV shows she never left her room."

"And Dr. Forrester's husband?"

"Was a little stiff in my opinion. Sad, but very controlled. Probably his personality. Very shocking event to process. I've seen all sorts of responses, from hysterical to cold. Says more about the personality than anything else, in my opinion."

"Have there been other disappearances in the area?"

"Just a teenager, who ran away to Christchurch. Came back a week later. And a wife who ran away from a violent husband."

"That's it?"

"Yes."

"How about disappearances in Christchurch or other places on the South Island?"

"Not really, I'm afraid. There is no obvious connection or pattern. Sorry."

"What do you think of the theory about the Iranian family?"

"Have a nice visit," Brown said, flashing a wan smile. He turned and left the room.

Dennis scanned the office's array of family photos one more time, then left.

⊙

She sat on the bed, fully clothed with her winter coat still on, crying.

"What happened? What's wrong?" he said. "Judy. Talk to me."

"My stepdad; he's had a heart attack."

"Oh god," he said. "Is it serious?"

"Mum doesn't know yet. They don't know whether he needs a by-pass or a stent. I don't know. Something like that. He's stable and they're doing tests. Mum is a mess. My sisters are a mess."

"You have to get back there right away," he said. "Have you checked flight schedules?"

"No, I'm too upset. Can you help me?"

"Sure," he said sitting down in front of the laptop.

⊙

"Every time I say goodbye to you, I feel like it's the last time I'll see you," she said, her faced buried in his shoulder.

They were standing in the terminal at the small regional airport in Marlborough. It was late afternoon, and Judy felt frightened and ex-hausted. Her stepfather—the only father she had known—was the rock of the family. With a mother and two stepsisters, her family life had al-ways seemed full of drama. Dad, on the other hand, was the only one who could calm the family down.

And he was sick, perhaps dying, for all she knew. Her hysterical mother was barely intelligible about his condition, and her sister Nan-cy was not much better.

She needed to get home and see for herself how her father was doing.

But there was the stress of her job waiting, and then there was Dennis.

Would he ever return? He was a complicated man.

"They're calling the flight, Judy. You need to go," he said, prying her arms from around his back.

She looked into his eyes, searching for something that might reas-sure her.

He smiled. "Stop it, your gaze is hurting!"

"Sorry," she said, reaching for her roll-on suitcase. "I miss you already."

"Not half as much as I'm going to miss you," he said.

"I worry about you," she said. "I worry about us."

"Stop worrying. You have enough stress in your life right now."

He kissed her hard. She noticed that he kissed when he could not find the words to express himself. *A man of action*, she thought. *I wish he could use words.*

⊙

Dennis was walking to his rental car in the parking lot when his phone rang. At first, he thought it was Judy, but the number was blocked.

"Shit," he said, stopping in the chilly wind.

"Cunningham, what the hell are you doing talking to Louise Nordland?" Simpson yelled from 9,000 miles away.

"I beg your pardon?"

"I said, 'What the hell are you doing talking to Louise Nordland?'"

"Since when can't I talk to folks at Langley? What the hell's got into you? I'm a contractor who works for the agency and has a million former colleagues there. Christ, Simpson, you're just a little too jumpy, don't you think?"

Dennis could hear Simpson breathe heavily, trying to compose himself. As deputy director of the Operations Directorate, Simpson had the unenviable weight of a thousand clandestine operations on his plate. And this project was the last thing he needed to deal with. Dennis was also aware of the internecine battles in the vast bureaucratic CIA empire, and that Louise and Simpson were competitors.

"Were you not directed to deal with me exclusively on this contract?" Simpson snapped.

"Yes, I was. But no one said I was prohibited from talking to anyone else at Langley. I don't know what's got into you. Do you want a rundown of what I've come up with, or do you want to keep complaining about the chain of command crap?"

"She said she gave you the five names of agency people who were seeing Forrester, is that correct?"

"Yes, I assumed the permission was cleared in Langley. Why is that so important?"

"You were supposed to go through me on that," Simpson said.

"You're a busy guy, and it just came up in a conversation with her. She said she might be able to help. Why are you being such a control freak?"

Again, he could hear Simpson breathe heavily to compose himself.

"Don't talk to Louise again about this case, Cunningham. Do you read me?"

"Louise Nordland is a thousand levels above my pay grade, and I'm not about to tell someone that far up the chain of command to screw off," he said.

"You are a real piece of work, you know that?"

"That's what I've been told."

"My clock says you have ten days left. Finishing sooner would be better."

"The headline is that the Ghorbani connection seems plausible," Dennis said.

"Well, that's good news," Simpson said, the tension sliding away from his voice.

"But there are parts that don't make sense, so I'm digging a little deeper."

"What parts?"

"The Ghorbani connection is completely circumstantial except for the DNA. If you take out the touch DNA, I'm not sure we have a strong connection."

"What the hell do you know about touch DNA? You were a goddamn investigator for OIG, not a CSI professional. You're watching too much TV in retirement."

"Touch DNA is a specious connection. And if *I* know that, *you* must know that. Do you want to kick off assassinations of Iranian agents as payback for something that isn't proven? Listen, the director said himself he wants another pass at this, and that's what I'm doing. I've got ten days to make my recommendation."

"Your recommendation is going through me."

"Yes, I understand that. And I need to get going if you don't mind."

Simpson hung up without another word.

Dennis stared at his phone, then slowly put it in his jacket, looked up at the partly cloudy, late-afternoon sky and breathed deeply. To the north, he could see the tops of a small mountain range over the buildings. Coming back from a golfing retirement was a lot less fun than he had thought.

⊙

Dennis sat at the small desk in the hotel room and looked through his notes, looking for a thread that might lead to another thread, something that could unify the perplexing elements of this disappearance.

But he could not concentrate. He could smell Judy's presence in the room. Was it her shampoo? Hair conditioner? The intensity of the loneliness surprised him. He pushed the notes away, stood up, and went to the bed. He picked up her pillow and put it against his nose. It smelled of romance, sex, soap, and longing.

He sat on the bed. There were times in his life when he could recognize the creeping appearance of depression, like the first wisps of fog. Dr. Forrester taught him through cognitive behavior therapy to change his thinking to focus on action, physical exercise, work duties, anything that would stop the chain of thoughts leading to a deep, black hole.

Today he didn't give a shit about taking positive steps. He was de-pressed and sat holding the pillow in his lap like he was comforting an old dog.

The phone, set to mute, vibrated on the desk like a wounded ci-cada. He stared at it but didn't move. It agitated again in a low hum. He tossed the pillow and grabbed the phone. He did not recognize the number.

"Hello?"

"Mr. Cunningham?"

"Yes."

"This is Dr. Caldecott. I was traveling with Jane when she disap-peared. We talked recently, remember? You called me and said I should call you if I remembered anything that might be helpful."

"Yes, I remember our conversation quite well."

"Well, I did remember something."

CHAPTER 9

He plugged his ear with his left forefinger, blocking out the sound of the bustling airport, while he pressed the phone to his other ear. It rang three times and went to a voicemail prompt.

"Hey, Judy, this is Dennis. Hope your father is doing well. I'm hoping everything is OK there. Just wanted to let you know that I'm heading to Washington. Something came up and I need to get back to the states. I'm in Auckland and catching a flight to Los Angeles, and then on to D.C. Please call or text me about how your father is doing. Bye. I miss you."

He looked around the airport, sighed, stood up, and walked toward a coffee shop. A flight to Adelaide, South Australia, was boarding next to his departure gate. How he wished he was going back to Australia instead of deeper into that cesspool of deceit, Washington, the District of friggin' Columbia.

Dennis sat at a small high-top table in the coffee bar and took a deep breath before calling. The phone rang three times until it went to voicemail.

"Simpson, this is Cunningham checking in. I'm heading to D.C.

and should be back there in a day. Call me if you need to talk. Can fill you in later on some developments."

The Air New Zealand flight to Los Angeles was twelve hours long but tolerable since he bought a business-class ticket. The non-American flight crews always seemed more solicitous, and he could not explain the difference. He prayed they would not run into turbulence over the vast Pacific Ocean, and except for a brief bump-and-run somewhere east of Hawaii, it was a smooth flight. He dozed off and on, nibbled at his meals and watched parts of three movies. When they were taxiing to the gate in Los Angeles, he turned on his phone and saw that he had a text from Simpson: *call me.*

After going through customs, he took a shuttle bus to another terminal, went back through security, and finally found a quiet area near his departure gate.

Simpson answered right away.

"What the hell are you doing coming to D.C.? Who said you could do that?"

"I need to check on a few things," Dennis said.

"Forrester disappeared in New Zealand, not D.C., you dipshit. Work this out in Kiwi land, not D.C."

"Maybe her disappearance had something to do with her work in D.C."

"Do you have Alzheimer's or something?" Simpson yelled. "You were asked to evaluate the assumption that the Iranians were behind her disappearance. The Ghorbanis are in New Zealand. The disappearance happened in New Zealand, not far from the Ghorbani's home. There is DNA evidence that Forrester was in the backseat of the Ghorbani's car, for chrissakes! What the hell are you going to D.C. for? Find out what happened to her in New Zealand!"

"Are you going to let me investigate this case, or are you going to investigate it? Because if the director wants me to do it, then you better let me do it my way. Either that, or I'll resign from this stupid case and make sure the director knows it was you who drove me away."

Dennis could feel his neck flush with blood as his anger crested quickly. He was feeling whipsawed between the director, Simpson, and Louise, and he had trouble getting his bearings on this case. Something was off, but he did not know what or who it was.

And when he was frustrated and confused, he would fall back to anger, a pattern that Dr. Forrester, of all people, had tried to break him of.

"Listen," Dennis said, "this case is very difficult for me to get my arms around. I'm sorry if we're getting off on the wrong foot. You're going to have to trust me that I'm doing what I think is best to get to a speedy conclusion. I'll keep you posted."

Simpson hung up without saying a word.

Well, that went well, Dennis thought, putting the phone in his pocket.

⊙

The trip to D.C. took twenty hours, including a layover at LAX. He arrived at Dulles International Airport at 5:30 p.m. a day after leaving New Zealand. He rented a car and staggered into his hotel in Rosslyn, Virginia, at 7 p.m. He had two single malts in the hotel bar and collapsed in his hotel room.

He woke the next morning and briefly thought he was still in Blenheim. After a groggy start, he gradually collected himself until he thought the whites of his eyes were more pink than red.

Dennis asked Louise to meet him at a Starbucks in Crystal City, the concrete jungle of buildings across the Potomac in Virginia.

He spotted her right away, with her white-blond hair, faint limp, and creaseless face. Dennis had not seen Louise in more than a year and had forgotten how diminutive she was. No more than five feet, she was easily lost in the crowd of people in line to order coffee. Like a well-trained street agent—which he was not—he didn't acknowledge her entrance into the bustling coffee shop. He browsed *The Washington Post* until she put her coffee on the table and sat down.

"Hey," Dennis said.

"Hey," she said.

Perhaps his negative interactions with Louise in the past had distracted him, but he was surprised how pretty she was. He had never considered her attractive, and it was a mild complication he was unprepared for.

"How's business?" he said.

"Same shit, different day."

He chuckled.

"I won't take up your time on this, Louise, but I'm sure you know by now that Simpson was bullshit that we talked."

"That's affirmative," she said, taking a sip of coffee.

"But I feel I can't work through him, Louise. He keeps trying to point me to the Ghorbanis and New Zealand."

"I can understand that." She took another sip, her thin lips leaving a delicate smear of lipstick on the coffee cup.

"But I feel like Forrester's death—well, I'm calling it a death though I guess she could be alive—is more related to her psychotherapy practice, and to people here, not in New Zealand."

"And why is that?"

"I can't say exactly, just a feeling. The DNA thing is just too specious. And I've got some new information that led me back here."

Louise, who had barely acknowledged his presence, now stared so hard at him that he flinched.

"What information?"

"From her colleague Dr. Caldecott, the one she was traveling with in New Zealand."

"What did Caldecott tell you?"

"That Forrester complained one night, over a couple of glasses of wine, that she had a pretty uncomplicated patient load, except for one patient."

"And?"

"Well, the patient was a male, and Forrester felt there was something odd about him. Caldecott said it was a vague feeling Forrester had, but that after so many years as a therapist, she said, you could often tell when you were dealing with a strange one."

"Strange one?"

"Yeah, like a sociopath. Or worse. Again, Caldecott wasn't saying this patient was dangerous; it was just that I asked her to tell me anything that might be helpful, anything at all."

"Let me get this right: you're saying that Forrester's friend told you that Forrester complained about a male patient that bothered her?"

"Yes."

"And you're suggesting, I gather, that Forrester's bothersome or dangerous patient figured out that she was going to New Zealand, followed her, kidnapped, and killed her?"

"Well, yes, that's a possibility."

"I've read the file, Cunningham, and it appears that she had nineteen active patients, only five of which were agency clients. We don't know who the other fourteen clients were. That information is not available to the agency, and it would take some heavy lifting from government sources to get that information. You've got only eight days to figure this out—according to my calendar— and you want to look into all her patients for males that could be sociopaths?"

"No, hang on. First, I have nine days, not eight."

"On my calendar, you have eight counting today; somewhere east of Fiji, if you remember, your plane flew past the International Date Line when you came here. You lost a day."

"Shit, you're right."

"So, what's your second point, if you have one?"

"Forrester's colleague said the male was a CIA employee."

Dennis did not think it was possible for Louise to sit motionless for so long, but she did. Leaning slightly into the table, with her small, child-like fingers around the Starbucks cup, her straight blond hair falling around her shoulders, Louise remained perfectly still. Her eyes seemed to focus on his chin.

"Say that again?" she said finally.

"Forrester said she was concerned about an agency male client."

"There's only one agency male client," she said.

"Yes, Kyle Keating."

Louise took a deep breath, swallowed, and shook her head slightly while leaning back, sending her hair swirling briefly. She looked idly around the coffee shop.

"Keating," she said.

"Did you bring the five agency patients' travel and vacation schedules covering the period of her disappearance?" he said.

"Yes."

"Can I see them please?"

Louise reached into her purse, pulled out an envelope, and put it on the table.

Dennis opened it and removed a sheet of paper that listed four names with vacation and absence schedules.

"Before you get your britches in an uproar, you can see that Keating was out of the office for two weeks during Forrester's disappearance. I checked, and he never left the country. He was at a religious retreat in Maryland with his church group."

"People in the agency still go to church?" Dennis said.

"Apparently one does."

"Have you ever met Keating?"

"Long time ago. He presented to a Mideast group. My recollection was that he was uptight and nervous, but competent. Knows an awful lot about Iran. Fluent in Farsi."

"Sounds like you're already alibiing for him."

"I just don't want you to go down a rabbit hole with eight days to go. He was in Maryland with his wife at a retreat."

"I'm still going to talk to him."

"Your choice. Just remember I recommended you for this job because I thought you were the right person. The director's getting impatient, and Simpson's boss in operations is getting impatient, and Simpson is getting impatient. And I'm feeling a little exposed because you're sitting here in Crystal City when you should be in New Zealand."

"Feels like everyone's trying to keep me out of D.C."

"Maybe they're trying to help."

"Maybe they're trying to mislead me."

"So much for my great instinct to tag you for this project."

"Relax, Louise. I'm going to get this done on time. It may not seem that way, but I appreciate your help and the difficult position you're in. And I have some other leads I'm following."

"I think I see a single crocodile tear being shed."

"Well, I've never been compared to a reptile before. That's a first."

"Just get the job done, OK?"

"Sure. And by the way, where's your schedule?" he said.

"My schedule?"

"Yes, you were one of the five agency employees seeing Forrester."

"Don't be an idiot, my schedule's not important. Besides, you just said it was a male that was Forrester's concern."

"I need your schedule, Louise."

"You're crazy. I'm not going to give you that. You already know I was seeing her in therapy, which is humiliating enough."

"I need your absence and travel schedule, Louise. Don't make me ask Simpson for it."

"You're such a prick, do you know that, Cunningham?"

"You could start by calling me Dennis; I call you by your first name, you could do the same to me."

"Fat chance on that, CUNNINGHAM," she said standing up, leaving her lipstick-stained coffee cup tottering on the table.

⊙

There were several machines hooked up to her father, and each had a different beeping sound.

"How are you feeling?" Judy asked.

"Fine, but they won't let me out. Swear I'll just get up and leave in me jocks."

"Dad, don't be silly. Mum says they're taking good care of you. They're just deciding when to schedule the procedure. They think you'll need a stent. Then you'll be right as rain."

"Well, I just don't like it here. Too many machines, all beepin' at me. Can't sleep."

Judy laughed. "They're for your own good. Just try to relax. Watch the telly, or read one of the magazines Mum brought you."

"Can't. Those bloody machines are driving me batty."

Judy sighed. "Dad, just relax, please. You'll be home soon."

"You headin' back to work?"

"Yes, later today."

"How's your Yank boyfriend doing? Your mum says he took a job in New Zealand."

"He's fine, and you should call him by his name, Dad, not my 'Yank boyfriend.'"

"He's your boyfriend, isn't he?"

"Yes."

"And he's a Yank, right?"

"Yes."

"Then he's your Yank boyfriend."

Judy shook her head. "I thought you liked Dennis?"

"I do like him, but I don't like the idea of my daughter moving to America."

"I've told you and Mum over and over, I'm not moving to America. Dennis said he's going to stay here."

"Then what's he doing in New Zealand?"

"Actually, he's in the states right now," she said.

"See, that's my point. He's a Yank and he intends to get you to go there. I like Yanks. But I like Yanks here, not over there."

"Oh, Dad. Please stop worrying about that."

⊙

"You look nice and rested," Daniel said, sitting on the corner of Judy's desk. "You must be thrilled to be back to work."

"Not likely," she said. "I feel a little conflicted about being here. Not sure I like this copper stuff anymore."

"What the hell? What has that Yank been doing to you?"

"It's not Dennis, it was that dust-up around the shooting in Golden Bay. Didn't like the way we were treated by that fellow back east."

"Forget about that wanker. I'm just glad you're back so I can rid myself of that new bloke Wilson. Thinks he's the smartest copper on the planet. You're my partner now."

"Calvin wants to see me at half-past three today," Judy said. "I can hardly wait."

"Don't worry about him. Let's just get back to being a team again. You'll get in the swing of things before you know it."

⊙

"You'll like working with Craig Wilson," Calvin Miller said, smiling broadly. "Just ask Daniel. He's a bright young man."

Judy fought to control her anger; the last thing she wanted to show her boss was an out-of-control woman.

"But Daniel and I have worked as a team for years," she said. "Why would you break up a good team? What's the purpose of doing that?"

"Judy, you know that we've mixed and matched teams over the years. It leads to solid police work, new ideas, fresh approaches."

"What was wrong with our approach?"

"Nothing was wrong; it's just time for a change. I'm sure you'll like it. This young man Wilson is good."

"Have you told Daniel about this arrangement?"

"No, not yet. I felt I should tell you first."

⊙

"Mum, Grandad said you're moving to the United States. You didn't tell me. Don't you think you should tell me these things?"

Judy laughed and threw her head back. "Trevor, for heaven's sake, I told you I'm not moving to the states. Your grandfather is a little confused these days. Regardless, he's wrong. I live here and intend to stay here."

"I'm not saying I wouldn't mind visiting the states, but you should tell me what's going on. I feel disconnected sometimes. Brenda's family is not like this; they tell each other everything."

Trevor was in his second year at uni and had a steady girlfriend Brenda Finn. Judy liked Brenda and thought she had a calming effect on her son, who despite his age, was still impulsive and emotional at times.

But then, being the child of divorced parents, whose lawyer father was serving time in prison for helping a narcotics ring in Western Australia, perhaps he was allowed some leeway.

They sat at the kitchen table in Judy's house. Trevor shared an apartment with another student in Claremont.

"You said you like Dennis," she said. "Has that changed?"

"No, I like him. He's got a dry sense of humor. He's gruff in a funny way. I just don't want you to move away."

"No worries about me moving to the states, Trevor. I'm not saying I won't visit there, but I'm not moving. Dennis is going to stay here."

"But isn't he there now?"

"Yes, but he'll be back soon. You'll see."

◉

"Hello, Judy, I'm Craig Wilson. The new bloke here."

Judy stood up from her desk and shook his hand, and then sat down. She was determined to put a good face on the decision to switch partners, though it pained her to part with Daniel. They worked so well together and had settled into a harmonious relationship. The dynamics of police partners was historically fraught with tension because of differing styles and personalities. Invariably, regardless of seniority, one of the partners sought dominance.

Judy was not certain where this partnership was going and dreaded more tension in her life.

He sat down across from her and smiled. He was perhaps five foot ten inches tall, weighed about one hundred and eighty-five pounds, had a shock of short, light-brown hair and hazel eyes. She guessed he was about thirty-five years old and was not wearing a wedding ring. Rumor was that he was divorced with two children, but Daniel's intel was notoriously inaccurate in matters like this.

Unfortunately, Craig was quite handsome, and Judy was aware that many of the women in the office—single or not—were swooning after him. One of the women in the records department had already sent her an email with the simple subject line: "lucky bastard!"

"So, Judy—it's alright to call you Judy isn't it?—you know that I was just transferred to the WA office after training. I'm new to AFP and was a patrolman in Queensland before joining the AFP. I worked with Daniel briefly. And I'm looking forward to working with you. You have a bonza reputation and I have much to learn from you."

"It's nice to meet you, Craig, and yes, please call me Judy. Welcome to Perth. Our office, as you already know, works closely with WA police and concentrates on more serious crimes including illegal drugs and human trafficking. There are several initiatives currently involving the importation and distribution of heroin, fentanyl, and meth. You don't have to read *The West Australian* to know how bad things have become lately. I've been on vacation and just getting up to speed on some of the cases on our plate. I believe you have the list of investigations we're been tasked with?"

"Yes, I've read the files. Bloody anxious to get going on them."

"Well, if it's alright with you Craig, let's run through them now to prioritize the list."

"Brilliant."

⊙

Dennis stopped calling it "instinct" a long time ago.

Instinct was an innate pattern of behavior in animals in response to a stimulus. The feelings Dennis had about people during investigations was not an innate impulse, like the desire to fly south in the winter, or hibernate; it was more like a finely tuned perception to a stimulus. And he felt it now, sitting in a living room in Bethesda, Maryland, listening to Nicholas Forrester talk about the disappearance of his wife.

"I can't tell you how unbelievably shocking it is to get a phone call from New Zealand, thinking it's your wife, when it's the police department saying she's missing. Missing!"

Forrester was in his mid-fifties, about five feet eight inches tall, with a receding hairline, hazel eyes, a firm, slightly flattened nose, and a sharp chin. He had a faint southern accent and was expressive and visibly upset about his wife's disappearance.

Dennis perceived a hint, or whisper, of something hovering over Mr. Forrester's conversation. *Was it guilt?* Perhaps he thought he should have traveled with her and none of this would have happened. *Was it fear? What was he fearful of? Could it be anxiety?* He had plenty to be anxious and depressed about.

But there was something that bothered Dennis.

"I know she saw patients in the home office downstairs," Dennis said. "Did she have another office?"

"No, just the one here at home. I'll show it to you. As I said earlier, I'm an economist with the Department of Agriculture and I work on Independence Avenue, so except for some evening patients, I really didn't see her at work. Patients would park in the street and enter through the side door and sit in a little waiting room. Jane had the office sound-proofed to prevent people waiting from hearing anything, if you know what I mean."

"Yeah, I remember sitting in that waiting room many times, wondering what was being talked about in the next room," Dennis said. "I was a former patient of hers."

Forrester's head tilted.

"Excuse me?"

"I was a former patient of hers. A while ago."

"Oh. So, you know the layout down there? I guess I wasn't aware that you saw her."

He smiled in what Dennis took to be polite confusion.

"Did she ever complain about her patients?"

"Complain in what way?"

"That they were dangerous?"

"No, she didn't see dangerous patients. That was not her expertise."

"So, she never complained about a particular patient?"

"I didn't say that. You asked about dangerous patients. She might complain about a patient being late, or canceling at the last minute, or being uncommunicative—stuff like that. But not because someone was dangerous."

"Is it possible that she was seeing someone she felt was dangerous, but didn't tell you about it?" Dennis asked.

"I suppose so. I mean, there are professional ethics about discussing patients outside of therapy. But I'm sure she would have mentioned something to me. Or I would have hoped so."

"Did you know she was an approved therapist for the CIA?"

"Yes."

"How did you know that?"

"She mentioned that a colleague had received approval to see CIA patients. I think she was intrigued by the idea. So, she applied and was accepted."

"Did she talk about her agency patients?"

"No. She was prohibited from doing that, obviously."

"Did she have a lot of agency patients?"

"I have no idea. As I said, she was prohibited from commenting on that part of her practice."

Dennis sat back in the upholstered winged-back chair and glanced around the well-appointed living room of an upper middle-class—or lower upper-class—couple in the prime of their lives: family group photos on shelves, original artwork and lithographs on the walls, books on white bookshelves, antique oriental rugs, bric-a-brac from foreign travels.

"What do you think happened to your wife?" Dennis said.

"If we're to believe the New Zealand police, she was abducted. I think that's obvious. Why do you ask?"

"I'm curious whether you have any other theories?"

Forrester frowned. "No. Why would I have other theories? That's an odd question."

"Was your wife upset about anything before she left? Was she unhappy or depressed?"

Dennis noticed a minute, barely perceptible twitch of his hazel eyes.

"They asked me that in New Zealand, and it's the same answer: no. Jane was looking forward to traveling with her friend Phyllis Caldecott. She was happy and content. She was the same Jane we all loved and cherished."

"OK. Let me ask you about the two men you met in New Zealand: Rangi Winchester and Colin McCarthy. I believe they kept you informed of the investigation."

"Yes, they did. They were professional and kind, given the circumstances."

"Did you know they were members of the New Zealand intelligence services?"

"Maybe they told us. I know there was a shift in jurisdiction since it was an American tourist that was missing. I can check with my son Jack, but I'm certain that's how they presented the change. Why are you asking about this?"

"I wanted to make sure you were aware they were not policemen."

"What difference does it make?"

"Policemen investigate missing persons; intelligence officials do other things."

"I don't get your drift if there is one, Mr. Cunningham. My wife is still missing, and I don't care if it's the Royal Canadian Mounted Police helping, I'd like to know what happened to her. And why."

"Do you know Phyllis Caldecott?"

"Yes. She's another psychologist and one of Jane's best friends. Phyllis is so upset she told me she's seeing a therapist herself. She feels like she should have gone out with Jane to the drug store and none of this would have happened."

"Do therapists go to therapy themselves?" Dennis said.

"They do if they require treatment. You seem ignorant about the mental health field for someone who was treated by my wife."

"Dr. Forrester was an excellent therapist, as far as I was concerned.

She helped me a great deal. I'm sorry to be pressing you on some of these things, but as I explained earlier, there is a great deal of urgency within the agency to validate certain facts about your wife's disappearance."

"I could care less about what the agency wants to do; that's hardly my family's concern. We want to know what happened to Jane. She may be alive, for god's sake. If the CIA can help, great. If not, I don't know why we're talking to you."

Dennis smiled sympathetically, leaned back and put his hands on the two armrests.

"I understand. Can I ask you a final question? I was wondering if I could see your wife's therapy notes. The ones she kept on her patients. In my sessions with her, she wrote things down in a notebook. I'm sure she has those stored in her office under lock and key."

Forrester's face wrinkled in surprise, then confusion.

"I can't show you those records. Those are protected by HIPAA and a host of professional ethical rules. Have you heard of the Health Insurance Portability and Accountability Act?"

"Vaguely. But if I could see those notes it might help me understand whether her disappearance was related to one of her patients here. At this point, I'm only asking to see the notes of her active agency clients. She must have kept those notes separate."

"I can't do that," he said. "I'm sure if the agency wants to get a court order, I suppose I have no choice. You really should familiarize yourself with HIPAA, Mr. Cunningham. It's not a trivial matter."

⊙

The bar was a nondescript joint in a small strip mall in McLean, Virginia, across the Potomac River from Washington, D.C. It was a mile from the George Bush Center for Intelligence, the official name of the CIA's headquarters.

The bland atmosphere, simple menu, and single TV set over the bar, made it the perfect gathering place for some of the old-timers in law enforcement and intelligence agencies. Bar regulars were retirees, some still employed, and some contractors—but all liked to drink.

Dennis said hello to the bartender, a tall man named Steve with a shock of white hair stretching skyward like the crest of a cockatoo. Steve always wore a long-sleeved white polyester shirt and black slacks.

"Where the hell have you been?" Steve said. "Thought you were dead."

"I pulled a Lazarus; I'm back."

"So, they got sun down there in Hades? I thought it was just plain fire and a little brimstone. You have a nice tan."

"You can get a tan from a hot fire."

"I guess. What can I get you?"

"You have a cabernet?"

"Shit, you have changed. Since when do you drink wine?"

"Since I rose from the dead."

"OK, one cabernet sauvignon coming up for the man who came back from the dead."

A heavy-set man with a belly protruding over his belt took up the stool next to Dennis.

"Got your message," the man said, slightly out of breath. "Nice to see you again. Thought you were dead."

"Everyone thinks I was dead. Why the hell is that?"

"Not many of us geezers around here anymore. Guys dropping like flies or moving to Florida. Hell, I have high blood pressure and I'm pre-diabetic, or that's what my doc says. What the hell does he know?"

"He's a doctor, that's what he knows. You should listen to him, Karl."

"Those doctors make too much money, that's what I know."

"What's that got to do with their advice?"

"I'm pissed off that he makes so much money and doesn't do shit except look at his computer screen. Used to be, they'd look at you and ask questions. Nowadays, they look at their computer screens when they ask questions, then they type. Feels like I'm seeing a stenographer instead of a doctor, for chrissakes."

Steve slid Dennis's wine glass over to him.

"What the fuck is that?" Karl asked.

"Lazarus here is now drinking wine," Steve said. "He said it was so hot in hell that they let him out because he was bitching so much. Now he's going high class so when he goes back, they'll keep the flamethrowers down a bit, you know?"

"Think I've seen about everything," Karl said, shaking his head. "Goddamn wine drinker."

"Take it easy, Karl, or you'll pop an aneurysm," Dennis said.

"What do you got for me?" Karl asked. "It sounded urgent."

"I need a background check and surveillance on someone here. Round-the-clock surveillance. Has to start immediately, like in ten minutes."

Steve brought Karl's Seagram and water, then left.

"Is this official work for a government agency we cannot mention, or is it something else?"

"It's both."

"Don't give me that shit."

"It's a contract from a government agency. I'm retired, or at least I was. I have an open checkbook on this."

"Now that's what I like to hear," Karl said, taking a long sip.

"Can you do it?"

"Yeah, I can do it. Cost you $5,000 cash to start, plus a grand a day until you're satisfied, or you drop dead, whatever comes first."

"You haven't lost your refined sense of humor."

"What can I say? It's the work we do. Gotta laugh sometimes. Who's your target?"

Dennis pulled out a piece of paper and slid it over to Karl, who looked at it, then put it in his shirt pocket.

"What's the deal?"

"Guy is the husband of a woman that disappeared on a foreign trip. He works for Agriculture, is a bit of a stiff, and I need to find out everything about him as fast as possible. Need to strike him off a small list. I'm in a rush. You sure you can do this fast?"

"Does a bear defecate in the woods? Of course, I can. Got an ex-D.C. cop who will do the tailing, and I'll use someone else for the backgrounder. How do I get hold of you?"

"I have a burner, and the number is on the piece of paper I gave you. Call me as soon as you have something. I need to know if he's a gambler, a cross-dresser, gay, straight, a neo-Nazi; everything."

"No problem. Where's my $5,000?"

"I brought $2,000; didn't think you'd be asking for $5,000 to start. Here's the two. I can meet you later today or tomorrow for the other three."

"No need. Just add it at the end."

"Happy hunting," Dennis said, pushing away the empty wine glass. "Remember, I need this fast."

"Alright already. Glad to see you're not dead."

"I am definitely not dead, at least I don't think so."

⊙

"How is it going?" Judy asked.

"Hell, I lost a day crossing the dateline, or that's what Louise told me," Dennis said. "This case is like grappling in the dark for something to hang on to."

"You're working with Louise again?"

"Well, 'working with' is a little strong. I'm tolerating her, let's say. Or maybe she's tolerating me. I don't know. I can't believe I got suckered into doing this damn thing. Everyone's yelling at me for going in the wrong direction, and time is running out. God, what a mess. But that's my sordid life. Hey, I forgot. How is your dad?"

"They put two stents in. Amazing what they can do nowadays. He's home and causing his normal trouble."

"I'm glad he's doing well. I like your stepdad. Piss and vinegar, but with a touch of sugar every now and then."

Judy laughed. "I've never heard you refer to him that way. That's very funny, Yank."

"And how about you? How's work?"

"Ah, yes, work. I have a new partner. He's young and full of energy. But it does make things a little complicated. I have to explain why I'm doing this or that; he asks a lot of questions. Daniel and I worked so well together. We never had to justify or explain things to each other."

"What happened to Daniel?"

"Nothing. He has a new partner too. I guess they wanted to shake things up. Though I have a nagging feeling—and Daniel agrees—that they split us up after the Golden Bay incident. Makes the partner change seem punitive, which is ridiculous. But don't get me started."

"I wish I was back in Perth," Dennis said. "I miss you. I'm living out of a suitcase again, and it seems like I never retired."

"You said you were bored."

"I was bored, but now I'm thinking that being a little bored is better than being squeezed from every direction by people I don't understand and trust."

"The good news is that you only have eight more days to make your report," she said.

"And the bad news is that I only have eight more days to make my report," he said.

"Just come back to Perth in one piece. I'm lonely."

"First plane out on day zero."

⊙

It was 9:30 in the morning and Dennis was still hungover from his flight and short stay in the D.C. area. His muscles ached, his eyesight blurred, and he found himself hunching forward when he sat as if he needed to concentrate to stop from falling asleep.

Kyle Keating was not happy to be sitting across from Dennis in a cold, empty office deep in the bowels of Langley. Dennis had commandeered a spare, unused office to chat with the agency's top Iran analyst.

Keating's chart said he was fifty-eight years old, but Dennis thought he looked like he was forty-eight.

Some lucky bastards just do not age, he thought.

Keating wore a blue, long-sleeved dress shirt, a maroon striped tie, a brown tweed sports jacket, and navy-blue slacks.

His wire-rimmed glasses tended to focus attention on his dark-brown eyes, the same eyes that were glaring at Dennis.

"Who are you again?" Keating asked, fiddling with a pen that he apparently intended to take notes with.

"Dennis Cunningham. I'm a former member of OIG here. I've been hired as a contractor for a special project run out of the director's office."

"OIG? What's that got to do with me?"

"I'm a *retired* staffer in OIG; this has nothing to do with that office."

"So, what's going on? I get a notice this morning from Simpson's office saying I need to meet with a Dennis Cunningham today on an urgent issue. No explanation, no details; just go to this office and wait. I can't ever remember being in this part of Langley before. These offices looked abandoned from the Vietnam-War era."

Dennis smiled—or his best attempt at smiling—in order to calm Keating.

"Please don't interpret our meeting as anything more than an attempt to clarify a few things that are of a sensitive nature."

"Everything we do here is of a sensitive nature," Keating said, throwing his pen onto his notepad. He sat back and crossed his arms in front of his chest in the universal body language of resistance.

"Let's get right to work then," Dennis said. "I'm investigating the disappearance of an agency contractor. This contractor is someone you are familiar with. This missing person had access to confidential medical information of agency employees. I've been asked to verify the official conclusion about the disappearance. Does this make sense?"

"If you say so."

Dennis struggled to find the correct approach with Keating. Of all the individuals connected to Dr. Forrester's disappearance, Keating had not one but two connections: he was a patient of the missing psychologist, and he was the top Iran analyst that presumably was involved in identifying the Ghorbanis as the likely abductors.

"How long had you been seeing Dr. Forrester in therapy?"

"Ah," Keating said, "this is about Forrester."

"Yes. Are you surprised?"

"No, I suppose not. I thought this was concluded already."

"Can you answer my first question, please?"

"I saw her for a little more than a year."

"How often did you see her; was it weekly?"

"Why do you want to know that?"

"As you can imagine, we are not privy to the detailed notes that Forrester kept, and I'm trying to determine if you saw her once a month, once a week, or once every couple of months."

"I saw her twice a week in the beginning, then we went to once a week."

"When was the last time you saw Forrester?"

"The last time?" Dennis noticed a slight hesitation in Keating's response.

"Yes."

"It was about ten days before she left on her trip."

"So, you knew about her trip to New Zealand?"

"Yes. She mentioned that we would be skipping a few sessions while she traveled abroad to New Zealand for a conference. She was a friendly person. By the way, are you interviewing everyone who was seeing Dr. Forrester, or just me?"

"If you could just stay with me on these questions, I'd really appreciate it," Dennis said. "I have a very tight schedule."

Keating frowned.

"So, you knew she was going to New Zealand because she told you in a therapy session?"

"Yes."

"When did you find out she was missing in New Zealand?"

For the first time in their interview, Keating sighed and dropped his guard a bit.

"That was a strange coincidence, and a little upsetting," he said.

"How was it strange?"

"I was pulled into a task force to evaluate the possible involvement of Iranian agents in the abduction of an agency contractor. I lead up the Iran desk here, and so it's not unusual that I get tagged to participate in anything to do with them. At the first task force meeting, the details of the case were laid out, and I was a little surprised at the coincidence that the contractor had disappeared in New Zealand. It never occurred to me that it was Forrester. I mean, what are the chances of that? And a psychologist? Never crossed my mind that an intelligence service would go after a psychologist who was seeing agency clients. I'm not sure I've heard of a similar case. Very strange."

"At what point did you find out it was Forrester?"

"In that first meeting; I remember taking notes and listening to Simpson lay out the details. Then he mentioned Dr. Jane Forrester's name, and I just froze. I mean, I knew her. I've been on plenty of task forces over the years, and it's rare that I personally know any agent, contractor, or asset that's being discussed."

"Simpson was presenting at this meeting? He's the deputy director of operations. Why would he be presenting and not one of his underlings?"

"I don't think he was happy about it, to be honest. He said there was tremendous pressure from the top to solve this thing quickly and put an action plan in place. Everyone in that room felt the pressure, believe me."

"When did you disclose that you had a therapeutic relationship with Forrester? And who did you tell?"

Keating looked down at the blank pad of paper, picked up the pen, and examined it briefly.

"That was awkward," he said, looking at the pen. "I pulled Simpson apart after the meeting in the hallway and told him I needed to talk privately. We grabbed an office and then I just told him."

"What did he say?"

"Nothing, really."

"Nothing?"

"He just looked at me for a moment, and said, 'noted.'"

"That's it?"

"Yes. I thought he would ask me some questions, but he didn't seem to care or think it was important. As I said, he seemed under a lot of pressure."

"Then I'm to presume that you were involved in identifying the Ghorbanis as people of interest in the disappearance?"

"I don't think I can talk to you about the Ghorbanis without permission," Keating said, putting down his pen and crossing his arms again.

"Listen, I've had access to the files and I've already met with the Kiwis on the intelligence side. I've been by the Ghorbani's house; I've seen sigint on their text messages. I know that there's an NSA listening post in the valley."

"Sorry. I need clearance to talk to you about them."

"Fine, get clearance ASAP, and contact me at this number when you do." Dennis wrote his agency mobile number on Keating's pad of paper.

"One more question for now. Did you go to New Zealand as part of this investigation?"

"I need clearance before I can go further."

"Jesus; go get your clearance and call me at any time of day."

Dennis stood.

"The least you could do is show me how the hell to get out of this building," Dennis said. "We're so far into the bowels of this facility that they'll find me weeks from now still walking around."

"Hell if I know where we are," Keating said.

⊙

"Boy, you keep returning like a bad penny," Peter Harbaugh laughed.

Harbaugh, a long retired senior agency official, maintained an odd-couple relationship with Dennis. The contrast between the two was so large that their relationship defied explanation. Harbaugh was erudite, a Yankee WASP, Yale graduate, patrician, dignified, and extremely well connected to agency matters even in retirement. Dennis was convinced that Harbaugh still had top security clearances.

Dennis, on the other hand, was working class, community-college educated, rough around the edges, direct, and confrontational. He had, Harbaugh teased, "a chip on his shoulder the size of a Winnebago."

And so, they got along famously, perhaps because each aspired to some of the other's attributes.

As usual for these random meetings, they met at a Starbucks on Wisconsin Avenue in Northwest Washington, D.C.

"I thought you retired to Australia after that London row," Harbaugh said.

Dennis, who was not an aficionado of film or TV series, repeated the only script line that he had latched onto over the years. In a terrible Italian immigrant accent, Dennis repeated the line uttered by the character Michael Corleone in *The Godfather*, later used in the TV series *The Sopranos*: "I thought I was out of it, but they pull me back in again."

Harbaugh laughed. "You love that line. It's a good one. The only problem is that it infers the agency is like the mafia."

"Like I said, 'they pull me back in again.'"

"Alright, you've piqued my interest! Are you really doing work for the agency again? After the last fiasco?"

"The short answer is: yes. The longer answer is: I have no idea why I agreed to do it."

"Can you hint about what you're working on?" Harbaugh said, leaning in to hear him above the din in the coffee shop.

"An abduction. A strange abduction, really. They want me to validate the conclusion that operations produced about who did the abducting, if that makes sense."

"Seems innocuous enough. Are you enjoying being back in the muck?"

"Not really. I admit to being bored in Perth, but now I think boredom would be better than this stuff. It's a ridiculous assignment that I'm beginning to think they—or some unidentified person—knew that I could never complete. I'm not saying I'm being set up, just that the terms of the investigation are so short and geographically spread out that a single person can't possibly do justice to it."

"That sounds about right," Harbaugh sighed. "Not much has changed, I suppose. Just younger people doing the same stuff. Is there anything that I can help with? You sounded a little urgent on the phone."

"Well, I was wondering what you know about Kenny Franklin?"

"Ah, Franklin. Are you in contact with him? That *is* a little odd. Why would the director be in contact with you? Now you definitely have my attention."

Dennis explained how Franklin flew into Perth on a side trip elsewhere and gave him the assignment. He told Harbaugh about the ridiculously short delivery date, as well as the requirement that he work through Simpson.

"Simpson?" Harbaugh said. "I've known him for years. Why would you be handled personally by the deputy director of operations? That's not kosher, or even sensible. Good heavens, what's going on over there?"

"Not only do I have to report to Simpson, but he's riding me all the time. Doesn't he have a million fires to put out each day?"

"But why you?" Harbaugh said, his long, gray eyebrows arching. "I'm not suggesting you're not an extraordinarily talented investigator. But why go half-way around the world to tag a retired OIG investigator? I don't even know what to say."

"Remember Louise Nordland? She recommended me for this assignment, and, voila, here I am making a fool out of myself while the clock ticks down. Should be playing golf on the west coast of Australia."

"I'm sure there's a reason why Louise wanted you involved. She trusts you, and she knows you'll stop at nothing to get to the bottom of it."

"Maybe. She's also involved, peripherally I hope."

"Well, that makes things complicated. How much more time do you have?"

"Seven days counting today."

"Let me poke around a little for you, if you don't mind," Harbaugh said.

"Be my guest. Rowing in circles makes me dizzy."

⊙

"Both of you have been tasked to help the Serious Crime Financial Task Force investigate the finances of a Perth-based mining company,"

Calvin Miller said. "I think you will find this work interesting. As you know, the AFP works closely with our Taxation office when it comes to white-collar crime. It is a major initiative of the government, and we've been asked to help."

Judy felt the orbits of her eye sockets tighten as she stared in wonderment.

"Judy, you seem perplexed," he said. "What's on your mind?"

"I've been working almost exclusively on criminal gang activity related to the trafficking of drugs. I have no experience in financial crime analysis. Craig and I have just started to work together to pick up the pieces on three cases, and you want to detail us to yet another investigation having nothing to do with drugs and gangs?"

"Craig here has a degree in finance, isn't that correct?" Miller said.

"Yes, but it's been a few years since my uni courses. I'm certainly not an accountant." Judy and Craig exchanged glances.

"To be clear," Miller said. "You will be assisting the Taxation blokes, not leading the investigation. And I don't expect it will take a lot of time out of your schedule. As you point out, you have more pressing issues to attend to."

Judy prayed her cheeks were not blazing pink as she grew angry. She ran the fingers of her right hand through her hair to expend some nervous energy.

"Judy, I think you and Craig will find this case interesting, and it will burnish your *curricula vitae*, as it were, with financial crime experience. This is a major initiative of the AFP and will be for some time. See this as a chance to expand your area of expertise."

After returning to her office, Judy sat down and picked up a pen and sullenly started to doodle.

Taxation investigation? she thought. *Has Miller started me down a long path of demotion? Why do I feel like I'm being punished for the Golden Bay shooting?*

Craig knocked on her open office door. "Got a sec?"

"Sure. Come in."

"What do you reckon Miller is doing sending us on this tax case?" he said sitting.

"I have no bloody idea. He's never done this kind of switching of expertise before, or at least that I can remember. It's a foolish idea."

"Suppose I can brush up on my economics, but it's a bit of a stretch for me, Judy."

"A stretch for you, perhaps, but an intercontinental leap for me," she said, painstakingly scratching out the word "Miller" on her pad of paper.

⊙

The Hyatt bar in Rosslyn, Virginia, was like any chain hotel bar; several TV sets on the walls showed eerily soundless sporting events, the food was ordinary but good, and the bartenders were attentive.

Dennis stared at the dark reflection on the top of his glass of red wine. Normally he would sip a single-malt whiskey with one or two ice cubes, preferably a Macallan 12, and toy with a plastic swizzle stick in boredom.

In retirement he realized it was not a good drink for him; he sipped too fast, ordered more often, and felt awful and depressed in the morning. Judy slowly converted him to wine, especially reds like cabernet sauvignon, merlot, and shiraz. She said Australia had developed a robust wine industry with many excellent wineries comparable to those in France, Italy or the states.

But Australia and Judy were a long way from the Hyatt in Rosslyn. Dennis missed her and the slow, predictable life of retirement.

Or so he told himself, as he stared at the mirror surface of his dark-purple wine. Dennis had not touched the glass in several minutes, and the wine reflected the blinding overhead lights of the bar. He sighed and opened the notebook he carried at all times. Maybe if he flipped through the notes on the investigation, something might jump out at him.

One of his cell phones vibrated and he reached into his sports jacket; it was his burner that was going off.

"Yup," he said.

"Got something," Karl said.

"Fire away."

"This is prelim, 'cause my two guys are not done yet. But the background is clean on your buddy there at Agriculture. Nothing in public databases shows anything whacky. No claims, no accidents, not even a fuckin' speeding ticket. Credit is excellent."

"A real Mary Poppins," Dennis said. "Great."

"Didn't say that; you gonna listen? I said the public database was clean. My guy doing the surveillance thinks your guy is a sugar daddy."

"Sugar daddy in that he has a girlfriend?"

"A young one; gal works in Agriculture too. He spent last night there. Unless they're working on a PowerPoint together over Chinese take-out, my guy thinks they're a couple. He's there again tonight."

"Your guy's got a camera, right?"

"Of course he has a fuckin' camera."

"I need photos of him leaving in the morning, or late at night, with the time stamp. Need them quick."

"We can do that."

"Thanks, Karl. Now I'm getting somewhere for once. Maybe I'll order another wine to celebrate."

"You and wine; doesn't seem like you, Cunningham."

"People change."

"I guess."

⊙

"What," Louise said. It was not a question, but a statement. Her voice was gruff and tired.

"That's a fine 'howdy-do'," Dennis said.

"What do you want, Cunningham? In case you hadn't bothered to check your watch, it's 10:55 p.m."

"Keating."

"What about him?"

"Can you get access to the geolocation data from his agency cell phone?"

Silence.

"Hello?"

"Why do you need that?"

"Because I'm curious. If you can get the data, I'd like to see it."

"Are you just grasping at straws or do you have something?"

"Louise, please, can you just get the data?"

"Christ. What time period do you need?"

"The month prior to Forrester's disappearance up to the month after."

"That's a lot of data. Just geolocation for his agency cell phone?"

"Correct, that's all I need."

"I'll see. I'm gathering you didn't try Simpson on this?"

"No. I need it ASAP. Simpson'll just say it's a stupid idea and why aren't I back in New Zealand. Please help me with this. Keep Simpson out of it."

She hung up without saying goodbye.

Dennis sat in his sterile hotel room looking out into the cluster of soulless skyscrapers. Peering between two concrete monoliths, he could see a small wedge of the Potomac River and into Georgetown and Washington, D.C.

The city looked benign enough by night, but he was not lulled by its similarity to normal cities. Washington was its own answer to the mystery of Russian nesting dolls. Just when you think you've found the last doll, there's another one inside. And another one.

Dennis hooked up both his agency phone and his burner to chargers, turned off the light and tried to sleep. He felt depressed and wondered if he should get up and watch TV or try to read a magazine. Depressed and stewing in bed for hours was a bad combination.

His agency phone lit up and shook like a wounded bat, flopping around the table top.

"Yes?"

"Gidday, is this Dennis?"

"Yes, who's this?"

"Colin McCarthy. NZSIS in Auckland."

"Hey, Colin. I'm in the states now. Forgot to tell you guys I was leaving."

"Right. We knew that."

"How'd you know?"

"We're in signals intelligence, Cunningham. You're somewhere in Virginia right now, if we've got this right."

"Whatever. How can I help you?"

"As a courtesy, thought we'd tell you that we found Forrester."

"Alive or dead?"

"Quite dead."

CHAPTER 10

t was a tip," McCarthy said. "Email came into Crimestoppers. They get a lot of useless stuff, and the police don't have the resources to check everything out. You know, pensioners who think their missing cat was kidnapped. Things like that."

"Yeah, so what was the tip?"

"Have the email right here. It said, 'That missing American psychologist can be found near the arch at White's Bay Beach.'"

"And?" Dennis said.

"Police found her body there. Buried in the sand up from the beach."

"Was there a positive ID?"

"Not yet, but they're pretty certain it was her. Partially decomposed. Same clothes she was wearing. Jewelry. Everything matches. They're expecting a DNA sample from the son any moment now. Husband has been alerted. Police recommended that given the poor condition of the body and the emotional stress from seeing that, that a DNA sample from the son would be a preferable method for identification."

"Autopsy?" Dennis said, moving over to the desk to turn on the lamp and get his notepad.

"No results yet. I'll keep you posted."

"Tell me about the email. Your digital forensics folks trace it?"

"Dead end, I'm afraid. The email header had a New Zealand IP address, but it was spoofed somehow. The sender certainly knew how to cover their digital tracks."

"Anything else stands out to the police there? How accessible is that beach? Is it popular?"

"Well, this time of year there's not a lot of folks going down to the water there, and it is a little isolated. Whoever took her down there had to carry her a bit. Good one hundred meters from the road."

"When will the autopsy be completed?"

"Not sure about that. Your embassy here is pressing the case, and Mr. Forrester is clamoring for some answers. Quite agitated he is. Are you coming here to finish up your investigation?"

"Yes. I'm not sure how quickly I can get a flight out. I'm going to want to talk to Detective Brown in Blenheim. And whoever is doing the autopsy."

"Not a problem. Let us know your travel plans. Cheers."

Dennis put the phone down and stared at the notes he scribbled in his notebook. He shivered, sitting in the air-conditioned room in his underwear.

He reached over and pulled the thick hotel curtains back and looked out into the Rosslyn nightscape. The buildings looked like black, glossy stalagmites. Over the top of a building, he caught sight of the throbbing taillight of a passenger jet approaching Reagan International Airport from the north down the Potomac River.

Dennis looked again at his notes, yawned, and then turned off the light. He reattached his phone to the charger and crawled back into bed.

He no longer felt depressed, just confused.

⊙

It was the mid-morning rush at the Starbucks, and Dennis grabbed a table that was marred with a spill of cold coffee and tiny sparkling white crystals of sugar. He used a napkin to clean it off and settled in reading *USA Today*.

He spotted her little blond head through the glass doors before she entered. Louise was dressed in a navy-blue pants suit with a light-blue blouse. He was aware again how attractive she was. Why had he not been observant before? Was it her personality? Her 'take-no-bullshit' approach to Dennis's 'don't-give-a-shit' approach?

Or had Dennis changed? Either way, it unsettled him.

She sat down with no acknowledgment, carrying a folded *Washington Post* under her left arm.

"Hey," he said.

"Hey," she replied, looking past him into the store.

"Thanks for helping out," he said. "I appreciate it."

"Whatever. Simpson's excited. Says they found Forrester's body."

"Yep."

"You going back there? How many days do you have left on this thing?"

"I'm supposed to fly out later today. Got six days left counting today."

"Supposed to? Sounds a little ambivalent," she said, finally looking directly at him.

"It's a long trip. I'm running out of time, and it will take me a whole day just to get there."

"Have you talked to Simpson?"

"I'm calling him right after you leave, why?"

"The Ghorbanis have skedaddled."

"Skedaddled where?"

"Ankara. They were on a tourist visa and never came back."

"Just left their house and belongings in New Zealand?"

"You got it," she said, cradling her coffee in both hands and taking a tiny sip. "Don't you think you should get back there and stop poking around here? This thing might be tied up now."

"As I said, I'm slated to leave later today."

For the first time, Dennis noticed Louise did not have her wedding band on. It was his turn to look away.

"I've got your data. I didn't bother looking at it. It's in the newspaper here. Chasing Keating seems like a dead end to me."

"Yeah, well, I think he's worth looking into."

"Maybe retirement suited you too well," she said standing.

He watched her walk with her slight limp out into the busy sidewalk and completely disappear.

⊙

Dennis was not an expert at reading geolocation data from cell tower pings, but years ago an analyst showed him the basics in a prior investigation. Louise had delivered Keating's agency cell phone location data printed on several sheets of legal-size paper, stuffed inside *The Washington Post* she left behind. Dennis sat in his hotel room poring over the rows of numbers and abbreviations.

He also had Keating's schedule of absences from work, including the dates around Forrester's disappearance. Keating said he was at a religious retreat for one week and took a week of vacation afterward, for a total of two back-to-back weeks out of the office.

Dennis identified the nearest cell tower to Keating's home in Vienna, Virginia, since it registered the most pings during the evening and early morning hours. Dennis knew the agency issued customized encrypted iPhones with special GPS chips. Cell tower pings were not accurate for detailing precisely where the phone was at any time, but the combination with GPS provided better accuracy.

Immediately he saw that during the period Keating was at a religious retreat in Maryland, and the following week on vacation, his cell phone appeared to be in Charlottesville, Virginia. It was there for almost the entire two weeks.

Either Keating was at a religious retreat in Virginia and not Maryland, or he was not at a religious retreat at all. It was also odd that the phone remained pretty much at the same location for the entire two weeks, not just the week he was on the retreat. Dennis did not have the time to request Keating's wife's cell phone records; she was a civilian, and those records would have to be requested formally.

⊙

"Dad, I can't believe you're back in the states and you didn't tell me!" his daughter Beth said. "Why do you do things like that? And you came through Los Angeles, I bet. You could have easily flown up to San Francisco to see us."

"Beth, I told you I was on a very tight deadline and I could not take time off," he said, squirming in the hotel desk chair. "When this thing's over, I'm coming to visit."

To his shock, she started to cry.

"Beth, what's wrong? Why are you crying? What happened?"

"I've got some important news to tell you," she said collecting herself. She put down the phone, blew her nose, then picked up the phone.

"I'm pregnant. We're going to be parents. You're going to be a grandfather."

Dennis had been a disappointing father by most standards, including his own. He spent his life ensconced in work, running from his own ugly childhood. Over the years, he managed to build a thin shell of insulation between him and the real world of honest emotional attachment. He was an excellent investigator with OIG, and a barely passable father and husband.

147

That eggshell of insulation cracked badly after his wife's death in a car accident. The fact that she was having an affair at the time of the accident created enough psychic damage that he fell into a deep depression and only climbed out with the help of an agency-approved mental health professional named Dr. Jane Forrester.

Slowly, and with great internal resistance from Dennis, Forrester brought him back from the brink, taught him to own his misfortune in life and embrace more life-affirming behaviors. That included trying to rebuild a fraught relationship with his adult child Beth.

"Dad, did you hear me?"

"Yes, I heard you. I'm just trying to process all this. Wow. You and Nathan are going to be parents. I'm going to be a grandfather. Holy shit. How are you feeling?"

"I feel good. Everything's normal. I'm only nine weeks in and have been warned that the first trimester can be iffy, so trying not to get ahead of myself. Still, it's very exciting. Are you excited?"

"Hell yes. I'm just caught off guard about being a grandparent. Who would have thought? Are you going to find out whether it's a boy or girl, or wait to be surprised?"

"Ha, Nathan wants to just wait and be surprised. I'm like, tell me whether it's a boy or a girl and I can get pink or blue clothes." Beth laughed, and Dennis found himself smiling.

"This is such great news," he said. "Listen, I promise I'm going to be done with this project in about a week. I'll check in beforehand. Maybe I can get Judy to come with me to visit."

"That would be so nice. I like Judy. I think she's good for you."

"I would agree."

⊙

"Here you go," Karl said sliding a large manila envelope to him at the hotel bar. "Like I said, this pal of yours has a girlfriend. Pictures of him leaving in the morning to go to work, time stamped. Even got some of her leaving for work a little later. Charming couple. My guy says they're very friendly, he patted her lovingly on her shoulder when they went shopping. Smiles a lot at her, stuff like that."

Dennis opened the envelope and slid out large color prints with time stamps. The first one showed Forrester walking into the high-rise condo complex with a small travel bag at 7:22 p.m. The next photo showed him walking out at 6:50 a.m. the following morning dressed for work with his travel bag. Two more photos showed the younger woman named Rebecca Cleary leaving the same day at 7:45 a.m.

A single sheet of paper was paperclipped to the two photos of Cleary, detailing her age—thirty-three—her address, job title at the Department of Agriculture, her alma mater, and other boring details.

Dennis looked carefully at the two photos. Cleary was about five feet two inches tall, with long, straight black hair that flowed halfway down her back. She wore plain work attire for a bureaucrat: tan slacks, a white blouse, a large pendant necklace, and no rings on her left hand.

"So, they're a couple," Dennis said. "Any idea how long they've been together?"

"No. That would take some time and you wanted this ASAP, right?"

"Yes, but it would help fill in some blanks if I knew how long this has been going on."

"My guy says that from the look of them—now this ain't scientific if you get my drift—but he thinks they've been together for a while. Very comfortable together, he said. Smiling at each other over dinner at restaurants, crap like that."

Dennis shoved the pictures back in the envelope and pulled out a letter-sized white envelope.

"Here you go. Thanks for your help on this, Karl. I wish I could say it helps clarify things, but it's made things muddier if that's possible."

"Thanks for the business," Karl said knocking back the remains of his Canadian Club and water. "Good to see you back in the game, you know?"

"Check back in about a week to see if I'm still around," Dennis said, staring into the glass of wine that he swirled on the bar. "People never stop surprising me, that's for sure."

⊙

Dennis took a walk in the concrete jungle of Rosslyn as dusk fell. It might be winter in the southern hemisphere but July in the Washington, D.C. suburbs was unpleasantly hot, with stifling humidity and heavy air.

He thought he'd navigate himself toward the Potomac, but the maze of traffic and the magnified sound of vehicles bouncing off the glass towers convinced him to turn around. He felt one of his phones vibrate and pulled out his burner.

"Hello?"

"It's Peter. How are you?"

"Well, I'm trying to walk around over here in Rosslyn to stretch my legs, but it's not very hospitable for pedestrians."

"Oh my, why would you stay over there, Dennis. That place is horrid."

"Can't stand being on your side of the river."

"Well, there is that," Harbaugh laughed. "I won't detain you in your exercise schedule, but I told you that I'd poke around for you regarding your project."

"Find anything?"

"Nothing definitive. But there is some scuttlebutt."

"About what," Dennis said, moving into the entrance to a building and plugging his open ear with his finger. "I can barely hear you, I'm afraid."

"Your benefactor, the one who recommended you; well, it appears that this person is being groomed by Kenny to take the deputy position at operations."

"But that's Simpson's thing," Dennis said.

"Precisely. He may be feeling the competition."

"They hate each other, you mean."

"Professionally, that is," Harbaugh said.

"Guess I'm not surprised. Nothing like unabashed ambition."

"I'm afraid that's all that I came up with," Harbaugh said. "Simpson's not a bad sort, Dennis. I've known him for a while. He can be a hard ass, I'm sure."

"I suppose. Thanks. That helps a bit."

"I'll leave you with a bastardized quote from Mark Twain if you'll permit me?"

"Ha. Please. Fire away."

"In the first place, God made idiots," Harbaugh said in a stentorian voice. "That was for practice. Then he made senior officials of intelligence agencies."

CHAPTER 11

The text message from a blocked number came into his agency phone at 11:43 p.m., while Dennis was gamely trying to sleep. Before bed, he talked to Judy about Beth's pregnancy and asked her to consider joining him in San Francisco to meet the happy couple.

Judy seemed distracted and it bothered Dennis. When the text pinged, he was wide awake.

this is Mr. Simpson's assistant James Canton. Simpson will see you in your hotel restaurant for breakfast at 6:15 a.m. sharp. He is expecting an update

Dennis tossed the phone onto the bedside table and waited for the screen to go dark. He sighed with a mixture of excitement at being a grandfather, and dread at having to see Simpson. And what was up with Judy?

⊙

"Why the hell aren't you in New Zealand, for chrissakes?" Simpson said, painstakingly eviscerating a breakfast sausage with the attention of a neurosurgeon. "Aren't you the great investigator? The one everyone's waiting to validate the conclusions already reached by professionals? The Ghorbanis got away while you were dicking around here."

They were joined at the breakfast table by Cameron, Simpson's administrative assistant. A small, thin man in his early forties, Cameron had combed his jet-black hair severely back onto his thinning scalp. He had a pronounced underbite that pushed his chin forward into a reptilian face, and the fact that he was chewing gum at 6:30 in the morning was strange. At the next table sat two squirrely faced men in black suits; Dennis took them for bodyguards. All five men were sitting cozily within four feet of each other.

"As I explained, there were a couple of things here in D.C. that needed to be looked at," Dennis said. "The director asked me to review the earlier findings and produce a recommendation on the accuracy of those findings. That's what I'm doing."

"What possible 'things' in the D.C. area do you think are that important?" Simpson said. "You should be in New Zealand. Any decent investigator would be at the scene of the crime. Why are you still here?"

"For one, there is Dr. Forrester's husband. I thought he should be looked at."

"He's a boring bureaucrat at Agriculture, Cunningham," Simpson said stabbing another piece of sausage. "You don't really think he had something to do with his wife's disappearance?"

"And there's Keating," Dennis tossed in quickly, distracting Simpson away from the subject of Mr. Forrester.

"Keating? You're kidding me. Keating? The Iran desk?"

"Yes. I gather you knew he was seeing Forrester in therapy."

"Oh please. If it wasn't for Keating, we might not have closed the loop on the Ghorbanis. So what if he was seeing Forrester?"

"As I explained, in order to be thorough, I need to review all options. I think the director would expect that much."

Simpson made a face that Dennis took to be either patronizing, or a scowl, or both. He put down his knife and fork.

"Kenny Franklin is the director of the Central Intelligence Agency. He's been in that position for thirteen months. Prior to that, he was a six-term congressman from Tennessee. The fact that he was a member of the House Intelligence Committee—not chairman, or vice-chairman but a member—does not provide him much experience in the intelligence business. As you well know, the president could replace him at any time, or Franklin could call it quits. Directors change, but the real work at the agency is done by permanent, long-time employees in operations and analysis."

"I understand that," Dennis said. "And I fully appreciate the task I was given by him. I intend to complete my work by the end of day fourteen. I was given a wide range to evaluate the findings, and that's what I'm doing."

Dennis was suddenly aware that Canton's gum chewing was very loud, like the slapping of wet feet on a pool deck.

"Do you mind not chewing gum while we're having breakfast?" Dennis said, pivoting to Cameron.

He froze in mid-chew, and then closed his mouth slowly and kept it closed.

"Thank you," Dennis said, looking back at Simpson. "I've got five days remaining, and I will do my utmost to complete it on time."

Simpson tossed his napkin on the table, took a final sip of coffee, then pushed his chair back. This prompted the two bodyguards to jump up and scan the room.

"Remember one thing, and this is the last time I'm going to say this. You were directed to work through me, and only me, at the agency. I'm your lead contact. You are not currently communicating with me on anything, and unless that changes, I'll be forced to complain to the director. It appears that you've been working with other senior agency individuals, and that must stop."

Simpson stood up, and the entourage flew out of the restaurant in a gaggle.

Dennis pulled out his burner and texted to Louise: *just met with simpson; told me not to talk to u anymore*

He had no intention of abiding by the order to avoid Louise, but knowing how much the two senior agency officials disliked each other, Dennis could not resist spreading discord and perhaps finding some new leverage. He finished his cold scrambled eggs, took a final sip of coffee, and saw his burner light up and dance around the table.

Glancing at the message, he laughed.

fuck him, Louise wrote.

⊙

There's bluffing when you have a good hand of cards and you guess your opponent doesn't; and then there's wild, reckless bluffing when you have no idea what cards your opponent has. Dennis was using the latter method of bluffing, as he sat across from Keating in another commandeered empty office at Langley.

Keating was not just displeased to be talking to Dennis; he was furious. His lips were pursed tightly, creating huge angry dimples on both cheeks.

"Can we get on with this?" he said, looking at his watch. "I'm missing an important meeting." Just then Keating's phone hummed on the corner of the desk between them. Dennis had purposely sat in the visitor's chair in the unused office and let Keating sit behind the desk. He wanted his interviewee to feel in control of the meeting.

Keating grabbed his phone and appeared to read an email or text.

"Shit," he said, sighing. "Can we start please?"

"Sure. I just have a couple of questions, and I think we'll be done. I appreciate you taking time out of your day for this." Dennis smiled but was met with Keating's quivering dimples.

"We noticed that you were absent from work at the time Dr. Forrester disappeared in New Zealand." Dennis used the pronoun "we" to imply—incorrectly—that there was a team working on this case scouring every bit of data. If Keating had anything to hide, the implication that others were digging up every bit of dirt would spook him.

"Yes, that's correct," Keating said.

"Your record of absences says that you were at a religious retreat for one week with your wife, which overlaps with the day Forrester disappeared. The following week you were on vacation."

"Correct." It might have meant nothing, but Dennis noticed that Keating's dimples sagged a bit.

"And just to be accurate, the retreat was in Maryland?"

"Yes."

"And for vacation, where did you go that week?"

"I think they call it a 'staycation' these days. My wife and I hung around here in Virginia. Took some day trips."

"Because of your status and expertise in the Directorate of Analysis, you would have been on call 24x7, so you had your agency phone with you at all times, correct?"

"Correct. Are we done yet?"

"Yes."

Keating stood up and grabbed his phone. "I hope I don't have to do any more of these interviews. This is tiresome. I keep repeating myself."

He walked two steps to the closed office door and yanked it open.

"Oh, just one more thing," Dennis said. "Charlottesville. What were you doing in Charlottesville for two weeks?"

Keating froze with his right hand on the knob to the open door. He stood perfectly still as if hit by a 1950's-style science-fiction ray gun.

"Hello?" Dennis said.

Keating made a snorting sound, pushed the door closed, and sat back down, clenching his cell phone tightly as if it were a primed grenade.

"Can you answer my question, if you don't mind?" Dennis said. "Your agency-issued cell phone was in or near Charlottesville for most of the two weeks you were out of the office. The phone was not in Maryland. Unless there's an error in the data, or you lent your phone to someone else—which is a serious breach of regulations—you were in Charlottesville, Virginia."

Keating's demeanor had changed dramatically. Gone were the dimples from taut facial muscles. Instead, his shoulders drooped, and he slumped forward refusing eye contact. He placed his phone on the desk in deliberate, slow motion. He licked his lips.

"So, this is how it goes," he said to Dennis, raising his gaze off the desk to stare directly at him.

"What goes?" Dennis said.

"Don't play around with me, you bastard," Keating said, his eyes now large and watering. "You've been planning this all along. Setting me up. Trapping me. Ruining me. I should have known you weren't on the up and up. You slimy bastard."

Dennis said nothing. The small office was painfully quiet. Keating's phone vibrated, but he ignored it.

"Were you even in Charlottesville?" Dennis said. "Did someone else have your phone? Were you someplace else?"

Keating's face suddenly contorted in fury.

"You know *exactly* where I was, you bastard. You fucking bastard."

⊙

Judy had a headache that felt like someone had driven a large tenpenny nail through her skull into her frontal lobe. She used the fingertips of her right hand to massage the area above her eyebrows.

She, Craig, and four other members of the white-collar crime team had spent six hours reviewing and matching dates on banking and tax records for Adonis Kadlec, a Greek-Australian dual citizen from Brisbane. Kadlec was under investigation for money laundering and tax evasion, and for using a West Australian mining company to help in this scheme.

"I think we're done for today, aren't we fellas?" Craig said, standing up from his computer monitor and stretching.

"Yeah," answered Phillip Connester from the Tax Office. "Think I'm stuffed. Let's be back tomorrow at nine?"

"How ya doing, Judy?" Craig said. "You alright? You look crook."

"I'm fine," she said. "Bit of a headache, I'm afraid."

"Feel like a pint after work?"

She was surprised, but not unhappy with the offer.

"Sure. A quick one."

They walked to a busy pub on Outram Street, making small talk and complaining about the boring work of tracking income and tax payments.

Judy's headache began to subside half-way through her glass of wine.

"I don't reckon I like this kind of police work, Judy," Craig said, rapidly moving through his beer. "Not sure why Miller chose us to help the tax blokes. You think he likes us?"

Judy smirked. "I have no idea. Not sure how we can keep up with the other cases when we're spending our days poring over spreadsheets."

"What do you think of Connester? A bit full of himself, cracking the whip like we're a mob of uni students. 'Let's get going, team. We don't have much time before Mr. Kadlec leaves the country again.' I think we all know what the stakes are."

Judy laughed. "You sound just like him. A bit much, isn't he?"

"Really, shouldn't accountants be doing this kind of work?" Craig persisted. "Not what I signed up for. Thought we'd be chasing drug dealers, stuff like that. Besides, it's better to be busy than bored, yes? Hey, another wine?"

"I don't know," she said looking at her nearly empty glass. "Haven't had much to eat today."

"Aw, come on, Judy. Have another. Keep me company. I can't stand going back to an empty flat so early. My shout."

"Sure. But this is the last one." Judy watched Craig walk to the bar, and she struggled with how handsome her partner was. She guessed he was half-a-dozen years younger than her, maybe more. He wore his thick, sandy-blond hair short, complementing his thick neck and broad shoulders. A small, diagonal scar ran across his chin, giving him a rakish, warrior look.

Judy had complained to her best friend Cilla about Craig's looks. "It's bloody distracting," she said over dinner recently. "He's so cute. And I think he's flirting a little with me. Or maybe I wish he was flirting with me. It's nice to be flirted with every now and then."

"You know how they define flirtation," Cilla said.

"No, how do they?"

"Flirtation is attention, *without* intention," Cilla said. "So be careful young lady. I thought you said Dennis will be back here in a week."

"Dennis," Judy had replied. "Will he ever return?"

"Judy, why are you so uncertain about him? When I've seen you two together, he's devoted to you. I love his brash sense of humor. Yanks can be so funny sometimes. What is going on with you?"

"I don't know," Judy said. "I'm lonely. And bored."

"That is a bad combination for an attractive woman like you," Cilla said.

Judy snapped out of her reverie as Craig returned with two drinks.

"Cheers," he said raising his beer and tapping it against her glass.

She looked into his hazel-colored eyes and smiled.

"I hope you don't think I'm too forward, Judy," Craig said. "But I heard about your former husband and his prison sentence. Must have been a difficult time for you and your son."

"People talk too much," she said. "I wish they wouldn't."

"I don't think anyone meant to be critical. Quite the opposite. You have a lot of respect around the office. Blokes told me I was lucky to team up with you."

"Really?" Judy said, taking a sip. "Well, they never say things like that to my face. If I'm so respected, what am I doing looking at spreadsheets?"

"Ah, Judy. Lighten up. You're too hard on yourself." Craig reached across and patted Judy's hand briefly.

For a moment she allowed herself to feel the thrill of a handsome, young man touching her.

⊙

With all his years wrestling with complicated investigations, Dennis had grown to expect anything from a cornered suspect. Once, after Dennis accused the Thailand station chief of embezzling agency funds to pamper his Thai girlfriend, the man reached into his desk, pulled out a .32-caliber revolver and placed it against his temple. Dennis barely had time to knock the pistol out of the man's hand.

So, he was completely unprepared for Keating's reaction to being called a liar.

"You enjoy ruining people's lives, don't you, Cunningham?!" Keating yelled, spittle flying out of his mouth. "So, they sent you to do the deed? Well, fuck them and fuck you. I've spent my whole career here, busting my ass to help this damn organization get out of its own way. And this is how they want to drop the ax? Away from prying eyes. Down in an abandoned office, with an asshole from OIG?"

Keating covered his eyes with his hands, apparently trying to block out the site of his interrogator.

"Keating," Dennis said quietly. "What were you doing in Charlottesville? Or were you even in Charlottesville?"

Keating kept his hands over his eyes and gulped several deep, measured breaths.

"Don't be mean," Keating said, his voice suddenly soft and weak. "I can't even look at you. The grim reaper cleaning out the agency of broken pieces. Nice work, Cunningham. You'll burn in hell if they'll even take you there."

Dennis tried again.

"Can you tell me about Charlottesville?"

Keating remained sitting behind the desk with his hands covering his eyes, breathing slowly. Dennis wondered idly whether Keating was capable of violence.

"Why do you act like you don't know?" Keating said. "Why do you have to be so cruel? You seem good at this stuff. You must really like it. You're a strange man, Cunningham."

"Put your hands down please, Keating. Come on. Look at me."

Keating dropped his hands slowly. Dennis could see that his eyes were wet.

"Charlottesville," Dennis repeated.

"You're serious? You want me to play along?"

"Yes, play along. Tell me about Charlottesville."

"Well," Keating said in a sing-song, mocking voice, "I was there for two weeks, and it was just like the last time. But you already know that. And, yes, it was helpful. And yes, I didn't tell the agency. It's never fun there, but, well there you go. Happy now?"

Dennis was utterly confused, and he kept bluffing. "Just tell me the name of the place. Let's start there."

"Right," Keating said. "I'm playing along to make it official. OK. It's called The Macon Center. Dr. Forrester had recommended it. It was my second time."

"Why did Dr. Forrester recommend it?"

"It's ultra-private. I could pay out of pocket. No money trail."

"For what kind of treatment?" Dennis said.

Keating put his hands behind his neck and arched back, looking at the ceiling tiles.

"Depression. Severe depression. They still use ECT there, which Forrester still believed in."

"ECT, help me on that one," Dennis said.

"Oh, I get it," Keating said. "You must be recording this; that's why you're making me go over all this stuff that you already know. It's for the confession."

"Keating. ECT."

"Electroconvulsive Therapy. Shock treatment. *One Flew Over the Cuckoo's Nest*, remember the scene? It still works for some people. Works for me, but I need to recover from it and can't go back to work immediately. And they make you go to daily group and individual therapy sessions."

"The Macon Center had you for two weeks for treatment for depression. Were you in contact with work while you were there?"

"Once, when there was an emergency. Dr. Forrester had disappeared, and the Kiwis thought it might be Iranians. Of all people, Dr. Forrester." He shook his head.

"When you returned, you were pulled into the task force on her disappearance."

"Yes." Keating still stared up at the ceiling, drained and exhausted as if he'd run a marathon.

"Did you or anyone at the Iran desk suggest it was the Ghorbanis, or did that tip come from somewhere else?"

"The Kiwis."

"And you vetted them from our side?"

"Yes. Everyone's been watching them for a while."

"There was no doubt from your end that the Ghorbanis abducted Forrester, presumably to coerce information about her agency patients?"

Keating dropped his hands, leaned forward, and stared with red-rimmed eyes.

"Why are you asking about the Ghorbanis? I just told you about Charlottesville. You got me. I'm toast here. Who gives a shit about the Ghorbanis?"

"Keating, you have not been listening to me. From the beginning, I told you my task was to evaluate the recommendation to punish Iranian intelligence for the Forrester abduction. Operations is planning a series of highly coordinated assassinations. I couldn't give a shit if you were in a whore house for two weeks, or an opium den; I'm only interested in your involvement in the Forrester case, especially your part to validate the Ghorbanis."

Keating swallowed twice in rapid succession, his Adam's apple bobbing aggressively.

"You're serious that you're not here to out me on my treatment?"

"Now you're making me mad," Dennis said. "Can you just answer the goddamn question?"

"Alright. The Ghorbanis. They were the closest hostile team near Forrester's disappearance. It made sense, as far as the geography went. But there was the DNA evidence that our guys got. I'm sure you know of that. And there were intercepts showing suspicious interchanges around the time she disappeared."

"If there had been no DNA evidence, would you be so inclined to finger the Ghorbanis?"

"That's a trick question."

"No, it's not. Answer it." Dennis could feel his anger growing by the second out of frustration. And Keating's battle with depression reminded him, perversely, of his own struggles.

"I probably would have held back my agreement that it was the

Ghorbanis," he said. "But there was tremendous pressure on the task force. It was obvious Simpson didn't like having to take this thing on himself. Scuttlebutt was that Franklin demanded it."

Dennis clicked the ballpoint pen he used for his notes, attached it on the inside pocket of his sports coat, and closed his notebook.

"Just so we're clear, Keating, I have no intention of doing anything with the information you provided about Charlottesville. So please proceed as if we never talked about it. Do you understand that point?"

A weary Keating nodded.

"But I have a question," Dennis said. "Why are you going through all this trouble—and personal expense—of hiding this stuff from the agency? You can't be discriminated against because of a medical condition. You were seeing Dr. Forrester already, and they were aware of that. Why all this cloak and dagger around Charlottesville?"

"I think you're being naïve about how the agency really works," Keating said. "I wouldn't be surprised if half the employees in this building are in therapy of some kind. But hospitalizations are not looked on the same way. They can say what they want in human resources, but my career is over as head of the Iran desk if this got out."

"Mmm," Dennis said standing up.

☉

"I'm tired of this thing," Dennis said, hunched over the bar in the hotel and holding the cell phone tight to his ear. "Some guy freaked out today. Felt bad for the bastard. I thought he was going to jump off a ledge."

"What did you say to him?" Judy said.

"Oh, the usual stuff. Caught him in a lie, though I thought it was a bigger lie than it turned out to be. To be fair, it was a big lie to him, but not a big one for me."

"Your life as an investigator is different from my life as an investigator. At least you don't have to look at spreadsheets."

"You're looking at spreadsheets? Don't they have forensic accountants to do that?"

"It's a long story. I'll tell you later. When are you coming back to Perth? How much time do you have left?"

"Tomorrow I have four days left. I can barely hear you, Judy. Where are you?"

"At a pub. Getting rid of a headache."

"With Cilla?"

"No, a mate from work. He's the new partner I told you about."

"Is work going alright? You seem a little tired too."

"No, work is going badly. I hate it now. I'm investigating spreadsheets."

"Well, don't do anything rash," Dennis said.

"Like what?" she said.

"Like quitting."

"Oh that. Not likely."

"I have to go, Dennis. Ta. Come home soon."

Dennis put the phone down and stared at the TV set behind the bar. There was a baseball game on, and he could not identify either team by their uniforms.

His agency cell phone vibrated, and he answered without looking at the number.

"Yeah?"

"Cunningham?"

"Yeah."

"McCarthy here from NZSIS. How are you?"

"Fine. What's up? Do you have results from the autopsy?"

"That's why I'm calling, actually. Thought you might be coming here directly, but it appears you're still in Washington."

"Correct."

"Well, the report says that Forrester died from two bullets to the back of her head."

Dennis lifted his eyes up off the bar and looked at the TV screen and squinted in concentration.

"What type of bullet?"

"Type?"

"Yes, caliber."

"Let me look. It says a .32 caliber. Is that important?"

"Maybe. Anything else?"

"Actually, there is. It seems that her body had been moved."

"Come again?"

"Her body. If you remember we received a tip that her body was buried near a beach. They found the body using sniffer dogs."

"OK, I remember."

"The assumption was, given the decomposition of the body, that she had been buried there after she was killed. But the autopsy report stated besides sand, her body had soil on it. The soil is not consistent with the sand she was found in. The coroner's conclusion is that she was buried somewhere else, then moved and reburied in the sand."

"Well, that's odd."

"Right. That's what we think."

"Was there any DNA evidence on her body or her clothes? Was she sexually assaulted?"

"No evidence of that. And no DNA from under her fingernails and places like that. But there does appear to be a fracture of three fingers on her left hand."

"Broken fingers? Wonder what that's about?"

"Could have happened after she was killed."

"And why would someone move her body, then call in a tip to the new burial site?"

"We thought you could help us on that. Are you coming back here?"

"I'm not sure. Have you released the body to the family yet?"

"Not yet. We needed to ensure you were satisfied. Should we release her body?"

"How's her husband reacting to all of this?"

"Mr. Forrester? I've had no contact with him. Rangi contacted him. Are you coming or not?"

Dennis looked at the TV again and watched a player strike out and slam his bat onto the ground in frustration.

"Feel free to release the body. And can you send me the autopsy report?"

"Right."

CHAPTER 12

Dennis was adamant that the end never justifies the means.

Well, most of the time, that is.

There were circumstances in his career where he bent his own standards into a pretzel of questionable morality. Today was one of those days when the straight line was going to be bent into a completely distorted shape.

It was a Saturday morning, and he told Mr. Forrester the prior night that he needed to speak to him immediately about his wife's disappearance. Forrester sounded agitated and complained that New Zealand authorities were not releasing his wife's body for transport back to the states for burial. Dennis reassured him they would release the body, but he insisted they meet the following morning.

He parked his rental car in front of Forrester's house and had a moment of déjà vu, conjuring up the times his gut tightened with anxiety before parking in the same spot for a fifty-minute session with the deceased psychologist.

Forrester opened the door before Dennis could push the buzzer.

"Come in, please," he said.

Forrester was dressed in a maroon, short-sleeved polo shirt, khaki shorts, and sandals.

"Sit down," Forrester said, pointing to the same wingback chair Dennis sat in before. "Can I get you a cup of coffee? Tea? Water?" In contrast to the last conversation in his house, Forrester seemed subdued.

"Nothing, thanks. Just had breakfast." Dennis smiled. He noticed that Forrester kept glancing at the large manila folder Dennis had in his lap.

"By the way," Forrester said, "I received notice that my wife's body has been released. You were right about that. My son is making arrangements with the airlines. I can't bring myself to do it." He sighed, shook his head, and looked at the floor. "How do things like this happen?"

"I hope this is not too disturbing, but did the New Zealand authorities talk to you about the cause of death?"

"Yes," he said, closing his eyes briefly. "Yes, they did."

The living room was silent except for the distant humming of an exterior air conditioning compressor.

"Why would someone do that?" Forrester said. "Why would you just shoot a stranger? Her credit cards were never used, or her ATM. I mean, what's the point, except madness? Of all things, a madman kills my wife, a woman who tried to help people struggling with madness."

Dennis shifted in his chair.

"What was it that you wanted to talk about today?" Forrester said. "It sounded urgent. I thought you might have some information about her abductor, or, I suppose, her killer."

Dennis stood up and walked the two steps between them and handed the envelope to Forrester.

"What is this?" he said.

Dennis sat back down.

"Can you tell me about the photos in that envelope?"

Forrester turned his head awkwardly as if attempting to better focus on Dennis.

"Pictures?"

"Yes. Can you look at the pictures in that envelope and tell me about them?"

Forrester slowly opened the unsealed envelope flap and removed five, large, color photos. He looked at the first one for thirty seconds, then slid it to the bottom of the pile. By the time he looked at the third photograph, his cheeks started to redden, and he made small vocal intonations. After finishing, he looked up at Dennis.

"I'm trying to figure out what you're doing, but I can't," Forrester said. "What *are* you doing?"

"I'd like you to tell me about those photos," Dennis said.

"What about them?" Forrester said, his cheeks now beet red.

"Who is the woman in the photos?"

Forrester closed his eyes and took a measured, deep breath, Dennis guessed, either to control himself or stop himself from passing out.

"Oh, I see," he said finally, opening his eyes. "You don't know. I thought you would have known, but why did I think that? You must have had someone following me, obviously, and they found me staying over at this woman's house. I see. Mmm."

He slid the photos into the envelope, stood up, and returned them to Dennis, shaking his head back and forth slowly.

"Her name is Becky Cleary," Forrester said standing in front of Dennis.

Forrester turned and walked into the kitchen without speaking. Dennis was caught off guard with Forrester's sudden disappearance from the room. He waited for almost a minute, and when he heard nothing, Dennis stood up and peered into the kitchen. Forrester had disappeared into a room past the kitchen.

"Hello?" Dennis yelled.

There was no response.

"Hello?" he yelled louder.

He heard a muffled grunt from the far room, and his heartbeat increased. It was never a good idea for someone being confronted to leave the room.

Forrester emerged from the room with a small, foot-wide box in his hands and asked Dennis to sit down.

He sat as directed, but only at the front edge of the chair. He felt a thin bead of perspiration gather above his top lip.

Forrester sat down and looked at Dennis. He tilted his head again as if measuring the distance between them. He opened the box and reached inside.

⊙

Judy was aware that something had changed, because she took an unusually long time to choose what to wear to work; she even tested a new, darker shade of lipstick.

The prior night she had stayed too long at the pub with Craig. She felt a mixture of guilt and pleasure at the attention Craig paid to her.

Steady, young lady, she thought, mimicking Cilla's warning. *Don't do anything stupid. Flirtation is attention without intention.*

When she entered the large meeting room the task force was using, Craig was already there. She wondered whether the prior evening's flirtations were something he intended or were just the silly male hormones at play.

"Gidday, Judy," he beamed as she sat down next to him at her terminal. "Hope I wasn't too cheeky last night. Feel like I sort of let my hair down."

"No worries," she said laughing. "I enjoyed going out. You were a perfect gentleman." This was girl-speak for: let's do it again.

"Just let me know when you get another headache," he said.

"Could happen at any time," Judy said. She signed in to her desktop computer just as Connester entered the room.

"Attention, please," he said, as everyone swiveled to see him. "We've received word that Kadlec himself is flying to W.A. today to visit the mining company up north. It's been decided we need boots on the ground to keep an eye on him. And, given the fact that us tax blokes are not field investigators, Judy, you and Craig drew the short straws."

"Really?" she said. "Are we looking to be seen or not? If he's in the air already, will we even get there in time to follow him?"

"Good questions, Judy, and we'll address that with you and Craig in my temporary office. These folks here need to keep crunching the data. Come along."

☉

"Hey," Dennis said to Forrester. "Take it easy. No need to panic. Just stay calm."

"Panic about what?" Forrester said, pulling out a photograph from the box and reaching to hand it to Dennis.

"Becky's my daughter from a previous marriage. That photo was taken with my first wife when Becky was in grade school. We divorced many years ago. Becky works in Agriculture. And yes, I did help her get a job there. I've been staying with her every now and then because she's taken out a restraining order on a former boyfriend. She's scared sometimes, though I don't personally think the fellow will do anything. I guess you never know. My son has stayed with her several times as well."

Forrester handed Dennis two more photographs showing his daughter as a cheerleader and wearing a gown and mortarboard.

"Becky is your daughter."

"Yes, but I'm not completely dense, Mr. Cunningham. I'm putting some pieces together, and I'm guessing you thought I might be complicit in my wife's disappearance, so you had me investigated. And your intrepid investigators did a negligent job figuring out that Becky was my daughter. They thought I was having an affair."

Dennis said nothing. He reached over and returned the photos.

"It's humiliating and infuriating that you thought that. On the other hand," he sighed, "I'm grateful that someone is trying to solve my wife's death. We feel like no one cares. The New Zealand authorities seem stumped. It's a nightmare that won't go away. And now you show up with these sordid accusations. Jesus."

"I'm sorry," Dennis said. "I should have pressed harder with the investigator. We could have avoided all this. But the photos I brought were a ploy to force you to show me your wife's therapy notes. I know how harsh that sounds, but I feel like there's something in those notes of her agency clients that's important. And I don't have the time to go through channels for a search warrant."

"My wife's notes?" Forrester said. "You really think they're that important?"

"Yes, I do. The agency gave me the name of the five employees who went through employee assistance to get your wife's information. But I need to see if there are any hints in those notes that can move me faster in the right direction."

"You really think Jane was killed by someone in the agency?" Forrester said. "I don't find that credible. Why in god's name would someone she'd been seeing want to kill her? She didn't see violent patients. And, for the sake of argument, if it was someone from the agency, why do it in New Zealand? I'm sorry. You're not making sense."

"Your wife was killed by two bullets to the back of her head," Dennis said. "That's not the work of a random psychopath. It has all the earmarks of a professional killing. She was shot with a small-caliber weapon, which is preferred by intelligence services. A .32-caliber bullet remains in the brain and bounces around for maximum damage; two bullets is one hundred percent fatal. I'm sorry to distress you on these details, but it's important you know. The current official theory is that a foreign intelligence service abducted and killed her. I'm trying to figure out whether that conclusion is correct."

"What do you mean by foreign intelligence service? What would they want with Jane?"

"If you think about it, you'll see that there might be perverse motives."

"You mean—wait, you're not suggesting they wanted to know about her patients?"

"It's certainly possible; at least one of her patients was a high-ranking agency official. We're not certain that is what happened, but we have to make sure."

"But they would have had to force her to provide information—" he stopped. "Jesus, I don't believe this. Oh god."

Forrester grimaced and closed his eyes.

He opened his eyes and said, "Fine. Come along. You can look at the notes. I don't know what to believe anymore, but you're the only person trying to help, or at least I think you are."

Dennis followed him through the kitchen, where he put the box down on the granite countertop and picked up a set of keys hanging on a hook. He continued into a hallway, then opened a door that led down a set of carpeted stairs. At the bottom was a finished basement to the left with some exercise equipment and another door to the right that Forrester unlocked.

The door opened into Dr. Forrester's office. Dennis had long wondered what was behind that door during his sessions with Forrester; he thought it was a closet and was vaguely amused that the door led to a fitness area.

Forrester walked past the two upholstered chairs that Dennis remembered well from his sessions. He sat at his wife's desk against the wall. Forrester unlocked and pulled open the center desk drawer. Inside he lifted a long horizontal drawer that held pens, push pins, and paper clips. Underneath was a small sticky note with several numbers on it.

"She was given strict rules for how to secure the notes of her agency patients," he said. "She had a background check, and we found out two of our neighbors were visited by FBI agents. If we'd known what was involved in this CIA crap, she'd never had done it."

"It's just a theory about her disappearance, but we need to pursue it, so please try to withhold judgment until we get some clarity," Dennis said. "Where did she keep the notes?"

"First," he said holding up the sticky note and replacing the drawer container, "I don't want you to mention this to the agency. She was not supposed to write down her combination and leave it around. Jane showed me and said I might need it one day."

He walked across the room and removed a large Monet print of an Impressionist exhibit at the National Gallery of Art. Behind the frame was a thick, shiny green safe with a number dial. Forrester followed the directions. At the end of the combination, he pulled down a lever and opened the safe.

Finally, Dennis thought. *Here we go.*

Forrester dipped his head down and reached into the small dark space. Dennis peered over the man's shoulder.

"Huh," Forrester said. "Nothing here."

"You sure this is where she kept her notes?"

"Yes. This is the safe that was required by the agency."

Dennis pulled out his phone and turned on the flashlight app. Both men's faces crowded the small open door to the safe.

"That's odd," Forrester said, turning to Dennis. "Why isn't there anything in the safe? You know, you're starting to bother me. You accuse me of having an affair, maybe even being involved in my wife's death, then you convince me to help you break every HIPPA rule for privacy in my wife's office, and there's nothing here. You *knew* there was nothing here!"

"Hold on," Dennis said. "Just wait a second. Maybe you misunderstood where she kept her notes."

"I told you already where she kept those notes; they were separate from her other patients' notes. It was part of the contract. You're not telling me everything, damnit. What are you trying to do?"

"Mr. Forrester, I know a lot of this today is a little strange, but—"

"A *little* strange?"

"OK, very, very strange. But let's keep our eye on the prize. Those notes are more important than ever. You said they were supposed to be in this safe. We can both see they're not there. She must have put them somewhere else. Let's focus on that. Where does she keep the notes for her other patients? Help me here."

Dennis could see Forrester struggling with how to proceed; he was justifiably confused and suspicious of him, but he was also trying to help solve his wife's death.

Forrester walked over to a low, horizontal, two-drawer beige metal filing cabinet. He found another key on the chain and unlocked it. He pulled out the top drawer, and it was half filled with hanging files and manila folders inside those.

"These are her non-agency clients," he said.

"Do you mind if I see if any of the agency clients' names are in there?"

"No, go right ahead."

Dennis knelt and flipped through each folder reading the name on the tab. They were in alphabetical order and he quickly went through them.

"Nope," he said standing. "None of the five. Where else could they be?"

"I have no idea. Unless you already stole them and are playing some kind of weird game. You're a strange man, Cunningham."

"Yes, well that may be, but your wife's notes are missing, and that's not a good sign. Can we at least look around to see if they're here?"

Forrester seemed to pout as he helped Dennis look through every possible place in the office that his wife could have stored her agency patient files. After twenty minutes, the two men sat down in the therapy chairs to take a breather. Dennis sat is his normal therapy chair and was comforted somewhat by that.

"Do you have an alarm system?"

"Yes. That was also required."

"Has it been set off recently for any reason? Have you lost power?"

"No."

"Is it a standard residential alarm service?"

"Yes. Most people on this street have the same service. It's advertised on TV."

"Alright. I think I've bothered you enough today. And I'm profoundly sorry for the photos upstairs. It was clumsy. But you have to believe I'm trying to figure out what happened to your wife. And the missing notes are not a good sign right now."

"I can't believe she took them with her," Forrester said. "This is very strange. I wonder if I should report it to the CIA?"

"No. Please don't do that just quite yet. Give me a day or two to check on a few things. Then, by all means, let them know. But I have one more small favor to ask. It's simple. I need you to call your alarm service and tell them that you need a report of all the activity for your alarm starting the week your wife left to New Zealand, until today. Now, they'll probably tell you that they can't produce that kind of report, but they do have the data. It's just a pain for them to pull it. You'll have to threaten them really hard."

"And what are you looking for?"

"I'm not sure. But I need that report ASAP. I think you'll agree with me that something is not right with your wife's office."

They stared at each other. Forrester sat in his wife's chair, and Dennis in his normal patient chair. He felt strangely comfortable, but anxious, just like the old days.

⊙

He prayed that Simpson would not answer his phone. It was a Saturday morning and the deputy director of operations of the largest and best-funded intelligence service in the world could be in Berlin, Germany or sitting in a McDonald's in Bethesda, Maryland, eating an Egg McMuffin.

Just don't answer the damn phone, Dennis thought. *I don't feel like talking to you today.*

On the third ring, it went to voicemail.

"This is Cunningham checking in. Have decided not to go to New Zealand. A lot more going on here. Have been reviewing Dr. Forrester's patients for leads. Also, folks at NZSIS say that Forrester's body was moved from another grave to the beach where she was found. I'm expecting the autopsy report from the Kiwis and will forward that to you. Some of the fingers on her left hand were fractured. She was killed by a double tap, .32 caliber, which tends to confirm the Ghorbani angle. I'm still planning to finish this up on time." He deliberately left out the part about Dr. Forrester's missing therapy notes. He would hold that back a bit longer.

Dennis hung up and sat in the Starbucks in Rosslyn. He took another bite out of his breakfast sandwich. His blood pressure was up; he could feel rhythmic throbbing through the arteries in the neck.

After Keating, he called Karl. Aware that he was in a public place, he hissed with invective.

"You idiot," he said, using his open hand to cup his mouth against the phone. "I want my money back. You and your lame team completely screwed this up."

"Hey, chill out. They did the best they could. You gave us a ridiculous timetable and we tried to meet that. If you would have given us more time, I'm sure we could have figured the daughter angle out."

"Don't give me that shit. You're incompetent, Karl. Maybe you're not just pre-diabetic but pre-senile as well. I want my fucking money back because you suck and your team sucks."

"You shoulda stayed retired. And stuck to the whiskey. The wine is goin' to yer head, my friend."

"Your goddamn incompetence is going to my head." Dennis hung up.

There was one more call he needed to make, and he did it quickly to get it out of the way.

She answered on the second ring.

"Cunningham," Louise said. It was a statement, not a question or a salutation.

"Yes. How are you?"

"Since when do you start off conversations with pleasantries? Did you fall on your head?"

"Not you too," he said sharply.

"What's wrong. You in a bad mood?"

"Yeah, it's only 11:10 in the morning, and my day really sucks. Go figure."

"Sorry to hear that. Guess I didn't help much."

"No, you didn't."

"Like I said, I'm sorry."

"Since when do you apologize?" he shot back.

"This call's going swimmingly," she said after a brief pause. "What do you want?"

Dennis took several deep breaths. The sound of the hissing milk steamers combined with the piped-in rock music to provide the modern version of silence.

"Cunningham, are you alright?"

"Yes. Actually no. I'm not alright. I told you, I'm having a bad day."

"Anything I can do for you? What do you need?"

Dennis realized he was rubbing his temple with his open hand.

"I don't know why I'm complaining. Bad habits."

"You sound depressed."

He swallowed. He *was* depressed and *angry* at everything and everyone: Karl, Simpson, Keating, the Kiwis, the Ghorbanis, the weather, the missing Forrester files…"

"Yes, I guess I am. It happens. I just need to take a walk to clear my head."

"Is it the Forrester stuff, or something else?"

Louise had never shown any interest in Dennis's state of mind, nor any sympathy whatsoever; their relationship was neutral at best and antagonistic at the worst. But he was feeling extremely vulnerable and dropped his normal guarded approach to her.

"It's everything."

"What's going on with you and Judy? Are you two going through a difficult time? These things happen. You'll get through it."

"It's this idiotic case. There're just too many layers. Usually, I get excited about the chase. It charges me up."

"That's why I recommended you. You're good at this stuff."

"Used to be good."

"Jeez, Cunningham. You don't sound right. Go take a walk. Get some fresh air."

"Sure."

Neither spoke for several seconds.

"I got an idea," she said. "I'm going out to dinner tonight with a group of friends. Why don't you join us? Couple of guys you'd find interesting, and a woman that works at the Pentagon. We're all single and love getting together when we don't have dates. You sound depressed and lonely."

"I don't think so. I'm not good company when I'm like this."

"Bullshit. You still at the hotel in Rosslyn?"

"Louise, I appreciate your interest, but it's really not necessary—"

"Be out front at 6:30."

"No," he said.

She hung up.

⊙

Judy and Craig landed in Meekatharra at 1:30 in the afternoon. She had raced back to her house, put together an overnight bag with clothes and personal items, then raced to the private airport for the AFP jet.

Craig was thrilled to be out of the office and kept up a steady chatter in the plane, while Judy tried to keep him on task.

"You have the camera?" she said.

"Right."

"You have the rental car ready at the airport?"

"Yes."

"Remember, Miller says we're tourists checking out the scenery. Kadlec is getting in around 3 p.m., and he's expected to head right for the gold mine. He and his accountant are staying in Meekatharra and will likely have dinner with the general manager of the mine, a Canadian named Phillipe Desaulniers. Connester says we need to catalog everything Kadlec does, including how long he's at dinner, how much he drinks, whether he looks relaxed or angry. Anything and everything."

"Judy, we've already gone over that. No worries." He reached over and grabbed her forearm and shook it reassuringly.

She did not like him touching her; not that the gesture was condescending or immature, but because it felt so warm and inviting. His smile, his good looks, and his rugged, almost care-free, enthusiasm were unnerving and enticing. She wished that Dennis would come back soon.

Their landing was bouncy as the small jet was tossed by the thermals roaring up from the hot, red countryside. It might be winter in Western Australia, but the interior was still warm.

After getting their rental car, they hung around the airport parking lot waiting for Kadlec's private plane.

"Do you think I look touristy?" Craig said, pulling the collar of his short-sleeve golf shirt.

"You look appropriately silly," she said.

"Well, you look smashing in those shorts and a tank top."

"You're are a bit of larrikin," she said.

They both heard the approach of a jet and got into the car.

"Welcome to sunny W.A., Mr. Kadlec," Craig said starting the Toyota Landcruiser. "My colleague and I will be watching you closely as you pinch loads of money from the taxman."

The day went from normal boring to extremely boring. They followed Kadlec and his accountant to the mine. Craig drove past the turnoff to the facility and pulled over a half-mile down the road. They took turns with the binoculars watching for Kadlec's return. As the afternoon wore on, Craig began to talk about what they would order for dinner.

"I'm thinking of a steak tonight," he said, sitting on the hood of the car. "Big juicy steak. You like steak, Judy?"

"Sometimes," she said, peering through the binoculars. "Not my fave."

"Bet you're a fish eater, lots of veggies. Health nut, I reckon."

"Oh please."

"You're in such good shape. Bet you're a runner too. How many miles do you run a week? Fifty?"

"Your mind is going all the time. You can't sit still! And food. Who thinks of food out here in the bush?" Judy pulled her eyes away from the binoculars and gave him an exaggerated frown. But, his comment about her being in good shape had not been lost, and she fiddled with the adjustment on the lens.

⊙

Dennis was more than a little agitated at Louise for cajoling him into going to dinner with her group of singles. What if he was feeling low? And since when did she care about his state of mind or wellbeing? She was simply trying to keep him together long enough to finish the project.

Louise pulled up in a metallic-blue BMW 3 series. The sun was low and sent long, towering shadows across Rosslyn.

"Hey," he said getting in the passenger side. "Wish you hadn't pulled this on me. You seem to think I'm going off the deep end or something."

"Oh, stop being a baby," she laughed. "Just enjoy yourself and get out of your funk."

Dennis shot her a quick look as she pulled into traffic. He could not remember a time when she laughed.

She wore fashionable round sunglasses, her pure blond hair bounced on her partially exposed shoulders from a light blue open-necked blouse. He could barely make out the faintest whiff of perfume or body lotion.

"What are you looking at?" she said, cutting aggressively through traffic to circle back onto Key Bridge into Georgetown.

"Nothing," he said.

She laughed.

"So, here's the drill tonight," she said. "There's six of us, including you. There's Sarah, a gorgeous black woman who works at the Pentagon; Steve, who's at State; Francisco, he's a mid-level diplomat at the Peruvian Embassy; and Mark, at DOJ. Mark's a hoot. And he's gay."

"All single?" he said.

"Yes, when we can't get dates, it's better to share a couple of bottles of wine at a nice restaurant and laugh it up, instead of sitting home and having a bottle of wine by yourself."

"I'm the stay-at-home-with-the-bottle type," he said.

"That's not healthy."

"Now you sound like Dr. Forrester."

That statement shut down the talk for a few minutes as Louise navigated crowded M Street.

"What happened to your husband? You were married last time we worked together."

"None of your business."

"Just asking."

"Didn't work out. Fifty percent of marriages don't work out."

"Sorry to hear that."

"Don't be sorry. It's better for him and me this way. Life moves on. People can stay stuck in something that doesn't work."

"No, I hear you."

"And how about you and Judy? Still an item all the way over in Australia?"

"Yes."

"Wedding bells in the wings?"

"Mmm. I don't know if I'm the marrying type. I don't know why we can't just live together."

"Does she want to get married?"

"I think so."

"And you don't?"

"Louise, come on. I'm not in the mood to talk about that stuff."

"Are you in the mood to be good company tonight? I told the group you were coming and were a funny guy."

"Me? Funny? Gee, thanks for setting me up."

"Would you just chill? Here we are."

Despite his trepidation going into the evening, Dennis found that he liked the group. Mark, the gay guy, was as funny as Louise said. Half the evening was taken up laughing at his jokes.

And Sarah was as gorgeous as Louise described. A tall, thin woman with skin the color of burnt almond, she had green eyes and a lusty, deep laugh.

"Now, Dennis, I have to ask, where did you get those blue eyes?" Sarah said at one point. "Lordy, they are like headlights on high beam. Louise here has blue eyes, but not like those 100-watt bulbs!"

Dennis laughed and just shrugged. "They came with the package. Mom, Dad, or a distant Viking relative. Who knows?"

"Well, you must be a woman slayer. Damn, Louise, you didn't say he was that good looking."

"He is a cute one," Mark said.

"Get in line there, my gay friend. I think Dennis is a lady's man."

"He just doesn't know how much fun the other side is," Mark said, sparking a round of laughter that even Dennis couldn't resist.

By the time they had dessert and more drinks, Dennis was a little drunk. He didn't need the McCallan 18, neat, with his chocolate mousse. But everyone was piling it on, and he was enjoying himself.

He was intrigued with Louise, who displayed a funny, self-deprecating sense of humor that he never guessed she was capable of. At one point she brought the house down when she described a spin class where her prosthetic foot almost fell off.

The group broke up at 10:30 and after the requisite hugs and handshakes, Louise and Dennis stood to wait for the valet to bring up her car.

"I think I drank too much," Dennis said.

"I think everyone drank too much," she said, laughing. "I try not to when I'm with this group, but they're so much fun."

"Fun they are," he said. "Sarah's a wild one."

After they got into the car, Dennis leaned back on the headrest.

"You alright over there?" Louise asked.

"Yep," he said with his eyes closed.

"How do you expect to get to your hotel room?"

"The same way I always do, on my hands and knees," he said.

While they drove, Dennis looked idly out the window. He wound down the window to get fresh air on his face.

"Nice night," he said. "Summer nights in our nation's capital."

She laughed as she pulled into a parking space.

"Where are we?" he said.

"My place," she said putting the parking brake on. "Come on, get moving."

"Louise, I can't stay at your place."

"I'm not leaving you in your lobby to meander through the hotel. And I don't feel like parking, walking you to your room, tucking you in, then leaving to drive back here. If you're going to drink that much, you'll have to sacrifice a bit."

"Christ, I'll take a cab," he said getting out.

Louise locked the car, went around and put her arm forcefully under his and pulled him toward the high rise on Connecticut Avenue.

"This is embarrassing," he said. "I think there's a cab there. Look."

"Yipes, I'll remember not to take you to dinner in the future," she said.

"Fine. I just want to go to sleep."

She navigated him through the set of double locked doors and said hello to Morris, the all-night guard in the lobby.

"Miss Nordland, can I help you?"

"No, all set, Morris. Have a good night."

"Yes, ma'am."

She helped Dennis into her spacious condo, plopping him onto the couch.

"Nice place," he said.

"Can I get you anything? Coffee, water, soda?"

"Got a beer?"

"No more for you tonight."

"You really won't let me go home?"

"Not like this. I'm going to change. There's a bathroom in the hallway. I'm going to put a new toothbrush on the sink with toothpaste. I also have some of my former husband's pajamas, and I'll leave them in there."

"Why do you have his pajamas?"

"He gets lonely. So do I."

"OK," he said. "I can't believe you're doing this."

But she had already left to get the pajamas. She dropped off the pajamas and went into her room shutting the door.

Dennis walked around the living room, looking at prints, photographs, books, DVDs, and other items. He finally made it to the bathroom, brushed his teeth, and changed into the pajamas. He folded his clothes, left them in the bathroom and wandered into the kitchen, where he opened the refrigerator.

He saw several containers of Greek yogurt, milk, butter, eggs, and the normal things you'd find in an American refrigerator. There was a half-empty bottle of white wine, and he took it out, opened several cabinet doors until he found a wine glass. He poured a full glass, put the bottle back, and made his way to the couch.

He picked up *The Washingtonian* magazine and flicked through some of the thick, glossy pages, taking a sip of wine now and then. Louise's bedroom door opened behind him, and he heard her pad out daintily.

"Dennis! More wine?"

"I couldn't sleep. I'm reading about the high and mighty in Washington society. I haven't found your picture yet, but I'm sure it's on one of the society gala pages."

"I don't think so," she said, moving around to stand in front of him. "Not my style nor demographic."

She wore a short-sleeve, green, satin pajama top, and long pajama bottoms. Her smallish, pointed breasts aimed directly at him, and his eyes veered down at the magazine.

"I hope I'm not keeping you up," he said. "Really. I can turn off the lights."

Louise walked into the kitchen and returned with a glass of wine. She sat at the other end of the couch, turned and pulled her legs up, and faced him. Out of the corner of his eye, Dennis could see the flesh-colored prothesis sticking out from below the left cuff.

"Why don't you like me?" she said suddenly.

He whipped his head around and looked at her. Perhaps it was the late hour, the alcohol, the absurdly confusing Forrester case, or all of the above, but he was completely unprepared for that question.

"Huh?"

"Why don't you like me? You've never liked me." She took a sip.

Dennis tried, through the late-night haze, to look at her face carefully. The Louise Nordland shell had cracked and there was another woman sitting at the end of the couch, vulnerable and sincere. Her honesty was unnerving, but Dennis had seen her manipulative side as well and was still guarded. Louise was as much a mystery as anyone he had dealt with in his life. Again, for the hundredth time that evening, he was aware of her understated beauty. The small nose, ice-blue eyes, Nordic straight blond hair, muscle-toned arms and shoulders.

He swallowed another sip of wine, stared hard at her with his puffy eyes.

"I can't believe you're asking me that question."

"I *am* asking you that question. What is it about me that you don't like?"

"There is nothing about you I don't like. Stop it. I don't like this conversation."

"Do you think I'm mean? You once said I was too ambitious. Is that it? Too self-serving? Unfeeling?"

"You're not going to trick me into saying something stupid, Louise. I don't know why you're doing this, but it's not making me feel comfortable. I mean, we worked together on that case in London, and you were my boss for a while in OIG. Typically, people's relationships with their bosses are not the same as those with their friends or peers. It's not like we were close at work, but I don't think it's supposed to be that way, is it?"

She sighed and shook her head.

"I don't think men like me. I think my ambition scares them."

"I can't speak for anyone else, but I respect you, including your ambition. I'm just not that ambitious. And perhaps it is intimidating for others when an extremely competent woman outperforms people around her. I don't know. But I'm not in management; I'm one of the guys who aren't always crazy about management."

"You're different, Dennis. You've always been different. I thought you'd be honest with me."

"I am being honest. You're smart, focused, intuitive, hard working—I mean, what can I say?"

She stood up, knocked back the glass of wine in one gulp.

"Whatever," she said walking into the kitchen. "I'll get you a blanket."

She returned from behind the couch and put down a plaid blanket next to him.

"Sleep tight," she said.

"Louise," he said standing up to look at her. "Um, I don't think I was very articulate. I like you, I really do. On a personal level. And I respect you on a professional level. And I appreciate you trying to pull me out of my funk today."

"Well, goodnight then." She turned, walked into her room, and shut the door.

Dennis sat back down.

God, what the hell was that about? he thought. *I have a feeling I messed something up.*

He put down the magazine, finished the wine, and took the glass to the kitchen. He turned off the kitchen light, went into the bathroom, looked at himself in her husband's pajamas, and felt stupid.

After the last light was turned off, he lay down on the couch and pulled the blanket around himself tightly. Maybe the air-conditioning was on too high, but he felt cold.

He tried to sleep but was bothered by the conversation with Louise.

The door to her room opened, and light from her bedside lamp cut sharply across the dark living room carpet. She walked around the couch and stood over him.

"You can sleep out here tonight, or you could sleep on my bed with me. If you sleep in my bed, I don't want any funny stuff. You can probably tell from tonight that I'm feeling a little self-conscious these days. I'm lonely. Maybe I'm even depressed like you. I'd like someone to sleep next to me but that's all. What do you think?"

"Whatever you want, I'll do," he said. "I feel bad about our conversation tonight."

She turned and walked into her bedroom, leaving the door open. He got up and followed. She sat on the other side of the bed and appeared to do something at her feet, then slipped under the covers.

Dennis jumped into bed and stared at the ceiling.

She turned on her side toward him.

"Is this too strange for you?"

"No."

She leaned back, reached over to turn off the light and stopped:

"Do you want to see my stump?"

"No."

"I'd like to show it to you."

"I don't think so, Louise. It's not necessary. I know how you lost it in Beirut. I think we all know that you were trapped in the building when it was hit with that car bomb. I'm sorry that they had to amputate it. You can't even tell when you walk."

"I'd feel better if I showed it to you."

"Why?"

"Are you scared? Do you think I'm disfigured?"

"No, that's not what I'm saying—fine, let's see it."

Louise pulled back the sheets and exposed her legs. Her right foot protruded from the right pant leg, but the left cuff was flat and empty about twelve inches from the bottom.

She looked at him and slowly rolled up the cuff of her good right leg, then did the same for her left. Dennis bit the inside of his lip. He was so unnerved by Louise's intensity and the strange intimacy of her sitting in a bed while showing him a missing part of her body.

About ten inches below her left knee, her leg stopped. The skin was puckered around the stump. There was some redness around the remaining calf muscle that must be caused by the prosthesis, he thought.

"Do you want to touch it?" she said.

"No, I don't—sure. I'll touch it. Will it hurt?"

"Not really."

He put his fingers around her leg several inches above the stump. Her skin felt warm, and the small blond hairs on her leg were soft.

"Sometimes it feels like it's still there," she said. "It's called phantom limb syndrome. Sometimes it hurts, but not often."

Dennis kept his hand on her leg and gently ran his fingers above the amputation site.

"I'm sorry it happened to you," he said removing his hand. "You were brave and tough to survive."

"I was lucky, that's all."

"Well, call it what you want," he said turning back to his side. "But I can call it brave."

She reached over and turned off the light, and they both stayed perfectly still on their sides facing away from each other, several feet apart.

"Dennis, would it be OK if I put my head on your shoulder? That's all. It's nice to have a man in this bed, and as we both know, it's not a good idea for us to do anything else."

"Sure, Louise. No problem."

She shuffled across the bed, and Dennis lay on his back. He lifted his left arm so that she could turn on her side with her head scrunched on his shoulder.

"Don't try anything," she said.

"Go to sleep."

Once during the night, he woke to find he was on his left side facing Louise's back. His right hand was on her small waist. He slowly pulled his hand away but was startled to feel her hand reach and put it back.

CHAPTER 13

I t sounded like a jet engine was inches from his face, and he sat up, startled and confused. It took a moment to remember he was not in his hotel room.

"Damn," he said rubbing his eyes, and jumping out of bed. Louise was in the master bathroom blow-drying her hair. The bathroom door was open, and she saw him in the mirror.

She turned off the blower.

"Hey," she said. "You snore."

"Yeah, well so do you."

"No, I don't."

"Kept me up all night."

She laughed. "Mr. Cunningham..."

Louise wore a thick, white terry cloth bathrobe. She put down the hair blower and proceeded into the bedroom, using a single gray metal crutch under her left arm to get to her side of the bed. The front of her robe had fallen open, and he could see one of her breasts as she sat down to put on her prosthesis.

Dennis rushed out of the room and into the spare bathroom. He got dressed, brushed his teeth, and folded the pajamas. He put them on the couch next to the folded blanket. Mercifully, Louise had closed her bedroom door, and Dennis relaxed.

She came out wearing a mauve blouse, tight-fitting jeans, and soft-soled shoes.

"Breakfast?" she said.

"I really should get back to the hotel," he said.

"Bullshit. You can join me next door for coffee and pastry."

"Sure."

They sat in the coffee shop looking at their phones and barely talking to each other. Dennis knew this was the modern way people shared quality time together, physically adjacent to each other but both privately ensconced in their devices.

Dennis ran through his emails on the agency phone. He then went through his burner. There were two texts from Judy: *how is the nz project going?* and *i miss u.*

Louise had three phones. She flew through the emails on the first one, her tiny child-like fingers tapping away furiously. The second phone she took more time reviewing and only appeared to answer one email. The final phone, which Dennis took to be a personal phone, she seemed to be texting.

She laughed and looked up at Dennis. "Sarah thought you were the most handsome white guy she'd seen in a while."

"I thought she was hot if that means anything."

"I'll tell her," and she typed.

His agency phone buzzed on the table and Dennis looked at it.

"Shit," he said putting it to his ear. "This is Cunningham."

"I'm commanding you to go to New Zealand and get to the bottom of Forrester's disappearance," Simpson said. "You only have three goddamned days left, and poking around Forrester's patients here is a waste of time. I thought I made it perfectly clear that we have several teams in place right now waiting for the thumbs up. We even have the Ghorbanis under surveillance in Ankara, and they've been added to the list. Get your ass over to New Zealand today."

"Listen, I understand the urgency," Dennis said. "You've made it clear all along. But I don't think there's anything to be gained by me spending a full day flying across the world to confirm information I already have. She was murdered in what looks like a professional assassination, was buried, then reburied for some reason. There's nothing more to learn over there. I'm close to getting some critical information on Forrester's patients. This could be key to the investigation. You'll have to trust me."

Dennis looked up and saw Louise staring at him; her face had taken on a tense, laser-focused demeanor. This was the business Louise; not the insecure, flirty Louise.

"Simpson, are you there?" Dennis said.

"You're an idiot," he said hanging up.

He put down the phone and looked idly as a young mother and her toddler ambled by.

"He wants you to go back to New Zealand?" she asked.

"Yeah."

"And you don't think that's a good idea?"

"No, I don't."

"You really think there's something about her patients that is more important?"

"Yes."

"Do you mean her agency patients or her non-agency patients?"

"My guess is that it's related to her agency patients."

"I'm one of her five agency patients."

"Don't I know," he said, frowning. "And you still haven't given me your absence schedule during her trip to New Zealand."

"Are you serious?"

"Of course I am. Were you at Langley when Forrester went missing?"

"No. I was traveling."

"Where?"

"I can't tell you. It's classified."

"For God's sake, Louise. Are you going to make me go to Simpson for this?"

"Yes."

"Tell me, why do you dislike him so much? Besides being a complete, self-serving jerk, what else do you have on him?"

"I don't like anything about him," she said. "I'm not saying he's not smart, but he has a habit of undermining anyone who works for him or competes with him. He's a masterful inside ballplayer. And he has a mean streak. Otherwise, he's a really great guy."

"Is it because you have sights on his job? First female to be deputy director of operations?"

"Please, that's just a little too pat, isn't it? Does that meet your narrative: brassy female feels like her aggressive male competitor plays unfair? Boo hoo."

"I'm just trying to figure out why you're not giving me your absence schedule, that's all."

"Let's get you back to your hotel so you can keep sleuthing," she said in what Dennis took to be a full-on pout.

They drove in silence through Northwest Washington and into Georgetown. The Sunday morning traffic was light.

"I have a confession," Dennis said, his face turned away at the passenger window.

"Really?"

"Yeah."

"Confess then. This should be interesting."

"I really wanted to have sex with you last night. You were very desirable."

"If that's how you felt, why didn't you start something?"

"You told me not to."

"Since when do you follow anyone's orders?"

"You have a point," he said turning to look at her. "But you seemed particularly vulnerable. I'd never seen you that way before."

Louise made a strange face that Dennis could not interpret. They drove in silence until she pulled into the hotel driveway and put the car in park. She turned to look at him but kept her sunglasses on.

"Well, I'm sorry you didn't fool around last night because that's the last time you'll ever have the opportunity. You had your chance. Your attempt would have been met with a very passionate response."

Dennis stared at her and conceded that she was a beguiling, mysterious, and beautiful woman. He got out and walked slowly around the front of the car and to her side window. He tapped on it and she lowered it, looking up at him into the sunshine.

"What?" she said.

"Just a second." He leaned down and gently pressed his lips against hers. When they parted, their lips stuck briefly together.

"And you'll never have another chance at that," he said.

He wished he could see her eyes, but all he saw were two round, dark, convex lenses, reflecting his confused and distorted face.

⊙

He entered the hotel coffee shop, bought a cup, and sat at an isolated table. He looked at his watch and did a quick calculation. Perth was thirteen hours ahead; it was 10:45 a.m. in Virginia on Sunday, so it was 11:45 a.m. on Monday in Perth.

He dialed, and she answered on the second ring.

"My wayward Yank," Judy said.

"Ha," he said nervously. "Wayward in what sense?"

"Wayward from me. I miss you."

"Well, I miss you too," he said staring into the top of his coffee cup. "I wish you could join me here. I'm lonely. People do weird things when they're lonely."

"What does that mean?"

"Nothing. Just that I wish you were here."

"My calculation shows you're almost done over there."

"I've got three more days counting today. Strange how I'm talking to you in real time, and yet we're in different times zones and days of the week."

"So how is the project going?"

"Simpson wants me to go back to New Zealand, but it's too late for that. I have a couple of wild ideas on what might have happened, but I just need some things to add up first. How are you doing?"

"I hate my job."

"What happened now? You just started back with a new partner."

"I wish you were here," she said.

"In less than a week, I'll be back in Perth. But what's going on at work?"

"It's too complicated to explain. Just get back here soon."

Dennis's agency phone started vibrating.

"Judy, I've got to jump off. Be home soon."

"I love you," she said.

"Love you too."

Dennis saw the number was blocked.

"Hello?"

"Dennis, this is Rangi—Rangi Winchester. New Zealand security bureau."

"Hey Rangi, how are you?"

"Fine, mate. How are you?"

"As well as could be expected, given the circumstances."

"Assume you're referring to the Forrester investigation?"

"Yes."

"That's why I'm calling, actually. I'd appreciate it if we kept our conversation confidential, to the extent that anyone's conversation is confidential these days."

"Well, I'm on an agency phone right now."

"I reckon that's about as locked down as they get."

"I suppose so," Dennis said. "Then again, who the hell knows. What's up?"

"Was talking to Colin yesterday. Remember, he's NZSIS. They handle sigint."

"Yeah, I remember."

"He mentioned in passing that they picked up some encrypted communications on the South Island about three hours after Forrester went missing, which would have been about three a.m. here. It an outbound call from the Marlborough area."

"Iranian agents?"

"Possibly."

"Is that all you wanted to tell me?"

"No, there's a bit more. Colin didn't want to bring it to your attention. He said it wasn't relevant."

"What wasn't relevant?"

"You can't repeat this, or I'm in a bit of trouble if you get my drift."

"No worries. What else is there to this outbound call?"

"It was a satellite phone, not a mobile phone."

"Interesting. What kind of sat phone?"

"The kind you blokes use."

"What blokes?"

"You blokes."

"The agency?"

"Right. Encrypted sat phone typically used by your people."

"You sure of that?"

"I'm repeating what Colin told me. He said sat phones are more difficult to triangulate and track, but he was certain it was you folks. Thought I'd tell you, in case that helps at all."

"I appreciate you letting me know."

"Cheers, mate."

Dennis hung up and took a sip of coffee.

His agency phone vibrated on the table again, rippling the calm surface of his black coffee.

"Hey, Louise," he said.

"Hey."

"Miss me already?"

"You shouldn't have done that," she said.

"Done what?"

"The thing at the end when you got out of the car. That was not called for."

"Too late to take it back now. Sorry if I offended you. But I thought I heard a little bit of a dare in the conversation."

She sighed.

"You're an interesting man."

"Is that why you called? You in the office?"

"Yes, I'm in the office, but no, that's not why I called. I didn't want you to bother Simpson about my absence schedule."

"OK, where were you when Forrester disappeared?"

"Melbourne."

"Melbourne, Florida, or Melbourne, Australia?"

"The latter."

Now he sighed.

"Why didn't you tell me earlier?"

"For obvious reasons. Thought you'd be overly suspicious and waste your time. I was in meetings for two days there, including the day Forrester went missing."

"Are there records of the meeting and your participation?"

"Those are confidential. You won't be able to see them. We were working on a plan to target a Chinese tech company operating in Australia."

"I don't know, Louise. I'll need to check, regardless."

"I'm telling you, aren't I?"

"What if I go ahead and ask Simpson now for more detailed records on your absence from Langley?"

"Go right ahead. But you're wasting your goddamn time."

She hung up.

⊙

It was clear now that Craig was flirting with Judy at any given chance. They had returned from their surveillance of Kadlec with little to show for their time in a dusty, small town, except that Craig was studiously flirting with her. Judy was troubled by the attention that Craig was showing her, not because she found it aggressive or inappropriate, but because she liked it. And liking it meant that she would have trouble telling him to stop. And if she had trouble telling him to stop, he would continue. And she would continue to like it, leading to a cascade of trouble.

Judy and Craig were given yet a new drug case in Fremantle, to add to their already overloaded docket. The Rebels Outlaw Motorcycle Club Gang, or Rebels OMCG, was suspected of starting up a small-time heroin ring in the Fremantle and Mandurah area. The Rebels OMCG was an Australia-wide gang that patterned itself on the Hell's Angels. The gang's unlikely insignia is a U.S. Civil War Confederate flag, with the image of a human skull wearing a Confederate cap inset in the middle of the flag.

Judy's initial reaction years ago to the Rebels was incredulity. She thought it was a poor joke of long-haired men, pretending to be American outlaws in leather jackets, driving Harley-Davidson motorcycles around in large, highway-clogging groups.

But the truth was that some Rebel OMCG members were danger-ous, and indeed, supported themselves by any means possible, including distributing drugs.

WA Gang Crime Squad Detective Stephen Saul, and Senior Sgt. Louie Fermi of the Fremantle District sat in a meeting room with Judy and Craig reviewing the case.

It did not take long for Judy to get angry.

During Judy's earlier years on the AFP, she deferred respectful-ly to the senior members of the force, as well as other interagency crime-fighting organizations. She had much to learn, and she listened dutifully to their direction and wisdom. The fact that their behavior to-wards her was often condescending and sexist was, unfortunately, part and parcel of those times.

Over the years, as police organizations employed more females, the pampering and condescension grew less overt and grating.

In this meeting, Craig unexpectedly took control.

"At first we received complaints about the sound of the motorcy-cles from two of their neighbors," Sgt. Fermi said. "When those Harleys start up, the noise is quite loud."

"But there are noise regulations, yes?" Craig said.

"Correct. In W.A. it's 95 decibels at 5,000 rpms. And I believe all of the bikes at this address are way over that limit."

"Well, why don't you blokes just cite them for that infraction then? Show those bikies who's boss," Craig said.

Judy rubbed her forehead in a display of irritation, and Saul from the gang crime squad looked at her. The two had worked on sever-al cases together over the years and maintained a respectful working relationship.

"That's not the best approach with these fellas, Craig," Saul said. "I'm sure Judy can explain. She's done this kind of work before."

Judy, still smarting from Craig's sudden grandstanding, had trouble keeping her voice calm and level.

"Craig, I'm sure district police will soon stop by and ask the bikies to be mindful of the disturbance they're creating in the neighborhood," she said. "It's the first step."

"First step?" Craig said.

"Yes," Saul said. "If we come down too hard on them now, they'll just move to another rental and start all over again. We want to nab them on more serious charges than having illegal mufflers."

"Well, if that's the way you do it, then fine," Craig said. "Seems a little slow, if you ask me."

Judy stared down at her notebook.

"We already have one of the bikers engaged in selling heroin in Cottesloe," Saul said. "Our goal now is to find out who's supplying them with drugs. And we believe they also have firearms in the house. Judy has been through this routine several times."

Craig crossed his arms in what Judy took for a pout. "Right. You're the veterans. Just seems a bit slow, if you ask me."

The moment Judy's car door closed, and before Craig started the car, she said, "Mate"—she could barely control herself—"don't you *ever* do that again. Next time we go into a meeting like that, you keep your bloody mouth shut unless you're either confirming some information or have a question about a fact. You are in no position to pass judgment on any aspect of an investigation with veteran police officers. And in the future, in interagency contacts, I'll take the lead in those discussions. Today you sounded like a bloody teenager."

"Well, it didn't make sense to me, Judy—"

"Damnit, Craig. Didn't you hear what I said? You're the junior member of this team. I've been doing this for ten years, for god's sake. If you have any questions, ask me. Next time shut your bloody trap. You sounded like a wankasaurus back there."

"Throwing a bit of a tantie, are we, Judy? I didn't mean any harm."

She looked out the passenger window at the light winter rain drifting down. The streets had a melancholy sheen, and she wondered whether she was tired of being lonely, or just tired.

⊙

"I don't know what it means," Forrester said, pushing the printout across the table to Dennis.

The Starbucks in Rosslyn had become Dennis's office. Forrester called him and said he had the report from his alarm service but could not make sense of it. He agreed to show it to Dennis in person, and the two sat side by side at the small table. Dennis was still a little groggy and confused about his night at Louise's.

"Well, this column here shows the dates," Dennis said, running his finger slowly down the first page of a thick, stapled set of sheets. "And it looks like this column, mmm, yeah, this one shows the time-stamp when the alarm was armed, and this one here is when it was disarmed. And this final one shows if the alarm went off, which I doubt ever happened."

Dennis started to flip the pages.

"OK. Let's start here," he said. "Your wife left on this date, so let's run through these timestamps to look for anything unusual."

Forrester adjusted his reading glasses and leaned in, while Dennis ran his finger across the columns. The dates showed a regular pattern. Forrester left for work during his wife's absence and turned on the alarm. When he returned in the late afternoon, he turned it off until he left to work the following day.

"You don't turn it on overnight?" Dennis said.

"No, not really. It's a pain, and once I forgot and opened the door in the morning to get the paper, and the stupid thing went off. Police came and I felt like an idiot."

They continued to look at the dates, and Forrester noted on some occasions that he stayed at his daughter's condo and did not return home until the following afternoon.

"Oh, this is the date that I left with my son for New Zealand," Forrester said. "I put the alarm on."

Dennis's finger stopped on the line that showed the second day of Forrester's trip. Both men leaned in as his finger moved horizontally across the page.

"What does that mean?" Forrester said as Dennis tapped his forefinger on a number.

"It means that your alarm was turned off on this date at 2:44 a.m., and then it was re-armed at 3:23 a.m."

"Not possible," Forrester said. "I was in New Zealand."

"Anyone else have the alarm code?"

"My son who was with me. We have a house cleaner. I'm not sure if she has the code, to be honest. Jane was always there when Maria cleaned the house."

"Anyone else you can think of? Your daughter that you had together?"

"She lives in San Jose; if she has it, she wouldn't be stopping by from the west coast at two o'clock in the morning."

"And your daughter from your first marriage?"

"She doesn't have it."

"Let's keep going," Dennis said, bending the corner of the page.

They continued to the final page and then returned to the page with the corner turned down.

"I'm guessing you think this is when Jane's notes were taken?" Forrester said.

"Yeah."

"But whoever did it must have known the alarm code and combination to the safe."

"Yeah."

"How is that possible?" Forrester said.

Dennis did not answer because he didn't want to stress Forrester. The answer was not pleasant.

"Do yourself a favor and change the entry code for the alarm," Dennis said. "Someone else has it."

"That's creepy. Should I call the police and tell them?"

"Not now, if you don't mind. I'd like just a few more days to work on this. Just change the code. I'd keep the cops out of it for now."

"It's as if no one cares about Jane," Forrester said, leaning back in his chair. "The CIA, the New Zealand police, our local police. Christ, what a depressing end to a wonderful life." His eyes watered and Dennis, for the first time, felt awful for this poor, proud man, whose wife had been caught up in something evil and inexplicable.

"Well, I care about her," Dennis said. "I'm trying."

"I appreciate it," Forrester said, standing. "But I don't hold out much hope. You're just one guy. Keep this printout. It's no good to me." He walked out of the coffee shop, his head held high, but his shoulders were stooped.

⊙

Dennis returned to his hotel room, pulled the chair to the desk, and re-read his notes in painstaking detail. He used another blank pad of paper to summarize items from his small notebook. After an hour he had reduced his twenty-two pages of notes into a single summary page.

At the bottom of the summary page, he wrote: "Someone or some group wanted Forrester's notes on agency clients. Why?" The "why" was underlined three times.

Underneath that sentence, he wrote: "For intelligence reasons or personal reasons? Which one? Find the reason, you'll find the killer. In three days!"

Almost as an afterthought, he wrote at the end: "NB: What does Louise have to do with any of this???"

Dennis stood up, took his burner off the table and positioned the camera over the one-page, handwritten summary, and took a picture of it. Then he sent the image in a text message to Judy and wrote: *Help! another set of eyes. what am I missing? 3 days left and all I have to show is a headache*

With studied reluctance, Dennis put down his burner and picked up the agency phone. He sent a text to Simpson that said simply: *can u send me louise's absence schedule for past 6 months?*

He looked around the hotel room and noticed it was later than he thought. The summer skyline had darkened in Rosslyn's cavern of glass skyscrapers. Dennis decided to take a walk before settling down for dinner at a chain restaurant nearby. This being a Sunday evening, he hoped it would be about as smog-free as it gets in Rosslyn.

When he got to the street, dusk had turned decidedly into night. The hot, muggy air from the Potomac River wafted over him like a fine, oily mist. He walked down North Lynn Street toward Gateway Park, a three-acre urban park that passed for nature in this part of concrete suburbia.

His head down and hands in his pockets, he started to sweat in the Jell-O-thick humidity.

"Hey," he heard from a car that had stopped next to him. "Get in."

Dennis was surprised, not so much by the driver, who he recognized, but because there was a man in the back seat. The driver leaned over and pushed the passenger door open.

Dennis got in and the driver pulled away quickly.

"What's with the guy in the back?" he said, motioning with his chin.

At that moment, with his head turned toward the driver, Dennis felt a sharp prick on his neck.

"What the fuck!" he yelled, grabbing his neck.

The gray, fuzzy darkness fell over him like a thick theater curtain. It was not painful, just confusing. He was aware of movement and voices, but that was about it. His name was mentioned several times, and he would have liked to answer but nothing worked; it was as if his battery had been disconnected.

⊙

Judy stared at the message and image from Dennis. It was 10:30 a.m. on Monday morning, and she was attending the weekly staff meeting. Since their recent altercation, Craig had kept his distance, and she was just as happy. Instead of seeing a handsome, sexy young man, she saw an immature, manipulative spoiled brat. How fast things change, she thought.

She tried to read the words on the image of a sheet of paper that Dennis sent her, but it was too small to read on her phone. She would print it out later and review. She was also thrilled that Dennis wanted her opinion on the case.

She texted back: *u have all the fun. will read later and send back dissertation! get home soon. miss u*

Later that evening, Judy sat in her parent's kitchen.

"Dad, you look good. I'm so happy they caught this heart problem."

"I'm right as rain," he said, tapping his chest. "These little stents are lifesavers, I'll tell you. Bloody amazing what they can do without opening you up. Send the damn things right up your leg artery."

"He just needs to take it easy," Judy's mother said.

They sat at the old kitchen table that Judy remembered fondly from her childhood. The accumulated smells of a thousand food items saturated the room. Judy could pick out hints of curry, fried eggs, breakfast sausage, butter, roasted chicken, and meat pies.

The phone vibrated in her purse.

"You work too hard, dear," her mother said as Judy pulled it out. "We worry about you sometimes."

"Oh Mum, you worry too much," Judy said, looking at the blocked number on the incoming call. "I think I need to get this."

"Hello, this is Judy," she said.

"Judy, this is Louise. Did I catch you at a bad time?"

"No," she said, as she waved to her parents and walked into the living room. "I'm fine. What's up?"

"Have you spoken to Dennis lately?"

"He sent me a text message this morning, why?"

"About what time did he send it?"

"It was 9:30 a.m. Monday, my time. Let me see, that would be 8:30 p.m. your time on Sunday if I got that right. Why? What's wrong?"

"We can't find him."

"Can't find Dennis?"

"Yes, Dennis. He's not answering phone calls or texts. He's not in his hotel room. His phones have gone dark. Do you know where he is? What was his last text about?"

Judy froze.

"Well, he must be taking a walk or went for a drive."

"No, I don't think so," Louise said. "Can you tell me what his last text was about?"

"Nothing. Just that he was hoping to get back here soon."

"Well, as you know, he was on a time-sensitive assignment and he's gone missing. If you hear from him, please tell him to contact me or Simpson ASAP."

"Yes, of course."

"I hate to ask this, but Dennis in the past was known for going on a bender every now and then. He had a bit of a drinking problem. Do you think he's on one now?"

Judy bristled. "No. I don't believe it."

"You don't believe he has a drinking problem or that he's on a bender?"

"He's not on a bender." Judy's teeth were clenched, and she was reminded of how much Dennis distrusted Louise.

"Please contact me if you hear anything. My number is blocked on your phone, so here it is."

Judy wrote it down and hung up.

"What is it, dear?" her mother said from the kitchen. "Is everything alright at work?"

"Yes, Mum. Work is fine."

CHAPTER 14

I t felt like a dream, but it was also *unlike* a dream.

Dennis could walk—or did he dream that he could walk? He could also talk, or it seemed that way, but the words he spoke were garbled.

Was he on an airplane? It looked small inside the airplane. Someone put on his seatbelt. He thanked them, but he wasn't sure they heard him.

He slept a lot. Or it seemed that way.

Someone would tell him to do something, and he would do it. It made no difference what they said, he felt impelled to complete any task given to him. None of this made sense, and he was not troubled by it. There was no panic or fear. Time flew past. Or did it crawl past?

Scenes of this dreamtime changed, like the moment a woman hugged him.

"Hey, David," she giggled.

"His name is Dennis. Call him Dennis."

"Does he talk?"

"Not much."

"He's kinda cute."

"You're all set, right?"

"You bet," she said.

"You bet," Dennis mumbled.

"He *is* cute!"

The lights were kaleidoscopic; he was moving fast and was mesmerized by the lights. He could not stop looking at them. He felt his forehead pressed against the cold glass. His mouth was open, and he felt saliva falling onto his chin.

"Mmm," he said.

"Yeah, Dennis. Lots of lights! Pretty, huh?"

"Dizzy."

"Yeah, baby. I bet you are. You're cute, you know that?"

"Yeah."

"You're funny," she said.

Later, there were too many people and noises, and Dennis felt more confused.

"Go ahead," she said. "Sign your name. Right there. Here. Hold the pen like this and sign your name. He's a little under the weather."

Dennis did not know who she was talking to, but he was certain that he was supposed to sign something, and he did his best.

"You don't have to take the pen with you, darling," she laughed. "Dennis, you're a hoot. Let's get going."

⊙

Judy stared at the print-out of Dennis's writing that he had sent her. It was a list of the key elements in Forrester's disappearance. Without Dennis to explain what the notes meant, she did her best to interpret. There was a primitive timeline that he drew starting from the day Forrester left on her trip. For some days there were notations like: "Phone tip/body found near the beach" and "autopsy: headshots, fingers broken/body moved?"

But the summation was clear: whoever wanted Forrester's therapy notes was the killer. And then there was the addendum. "NB: what does Louise have to do with any of this?" Judy was curious why Dennis used the abbreviation of the Latin phrase *nota bene*, translated roughly into "take special notice." Why was he so concerned about Louise?

Judy gave up calling and texting Dennis; the calls went to voicemail and the texts were unanswered.

She knew Dennis could become so transfixed during an investigation that he failed to pay attention to common courtesies, like answering a text.

Judy was angry Louise brought up Dennis's drinking; in the past, he had been a hard drinker, but she resented Louise's insinuation that he was a drunkard on a binge. She could not remember the last time he was blotto, certainly not since he lived in Perth.

Still, where the hell was her Yank?

⊙

"Why?" Dennis asked.

"Why, what, silly?" she said.

"I don't know."

"You really are messed up, aren't you, Dennis? Boy, they weren't kidding. OK, so Dennis, are you paying attention? You put this pipe in your mouth like I did, and I'll light the bowl here, and you breathe in. Watch me."

"Holy shit!" she said. She leaned back in on the sofa. Dennis watched her. She finally sat up, her cheeks pink and flushed, and showed Dennis how to do the same thing.

He coughed.

"Let's do it again, do it slowly."

This time he felt very good, though he coughed for several minutes.

"What do you think of that, Dennis, baby? Fucking incredible, yeah?"

Dennis nodded.

"Mmm," he said.

"Let's do some more, OK?" she said.

Dennis had difficulty focusing. He wanted to stand up and leave, but he also felt very tired.

"More?" she said.

Dennis shook his head.

"We have to do more. Come on, I'll help you."

Later, he realized he was in a car moving again. The lights outside were not as bright as before. The woman was talking a lot, but he could not understand her.

"Shit, is this where I'm supposed to go? Shit, shit, shit," she said.

The car stopped near a building. She turned off the car and parked.

"Should we do more, Dennis? I have a lot. Too much really. What do you think? Let's do more, OK? Yeah, why not. Fuck it, it's free."

They did more, and this time Dennis felt very strange.

"No," he said.

"Fine, no more for you," she said.

Dennis closed his eyes. Someone spoke to the woman, and she opened the door. There was a commotion outside. Dennis's door opened, and he was helped outside into the cool, dark air.

The woman was sitting on the ground with her back against a building. The front of her shirt was red.

"Oh my god," she mumbled.

Someone pushed Dennis to his knees in front of the woman, took his right hand, wrapped it around something, and pushed it toward the woman's stomach.

Dennis resisted. "No," he mumbled.

Someone smacked him on the side of his head and pushed his hand again.

The woman was quiet.

"Hey," Dennis said, sitting in front of her on the gravel parking lot. He touched her face.

"Sorry."

Later he tried to walk but kept falling. He crawled on all fours, making strange sounds with his mouth. He tried to stand again but fell, so he continued to crawl. He was cold. And angry. People were bothering him.

⊙

Judy couldn't wait any longer and she dialed the number. It was 10:45 p.m.

"Have you heard from him?" Louise said.

"No. Have you?"

"No."

"Have you checked his hotel room?" Judy said.

"Yes. We had some people go by today. He's not there. Nothing has been taken that we can see. His computer is there, though not his phone. I think he had a burner too. That's gone. It seems that he left the hotel and never returned. A surveillance camera in the lobby showed him walking out at 8:58 p.m."

"His cell phones?" Judy said. "Did you ping them."

"Both are offline. No pings. Last geolocation was from Rosslyn yesterday. No other CCTV of him."

Neither spoke for several seconds.

"Has he done this before?" Louise asked.

"Done what?"

"Gone off. Disappeared."

"No."

More silence.

"Maybe he took a walk and was hit by a car or fell down an embankment," Judy said. "A freak accident."

"Not corroborated by any reports from hospitals in the area," Louise said.

"Something is very wrong," Judy said.

"Are you aware of any problems he's had with drugs?"

"For god's sake, no," Judy said. "Never."

⊙

Dennis opened his eyes, but the glare was blinding, and he shut them again.

"I think he just opened his eyes," someone said.

"Sir, can you hear me?" a man's voice floated from far away. "Hello? Sir, can you open your eyes?"

He opened his eyes again, closed them, and finally squinted through thin, watery slits. A man's face was only a foot away.

"Sir, can you hear me? Just nod if you can hear me."

He nodded.

"That's great. Can you open your eyes? Can you look at me? Yes, I'm right here. Can you see my hand? I'm waving it."

He nodded.

"Great. How are you feeling?"

Dennis stared up at the face of a young man with short, dark hair and a white coat.

"Can you talk, sir? Can you tell us your name?"

He felt immense confusion as if he was locked inside a white room with white walls, a white table, and a white light. He tried to speak, but his lips felt leathery and cracked. He tried to raise his right hand to his face, but his hands would not move.

He craned his neck up from the pillow and looked at his hands. They were bound to the sides of his bed. He dropped his head back onto the pillow. He coughed.

"Sally, can you give me the water?" the man said.

He felt something on his lips and saw that the man in the coat was pressing a straw from a container against his lips. He sucked and his mouth filled with cold water. He gulped huge amounts of the liquid, until the overflow streamed down his chin and onto his chest.

"There you go, sir," the man said. "That should help."

He coughed, cleared his throat, and tried to speak, but only managed to gargle. He heard a motor humming and felt his head being raised.

"That should be better for you," the man said. "Now, can you speak? Can you tell us your name?"

Dennis tried to speak, but it felt like his tongue was fighting a mouthful of steel wool. He managed a word.

"What was that? What did you say?" the man said.

"Hand," he said.

"Hand? Did you say 'hand'?"

He nodded.

"I see. Of course. Your hands. Your hands are being kept in restraints. You're in a hospital. I'm afraid we needed to use restraints before you hurt yourself or someone else. Do you understand? You were brought into the hospital last night by the police. You were naked and had no identification. We'd like to know what your name is. Can you tell us? It would help us a great deal if we know who you are."

He closed his eyes. *Naked. No name. Hospital. Police.* He shook his head.

"You don't know your name?" the man asked. "Did you fall and hit your head? Did someone hit you? Were you taking any drugs, or were you drinking heavily, sir? Is there anything you can tell us about what happened last night? Do you even know where you are?"

Dennis rocked his head back and forth on the pillow.

"Sir, you're in Las Vegas. Do you remember coming to Las Vegas?"

"No."

"Do you know what hotel you're staying at?"

"Hotel?"

Dennis watched a uniformed policeman enter the back of the room.

"I think we got him ID'ed, Dr. Kellis," the policeman said, handing something to the doctor.

The man with the white coat leaned in close. "Sir, are you Dennis Cunningham?"

Dennis nodded slowly, then closed his eyes.

"Good," he heard the policeman say. "Now we're getting somewhere."

⊙

"Murder!" Judy yelled into the phone. "What? You're off your bloody rocker!"

"You're not being helpful," Louise said. "Can you just calm down for a second."

"Calm down! How the hell can I calm down? I can't believe this."

"Do you want to call me back later?"

Judy closed her eyes, took several deep breaths, then said, "Go ahead."

"He's in a Las Vegas hospital—"

"Las Vegas!"

"Jesus, Judy. Call me back later." Louise hung up.

Judy stood up from behind her desk, walked around it, and looked out the window into the Perth skyline. The sky had a gray cast to it, with thick, billowy clouds scudding across her view. She bit the inside of her lip absently, held the phone up, and dialed.

"Keep going," Judy said, as if the conversation had never ended.

"He's in a Las Vegas hospital. But before I go on, you've got to listen and don't lose it on me. Just listen. I have no idea what's going on, and I'm hoping you can help because none of this makes any sense. I know Dennis a little bit—not as much as you, certainly—but this situation is very bizarre. Should I continue?"

"Yes."

"As I said, he's in a Las Vegas hospital. He was brought in last night at around 3 a.m. their time. I know this is going to sound strange, but here we go: he was naked, disoriented, hostile, and covered in blood. When EMTs tried to calm him down he attacked one of them, and they had to restrain him. He was a John Doe at the hospital until police found the body, his clothes, his driver's license, and government passport. The passport is what led them to Langley, and finally to me."

"Body?"

"A woman. A prostitute and drug addict named Pamela Stanton. She was found next to her car, stabbed multiple times. There was cocaine and crystal meth in the car. Dennis's clothes, heavily blood-stained, were found in and outside the car. Police are investigating this as a homicide. They have Dennis and the woman checking into the Bellagio earlier that night. They're checking for video at the casino, though it will take an administrative subpoena and a few days for that to come back. One eyewitness on the hotel staff said Dennis was under the influence because he was propped up by the woman throughout their stay. He was in the hotel for less than eight hours."

"I don't believe any of it," Judy said.

"Let me finish. Her car was found in a seedy section of Las Vegas called the Boulder Strip. They think she was buying drugs. At this point, they have a knife that they think is the murder weapon, and they're testing blood on Dennis's clothes and his skin to see if there is a match. I used the CIA connection and claims of national security to free up some information from the DA there. He told me they consider Dennis a person of interest. But they can't get much out of him. He's apparently agitated and confused. And they're trying to get information on the dead woman."

"I don't believe any of it," Judy said.

"I'm not sure it matters whether you believe it or not, Judy. He's in serious trouble. My guess is the DA is trying to determine if Dennis is a suspect or a victim in the same attack. If they find probable cause that he's the killer, they'll charge him. And as a side note, Dennis was supposed to be on a case for me. His report was due today. While you ponder this, can I ask you just one question?"

"Yes."

"Have you ever known Dennis to do hard drugs?"

"Never. The things you just told me have no relationship to the Dennis that I know."

"I'm leaving in about an hour for Las Vegas to see if I can bully my way into seeing Dennis. I found him a lawyer. I'm only intervening in this case for business reasons; he was a critical piece of an investigation, and I need to close that up. Moving forward, I would think you'd want to be involved because I won't be. I'm going to text you his lawyer's name and contact info. Please get hold of the lawyer soon."

"I'm going to Las Vegas myself," Judy said. "Please share any information you have. It'll take me a day to get there, and it's possible that we may not meet up."

"Good luck," Louise said.

Judy hung up and continued to look out the window on the tall buildings in Perth. Raindrops started to pepper the window as she bit the inside of her lip.

⊙

"I'd like to leave a message for John Ruby," Judy said, pressing the phone hard against her ear to block out the sound of the airport boarding call. "Could you ask him to text me? My name is Judy White and I'm calling about Dennis Cunningham. I'm in Sydney, Australia, and I'm going to be boarding a plane to the US in an hour. I'll be on a plane for a while, so texting would be best. I think the plane has Wi-Fi."

Judy gave the woman her phone number, reminded her of the

country code, and spelled her name. She noticed a wine bar near her departure gate, and she sat on a stool and ordered a glass of red wine.

Her phone vibrated, and she saw the call was from the U.S.

"Hello?"

"Is this Judy White?" a man asked.

"Yes, who is this?"

"John Ruby, attorney at law here in sin city, USA."

"Ah, yes. I was led to believe you have been retained to represent Dennis Cunningham."

"I've been asked to represent Mr. Cunningham, but I haven't decided to accept the case. My fees are pretty hefty, Ms. White, and I like to start there."

"Do you require a fee before you even take the case?"

"No, but I need to know what the case is, and who the client is. I've been contacted by someone in the federal government who asked me to represent Mr. Cunningham, but I haven't had time to contact the DA's office. I don't believe there are any charges yet. What relationship do you have to Mr. Cunningham, if you don't mind me asking?"

"I'm his friend. A close friend. I'm about to fly to Las Vegas, though it will take me a while to get there. I'm in Australia right now."

"I see. Well, I'll contact you by text since you'll be on an airplane. The only thing I know about the case is what I read in the paper this morning. What time is it there?"

"It's 2 p.m. on Tuesday."

"Well, it's 7 p.m. here on a Monday. I'll know more tomorrow, or even later tonight. I'll be in touch."

"Thank you," Judy said and hung up.

She took a huge gulp of wine.

Murder, she thought. *Drugs. Prostitute. Dennis, what the hell happened to you? Jesus, Mary, and Joseph. I thought I knew this man.*

⊙

There was now a uniformed policeman outside Dennis's hospital room at all times. They had removed his restraints, but he noticed the medical staff were careful around him.

He was aware that he was in trouble for some reason, but that was all. Everything else was a blur. Every now and then, he felt a wave of anxiety overwhelm him: *What is happening to me? What did I do? Why can't I remember anything? Am I having a nervous breakdown? What happened to that woman? Did I hurt her?*

Dennis heard some people talking outside his room, and then two people entered: a tall, dark-haired man in a white coat and a short, thin, blond woman with pale blue eyes.

The blond woman walked over to the bed and stared at Dennis intently, saying nothing.

He stared back, searching his memory banks for information on this woman.

"Dennis, do you know who I am?"

He stared, looking at her straight blond hair and her intense eyes.

"Not sure," he said.

"Where do you live, Dennis?"

He shook his head.

"Where do you work?"

He shook his head again.

"Have you ever heard of a woman named Dr. Jane Forrester?"

Dennis tried very hard; he closed his eyes, considered the name, and came back blank.

"No."

"Do you know why you're in a hospital?" she said.

He shook his head slowly back and forth.

"Christ," she said. "What the hell did they do to you? Those fuckers."

"Who?" the man in the white coat said.

Dennis watched as they left the room.

"Hey!" Dennis yelled.

They returned.

"Can you get me out of here?" he said to the woman.

"No, I'm sorry, Dennis. I can't do that."

They left again.

The uniformed policeman poked his head briefly into the room, then returned to his chair outside.

Dennis felt tired, though maybe he was depressed. He closed his eyes and found himself lost in a strange dream that included a woman and a lot of blood. For some reason that he could not understand, he felt guilty about the woman who had blood on her.

He slept for a long time. He knew it was a long sleep because the next time he woke it was dark outside the hospital window.

Men's voices could be heard outside his room. It was not quite an argument, but the conversation was strange.

"You're the attending, Dr. Kellis, and we'd like your permission to talk to him. We have just a couple of questions. Nothing too heavy."

"He's very confused. We're not sure what's wrong with him, to be honest. He could have had a psychotic break, or perhaps it was drug induced. We don't see any signs of head trauma. We're just not sure what's going on."

"But can't we talk to him for just a few minutes? He could help clear up a couple of things."

"Let me see. Please stay here."

Dennis watched the man with the white coat come into the room and stand next to him.

"How are you feeling, Mr. Cunningham?"

Dennis shrugged.

"Do you know where you are right now?"

"Hospital," Dennis said.

"Can you speak? Are you having trouble using words?"

"Little."

"Is your memory getting better? Do you know where you were last night?"

"No."

"Does your head or neck hurt?"

"Maybe."

"How often have you done meth before?"

Dennis shook his head.

"You haven't done it before?"

"No."

"Well, just stay here and rest. I'm sure you'll start feeling better very soon."

He left, and Dennis heard the conversation continue outside his door.

"Not now, detective," the man in the white coat said. "He's still not cogent. Just give him some time."

Dennis went back to sleep. It was easier to sleep than to talk.

Later—it felt like the middle of the night—Dennis heard voices outside.

"You're a new cop," someone said. "Been on the force for a while?"

"Couple of months."

"Got an order to pull blood from this guy."

"Let me see your name tag."

"You rookies are funny. I've worked here longer than you've been alive."

"Time to wake up," a new man in a white coat said. "They've asked for another blood sample, pal."

The man in the white coat tied a blue rubber strip around his left bicep.

"Squeeze this ball here, would you, pal?" the man said.

The man gently slapped the inside of Dennis's elbow.

"Here's a good one," he said, fondling a vein with his gloved forefinger. "Just a little prick here."

Dennis watched two vials fill up with his blood.

"OK, pal. Press this down until I get a band-aid. Good. Have a nice night."

Dennis felt strangely numb, except for the slight discomfort where the band-aid sat.

⊙

Judy was somewhere near Hawaii, crammed into the aisle seat of the Qantas A380 when she received a text.

atty ruby here; have been paid a retainer by a louise nordland to represent cunningham. she said u will direct me. please contact me when u get to lv. no charges yet

Judy put down her phone on the seat-back table and tried to concentrate on the movie she was watching, but it was no good. She felt a crushing sense of sadness and fear. She thought she knew Dennis, but this latest turn was too much. *Murder.* She was a policewoman and knew all too well about murder and its aftermath. Her eyes welled up, and she discretely dabbed at them so that her seatmates wouldn't notice.

Her phone vibrated again.

mum, where are u? grandma says u r going to states?

She texted back:

sorry trevor; a bit hectic now. will explain later. love u

Judy forgot to tell her son she was leaving. How quickly life comes undone with Dennis, she thought. Is all this worth it? Was Dennis worth it? She was not sure any longer.

At San Francisco International Airport, Judy had to change terminals to get the domestic flight to Las Vegas. While she was in the

AirTrain she got a text from Louise: *u in US yet?*

yes, changing flights at SF airport. will be in vegas in 2 hours. where r u?

in dc; need to talk. call me at this new number asap. please buy a burner to call me. do NOT use my other agency number

Judy was jostled in the elevated train and held on to the stainless-steel post as if it were the only stable thing in her life. During the long, depressing flight to San Francisco, she had grown less eager to visit Las Vegas. She was not anxious to see Dennis, nor Louise or the attorney. She wanted to crawl into a hole somewhere and curl up into a tight ball.

The flight to Las Vegas was only an hour and a half, but getting through immigration and changing terminals in San Francisco took longer. By the time she landed at McCarran Airport in Las Vegas, the sun was setting, and she was utterly exhausted. She pulled her roll-on through the airport with all the enthusiasm of a prisoner on work detail.

Judy stopped at a kiosk and purchased a disposable phone. She activated it and found that it was charged. She sat down and called the number Louise gave her.

"Louise, this is Judy. I have a disposable phone."

"How are you doing?"

"So-so."

"I can understand that. Must be a shock," Louise said.

"A big shock."

"Yes, well. I want to tell you a couple of things that are very important. I know you must be pretty tired and confused right now, but please try and pay attention."

"Alright."

"You sound really depressed," Louise said. "Maybe we should talk later."

"For god's sake, Louise, just get going."

"OK, here goes. I saw Dennis in person yesterday. He's in very rough shape mentally but I'm pretty sure I know why."

"Yeah, well, you cut up a prostitute like a roast chook, you'd feel a bit off too," Judy said.

"Chook?"

"Nothing, Louise. Just go on please."

"Judy, there is something else going on, and it's related to Dr. Forrester's disappearance."

"Oh please—"

"Listen to me," Louise said. "Just listen. When I saw Dennis yesterday, he was clearly suffering some strange cognitive issues. I talked to the attending physician, and there is no evidence that Dennis had head trauma. And yet he shows every indication of profound amnesia. The physician admitted that people who overdose with cocaine or meth can have psychotic reactions, but they don't typically have such severe amnesia. Dennis didn't know who I was, though I could see him trying to remember."

"I think we know he's not himself," Judy said slowly, "but to be honest I don't know who he is. I mean, I thought I knew who he was, but he's always had a dark side…"

"Dennis is not *that* dark," Louise said.

"Well, it seems that way now."

"Listen, I'm waiting for a report. I'm pretty sure what it's going to show. And assuming I'm right, then we need to be extremely careful. Use your burner to contact me, and don't use it for any other communications to your family or anyone. If I ask you to use another phone, then buy a new one and toss the old one."

"What?"

"And I've paid $10,000 to that attorney Ruby. He's agreed to take the case. I gather this guy Ruby is pretty good. I think it's safe to say once Ruby takes the case, that he'll be under surveillance as well. So, think about that when you talk to him. Make sure Ruby understands that there's something else at play, and he should be even more discreet than normal."

"I'm sorry, Louise. I know I'm tired and depressed, but this sounds absolutely and bizarrely paranoid."

"Hey! Do you want Dennis out of this mess?"

"Of course I do."

"Then do what I say. Now go see Ruby."

Judy hung up. Sitting in the terminal she was hunched so far forward that her face was touching the top of her roll-on suitcase. She sat up straight, looked around, and could see a mountain range in the distance through the huge floor-to-ceiling windows at the airport.

She stood and waddled her way to the taxi area, exhausted.

Something else at play, Judy thought, replaying Louise's admonition. *I really hope you're right, Louise, because I've just about had it with Dennis. I can't take his troubled, twisted world any longer.*

⊙

They met in a small Italian restaurant two blocks from the Las Vegas Strip. Judy chose not to stay at one of the huge casino complexes, but instead at a Hyatt nearby. She took a short nap after calling Ruby, and then got up, showered, dressed lightly in a skirt and sleeveless blouse, and walked the five blocks to the restaurant. The evening was warm but very dry. She started out in the winter in the southern hemisphere and was now sitting in the summer in the northern hemisphere. Everything in her life was upside down now. The lights from the Las Vegas Strip lit up the sky.

Ruby told her to look for the "big guy" at the bar drinking a Crown Royal on the rocks.

She saw a broad-shouldered, heavy-set man at the bar talking on his cell phone. He stopped talking when she stood next to him.

"Call you back," he said into the phone.

"John Ruby?" she said.

"Yes," he said standing. "And you're Judy White?"

"In the flesh," she said.

"Let's grab a table, if that's alright with you, Ms. White."

"Please call me Judy. And yes, a table would be fine."

"Jimmy," he said to the bartender, pointing to the dining room, "on the table."

"You got it, Johnny," the bartender said.

He led her over to the hostess, who took them to an open table and produced two menus. Ruby smiled, but neither spoke as they sat down.

"So, for the record, this is a little unusual for me," Ruby said, swirling his drink. "I was retained by someone who said she works for a government agency, and she directed me to answer to you on this case. I asked her to put it in writing, but she refused. She did provide a check for $10,000 that cleared the bank. So, I guess I'm using you as my contact. I've talked to the DA's office and got some preliminary information, and I'm prepared to represent Mr. Cunningham. It's a serious case, as I'm sure you're aware."

"Yes, I'm aware," Judy said.

"But before we proceed, do you mind telling me what your relationship is to Mr. Cunningham? You were a little vague on the phone earlier."

"I guess you'd call me his girlfriend."

"I see. Well, that suffices. Where are you from? Your text said you were coming from Australia, and your accent seems to be from that part of the world, though I couldn't tell an Australian accent from a New Zealand or a British accent if they waterboarded me."

"Yes, I'm Australian. And I'm also a member of the Australian Federal Police."

"You're a cop? That's interesting."

"I'm on leave right now."

"So, you and Cunningham are an item, then?"

"If that means we're a couple, then yes."

"Do you know Louise Nordland?"

"Yes."

"How do you know her?"

"She was Dennis's former boss, and we were in contact on some other issues."

"OK," he sighed. "So, here's the deal. Cunningham could be in serious trouble. My guess is—and it's only a guess—the DA is building probable cause to arrest him for involvement in this woman's death. The DA is trying to piece together what happened with this woman and Cunningham. I checked around, and the dead woman was a working prostitute with a drug problem. And Cunningham tested positive for cocaine and meth. Crazy combo of drugs. But we're early in this thing."

"Do they have a strong case for murder?"

"No. They got no witnesses that I've heard of. There was a knife next to her body. If his prints are all over it, well, that's a problem. They can't pull prints from him directly, at this point because he's not a suspect. But they'll run prints found on the knife through the national database. Could take a while. Then there's possible DNA matching. Could be some of the killer's DNA on the knife. They have Cunningham's blood from the hospital, so let's hope his DNA is not on the knife. DNA could be a problem. You never know. But all they got is a dead, drugged out prostitute, and a naked guy crawling on all fours around Las Vegas splattered with blood. I'm sure it's her blood since he only had some scratches on his knees from crawling. There's apparently a video of the girl and him checking into the Bellagio."

The waitress came to take their order, and Judy ordered a Caesar salad. Ruby ordered cheese ravioli and a Diet Coke.

"That all you're going to eat?" he said.

"I'm not very hungry."

"Tell me, did Cunningham have a drug problem? He was pretty lit up when he got to the hospital. Did he go on sprees every now and then? I'm just trying to know what I'm dealing with here."

"I've known him for several years, and I've never seen him touch drugs. If anything, he likes a drink every now and then."

"You know we have a lot of guys come to Vegas and sort of let loose, you know? And women too, especially bachelorette parties. They do crazy things. I'm just trying to get some history here on Cunningham. Sometimes there's another side to a person, you know, that people don't see until they get into trouble."

"Listen, Mr. Ruby—"

"Call me John."

"Listen, John, I'm not a child and I don't pretend to know every single detail about Dennis's life, but he's never done drugs that I know of."

"Has he used prostitutes before?"

Judy felt her forehead crease into deep, horizontal wrinkles as she fought the temptation to punch the attorney who was supposed to save Dennis. Or maybe she wished she could punch Dennis.

"Not that I know of," she said.

"This woman Nordland led me to believe that Cunningham works for the CIA. That true?"

"He used to be an employee of the agency, but he retired about a year ago. Recently he was contracted by them to investigate a disappearance. Unfortunately, he won't be able to complete his report as a result of this incident."

"Mmm," Ruby said, polishing off the remainder of the Crown Royal. "This Nordland woman tried to warn me the case was complicated. She said that Cunningham is involved in some kind of intelligence work. She buffaloed the DA here into talking to her. She's a tough broad."

"Yes, she is. She also wanted me to say that you might be under surveillance now that you took the case."

"What, from the IRS?"

"No. Other people."

"What kind of surveillance is she talking about?"

"She didn't say, but I'm sure your phones will be an obvious place to start."

"Seems to me that this is just a case of a high-strung CIA guy gone off the rails. I mean, this stuff happens out here. This is where they come to go crazy."

"It's *our* firm belief that you're mistaken, John. This is more complicated, and you should be very careful." Judy felt buoyed by the spontaneous use of the possessive pronoun *our*; it was emotionally satisfying to treat Louise and her as a team to save Dennis. If nothing more, it gave her cover to avoid the opposite proposition: that Dennis had gone very darkly off the rails and she was alone fighting for him.

The food came to the table and they ate in silence.

"You gamble?" he asked.

"No. Never. I gambled in the choice of my profession, but that's about it."

"And this Australian Federal Police. What's that?"

"Similar to your FBI."

"Really? Interesting. So, you're a real cop?"

"What did you think I was, a meter maid?"

He laughed heartily. "Funny."

After several seconds of silence, Judy suddenly said, "Do you think he did it?"

"Cunningham? Did he kill the prostitute?"

She nodded.

"I have no idea, to be honest, Judy. None. And I don't care either way. He needs representation, and I'm going to give him the best help

I can muster. That's how it works. I'm sure it works the same Down Under."

⊙

Dennis suddenly remembered who the blond woman was.

"Her name is Louise," Dennis said to the empty hospital room.

The policeman outside the room poked his head in.

"That woman that came in. The little blond woman with the limp. Her name's Louise."

"Don't talk to me. Your best bet is just to shut up. You got enough problems."

"Her name is Louise, but I can't remember her last name," Dennis said.

"Jesus," the policeman said, returning to his chair outside.

Dennis was not nearly as tired as before. He felt rested, alert, though still confused.

"Am I in trouble or something?" he asked.

"I'm not talking to you," the policeman said from outside.

"I think I'm feeling better."

CHAPTER 15

I n a single wild swing of her left arm, Judy knocked her business phone off the bedside table as the alarm sounded. Cursing, she fell out of bed trying to find the phone. She grabbed the charging cord and slowly retrieved it. After turning off the alarm, she put the phone back on the table and flopped back in bed.

Judy started to sit up but fell back into bed.

God, I'm tired, she thought. *Half-way around the world to end up in one of the strangest cities on the planet. Dennis, what were you doing here? What is wrong with you?*

The burner rang. It was on the dresser on the other side of the room charging, so she jumped out of bed and grabbed it. She saw the incoming number.

"Hello, Louise."

"Got a problem," Louise said.

Judy did not appreciate Louise's grunting, abrupt manner of speech. The tiny blond seemed to enjoy leaving out pronouns and other useful parts of speech. Or maybe she was just economizing her communications. Either way, it was irritating.

"What's that?" Judy sighed, rubbing her eyes with her free hand. She glanced in the mirror and quickly turned her eyes away: the sight of the jet-lagged, depressed woman was not pretty.

"Dennis's hotel here in Rosslyn. The Hyatt won't let me have access to his personal belongings."

Judy was still foggy from waking up.

"What about his belongings?" she said.

"After he went missing, they packed up his belongings into his suitcase and stored them with the concierge. I can usually bluff civilians by showing my agency ID. Most get rubber legs when I do that, but those jerks from Hyatt won't buckle. I'd get someone to break in there, but it would be a real mess if they were caught."

Judy yawned. "Why are you telling me this?"

"They'll only release it to a family member."

"I'm not a family member, Louise. We're not married. You know that."

"Yes, but he's got a daughter. I had them call her in California. Beth's her name. She can give them permission to release his stuff to you. She doesn't know me from a hole in the wall and won't do anything I ask her to do. Call his daughter. Here's the number."

"Damnit, Louise. I just woke up. Hang on." She walked across the room to get the complimentary hotel pad and pen. "Go ahead." Judy wrote it down.

"After you get her to send in the release, get a flight first thing to D.C. I need you to get his suitcase to see if he has anything I could use."

"I just got here, Louise!" Judy said. "I haven't been able to see Dennis yet."

"Work through Ruby. Call the daughter." Louise hung up.

"Bitch," Judy said under her breath as she hung up.

She sighed and sat down on the corner of the bed, her shoulders hunched. She glanced at herself in the mirror. Her hair was plastered to one side of her head, her eyes were the color of a bright-red hibiscus blossom, and her left cheek showed the slashing dent caused by a twisted bed sheet.

The burner rang again.

"God," she said looking at the number.

"Hey, this is Ruby."

"Hello, John," she said.

"I have some bad news. They're moving him to the Clark County Detention Center. He's going to be arraigned on murder one later today. I gather they have DNA, probably on the knife, that makes him a suspect and not a victim. And he said some ill-advised things to the doctor and investigators that interviewed him. It sounds bad, but this case has a long way to go."

"What ill-advised things?"

"He apparently said he was sorry about hurting the woman. He kept apologizing. I wish I could have been there when the cops talked to him at the hospital. Unfortunately, they can use utterances like that in building a case."

"Oh Lord," Judy said, sighing. "Will he be granted bail?"

"Not likely."

"Can I see him at the arraignment?"

"Sure. But I want to warn you that some people don't like to see their loved ones in handcuffs. But you're a cop and you know the drill."

"I don't quite know it from this side of the fence," she said. "Give me the address and time. I'll be there."

⊙

It was one of the worst decisions she made in her life.

The clerk called Dennis's case, and he was led into the courtroom in handcuffs. That was bad enough, but his bright orange jumpsuit with the letters CCDC on front and back, and his strange, disheveled appearance shocked her. She tried to catch his attention, but he did not look her way. The judge, a frumpy older woman, asked him whether he was Dennis Cunningham, whether he understood the charges. Dennis said he did. She asked whether he had an attorney, and he said he did. Ruby whispered several times to Dennis.

Dennis was asked to make a plea, and he said, "not guilty" in a small, insignificant voice. The judge declared Dennis was going to be denied bail due to the seriousness of the crime.

And then it was over. Dennis never looked for Judy. She almost cried.

Outside in the withering Nevada summer sun, Ruby said, "I'm not sure you should have come. I thought you knew these things are not pretty."

"He didn't even look for me. I was waiting for him to see me, but he never looked. Jesus, what happened to him here? That's not the Dennis I know." A tear slid from underneath the right lens of her sunglasses. She let it sit there, collecting makeup and eyeliner.

Ruby put his massive arm around her and gently hugged her.

"Judy, I'll do the best we can for him, I promise you that. He's allowed phone calls in the Clark County Detention Center, but he says he doesn't know who to call. He may be putting on a good act, but to me, he's not sure what happened to him or what he's doing here."

He released her from his reassuring hug.

"Let's take a walk. There's a coffee shop right around the corner. Come along."

Judy wiped the tear away and followed, her head bowed. She was utterly and completely shocked by Dennis's appearance and demeanor. The multiple feelings of fear, anger, exhaustion, and shock came through in a firestorm and left her a whimpering, shell of a person following a large, broad-shouldered man on the hot Nevada pavement.

They sat down at a table, and Judy squinted out the coffee shop window into an orangish glare. It reminded her vaguely of the outback.

Ruby brought over two cups of coffee and sat down.

"Should I give him your number and ask him to call you the next chance he gets?" Ruby said.

"I don't know. From the look of him, I'm not even sure he'll recognize me."

"We don't know that," he said, taking a sip. "I obviously don't know Dennis, but it looks like he had some kind of breakdown. Has he done this before?"

"Done what?"

"Showed symptoms of a psychological break?"

"Not that I know of, though perhaps I'm missing something about his life. He was depressed after his wife died. I know he was in therapy for a while. He had a tough family life growing up."

"It's been a couple of days since he was brought into the hospital, and he's only made a little progress. The judge asked for a psych eval. Guess we'll find out if he's got some psychological issues that might explain his behavior."

Judy took a sip of coffee and continued to look outside, avoiding Ruby.

"I just wish the attending would have kept the investigators away from him," Ruby said.

"What did he say to them?"

"Something like, 'I'm sorry about the girl.'"

"The girl? You mean the prostitute?"

"That's what they're taking from it, the prostitute."

"God," she said, shaking her head.

"He did say something else to me though," Ruby said.

"Huh?"

"He said, 'something happened to me.'"

"That's it?"

"Yeah. To be honest, he looked like a lost child. Completely harmless and lost. But he was intense when he said, 'something happened to me.' Then he went back to that blank look. Sorry. I mean that's all that I have."

"Did you tell him I was out there in the courtroom?"

"Yes."

"And what did he say?"

"He didn't say anything."

She shook her head.

"Listen, we don't know anything about the forensic evidence. The knife, the blood on him. The DNA. Don't give up hope, Judy. You're a cop. Get tough."

"I probably need that pep talk right now," she said. "I feel so depressed. I mean, to think I just flew halfway around the world to see Dennis in handcuffs. What a shock. I'm just—I don't know what to say."

Ruby's phone rang. "I have to get this. It will only take a second."

He chatted to what sounded like his secretary or paralegal for a few minutes, then hung up.

"Sorry about that. I'm afraid I have to get going."

"Of course."

"Dennis will be allowed visitation rights," he said standing. "Do you want to see him?"

"I suppose so," she said, fidgeting with her coffee cup.

Ruby sat down and gently grabbed Judy forearm.

"Can I suggest something?" he said.

"Please do."

"Why don't you wait just a bit longer to see him? I don't think he's got his shit together right now."

"But I want to see him."

"I understand, but you don't want to see him like this. Just give him a day or two."

"Maybe he'll feel better when he sees me."

Ruby looked down at his empty coffee cup.

"I lied to you," he said.

She grimaced. "Lied to me about what?"

"I *did* tell him that you were in the courtroom. I said, 'Judy is out there.' Then he said, 'Who's Judy?'"

⊙

The phone call to Dennis's daughter was a disaster. Judy tried to steel herself to the interchange, but Beth was disconsolate. She cried. Then Judy cried.

Finally, Beth agreed to send a release to the Hyatt in Rosslyn to allow Judy to recover his belongings. Judy told Beth that she was flying to Washington within the hour and begged her not to go to Las Vegas to see Dennis since he was not "in a good place." Beth, who was pregnant, continued to cry until Judy hung up.

Judy texted Louise detailing her travel plans. She texted Ruby to say she was leaving town for a day or two but would insist on seeing Dennis when she returned.

good idea to leave dodge, Ruby texted back. *will keep u posted*

Judy did not know what "dodge" meant, but it didn't matter. She was now running from Dennis or the man who pretended to be Dennis.

At the airport, waiting for her flight, Judy got a text from Louise:

did u tell ruby to be careful?

yes. he was skeptical of being watched, she answered.

he's a lawyer, what do u expect. have interesting stuff to share; call me when you land. go right to hotel and get his suitcase

Judy wrote back: *decided to stay at same hyatt; will take his suitcase to my room*

excellent, Louise responded.

⊙

Dennis shared a cell with a small, wiry black man named Chili.

Chili didn't talk much, except to ask Dennis periodically if he had any cigarettes. Smoking was not allowed in the cells, and Dennis repeatedly told him that he didn't smoke. But that didn't deter Chili from asking every thirty minutes or so whether he had any cigarettes.

Dennis was lying on his bunk when he suddenly sat up and looked at Chili.

"I know Judy!" he said. "Chili, I know Judy!"

"I know Judy too," Chili said. "She gone. She moved a long time ago. Back to L.A."

"Yes! Damn, damn, damn," Dennis said. "Judy!"

"Judy gone," Chili said.

"Naw, she's here," Dennis said.

"She gone, man."

"Naw, she's going to visit me, probably tomorrow. Hey Chili, this is a jail, right?"

"No, it's a McDonald's, man. Shit, of course it's a fuckin' jail. Now you mention it, I could use a Big Mac right now."

"What did I do?"

"You kilt someone."

"I *did*?"

"Fuckin' A you did. A whore. You're a bad dude. You scare me."

"A whore?" Dennis said. "I killed a whore?"

"I didn't kill no whore. You the one who kilt her."

"That doesn't make any sense," Dennis said. "Wouldn't I remember something like that?"

"I sure as shit would. But you crazy white dudes, you do all them drugs and shit, you get crazy. Not me. I don't do no drugs. Anymore. I used to. Not now."

"Chili, I didn't kill a woman. How could I kill a woman?"

"Dude told me you cut her up."

"Me?"

"Well, who do you think we talkin' about? 'Course it's you. You cut that poor girl up bad."

"I did no such thing," Dennis said. "Hey, do I have a lawyer?"

"Don't ax me. I don't know that kinda stuff."

"I must have a lawyer. Man, I feel different right now."

"You just calm down there. I don't want you gettin' all worked up. Don't make me call the jailer."

"I'm not getting worked up. I'm just remembering things."

"Keep your 'memberin' to yerself. Yer the one that kilt that girl."

Dennis leaned back in his cot, and for the first time in what seemed like years, he felt giddy. He remembered things.

"Hey, man," Chili said, "you got any cigarettes."

"No. Sorry, Chili. I don't smoke."

"Jus' askin'. Sure could use a smoke."

⊙

Judy slept on the long flight back to Reagan National Airport. She drank two glasses of malbec and had a bad dream about a desert plant that came to life and bit her.

It was 8:30 p.m. when the American Airlines flight turned for its final approach north up the Potomac River. Judy was in the window seat on the right side of the plane and saw the Capitol dome and the Washington Monument lit up. It was an impressive sight for a city that she had grown to loathe.

She decided to rent a car, though she was not sure why. There was something about Louise that bothered her, and she thought it better to have complete freedom of movement. The last thing she wanted to do was be trapped inside Louise's car with the little blond ball of intensity.

Google Maps got her to the Hyatt, and she had the car valeted. Checking in was easy, but getting the release of Dennis's suitcase was not. The hotel manager had gone home for the day, and the assistant manager—a short Hispanic man with a thin mustache named Rodriguez—refused to hand over the suitcase until the manager arrived in the morning.

Stressed, exhausted, and suddenly very angry, Judy unleashed on the assistant manager, to the extent that other guests walking by stood and watched. Judy demanded that she be given the suitcase *now*.

"Mr. Rodriguez, call your manager right now, and tell him that I've just arrived and demand access to that suitcase. You have received the appropriate clearance letter from Mr. Cunningham's daughter. Give me the goddamn suitcase, or I'm calling the police and my lawyer."

Judy did not have a lawyer and had no intention of calling the police, but she was angry.

The assistant manager did his best to mollify Judy, but she insisted that unless he gave her the suitcase, she was going to go into the back room and get it herself.

Rodriguez disappeared to make a phone call. He returned ten minutes later and asked to see her identification. She showed her passport; he looked at it closely. He pushed a form across to her and asked her to sign it. Then he disappeared behind the counter, into a room that required a key to unlock. He returned, pulling Dennis's black roll-on.

Without a thank you, Judy pulled the two suitcases to the elevator, with her purse awkwardly strapped around her shoulder.

She put her suitcase on the bed and started to unpack. The burner rang.

"I'm here, Louise," she said. "Room 421."

"Do you have the suitcase?"

"Yes. But can we do this tomorrow? It's late."

"I'm on my way now."

"Fine." Judy hung up and stared at Dennis's suitcase.

What the hell did Louise think she was going to get from Dennis's belongings? she thought. *And why right now? Jesus, that woman is crazy, or I'm crazy, or we're both crazy.*

Twenty minutes later there was a knock at the door. Judy opened it to see Louise standing there, wearing skinny jeans, a light-blue silk blouse and muted, dark-blue dangling earrings.

"Hey," Louise said stepping inside.

"Welcome to my home away from home," Judy said.

Louise dropped her purse on the dresser. Judy had forgotten—or perhaps she had chosen not to notice—how attractive Louise was. While she was no more than five feet tall in raised heels, her medium-length, Nordic white-blond hair hung in a modern page cut. Her ice-blue eyes were striking, and her face—except for the area at the outside of her eyes—was creaseless. She walked with a mild limp, and Judy remembered her prothesis.

"Is that it?" Louise said pointing to the suitcase,

"Yes."

"Have you opened it?"

"No. I was waiting for you."

Louise went over, grabbed it by the handle, and threw it onto the bed with a flourish.

"What are you looking for?" Judy said.

"I don't know. Something to help me make the case."

"What case?"

"That someone at the agency was trying to stop the Forrester investigation."

Louise unzipped the suitcase and flipped both sides open. The clothes were haphazardly packed into the suitcase, and Judy suddenly felt proprietary ownership of Dennis's clothes, as Louise ran her hands through the contents. She tossed his underwear, shirts, and socks onto the bed like she was playing in a pile of leaves.

"Shit," Louise said. "Didn't he have a notebook? I saw him writing notes down. Where is the damn thing?"

"Yes, he did have a notebook. Must be there somewhere, unless he took it with him."

"There was no notebook found with his clothing, according to the Las Vegas police report. And it wasn't in his hotel either."

Judy was irritated at Louise's brusqueness with his clothes, as if they demonstrated some intimacy between Louise and Dennis. She sat down and took a sip out of her clear, plastic cup that held the remains of a cheap white wine from the mini-bar.

"You want something to drink?" Judy said.

"No," Louise said, unzipping Dennis's toiletries bag. She looked up and saw Judy's wine. "Actually, yes. Is there a red wine in there?"

Judy got up, opened the mini-bar, and removed a small bottle of cabernet sauvignon. She unscrewed the tiny metal top with a twist and poured it in a clear plastic cup.

Louise walked over and took it. She held it up, and Judy reciprocated by holding her cup up, and they touched them together.

"Cheers," Judy said.

Louise took a sip, then returned to the contents of Dennis's suitcase.

"There's no notebook," she said. "Just this blank pad of lined paper." Louise took another sip with her left hand and with her right hand picked up the pad. She held the pad up to the light. "He wrote something but it's very light. I don't think they'd be able to pull anything off this. Shit. I bet they got into this room and cleaned it out. They had his room cardkey."

"Louise, who is 'they'? You're not filling me in. You said you had something interesting to share."

Louise sighed, drained the remaining wine in a single, impressive gulp, and walked around the bed and sat facing Judy.

Judy plopped down in the hotel desk chair, and they stared at each other from three feet apart.

"As you know, Dennis was tasked to evaluate the conclusions reached by operations regarding who kidnapped Dr. Forrester. I was the person who recommended Dennis for this effort. I thought we needed someone good, who would work fast, and was not beholden to anyone or group within Langley. *Ergo*: Dennis. For context's sake, operations was furious that the director wanted another set of eyes on their recommendation. They had everything teed up for a series of actions on Iranian operatives across the globe. Intelligence agencies do this silly tit-for-tat crap all the time. So, that's how it started. The only complication was that the director gave it to the director of operations, who is Simpson's boss, who in turn gave it to Simpson—remember he's the deputy director of operations. Simpson insisted that he be the lead contact for Dennis. For the record, I don't like Simpson; he doesn't like me."

Judy stirred in her chair. She was not particularly interested in the byzantine bureaucratic battles at the CIA, but she let Louise proceed, as long as this history lesson got around to Dennis and his problems.

"Simpson was pissed off from the get-go and wasn't happy with Dennis's focus on Forrester's agency patients, or her husband, or anyone in the U.S. He thought Dennis should have stayed in New Zealand. But as time ticked down—by the way, his report is now overdue—Simpson was furious that he didn't know what Dennis was doing. And to be honest, the director was getting pissed off too. And I was feeling exposed because nothing seemed to be happening on Dennis's investigation, and I was the one who recommended him."

"I don't mean to sound unsympathetic," Judy said, "but I'm one hundred percent focused on Dennis right now. He's in jail in Las Vegas on charges that could keep him locked up for the rest of his life. I don't care about Forrester, or Simpson, or New Zealand, or your problems with the director. I'm sorry, but that's where I stand right now. I'm flying back to Las Vegas tomorrow to see what I can do to help Dennis, or at least the Dennis that I once knew. This new Dennis is not the man I know."

"Got any more wine in there?" Louise said, pointing her chin at the mini-bar.

"Sure," Judy said, a little taken aback at Louise's change in topic.

Judy rustled around in the small refrigerator. "Malbec?"

"Fine."

Judy ripped the screw cap off and poured the small bottle into Louise's cup.

"When I saw Dennis in the hospital, I knew something was wrong," Louise said. "He didn't know who I was. I saw him struggling to place me, but he was just burnt toast. Nothing there."

"Yes, I know," Judy said quietly.

"And I recognized it right away," Louise said. "It's called C24. Or that's our name for it."

"What are you talking about?"

"It's a drug, a very powerful drug that's similar to gamma-hydroxy-butyric acid. But worse."

"The date-rape drug?" Judy said.

"Yeah."

"You call it C24? That sounds like a joke. I'm sorry, this is too much."

"Ever heard of WD-40? It's an oil in a spray can."

"I think so. Why?"

"It's called WD 40 because the guy that invented it kept running through a ton of different formulations. Formula number 40 is when he hit pay dirt. So, it was named WD-40, for water displacement formula number forty."

"You really are talking gibberish," Judy said. "And you're giving me a worse headache than before you arrived."

"Well, the researchers were looking at a host of different combinations of drugs to get what they wanted; at version twenty-four they got what they wanted. The 'C' stands for compliance and consciousness. So, C24 it is."

"You people are strange."

"Whatever. But the only thing you need to understand is that C24 is more powerful than the date-rape drug. We've used it sparingly in some sensitive operations where we needed to disable an individual and put them in a compromising situation. Depending on the dosage— remember, I'm not a doctor, but this is what the agency's medical team presented—the person under the influence has severe, but mostly temporary, amnesia. And they're compliant; very compliant. That's why the ops folks like it."

"What do you mean 'compliant'?"

"The person under the influence does pretty much what they're told. If the dosage is too high, they pass out; if it's too low, they aren't compliant. It has a long half-life too. So, when I saw Dennis, I just knew it. He was fried. But I needed proof, so I had his blood tested."

"Wait," Judy said standing up, "you had his blood tested where? And how?"

"I had one of our contractors go in and pull his blood."

"I'm sorry. You just ordered someone at the hospital to take Dennis's blood? Even I don't believe you can do that. Please, Louise, I'm not an idiot."

"No, I couldn't do that," Louise said, taking a big sip of wine. "We have contractors everywhere, especially in places like Las Vegas, Macao, Bangkok. Important people get crazy in places like that. It's handy to have contractors on hand. They're well paid. And remember, a contractor hasn't the faintest idea whether a mission was sanctioned by the president of the United States, or a disgruntled chief of station looking for revenge. That's the weak link."

"They pull blood?" Judy said, incredulous. "Come on, Louise. Please."

"No, it's true. Sorry if you don't believe it. I got in contact with one of our guys in Langley that runs the group in Vegas, and I told him what the problem was: can they get me someone to put on scrubs and walk into the hospital and pull blood from a patient under police observation. The answer was yes, of course they can. You'd be surprised what someone wearing scrubs can get away with walking around a hospital with a fake name tag."

"Jesus," Judy said, downing her wine. "I don't know whether to believe you."

"The blood was flown back to our lab here, they ran the test, and found C24."

"Are you serious?" Judy yelled.

"Hey. Calm down. I don't want hotel security running up here."

Judy walked around the room running the fingers of her right hand through her hair. "I can't believe it. I just can't believe people do things like that. But wait," she said, "why?"

"Why did someone bother to set him up like this?"

"I think the answer is obvious, Judy; someone or some group thought Dennis was close to nailing the Forrester case. This is just a theory now, but it's a good one. No one uses C24 except the agency. Well, that's not entirely true. We gave it to the Israelis, and they use it a lot. Our lab can test for it because it's not a publicly known drug. My guess is that Dennis was nabbed in Rosslyn, drugged, taken to Vegas on a private jet, and set up to look like a drugged-out guy getting laid and on a bender. This way his investigation is never completed, and he looks like a complete, unreliable fuck up."

"So do something about it! Tell the police, tell your boss. Just get Dennis out of jail!"

"Wait, Judy. Hang on. I told you, this is a theory. I was hoping that Dennis would have left some notes that would confirm he found who nabbed Forrester. I just need something else."

"What about the C24? Isn't that enough?"

"Well, it would help. But by itself, it might lead down a rabbit hole to yet another investigation about who had access to C24, whether the Israelis were involved, or whether they sold it to someone else."

"They would do that?"

"Yes, the Mossad's completely unprincipled, if that's even possible in this business. If I just had something else that tied Dennis's arrest in Las Vegas to the Forrester case, I could get them to stop this Iranian operation. And my reputation wouldn't end up in the shitter."

"I don't care how many Iranians you folks kill, and your reputation is the last thing on my mind, Louise. In fact, I find it disgraceful that you're concerned about your career while Dennis sits in that damn jail."

"Then help me find his notes, goddamnit! I need something more."

"Wait," Judy said. "He sent me something."

"He what?"

"Dennis asked me to look over a written summary of the investigation. I think he wrote it on the pad in his suitcase. I'm guessing someone took the page. But I have a copy."

"Well shit, Judy, let's see it. For chrissakes, why didn't you tell me? We've been sitting here all the fucking time, and you had his notes!"

"I'm sorry," she said fumbling for her business phone. "I should have thought of this earlier. My brain is upside down. He sent me a photo of the page, but we can make it work. Remember, I said these aren't his notes, this is a one-page summary of his notes."

"I don't care, just show me what you have."

Judy found the image and turned her phone sideways to make it more readable. The two women's heads were six inches apart as they squinted at the picture Dennis took of his summary page. Judy clumsily enlarged and then reduced the image size.

"Holy shit," Louise said. "Someone stole Forrester's notes on agency clients? Well, that's what I need. This is enough along with the C24.

Incredible. Can you send me this image?"

Judy fiddled with the phone and sent the image to Louise's burner. Louise never mentioned the last line of Dennis's note, and Judy let it pass. It read: "NB: What does Louise have to do with any of this???"

Louise looked at her watch: it was 11:50 p.m.

"I'm calling Simpson," she said. "He needs to see this."

Louise pulled her agency phone out of her purse; it was inside a metallic bag. "What's that for?" Judy asked, pointing to the bag.

"Black-out bag. Locks it down. No tracking, no incoming or outgoing. I've been very careful since I suspected someone in the agency is behind this. I don't want anyone to know where I am."

Louise dialed and waited.

"Hello, is this Daria? This is Louise Nordland. I know it's late but it's important I speak to Phil. Yes, I can wait."

Louise walked slowly around the room with her head down looking at the floor waiting for Simpson.

Judy was confused, but also elated. If Louise was being truthful, Dennis was innocent. There was no better outcome she could have wished for. But she also kept returning to the last sentence of his notes: what did Louise Nordland have to do with any of this? He was always suspicious of the diminutive woman—should Judy be careful of her as well? At this point, Louise was the only person in the world who could prove Dennis was not responsible for what happened in Las Vegas. Judy had not recorded their conversation, and the moment Louise walked out of the hotel room, she took the proof of Dennis's innocence with her.

"Phil, I know it's late, but I've just stumbled on something about the Forrester disappearance that you need to know. Someone broke into Forrester's house and stole her notes on her agency clients. And there's something else about Cunningham that you need to know about. I think there's someone inside who's responsible. I have no idea who, but I think we should call off the Iranian project ASAP. I can explain everything in person."

Louise listened, while she toyed with the earring on her open ear.

"Sure. It's late, but I can do it. You're not far. OK."

Louise hung up and looked at Judy.

"I'm going over to Simpson's house. He lives in McLean. It's not far, especially this time of night. He's going to shit a brick when he hears about the C24. What a clusterfuck. The only problem is that I have to see his wife, Daria. I can't believe he lets her answer his agency phone at night. Weird couple."

"Huh? His wife?" Judy said.

"Daria. She's this six-foot, gorgeous, blond Ukrainian. Probably thirty years younger than him. Wears her hair in a pulled-back bun. We call her Broom-Hilda. No one's ever seen her smile; not at last year's Christmas party at his house or any other function. We think she's a robot. He brought her back from an assignment in Ukraine like she was a toy or something."

"Louise, is there any chance you could write down a summary of what we just talked about? Just for my records?"

"Sorry, can't do that. You're not authorized to know any of this, and I'd be in a shitload of trouble if they knew I told you. But don't worry. We'll get Dennis out of there, I promise. I just need to get Simpson involved. And guess what? Dennis's report on Forrester's disappearance—delivered through me—will only be a couple of days late."

"Um, are you sure you can't just write down that C24 stuff for me?"

"No! I can't, Judy. But trust me. Dennis is safe now."

"Mmm," Judy said.

"I've got to pee," Louise said. She cupped her hand over her mouth and breathed. "Do you have any mints? I don't want Simpson to think I'm hammered."

"Yeah, you go pee, and I'll dig them out."

"Thanks." Louise went into the bathroom and shut the door; the bathroom fan came on automatically.

Judy reached for the hotel phone and dialed the front desk.

"Can you have my car brought up?" she said. "It's 76554 on the stub. Yes. Fast please."

The toilette flushed and Louise came out.

"Forget the mints, I just used a dab of your toothpaste. Hope you don't mind. And hey, can you call for my car? Here's the stub," she said, reaching into her front jeans pocket.

Judy called for Louise's car.

"We'll be in touch," Louise said. "Not to worry. We'll get Dennis out of there, and we'll nail Forrester's killer at the same time. We're finally getting somewhere."

Judy looked askance at her purse and her own valet stub and nonchalantly moved them together near the TV set. She walked Louise to the door.

"Good luck, Louise. Please call me first thing tomorrow? I hate to sound nervous, but I am. I need to get Dennis out."

"Not to worry." Louise bolted out the door, and Judy watched as she limped down the long hallway toward the elevators. Judy turned her head in the opposite direction and saw the emergency exit sign leading to the stairs. If she ran, she could get to her car and beat Louise out into the street. She had made up her mind to follow her. If Louise did not go to a private residence, and instead went somewhere else, Judy was going to do anything—including ramming her car—to force Louise to record details of Dennis's drug-induced set up in Las Vegas.

She rushed back in the room, grabbed her room key, parking stub, and purse, and flew out the door and toward the emergency exit stairwell. She bounded down several steps at a time, and almost tripped at one point. At the ground floor, she opened the heavy metal door that exited onto the side of the building. The door closed behind her, and she realized she didn't know where the entrance was, but the door was locked when she tried to get back in.

"Shit," she said and ran down an alley to what she hoped would be the entrance. Peering around the corner, she was relieved to see the well-lit covered entrance. Her car was being pulled up and she ran to the valet driver, showed her stub and jumped in. She didn't bother glancing into the lobby to see if Louise was there. If she was caught, so be it.

Judy drove down the exit ramp and stopped. In her rearview mirror, she could see a blue BMW being brought around to the entrance. Judy spotted several parking spaces that were marked for hotel staff. She pulled into an open spot and turned off her lights but left the car running.

In a flash, she saw the BMW race down the ramp with Louise behind the wheel. The BMW barely slowed as it entered the main street, then tore off to the right. Judy reversed, put her lights back on, and roared out onto the street and saw what she assumed was Louise's taillights moving quickly away. She accelerated as fast as the rental car could go, but the taillights were receding quickly. A traffic light turned red in front of her, but Judy roared through it chasing those tiny, receding taillights.

Then, just as quickly, she came up directly behind Louise's car at another light. It turned green and Louise was off again. She did her best to remember some of her AFP lessons on tailing a car: keep an eye out for a unique physical characteristic of the car lights, remain two cars behind at the closest, no sudden, obvious attempts to keep up. Drive past the car when it parks, if possible.

It was a struggle to keep up with Louise, but it was more challenging to remember to drive on the right-hand side of the street. At one point she slid momentarily across the dividing line into oncoming traffic. Finally, after twenty minutes on a busy road, Louise pulled into a neighborhood of large homes. Now, it was just the two of them on the street, and Judy stayed much farther behind; she could easily see

Louise's car in the distance.

Suddenly, there were brake lights on Louise's car, and then nothing. Judy kept driving past the BMW and saw Louise get out of her car and walk up the sidewalk to a large colonial-style brick house with an attached two-car garage. In her rearview mirror, she saw a tall woman open Simpson's door.

Must be Broom-Hilda, Judy thought.

She drove down the block, turned, and drove past the house now on the left. Lights were on downstairs shining through thick curtains. Judy continued down the street, turned around, and returned toward what she presumed was Simpson's house on the right. It was an upscale neighborhood with a wide street, and there were cars parked on the street. Judy parked two houses away from Louise's parked car and turned off the car.

What the hell should I do now? she thought. *Louise did what she said she was going to do. This must be Simpson's house.* She looked at her watch. It was after midnight. Judy yawned. She looked around the neighborhood. Many of the houses had lights on, though some were already dark. She crossed her arms and yawned again. She closed her eyes, opened them, and closed them again.

She opened her purse and pulled out her burner. She dialed and waited; it went to voicemail.

"Hey, Ruby, this is Judy. I know this is going to sound crazy, but Dennis is off the hook. We have proof. I'll call you when I'm heading back tomorrow to Vegas."

Judy hung up. She was giddy, nervous and exhausted. She closed her eyes again and realized she should get back to her hotel before she fell completely asleep. She felt hot inside the car and wound down the window. The soupy, warm summer air only made her groggier.

Her burner rang.

"Ruby here. What's this about Dennis getting off? Defense lawyers don't get these calls very often."

"The woman who retained you—Louise Nordland—she provided some extraordinary information today that will exonerate Dennis."

"Well, shit, tell me. What is it?"

"I can't. I think there are national security issues involved. But Louise swears she'll get Dennis out as soon as possible."

"To be honest, that doesn't excite me, Judy. I like facts and not promises. Do you believe this woman?"

"Yes. Mostly."

"Mmm. OK, well I'll have to wait for you to explain in person. You'd be glad to know I have some good news for you as well."

"Really?"

"Yes. It's Dennis. He's a different person. He's come out of that funk or crazy state of mind he was in. He's asking for you. He's allowed to make calls from jail; he made one to his daughter today. It's too late for a call now. But they'll let him call tomorrow morning early. When are you flying back?"

"There's an early morning flight if I can get on it. I'll text you. I can't wait to talk to him. Thanks for your help, John."

"I haven't done anything, Judy. Thank me when he's out. By the way, you sound exhausted."

"I am. But it's happy exhaustion."

"Get some rest. We'll see you tomorrow, I hope. Bye."

Judy hung up and sighed. She could see Louise's car parked about fifty yards ahead.

She closed her eyes.

Louise better come through on her promise, or I swear I'll crush that little woman, she thought.

The next sound she heard was the distant rumble of a garage door opening and a car starting up.

"Shit," Judy said under her breath.

Her watch showed it was 2:13 a.m. She saw Louise's car start up, and she saw a large black SUV backing out of the Simpson garage.

Maybe Simpson and Louise are going to headquarters in Langley, Judy thought.

The SUV stopped halfway down the driveway, and the driver got out; it was Simpson's wife. She walked over to the BMW's driver side window and said something, then stood up and scanned the neighborhood. The woman returned to the SUV and got in. The BMW pulled out slowly and the SUV backed out and followed behind.

Judy felt a frisson of alarm. This did not seem right. She started her car and followed the two cars. There were few vehicles on the road, and Judy made sure to hang farther back. She ran through one stop light and two stop signs in order to keep up.

After a series of turns, she found herself flying down a highway that appeared to be in a heavily forested area; tall black, leafy tree silhouettes bordered a grassy median. On her right, she could see down to a sparkling river in the distance and buildings on the opposite bank. Judy was so distracted by her surroundings that she didn't realize the two cars had pulled into a small, empty rest area. It was too late to stop, so she drove past them.

Nearly one hundred yards farther she pulled onto the shoulder and turned off the car. A taxi whooshed past her doing around sixty miles per hour.

She got out of the car and jogged back toward the two parked cars, staying off the highway shoulder and running deeper through the grassy area and between trees.

What the hell was Louise doing? she thought. *I don't trust that woman. Shit, what is going on?*

Judy stumbled over a tree root and fell flat on her face. She got to her feet and kept running, brushing grass and pieces of dirt off her face. Out of breath, she finally came to the deserted parking area with only the two cars next to each other. There was no sign of movement. The cars were turned off, and there were no interior lights on. Judy crept within fifty yards, hidden by shrubs and trees.

Nothing happened for several minutes. Judy moved closer. She was thirty yards away when the interior lights of the BMW came on as the driver-side door opened and a man got out.

The man went around and opened the passenger door. Judy tried to get closer for a better view but was obstructed by the branches of a bush. It looked like the man was carrying something, and then he closed the driver-side door and went around to the passenger side and went inside, closing the door. After several seconds, the interior lights went out, and there was nothing but the sounds of insects chirping, and the periodic whoosh of a lone car racing by.

The sudden flash of light and muffled explosion jolted Judy.

"What the—" she whispered to herself, pushing a branch aside to see the man get out of the passenger side and into the SUV that had started up. The SUV backed up, then drove by, briefly illuminating the area where Judy crouched behind a shrub. The SUV disappeared in a roar onto the highway.

Her palms were wet as she watched the SUV's taillights disappear. The insect kingdom slowly resumed its nightlife, and the scene took on a surreal quality as Judy walked toward the BMW. She whipped her head around for the return of the SUV, or any car for that matter.

Ten feet away she saw Louise sitting in the driver's seat, her head tilted to the side. She walked up to the windshield and strained to see what Louise was doing. Then she screamed. The top of Louise's head was torn open and blood dripped down her perfect skin and onto her silk blouse. A pistol had fallen into her lap. The light from a street lamp glinted off one of Louise's earrings.

She ran as fast as her legs would move back to the rental car. She started the car and pulled out into the dark, empty highway and drove, her mind whirring in a maelstrom of troubling thoughts. She drove and drove, following a sign that led to a much larger highway. She kept driving.

Simpson killed Louise; his wife helped.

Judy estimated that she fell asleep in her car around 12:30 a.m. Almost two hours had passed when she woke. What happened in that house for two hours?

The sight of the petite, aggressive, attractive Louise with the top of her head mangled was shocking. Judy was numb as she whisked down the huge American highway with only tractor trailers for companionship in the early morning. She was scared, tired, and lonely. Should she go back to her room at the Hyatt? Judy worried now that the forces that conspired to put Dennis in prison and kill Louise were poised to harm her.

Or was that just the terror of a traumatized, confused woman? If Simpson killed Louise, why would he want to kill Judy? Did Simpson and his wife coerce information from Louise that identified Judy as a co-conspirator? And there was the jaw-dropping fact that the only person capable of getting Dennis out of his predicament was now dead.

After a while, with the initial adrenaline rush over, fatigue began to drain Judy. She started to slow down and drift in her lane as if she was drunk. A street sign showed lodging available at a place called Gaithersburg. She took the exit and found a motel and checked in. The man at the front desk said almost nothing to Judy, except where to park and how to get to her room.

She drove around to the side of the motel, found her room, took a paranoid look around the parking lot, then ran into the room and locked herself in. The clock radio showed it was 4:11 a.m. She kicked off her shoes, slid out of her shirt and brown slacks, turned off her phone to save battery life, and jumped under the covers.

Judy assumed she would fall asleep immediately, but it didn't happen that way. She kept looking at the motel room door with the safety chain hooked up, expecting someone to break in. And she thought about Louise, with the top of her head torn open. And Dennis; poor, incarcerated Dennis, sitting in a jail cell without a clue to what happened.

CHAPTER 16

She bolted out of bed in a panic, stumbling because the bedsheet was twisted around her legs. Daylight streamed in around the curtains. A car had roared to life outside the door, waking her out of a deep, troubling sleep.

Judy sat on the end of her bed to gather herself. She unwrapped the small bar of soap in the bathroom and washed her face. She ran her fingers through her hair to tease some life into it, then put her clothes and shoes back on.

She pulled into a nearby McDonald's and bought a breakfast sandwich, an orange juice, and a large coffee. Judy remembered her phone was off, so she turned it on and noticed she had thirty-two percent of her battery life remaining. She figured that would be enough for her to get back to the hotel using Google maps. The daylight gave Judy some courage that had been missing in the early hours. She would return to her hotel regardless of her fear of being hunted.

Her phone rang.

"How you doing?" Ruby said.

"Not good."

"What's wrong?"

"I don't know where to start, or even if I want to start."

"Yesterday you were giddy."

"Louise is dead."

"Louise Nordland? The one who hired me?"

"Yes."

"Shit, what happened?"

"I'm not sure I want to go there yet," she said, taking a sip of coffee. "I'd still be talking an hour from now. I need to talk to Dennis. Will he be allowed to make a call today?"

"Uh, yeah, he would. But it's only 6:30 in the morning here. I can call a contact I have at the corrections center. A good guess is he'd be able to call around 10 a.m. our time; that's 1 p.m. for you. Would that work?"

"Yes. You said he was better now, right?"

"Yeah, he's a different guy. He really wants to talk to you."

"Then *please* have him call me today. I can't tell you how much I need to talk to him."

"You sound really stressed. You sure there's nothing I can do for you?"

"Just make sure he's on the phone at 1 p.m. my time."

"I can do that. If the time changes, I'll text you. Hang in there, OK? And remember, his calls will be collect calls."

"Just get him on the phone."

⊙

Judy valeted the rental car at the Hyatt, went to the front desk, and asked if she could get someone to accompany her to pick up and store some luggage for her. They sent a tall black man along and the two made small talk in the elevator. She was nervous about going into her room alone and concocted the ruse of needing help with a suitcase when she opened her door.

There was no one in her room. Nothing seemed to have been disturbed. The empty plastic wine glasses were still there, as were Dennis's clothes tossed all over the bed. Judy apologized to the bellhop for not having packed yet and threw most of Dennis's clothes haphazardly into his suitcase. She gave the bellhop a $10 tip and asked to have the suitcase stored.

After he left, she stared at Louise's plastic glass; it had a thin residue of red wine at the bottom. The image of the woman with her head wound was horrifying, and Judy sat down on the bed, in almost the same spot that Louise had sat the night before while explaining her suspicions for what happened to Dennis.

Now there was no Louise and no evidence that exonerated Dennis.

She connected her burner to the charger, then took a long hot shower, desperately scrubbing the foulness of the prior night's events from her body.

Afterwards, she grew increasingly worried, and attached the "do not disturb" sign on the outside of her door, relocked it from the inside, put a spare towel at the base of the door to prevent electronic eavesdropping cameras from seeing into the room, and also used a tissue to plug the inside of the door's peephole to prevent observation inside.

She dressed in a pair of jeans, a beige cotton blouse, and black flats. She took an unusually long time to apply makeup, not because she was concerned about her appearance, but because looking in the mirror allowed her to slowly review the events of the previous day and night. And with each bit of foundation, eyeliner, and a modest dab of pale lipstick, Judy grew angry.

For all the wild, confusing theories that rattled around in her head, she began to settle on a simple truth: Simpson had killed Louise at the very moment she provided proof that someone inside the agency was interfering with the Forrester investigation.

Simpson had to be involved.

But Louise didn't *know* Simpson was involved; she would never have gone to his residence that night if she felt in danger.

Judy did not need to understand the swirling dark forces at play. For her, the math was simple. She knew that Simpson killed Louise; Simpson's arrest for murdering Louise would lead to Dennis's release.

The difficult part, she knew, as she delicately tightened the small cap on her eyeliner container, was how to nail Simpson. Judy was the only witness to Louise's death; Louise and her conversations in the hotel room were not recorded, and there was no one except Judy to recount them. Even Louise's cell phone could not be linked to Simpson's house the prior night; she had it locked in a blackout bag.

If Simpson was as clever and diabolical as Judy now believed, he might concoct a scenario in which it looked like *Judy* killed Louise in that rest area.

She suddenly panicked. Had she imagined that Louise had been killed the prior night? Was she so exhausted after falling asleep in the car that she *dreamed* Louise was killed?

"My God," she said out loud. "Maybe Louise isn't dead after all!"

She called the front desk and asked for her car to be brought up. In the lobby, she put on her best clueless tourist impersonation and told the concierge that the prior day she had driven down a scenic drive that was near a river close by the hotel. After a couple of minutes of give and take ("did you see a military graveyard?" "did you see the Pentagon?" "did you see an airport?"), the concierge determined that Judy had been on the George Washington Parkway heading northwest toward Maryland. He used her phone to plug in a Google Maps address that would put her on the parkway.

Initially, she did not recognize any of her surroundings; the streets did not look right, nor did the strip malls she passed. Eventually, she found herself on the George Washington Parkway. This part was vaguely familiar. Off to her right, she could see through the landscaped scenery and the Potomac River below. There were buildings and church spires across the water.

Judy looked desperately for parking areas, but she saw only one that was nearly empty. There was no BMW parked there. Surely if a woman had been found with a gunshot to the head that morning, there would still be a police presence.

As she drove up the busy parkway she began to hyperventilate. Maybe she did dream the entire incident, and that thought disturbed her profoundly.

I'm going crazy! What has happened to me? Am I so caught up in Dennis's bizarre evening with the prostitute and drugs that I'm decompensating?

And in a flash, she drove past two US Park Police cars, a blue BMW with yellow tape around it, and three black SUVs. Judy put on her hazard lights and pulled over on the shoulder in almost the same spot she had the prior night. She could see nothing in her review mirror, so she got back on the highway and after several mistakes, managed to get off and then back on the parkway heading in the opposite direction.

She saw the police cars and the BMW from the other side of the parkway as she drove by.

"Damnit!" she yelled as she drove by, pounding the steering wheel.

⊙

Dennis mulled the scuffed black telephone handset. It felt heavy and old fashioned, but it was the only phone prisoners could use. It was already five minutes past 10 a.m. in Nevada, and Dennis struggled about calling Judy. What would he say to her? He was powerless to explain what happened to him. One moment he was walking in a Washington suburb, and the next thing he knew he was naked, covered in blood, and struggling with an EMT in a gravel parking lot in Las Vegas.

What could he possibly tell Judy that made any sense? He was charged with murdering a prostitute, but he could barely remember anything about the woman, nor how he got to Las Vegas in the first place. His brain felt strange, as if he'd had a seizure. The only good news—if that made any sense—was that his memory had returned.

He knew who Judy was. He remembered he was investigating the disappearance of Dr. Forrester. In one of his allowed calls from the jail, he phoned his daughter Beth, but she sobbed throughout the conversation, and he was so numb with shame, confusion, and depression that he hung up quickly.

What happened to me? Did I have a psychotic break?

He sighed, looked at the large wall clock, and dialed.

There was an announcement saying it was a collect call. The recording offered voice prompts to accept or decline the call.

"Dennis!" she yelled after accepting it.

"Hi."

"My god, it's good to hear your voice," she said.

Silence fell between them, like a two-foot thick sheet of plexiglass.

Judy finally spoke: "Dennis, how are you?"

"As fine as could be expected, given the circumstances."

"Ruby said your memory was returning. Is that true?"

"Yes, pretty much. Well, not all of it. But most of it."

"Do you remember the Forrester investigation?"

"Yes."

"And Louise Nordland?"

A pause. "Yes, I remember Louise."

"Do you remember going to Las Vegas?"

"No. I know that sounds outlandish, but I just can't remember. I've tried. I remember a casino, I think. And a woman talking to me, but that's about it."

"Do you remember the last person you saw in Rosslyn?"

Pause. "I think I saw Louise."

"No one else?"

"I don't remember."

"I have something to tell you about Louise that is disturbing. And I really need your help. I don't know what else to do."

"You mean more disturbing than what's happened here? Judy, I'm in jail charged with stabbing a prostitute to death."

"I'm sorry. That didn't sound right. I can tell you're very depressed. But try to stick with me. I need you to listen and help me because it will help *you*."

"Nothing will help me. Maybe a noose."

"Jesus, Dennis. Don't talk like that."

Silence.

"Dennis!"

"Yes, I'm here. Go ahead. I'm just tired."

"Louise is dead."

Pause. "I'm sorry, what did you say?"

"Louise Nordland is dead."

"Louise? What, what—"

"Here's the sordid little story. Let me get through it once before you ask questions."

"Louise is dead?"

"Dennis, please pay attention. Are you ready?"

"Yes."

And she told him about Louise's visit to her hotel room, her explanation for what happened to him including C24, the sharing of Dennis's investigation summary with her, the call and trip to Simpson's home, and the early morning shooting in the rest area.

"I don't believe it," Dennis said when she finished.

"What don't you believe?"

"All of it. Louise can't be dead."

"Jesus, you are in tough shape."

"And I don't believe there's anything called C24. Never heard of it."

"Why would you have heard of it?" she asked. "You weren't in operations. You were in the Inspector General's office. Why would you know about their methods and drugs?"

"I need to talk to Louise."

"For chrissakes, Dennis, she's dead. Don't you understand? She told me you were poisoned with that shit, and you didn't kill that woman. Someone wanted your investigation on Forrester to stop. And it stopped. You're in a Las Vegas jail, you're thoroughly discredited as a drug addict and murderer. And you never turned in your report. The only person who knows the truth is now dead. But I know one thing: Simpson killed Louise. I saw it. But Dennis—Dennis, are you there?"

"Yes."

"I don't know who to talk to. I could go to the police, and I'm tempted. But I don't know if my testimony is enough. There's probably no electronic evidence that Louise visited Simpson that night; her cell phone was in a blackout bag, so it wasn't pinging cell towers. There would be electronic evidence that *my phone* was in front of Simpson's house for several hours, and that it was also near where Louise's body was found. It would lead police to think *I* should be a suspect, not Simpson."

Silence.

"Are you there?"

"Yes. I'm just trying to process all of this. It's confusing."

"While you process that, remember that Louise had the results of your C24 blood test. I don't have the results, and you don't have them. Simpson may have already wiped that test clean from the lab. But I need proof of what Louise told me; *we* need proof because you'll end up in prison for a long time."

Judy could hear Dennis breathing into the mouthpiece.

"Dennis?"

"I'm here. I'm thinking. Is she really dead?"

"Yes! Dennis, Ruby said you only have a while to talk on the phone. Please help. What should I do? Who do I talk to?"

"I'm so angry I could kill someone."

"That's not helpful, Dennis. Concentrate. What should I do?"

She heard him swallow hard and could visualize his Adam's apple bounce.

"Alright," he said. "So, it's Simpson."

"Well, it's Simpson who killed Louise. I don't know who else is involved."

"One is enough," he said.

"Yes. What do I do, for god's sake? I'm scared. I don't know if they know Louise met with me. Maybe they'll come after me. I don't know."

"I'm not sure who at Langley could help you," he said slowly. "Louise would have been the perfect person."

"Can you think of anyone else? A friend you trust?"

"If we could get Simpson to admit it, and record it somehow, that would be evidence enough to get the ball rolling. Maybe I could pay Karl enough to help out."

"Who's Karl?"

"He's a contractor who does anything for money, even if it's a little crazy. He might do it. I just don't know how he'd get in front of Simpson. Karl's a rough looking guy, and he might not get past the front door. But it's worth a try for sure."

"What if I did it?" she said.

"Did what?"

"What if I went to Simpson's house and confronted him with what I saw that evening? I could tell him that I followed him to the parking area and saw the shooting. I mean, no one else could possibly know those exact details except me, Simpson, and his wife. Wouldn't he freak out and say something incriminating?"

"He might, Judy. But you'd be in danger. If he killed Louise, why would he stop there?"

"If I had a recording device, and Karl outside to protect me, then we'd have what we need. And we'd have it quickly. Simpson's the only person that can exonerate you."

"I don't like it. Better to send Karl in."

"No, I don't think so. I go in, Karl stays outside for backup. I have a feeling that I could really rattle Simpson. In fact, I'm dying to see his face. If we record it remotely, and I tell him we have him taped, then case closed. And you get out of jail *now*, not twenty years from now."

"Judy, I don't know. I don't like this plan. Karl could handle this."

"You don't have much say right now, Dennis. Give me Karl's number. I'll figure it out with him."

Dennis recited Karl's phone number. "I think that's it. Shit. Let me think. Did I get the number wrong?" He repeated the numbers slowly. "No, that's right."

Judy wrote it down.

"Are you sure?" she said.

"Yes. Hang on. There's another person you should contact. His name's Peter Harbaugh. I can't think of his number right now, but he lives on Wisconsin Avenue in Northwest Washington. Look him up online and call him. Maybe he'll go into Simpson's house with you, and Karl could remain outside. Harbaugh's an old-timer at the agency but very well connected."

"So, you're OK with me confronting Simpson directly?"

"No, not really. But nothing makes any sense. And Louise—dead. I don't understand. Whatever you say, I'm going to support, only because I don't have another plan. But you need someone in there with you. Don't you dare go in alone. Leave Karl outside, and go in with Peter. Beg him, if you have to."

"Our time's up," she said. "Are they going to cut your call off?"

"Yes, looks that way. Please be careful. Oh, jeez, I don't know, Judy. Let's talk some more about this plan tomorrow."

"No. You've always told me in the past that speed is critical in your investigations. Get the perpetrator when they're fresh and don't have time to scheme. You've said over and over that field people in intelligence are trained to lie and obfuscate in order to protect their identities. You called them professionally trained liars, and that the ones that go bad are hard to spot. But once you find them, get them before they concoct another, better lie."

"Did I say that?"

"Too many times. Now I'm going to put it in action."

"Judy, I—"

The connection was cut.

CHAPTER 17

Karl insisted on meeting Judy in person.

"I don't mean to be impolite or anything," he said to her, "but talkin' on the phone about this kind of stuff is unnerving, especially if I don't know who I'm talking to. I know Dennis Cunningham, but I don't know you. Sorry, but that's how these things work."

Judy recommended a Starbucks nearby.

"I ain't a Starbucks guy; never had one of their coffees in my life. There's a Dunkin Donuts in Crystal City. Can you get there?"

"Yes. What do you look like?"

"Look for a fat guy with a yellow pencil doing a crossword puzzle."

"Can we get together right away?"

"Like how 'right away'?"

"Maybe an hour and a half?"

"Jeez, lady. I guess so. Something happen to Cunningham?"

"Yes. I can fill you in."

"Uh, in case he didn't tell you, I work for money, not for patriotism. I can't tell who the real patriots are anymore. Those who pay are patriots to me."

"Do you need money right away?"

"Yeah, to get things going. But I don't know what you want. Let's chat first."

○

The call with Harbaugh was more restrained and difficult. While Judy found him gracious and polite, she had trouble getting him to commit to meet her.

"Dennis has talked a great deal about you, Judy. I'm so glad to make your acquaintance, even if it's only by telephone."

"He's spoken very highly of you, Peter. I think he's seen you as a mentor."

"Well, that's very kind of him. I like Dennis. He had a very unusual career in OIG. He took on some very difficult cases, and to be honest, I was hoping for his own peace of mind that he would stay retired. But he told me about being plucked out of Western Australia—if I have my geography correct—and tossed back into the muck. I hope he's doing well."

"Peter, he's not doing well. I'm afraid he's in very serious legal trouble right now. It's very complicated. He suggested I get hold of you to see if you would help."

"Ah, well, I'm an old man, Judy. I'm sure he's told you that I retired a long time ago. I've not heard of any trouble he's in. I assume he's had a run in with folks at Langley and needs some advice. Why don't you have him contact me directly?"

"That's difficult right now, Peter. Dennis is in jail."

"I beg your pardon?"

"Dennis is in jail."

"Good heavens. Why is he in jail? A military jail here? Did he take something that was classified?"

"No. He's in a jail in Las Vegas."

Silence. "What is he doing there?"

"Can we talk in person? Seems inappropriate to go over this on the phone. It would take a while."

"Judy, I have to say that I'm not sure how I can help Dennis. I don't have any contacts in Las Vegas. Does he need a lawyer? Perhaps I can call around."

"Is there any way we could talk today? Perhaps around 4:30 this afternoon?"

"Oh, I think that might be difficult. We have some plans this evening."

Judy decided on a more direct approach.

"Dennis said he could count on you, and he needs your help right now. Today. It's very important."

"I would like to help, but perhaps later this week we could catch up?"

"Today at 4:30 is the best time to catch up. Dennis needs your help *today*, not later this week. I'm sure you can meet me near your home in Washington. Where do you suggest?"

He sighed. "I suppose the Starbucks nearby. Dennis and I've met there many times. It's on Wisconsin Avenue, near the Naval Observatory."

"I'll see you there at 4:30. I'll be wearing denim jeans and a yellow blouse."

◉

At 4:50 p.m., Judy found herself pacing around the interior of the Starbucks. She once approached an elderly man sitting at a table and said, "Peter?"

The man simply shook his head and continued to read a newspaper.

A smartly dressed, elderly gentleman walked in and caught Judy's eye. He waved and pointed to the coffee counter, which Judy took to mean he was going to order a coffee. She sat down at a small table and waited.

"Judy," he said when he came over. "A pleasure to meet you finally." They shook hands.

He wore a pair of beige, double-pleated slacks, an open-necked, starched blue dress shirt and a navy-blue blazer with gold-colored buttons. Judy thought he looked elegant and refined. His face was tanned, narrow, and handsome. His nose pointed upwards slightly, drawing attention to his intense, hazel eyes. He sported a full head of dark gray hair, though it was receding at the temples.

She thanked him again for meeting her on short notice.

"Oh please," he said. "Not to worry. Anything for Dennis."

Without a lengthy preamble, Judy dove right in, starting with the impromptu visit by Director Kenny to Perth International Airport, the assignment to evaluate an earlier report on Forrester's disappearance, Dennis's visit to New Zealand, and his trip to the Washington area. She talked non-stop for what seemed to her like ten minutes but was thirty minutes when she looked at her watch. She had not got to the Las Vegas part, nor the conversation with Louise, or the bizarre events at Simpson's house and the highway rest area.

Harbaugh never asked a question; he just listened intently, sipping his coffee now and then.

"Does that make sense?" she asked. "Did you follow those parts so far?"

"Yes. Please continue."

Judy plowed in again, detailing Dennis's disappearance and re-emergence in a hospital, his confused state, and the murder of a prostitute.

"Oh my," was the only response that came from Harbaugh's lips after she described the charges against him.

Finally, she ran through the events with Louise that ended with what she suspected was a posed suicide.

Exhausted, Judy rested as if she had just finished the defense's closing arguments in a trial.

When Harbaugh said nothing, Judy said, "He told me to get hold of you and a man named Karl. We agreed that I would show up at Simpson's house unannounced, with Karl as backup out front, and with a remote eavesdropping device, recording what happens when Simpson is confronted. Dennis was hoping you could go with me into Simpson's house."

Harbaugh said nothing.

"He'll deny everything, of course, but I'll keep pressing until he realizes that I really witnessed the killing and will be turning the information over to the authorities. My job is to get him to lose his composure and say something incriminating. We'll have it recorded, and then I'll tell Simpson that Karl is outside calling the police."

"Mmm," Harbaugh said. "Does Dennis really think this is the best approach? I mean, what if Simpson simply denies it?"

"My job is to provoke him to say something incriminating. Obviously, Louise would have been the perfect person to go with me to Simpson's, but, well, that's not an option."

"I see," he said, rubbing his chin. "I think I could do that. But who is this man Karl? Can you trust him?"

"Dennis said he's about as good as we're going to get right now. It will cost some money, but I don't care. It's money well spent if it gets Dennis off the hook and some justice for Louise."

"I heard about Louise," he said. "Very sad."

Judy sat forward in her chair. "What did you hear?"

"That she was depressed after her divorce, had seen a therapist, or so I heard. She was very depressed and shot herself. Tragic for such a talented rising star in the agency."

"Well, you don't still believe that, do you? I just told you what happened to her."

"Yes, I heard that. Simpson. Mmm. But why would he do something like that? I'm not doubting what you saw, but why would he kill Louise? To what end?"

"To stop the Forrester investigation."

"But why would Louise go over to his house at night, alone, if she suspected him?"

"I'm sorry, Peter. I'm not making it clear. She *didn't* suspect him; she must have suspected someone else that she didn't mention, at least to me."

"I see. Well, it's a very dark stain on the agency if this happened. And there's Dennis's situation, which we need to fix ASAP. Poor man."

"Have you ever heard of C24?" she said.

"I can't answer that. I hope you understand. I'm bound by confidentiality agreements."

"Yes, I suppose."

Harbaugh leaned back in his chair and raised his eyes to the ceiling, thinking. Judy remained quiet and waited.

"You are sure it's Simpson who did this?" he said, lowering his eyes at her.

"Yes. And his wife."

"Well, then. If you'll permit me, I'd like to vet this man Karl. I've never heard of him, though that's not new. I've been out of the swamp for a while. Assuming he's a solid backup, I propose to get you a very interesting, state-of-the-art, wire to wear when you meet Simpson. It's tiny, and you don't have to do anything except wear it. When do you intend to do this intervention, so-to-speak, with Simpson?"

"Tomorrow night. I just need your help with one more item."

"And that would be—?"

"Verify that Simpson is in town and not on some venture overseas."

"I can certainly do that."

⊙

"You got any cigarettes?" Chili asked.

"Damnit, I told you I don't smoke, and they don't allow smoking in the cells anyway," Dennis said, pacing back and forth. "Chili, why don't you ask me something else, like do I have any gold bullion or Big Macs on me? Jeez."

"Jus' askin'."

"I know, but you *keep* asking. All day. The only time you don't ask is when you're asleep."

"I can't help it, man. I like to smoke. Calms me down. I git the jitters when I don't smoke."

Dennis shook his head and continued to pace the three steps to the front bars, then back again, over and over.

"I'm hungry," Chili said. "Why did you bring up them Big Macs? Why can't they give us Big Macs in here? They have to be such hard asses."

Dennis turned at the back wall, took a step and stopped.

"Shit," he said. "Hard ass. Oh crap."

"Don't get all pissed off now," Chili said. "I can't help if I got hungry."

"Jailer! Hey, jailer. I need to talk to my attorney," Dennis yelled.

"Shut up, you motherfucker," someone yelled from a nearby cell.

"You talk too much to yer lawyer, man," Chili said. "He didn't cut that whore, you did."

"Jailer!" Dennis yelled.

"Shut the hell up," someone else yelled.

⊙

Karl sat in the booth, staring at Judy across from him. The restaurant was busy during the lunch-time rush.

"Why did you have this guy Harbaugh check up on me?" he said.

"Dennis told me to contact Peter and get him involved," she said.

"I ain't crazy about this new plan, to be honest. But it's your money. You got it, right?"

"Yes," she said pushing an envelope over to him. "Cashier's checks. Three checks for $5,000 each. Just like you asked."

"Well, I thought I was only dealing with you. Now, this guy Harbaugh acts like he's calling the shots. What's the deal?"

"He'll be here in a few minutes. I like his plan. He'll go in with me, and you're outside. He's going to give me a wire of some sort, and you're going to have the remote recording device in your car, listening in. The moment you hear me say, 'Karl, let's get going,' you call the McLean police department, and then go to the front door and start knocking."

"It's not the McLean police; it's Fairfax County police."

"Call the FBI; I don't care. Just call the right folks."

"You trust this guy Harbaugh?"

"He asked me the same thing about you."

"Well, there you have it. Two suspicious people doing what they do best. It's a crappy business."

"Here comes Peter now," Judy said.

Harbaugh, dressed more casually in jeans and a blue polo shirt, dodged a waitress inside the bustling Applebee's Bar & Grill in Falls Church, Virginia.

"Hello, Judy," he said smiling broadly. He sat down on Judy's side of the booth. "And you're the famous Karl."

"Yeah, that's me."

Neither man shook hands, which Judy found odd. She was nervous enough about the entire venture and wanted the team to work well together, but this was not her realm and she deferred to the apparent testosterone at play.

Who cares if they don't like each other? she thought. *Just get the damn thing over with.*

Harbaugh brought a black briefcase and put it beside him on the booth seat.

"So, are we all set for this evening?" Harbaugh said. "Simpson's in town today and leaving the country tomorrow, so tonight's the night."

"You got the device?" Karl said.

"Yes. But before I unpack it, let's review. It's been a while since I've had to employ some street craft, and I find it kind of exciting. But preparation is always key, so can we review?"

They went over their parts, with Karl picking up Judy and Harbaugh at her hotel, driving to Simpson's and parking in front. Judy and Harbaugh would talk their way into seeing Simpson. Judy would wear a wire, and Karl would record outside, listening in. Assuming Judy and Harbaugh could provoke Simpson into incriminating himself, Karl would wait for the audible signal from Judy to "get going," he would contact Fairfax police with an emergency and go the front door and start knocking.

"What happens if this guy Simpson starts acting crazy?"

"You mean, gets violent?" Harbaugh said.

"Yeah. What are you two gonna do? If the front door is locked, how the hell do I get in?"

"I need a gun," Judy said. "Karl, can you get me a small handgun?"

"That might be helpful if you ask me," Karl said. "What kind of gun?"

"Something small, a .32 caliber. Any chance you could get a Beretta Tomcat? You familiar with that one?"

"I can look it up and get something like it."

"Is that necessary?" Harbaugh asked.

"I think so," Karl said. "Am I missing something, but aren't we thinking that Simpson already popped someone?"

"I'm taking a gun with me," Judy said. "Simple as that."

"Fine," Harbaugh said. "Now, let's get clear on how this wire works.

I'm told this is extremely reliable and good up to two hundred yards in distance. Farther than that and it won't broadcast a strong enough signal. You understand that?"

"Yes," Karl said. "I got it. If I'm parked outside, we're well within range."

Harbaugh took a glance around the restaurant, then opened his briefcase. He took out a plain brown cardboard box. He opened it slowly but did not remove the contents. With the lid up, he turned it to face Judy and Karl. Inside was a device with two meters on the front and several dials. A set of earbuds was placed on top inside a small plastic bag. Another plastic bag held a piece of jewelry.

Harbaugh opened the jewelry bag and pulled out a gold-colored, half-moon shaped pendant attached to a gold necklace.

"Judy, this is the wire. The necklace is the broadcast antenna. Please do not cover it with a scarf or any material. And this," he tapped the pendant, "is the microphone. Under no circumstances cover this with any fabric or let it, um, fall too low into your clothing, if you know what I mean."

"How does it turn on?" Judy asked.

"Karl turns it on remotely with this button here," he said pointing to a red button on the face of the device. "We'll make sure it's working before we head in. Karl will confirm that he can hear clearly, and then we'll knock on the door."

"So, once I get the signal, I have the cops on autodial and tell them there's a disturbance at the Simpson address. But what if he just lets you guys go and doesn't do anything crazy, even though he admits it. Why do we need the cops?"

"We need something official to happen," Harbaugh said. "We need a police event to make Simpson know we're for real. I've talked discretely to someone at Langley, and they will also be on notice if I haven't called him by a certain time."

"I hate to be Debbie downer here, folks, but what if Judy can't get this guy to incriminate himself?" Karl said.

"If on the outside chance the plan doesn't work, then we'll just leave by the front door," Harbaugh said. "End of plan."

"Don't count on it," Judy said. "I'll get the bastard going."

Harbaugh smiled, closed the lid of the box, and slid it to Karl. "Pick us up at eight o'clock tonight from Judy's hotel in Rosslyn," Harbaugh said. "This is fun."

"Mmm," Karl said.

⊙

Dennis called Ruby again. His secretary Phyllis accepted the collect call.

"He's not here, Mr. Cunningham," Phyllis said. "I gave him your other messages. He's in court. I'm sure they'll break soon. But he's really busy today."

"It's urgent," Dennis said. "Please, Phyllis. I need to talk to him."

"I'll tell him," she promised.

Dennis quickly dialed Judy. It was 4:15 p.m. in Washington, and he was desperate to reach her. She did not answer the collect call.

"Shit," he said.

⊙

She ran along the Potomac River in the late afternoon, past spartan Marine Corps runners, Capitol Hill interns and Pentagon workers. It was hot and humid, but she pushed herself to sweat out today's tension from her body. The perspiration ran in rivulets down her cheeks and onto her sleeveless runner's shirt.

She was out of shape, and the first mile was horrid; her knees hurt, her lungs ached, and she gulped air like a giant koi fish at the surface of a pond. The second mile was worse than the first, but the third mile felt better as the endorphins broke through to block the pain. On the return path, even the endorphins failed her, and she resorted to the runner's dreaded walk-run that signaled failure.

She walked the quarter mile from the running path to the Hyatt, dodging traffic and trying to cool down. The muscle pain and overheating helped mask Judy's nervousness about the evening's plan to ambush Simpson. On the one hand, it seemed simple and straightforward—drive up, put on a necklace, knock on the door, confront Simpson and his horrid wife, then leave him sputtering. On the other hand, it was audacious and dangerous: was Simpson capable of more violence, even though he knew he was being recorded?

In her hotel room, Judy left her door jammed open while she looked through her closet and bathroom, including under her bed. Her paranoia had increased dramatically since Louise's death. After checking the room, she locked the door behind her and took a long, cool shower. She toweled down and looked in the mirror. Her cheeks were still flushed red from the run, so she put on her underpants and threw on the hotel's terry cloth bathrobe.

She checked her phone and saw that there was an uncompleted collect call from Dennis.

She sat down and called Ruby. His phone went to voicemail.

"Hey John, this is Judy. Have you talked to Dennis today? Just curious. Looks like he tried to call me. Is everything OK there? Call me."

Judy fussed around the hotel room, watching a little TV news while her body cooled down. Outside she could see the shadows lengthening as the afternoon slid into dusk. She ordered room service and ate a salad and had a glass of chardonnay.

At 7 p.m. she got dressed and rehearsed how she intended to entice Simpson's wife into letting Peter and her see her husband. She was going to ask Peter to make up some intelligence emergency as a pretext. Inside, she was going to switch gears and ask about Louise's disappearance and accost him with the knowledge that she followed Louise to his house the night she died. Judy anticipated he would protest until she dropped the bombshell of what she saw in the early hours at the rest area on the GW Parkway.

She did one final check in the mirror, before leaving the hotel room at 7:40. In the lobby she sat in an overstuffed chair, tapping her fingers on the armrest nervously. At 7:50 her phone rang; the number was blocked.

"Hello?"

"Judy, this is Peter."

"Are you running late?"

"Actually, something has come up. My wife has had a heart attack, or we think she's had one. An ambulance is on its way over. They don't think I should drive her. I'm sorry."

"Oh, well that's pretty serious. It throws our plans out a little."

"Are you comfortable going through it by yourself? I feel so bad—" Judy heard Peter talking to a woman in a reassuring voice. "Sorry," he said. "She's nervous. I guess I am too."

Judy sighed heavily, less out of sympathy than out of exasperation. She had pumped herself up to confront Simpson, and now she was confused. *Delay or just go for it? What would Dennis do?*

"I feel bad for you, Peter. Good luck with your wife. I hope everything is fine."

"Do you intend to go ahead?"

"Yes. I have Karl with me. I'll get this thing over with."

"Are you sure?"

"Yes, I'm sure. The tension is driving me batty, and you said he's traveling tomorrow. I'm a nervous wreck and I think I'm going to explode. I need to save Dennis, and this is the only way out."

"Would you call me afterward, please?" he said. "Leave a voicemail if I don't answer."

"OK. Good luck."

"Good luck to you."

Just as she hung up, her phone rang again.

"Ruby, how are you?"

"Fine. What's up?"

"Have you talked to Dennis today?"

"No, I'm sorry I haven't. He called my office five times today. He thinks he's my only client. I have a trial today and an arraignment. If I get hold of him, I'll let you know."

"OK."

Judy hung up and walked outside. The blast of humid air instantly began to curl her hair and she self-consciously tried to flatten it with gentle pats. She felt funny worrying about her appearance at such a fraught moment, but it gave her something else to concentrate on instead of Simpson and Broom-Hilda.

Karl pulled up in a Cadillac CTS and Judy jumped in.

"Fancy car," she said snapping the seat belt into place.

"Where's Harbaugh?"

"He's not coming. His wife is sick. I told him I didn't want to postpone."

"I don't like this. It's not the plan. You can't change the plan at the last moment."

Maybe it was the heat, or her emotional tether being stretched a tad too far, but she said, "Goddamnit, Karl drive the fucking car."

He shook his head and pulled out.

"I don't like it," he mumbled.

"Do you have my gun?"

"Yeah. Not a Beretta. It's a Kel-Tec. Let's hope you don't have to use a gun tonight. Once you fire a gun, things get complicated. Reach under your seat."

Judy found the pistol and gingerly pulled it out. Its compact size

was perfect. She pulled out the magazine, slid it back in place, and toggled the safety off and on. She made sure the safety was on and cham-
bered a round.

"Thanks," she said.

"Thank me later. You sure you want to do this?"

She gave him a withering stare.

"Roger that," he said.

They drove in silence except for the radio; it played songs from the
1970s and 1980s.

When they pulled onto Simpson's street, the sun had set, though
there was still a pink glow on the western horizon.

"In the glovebox is the necklace," he said.

She opened the compartment, removed the small ziplock bag, and
pulled out the necklace, untangling the chain. She undid the clasp and
put it on. The pendant sat right below her neck, perfectly exposed. He
shot a quick glance at it.

"Perfect."

The only problem Judy had at this moment was that her palms were
soaking wet as if she had plunged them into a bathtub. She wiped them
off on her jeans. She swallowed hard at the memory of pulling up behind Louise in front of the same house.

Karl parked a half block before Simpson's house. He reached around
onto the floor of the backseat and pulled out the listening device. He
plugged the earbuds in, turned on a switch and fiddled with a knob.

"Say something."

"Testing one, two, fucking three."

"Um, OK. Let's do it."

He pulled out and drove to Simpson's house. The light was on over
their front door, and the first floor was lit up inside. Judy had not paid
attention to the neighborhood but now realized the homes were large
and very expensive.

"If this thing goes sideways, just yell for me, and I'll bust that god-damn door down," he said.

She took out her business cell phone and unlocked it.

"What are you doing?" he said.

"As a backup, I'm going to leave my voice recorder on while I'm in there."

"Are you sure you need that? Will it even work in your back pocket like that?"

"Doesn't matter; it'll make me feel better."

"Your call."

"Thanks, Karl. Everything is going to be fine. I have truth on my side if that means anything. Dennis says that's the only partner you need."

Judy leaned forward, pulled up her loose-hanging blouse at her back, and jammed the gun into the belt. She did not have a purse; instead, in her right front pocket, she had a rubber band around her plastic AFP photo identification and her W.A. driver's license. She pulled the blouse over the gun, got out, and walked steadily to the front door.

CHAPTER 18

Jesus, I've been trying to call you all day, Ruby! Where the hell have you been?"

"You're not my only client, Dennis, and you know that. It's been a long day. What can I do for you?"

"Call Judy and tell her not to go ahead with her plan. Tell her to stop."

"What plan?"

"Doesn't matter. Just tell her that."

"I talked to her a little while ago."

"You did? What did she say?"

"She said you tried to call her."

"Damnit Ruby, call her now."

"I tried a minute ago and it went to voicemail. I'll call again in a while."

"Tell her to nix the plan."

"Got it. Talk to you later."

⊙

She rang the doorbell three times before it opened.

A tall, blond woman with high, prominent cheekbones answered the door. Her blond hair was pulled severely into a bun at the back. Her brown eyes and dark, manicured eyebrows peered down at Judy.

"May I help you?" the woman said in a heavy accent.

"Yes, I'd like to see Mr. Simpson, please. It's very important. I'm afraid I need to talk to him in person."

The woman wore a dark purple, long-sleeved silk blouse, stressed by an ample bosom. Judy was struck by the woman's almost painful attractiveness, yet her facial expression was hard and cold. Judy thought she was the woman who got out of the SUV in the early morning and consulted with Simpson in the BMW.

Instead of pressing Judy for more information, she said, "Come in."

She closed the door behind Judy and pointed down a twenty-foot hallway adorned with several paintings, an umbrella stand, and an antique marble-top table with a lamp on it.

Judy walked down the carpeted hallway past a huge, granite kitchen on her left. The hallway led to a large formal living room, with a fireplace, a large sofa with a coffee table planted in front, and several formal, wingback chairs spaced about. Her palms were wet again, and she wiped them quickly on her thighs.

A man sat diagonally across the room to her left in a chair reading a book under a lamp; he looked up over his reading glasses. Judy estimated he was perhaps in his late-fifties, gray-flecked brown hair, a pointed nose and a square chin with a pronounced dimple in the middle of it. She could not identify him as the man who was in Louise's BMW that night since she was too far away to see clearly. But this was Simpson's house, and this was the house that Louise entered.

"Hello?" he said. "May I help you?"

Judy nervously fingered the pendant, then dropped it quickly.

"Phillip Simpson? Deputy chief of operations at Langley?" she said. He smiled.

"Well, that may be or not be. Who are you? What do you want? You don't appear to be selling Girl Scout cookies."

"I'm here to talk about Louise Nordland, Mr. Simpson. And Dennis Cunningham."

He laughed, which caught Judy off guard.

"Excuse me? Louise Nordland and Dennis Cunningham? Who are they?"

"How about Dr. Forrester? Does that name ring a bell?"

His mouth twisted in concentration.

"Dr. Forrester, you say?"

"Yes. A psychologist."

"Perhaps, perhaps not. What is it you want? Why are you here?"

"I'm trying to save Dennis's life, is the short of it. And get some justice for Louise."

He chuckled, which surprised her.

"What's your name?"

"Judy White."

"You're Australian."

"Yes."

"Australian and South African accents are easy to pick out. I have trouble with some New Zealand accents, though. They almost sound British."

Judy again fingered the pendent unconsciously.

"Dennis is in jail in Las Vegas right now. I'm sure you know that."

"Mmm," he said. "Why don't you sit down?" He pointed to the couch next to her.

"No, I think I'll stand." Judy was aware that his wife was out of view. She turned a little to see Daria standing to the far left, near another opening to the kitchen.

"Daria, can you get our guest Judy a glass of water?"

"I'm not thirsty."

"Well, then you could bring me a drink, please. Bourbon and water would be nice."

Daria disappeared into the kitchen.

"If we're going to talk, Ms. White, you'll need to sit down. It's not polite to stand. Please sit."

Judy debated briefly whether to comply and decided that her jittery legs could use a place to hide. She sat at the far end of a fabric-covered couch with the coffee table in front of her.

Daria returned silently to the room; for a woman who was easily six feet tall, she walked like a panther.

"Thank you, darling," he said. "Why don't you leave Ms. White and me here for a few minutes to discuss some things?"

Daria looked uncertainly at Simpson, then lowered her eyes and returned to the kitchen. Judy sat ten feet away from Simpson and tried to keep her bearings. The hallway to the front door was almost directly behind her, which she found comforting. And she liked the metallic warmth of the pistol digging into her back.

Simpson took a long sip and put the drink down on a coaster.

"Do you read much history?" he said.

"No. Sorry, I don't."

"I'm nearly through a history of the Vietnam War by Max Hastings. Excellent story of a sad, tragic war. For all sides, not just ours. Heavens, the north suffered horribly. It's difficult to know how the U.S. went off the rails so quickly and then stayed off the rails. Fascinating, really. But you know, we do that all the time, this great country. Off the rails with abandon and gusto, it seems."

"I'm here to talk about Dennis and Louise, not the Vietnam War."

"Yes, of course. You'd like to know what happened to them and why."

Judy stiffened. She hadn't asked the question in just that way, but indeed, that was why she was there.

"Daria?" he said, raising his empty glass. She entered from the far left again as silent as a cloud across the sky. "Another one please, darling." She flowed in, took his glass, and returned almost immediately with a fresh drink.

"Sit," he said to her. She sat in a leather armchair to his right.

"So, Ms. White. Do you want to know what happened to Cunningham? Is that correct?" The shift in his conversation—from apparent confusion and vague denials—to a friendly casualness unsettled her. She sat forward on the couch. Something was not right. She felt a drop of perspiration fall from her right armpit onto the inside of her blouse.

"Well, Cunningham got into trouble on his own. I tried to help him. I really did." He looked to Daria as if seeking reassurance. "But he just wouldn't give up on Forrester's patients." The two looked intensely at each other. Judy felt a strange sense of extraordinary intimacy between them.

"I'm confused," Judy said quickly. "What do you mean that you tried to help Dennis? What are you talking about?"

"I'm trying to explain how he ended up in a jail in Las Vegas. I mean that's why you're here, right?"

Judy said nothing. She had not mentioned Las Vegas to Simpson. They had not got that far. Another drop of perspiration fell on the inside of Judy's blouse, and she closed her right arm against her side to hide the expanding sweat stain.

"Your fellow there insisted on poking around in Washington. I told him he should be in New Zealand. But no, he insisted on fussing around with Dr. Forrester's agency patients here. And he confronted poor Mr. Forrester. That was uncalled for." He looked at Daria again, as if in confirmation.

Judy licked her dry lips.

The ambush was up. *Why waste time,* she thought. *I have Karl outside. Let's do this.*

"Can we quit fucking around here?" she said. "Why did you set Dennis up? Why was it so important for you and whoever else is involved to stop the Forrester investigation? Why?"

"Oh, such language!" Simpson said to Daria, chuckling. "Well, I thought that would be obvious. But I guess not. I mean, Louise got it right away when I explained it to her. But I can't expect you to have picked up on it. I mean, really. You're just a divorced, working mother with an unsavory, incarcerated, former husband and a washed-up OIG investigator as a boyfriend. Why would you know *anything*?"

Judy's mouth began to gum up; her saliva felt like overcooked oatmeal. She licked her bone-dry lips again.

"Since you asked, we'll let you in on it, should we Daria?"

Daria shrugged.

"Oh, I think she deserves that much." He turned and smiled at Judy.

Her heart roared in her chest, creating a loud thumping sound in her eardrums.

"You see, I started to see Dr. Forrester in therapy myself. I had to see someone. In the beginning, I was ashamed. It felt dirty. Why not see someone who could help sort it out? So, I found out that Dr. Forrester was on the approved list of therapists, and I started to see her. But I know how the agency works, and I wasn't about to let those gossipy fools know I was seeing her."

For the first time that evening he spoke with anger and resentment.

"They're always looking for weakness, you know. Constant appraisals, evaluations, 360 reviews. You name it. So, I simply went to see Forrester without telling the employee assistance program. You know, Ms. White, at most *honorable* companies, you don't even need to notify employee assistance or human resources that you're consulting with someone on the list. But at Langley, oh, they need to know everything.

Everything!"

"Why did you need to see Dr. Forrester, if you don't mind me asking?"

"Heavens no, I don't mind at all. The reason I went to see her was that I liked it too much. I suppose I felt it was wrong to like it. But of course, there's nothing wrong with liking it. Dr. Forrester tried to convince me otherwise, the stupid bitch."

"I'm sorry," Judy pressed. "What did you 'like' too much?"

"Making them suffer."

"Who?"

"The prisoners," he said.

"Prisoners where?"

"Abu Ghraib. Surely you heard of that place?"

"The prison outside of Baghdad, where the prisoners were tortured by the CIA?" she said.

"Yes, and get that dripping condescension out of your voice, young lady," he said sternly.

"Sorry, I didn't mean that. I was trying to understand, that's all."

"What's to understand? We were trained by psychologists to break those prisoners. So, we broke them. We had *orders* to break them! Is it my fault that I liked it? The waterboarding was messy but effective, I suppose. Too much gargling and slobbering for me, to be honest. The dogs were the best, though. We put the dogs on those men, and they were absolutely frightened out of their wits. Some of them actually soiled themselves just hearing the dogs. The blindfolds were a stroke of genius, though. First, we let the dogs go insane near a prisoner who could plainly see those apoplectic German Shepherds. Then we let the dog take a good bite. In the follow-up session, we blindfolded the prisoner and put them next to the dogs. Just hearing, but not knowing, whether the dogs were going to bite drove those men nuts. We learned a lot of important intelligence after the prisoners broke—and they *always* broke. Those psychologists who trained us were great patriots. Unsung heroes in the war on terror."

"You told Dr. Forrester that you *liked* torturing those prisoners?"

"It's not torture!" he barked. "That's propaganda from the media and left-wing nutjobs. It was enhanced *interrogation*—" he drew out all six syllables as if he was teaching English as a second language.

Judy could see Simpson's rising agitation; she noticed he had started to clench and unclench his fist.

"Did Dr. Forrester help?"

"Help? Hardly. She made me feel dirty. Like I was filth. Like I was sick."

"Did you stop going to see her?"

"Yes, of course. I had no choice but to stop."

"Why?"

"I think she grew a little frightened of me. And I know this is going to sound strange, Ms. White, but the more she was frightened of me, the more I *liked* her being frightened."

"What happened to her in New Zealand?" Judy said quickly; the more Simpson talked, the more agitated he became. Her instinct told her she needed to break up his monologue with questions.

"Oh, that. I had her killed. She would have turned me in, I'm sure of it. The bitch."

Judy kept both arms tight against her sides to cover the huge sweat stains spreading into her blouse.

"Did you do it yourself?"

"Do what myself?"

"Kill her?"

"God no! I just put out an order to a group we work with a lot. I kept it off the books. It's done all the time."

"What did they do to her?"

"You are a nosy one, aren't you? Well, if you must know, they were ordered to rough her up enough to get that damn safe combination in her office and alarm code to her house. For noncombatants, it's often enough to smash a finger or two in order to get what you want. The hand, you know, has three nerves: the median, ulnar, and radial nerves. Quite painful to crush a finger."

"What happened to her afterward?"

"Oh, they shot her. All gone. Poof. No more Dr. Forrester and her condescending judgment."

"Why did you have her body moved? Dennis said her body was moved to a beach after being buried somewhere else."

"I needed to get that stupid boyfriend of yours out of Washington and back to New Zealand. I thought he'd go back after they found her body was moved. I thought he'd be curious about that. But no! He stayed here and found out that someone stole her therapy notes. You know, it took a lot of work and planning to make it look like the Ghorbanis had kidnapped Forrester. They scraped enough skin cells off that woman to fill a jar, and then spread it all over the back of the Iranian's car."

Judy was petrified; she instinctively tried to keep Simpson engaged with questions that he seemed almost gleeful to answer.

"Do you think Dennis suspected you all along?"

"You know, I'm not sure. But why take chances? And that ambitious little twit Louise started poking her upturned nose into stuff. I think she had eyes on my job." He looked at Daria and they shared a smirk.

"How did you get Dennis to Las Vegas? Was it C24?"

"That Louise could never keep her little mouth shut. Yes, it was C24. We picked up Cunningham walking the streets of Rosslyn, for god's sake. Easy peasy. He never knew what hit him. That stuff is truly amazing."

"Who killed the prostitute?"

"Who cares? The team paid this idiot prostitute to check him into the hotel, get him as high as possible, then meet up off the Vegas strip somewhere nice and seedy. I gather Cunningham was a total wipeout at that point, and the contractors carved up the woman like a Thanksgiving turkey. They made sure your good friend Cunningham had his slimy little paws all over the knife, and they let him go. They said he removed his clothes on his own volition. Brilliant move. Loved it."

"Why Louise?"

"Well, she figured it out, or most of it, didn't she? She just didn't know it was me." He chuckled. "She was always a little too smart for her own britches."

"When Louise came here that night," Judy said, "you decided she knew too much and needed to be removed."

"Poor thing was depressed about her divorce. It was too much for her and she killed herself."

Judy's throat was parched.

"I saw you shoot her," Judy said, fingering the pendant again.

"Yes. We know that, don't we Daria?"

She nodded.

"Oh, and stop with that recording device thing on your neck. It's *not* a recording device."

Judy's fingers froze with the pendant between them.

"What are you talking about?"

"It's not a recording device, silly!" he laughed, and for the first time, Daria laughed out loud too.

"Karl, get moving. Now!" Judy said into the pendant.

Simpson and Daria looked at each other and smiled.

"Karl!" she yelled.

Daria stood and slithered into the kitchen with Simpson's glass.

"Karl works for me, Ms. White. At least now, he does. I'm sorry. I pay better than you. Did you know Peter Harbaugh and I are old friends? And like old friends, he was sympathetic to my problem. He filled me in on your plan. All I had to do was reach out to Karl and make a counteroffer; he was just as happy to go along with *my* plan. He's got your $15,000 and another $50,000 from me. He wasn't thrilled to turn on you, but he likes money. Though, to be honest, Daria and I think he's a little rough around the edges."

Judy tried to clear her throat, but it felt as dry as a ravine in the Gibson Desert.

"Why don't you look in that box on the table in front of you?" Simpson said, taking another sip of his drink. "Go ahead. Open it."

"I don't want to," she said. "I think I've seen enough today."

"Don't worry about there being something ghoulish in there; it's just a box of mementos. Really, you should see them."

She did not want to open the box, but she needed to keep the conversation going with Simpson because she was afraid of what would happen when he stopped talking. She had trouble believing that Karl and Harbaugh had turned on her, but then, this entire visit felt upside down.

Judy leaned forward and opened the expensive, hand-made wooden box. She was half expecting to see a severed finger, ear, or another body part; instead, there lay random items, including several different earrings, a magnetic hotel room key, a physical key, and some folded papers.

"See anything familiar?" he said, almost giddy with excitement.

Judy leaned closer and stabbed the items with her right forefinger, moving them around.

"No."

"How about one of the earrings?" he said.

She leaned in closer and noticed there were two different single earrings. She tried to appear engaged with the contents but kept an eye on Simpson on the far side of the room.

"Huh," she said, picking up a small earring. "Who's earring is that?"

"Excellent!" Simpson said. "Louise wore them the night she visited. I like to keep mementos."

Judy remembered Louise's earrings and felt a combination of disgust and cold fear as she fingered it.

"Why not look at those folded papers in the box?" he said, looking alternately at Daria and Judy as if he was showing a set of jewels.

She reached for the folded pieces of lined paper and opened them. There were at least five pages stapled together at the top left. Judy strained to read the writing, and quickly surmised that there were dates followed by phrases and half-sentences. Each new date was separate from the prior date with a hand-drawn horizontal line.

"Look at the last page," he said.

Judy flipped the pages to the end, and saw a date at the top followed by the scrawled words "DSM diagnosis," "sadistic tendency?" "violent?" "personality disorder?" "refer to Dr. Mattusch?"

She refolded the papers quickly and tossed them into the box and slammed it shut.

"I gather those are Forrester's notes she took on you. Looks like she was going to refer you out to someone who could help with your particular disorder."

"It's not a disorder!" he yelled, a tiny fleck of spittle flying out of his mouth.

Judy stood and shoved both hands into the front pockets of her jeans. "There are a lot of items in there, so you must have been a busy person. And I don't believe what you said about Karl and Harbaugh."

She reached behind her back and pulled out the gun. She flipped the safety off and pointed it at him. Daria came out of the kitchen with another drink at the same time and chuckled.

"The gun doesn't work, Ms. White. Do you think Karl was going to give you a working gun? Please! Go ahead, shoot me. I'm serious."

Judy took two steps toward Simpson.

"Don't make me do this," she said. "Karl will be here in a second."

"Good lord, you really don't believe me. Karl's outside to make sure you *don't* get away."

"I don't believe it."

"If you don't believe me," he said taking a sip, "then shoot a hole in the ceiling. Daria, darling, are we really almost out of this bourbon? Is it Pappy Van Winkle?"

She nodded and went back into the kitchen.

"We'll get some more tomorrow," he said, watching her move about the kitchen. "Put it on the grocery list, would you?"

Judy pointed the pistol at the ceiling and pulled the trigger, wincing as she prepared for the explosion. The trigger hinged backward, but nothing happened. She furiously toggled the safety off and on, then tried again. Nothing.

She backed up slowly.

"Karl said he fixed it so the trigger wouldn't work. I guess he really is good at this stuff. He's outside the front door, or maybe he's in the car," Simpson said. "I don't know. Either way, you're not going anywhere in a vertical position." He laughed. "I'm sorry. I only wish I had a German Shepherd to keep things exciting."

Judy inched backward, keeping the malfunctioned weapon pointed at Simpson in a reflexive but useless gesture. She stepped back toward the hallway behind her. If nothing else, she could throw the stupid gun at Simpson and run for the front door.

The edge of the couch rubbed the back of her legs, and she tried to skirt around it. Simpson looked amused and not the slightest bit alarmed. If she was confused about the apparent double-cross from Karl and Harbaugh, she was equally astonished by Simpson's nonchalance.

And then it happened with stunning viciousness.

Judy screamed, but her voice was muffled by the thick, clear plastic bag pulled over her head from behind. Daria had disappeared and reappeared behind, slamming the bag tight around Judy's neck and forcing her down onto the couch. In a panic, Judy dropped the gun.

Each giant breath Judy struggled to inhale was blocked by the plastic sucked into her mouth. Judy's eyes bulged as her fingers clawed at Daria's hands, but the woman was standing behind the couch with her forearms pressing Judy's shoulders down.

Judy squirmed furiously in a sitting position on the couch and kept pulling at Daria's hands.

Through the gauzy plastic, she could see Simpson moving toward the struggle. He sat in front of Judy on the coffee table and stooped forward. He grabbed Judy's wrists and held them down on her lap. She felt completely and utterly helpless, and it occurred to her that Louise had been disabled in the same way. They probably suffocated Louise until she passed out, then administered C24.

"Relax," she heard Simpson yell, through the amplified crinkling of the plastic. "Just relax, you poor woman."

She could see him smile through the plastic. His cruelty and audacity were enough to spark a final attempt to save herself.

Judy gave in to Daria's downward pressure by sliding lower into the couch. As a result, Daria was forced to lean forward over the back of the couch to press down and to keep the bag tight around Judy's neck.

Scrunched very low in the couch, Judy simultaneously pulled her legs up into her chest. With her back pressed hard against the couch, Judy slammed her feet into Simpson's chest and sent him flying backward off the coffee table onto the living room floor. With her hands now free, Judy reached up and grabbed both sides of Daria's long neck and sank even farther down into the couch. She managed to pull Daria forward into an awkward position so that her stomach was over Judy's head.

Judy barely had the strength to plant her legs down on the floor and, using her forehead in Daria's stomach as a fulcrum, she jerked the woman further forward. It took every bit of her runner's thighs and hamstring muscles to stand up while pulling Daria and flipping her completely over. Daria's back came down hard on the coffee table and onto Simpson, who had gained his footing.

Judy ripped the plastic off her head and careened over the back of the couch and onto the floor. She sprinted toward the front door but stumbled as she struggled for air. Scampering on all fours she grabbed the front door and yanked it open, sucking in huge gulps of air.

The warm summer air hit her at the same time she saw a startled Karl at the base of the front steps.

"Hey!" he said, reaching into his pocket. He pulled out a Glock and pointed it at her.

"Sorry," Karl shrugged.

Judy slammed the door shut and turned to look back in the living room. She was shocked to see Simpson kicking Daria, oblivious to Judy.

"You stupid bitch!" He leaned down and punched her twice, creating a sickening fleshy thud.

Judy fled to her left into the kitchen, quickly scanning for a weapon. But she heard banging at the front door and Karl's voice, and she kept running through the kitchen and into an unlit large family room beyond. She tripped over a small leather ottoman but bounced up in front of two large windows facing the dark street. She tried to open one of the windows but there appeared to be some anti-burglary device locking the double-hung windows in place. She could see the windows were triple glazed. It would take something heavy to break those windows, and she looked around the darkened room.

"Shit," she said under her breath. The ottoman looked too soft and round to break a thick window. She heard the front door open and Karl's voice.

"Look around the outside the house," Simpson said to Karl. "Check the windows. We'll search inside."

"Judy could make out a large, wall-mounted TV screen, several bookcases, a couch, and several large leather chairs. The room had two closets, and though it was the most obvious place to hide, she quickly opened one of the louvered, bi-fold doors and closed it behind her. She had no choice.

She tried to bury herself under what felt like a pile of blankets, but it was no use; there was only a single blanket.

Judy remembered her phone, pulled it out, and dialed 911.

"This is 911 Emergency Services," a woman said. "This call is being recorded."

"I'm being held against my will in a house in McLean, Virginia. My name is Judy White. Please send police."

"Judy, what address are you calling from?"

She gave Simpson's address.

"Can you give me a number to call back in case we get disconnected?"

Judy gave her the number.

"Judy, you are whispering. You said you're being held against your will?"

"Yes."

"Does the person have a weapon?"

"One of them does."

"How many people are holding you?"

"Three: two men and a woman."

"I'm sending police to that house. They'll be there within ten minutes. Please try to stay on the line."

"Don't let the police leave here without looking for me."

"Judy, I read you loud and clear. They will certainly search the house. Are you injured?"

"No."

"Is anyone injured?"

"Not yet."

Judy heard Simpson in the kitchen; he was furious.

"How could you let that woman get away?" Judy heard what she took to be a slap, then another one. And then what sounded like a loud thump, followed by something or someone hitting the kitchen floor.

"Get up, you bitch. Now go look in the family room; I'll look in the spare bedroom. Use this if you find her."

"I can't talk any more," Judy whispered into the phone. "I'm going to hang up."

"No, Judy! Do not hang up. Keep the line open. I won't speak unless you ask me to. Let me know when you hear police sirens by tapping with your fingernail on the phone two times, then wait and tap again. Do you understand?"

"Yes."

Judy saw the lights in the family room come on, their glare creating horizontal shafts of light through the louvers. She could barely make out Daria's soft steps as she traversed the room, looking behind the chairs. But it did not take long for Simpson's wife to search the only places left, the two closets.

Judy heard the closet bi-fold doors open on the other side of the room, and then close. Daria walked over in front of the closet Judy sat in. Judy could see the shadow outside through the louvers. Simpson had given Daria a weapon to use.

Judy's heart pounded as she waited. She decided not to launch herself at Daria. If she had a gun it would be over in seconds. Better to get captured and play for time, presumably they didn't know she called 911.

The bi-fold door opened. Judy looked up at Daria, who had taken several steps backward. The woman had a taser in her right hand. Judy raised her hands in a feeble attempt to surrender.

Daria had been crying; the mascara was smudged below each eye. She had a noticeable bruise and swelling on her left cheek. The two women stared at each other. Judy waited for the taser. Nothing happened. They stared at each other. Daria turned her head toward the kitchen as Simpson yelled, "Where the fuck is she?"

Daria slowly closed the door. Judy heard her feline feet walk out of the family room. She turned off the lights.

Judy didn't know if Daria intended to return with Simpson, or whether she was going to do absolutely nothing. It was clear, at least to Judy, that Daria had been beaten and perhaps sustained worse in that house over the years.

Finally, after several more minutes in the dark, Judy heard sirens and she tapped the phone twice.

"Judy, can you talk?"

"Yes."

"You hear sirens?"

"Yes."

"Where are you in the house?"

"In the family room. First floor. In a closet."

"We'll make sure they check the closet there. Just stay quiet and we'll get to you, OK?"

"Yes."

Judy could see flashing blue lights through the louvers.

"They're here," Judy said.

"Stay where you are."

"OK."

She heard the doorbell ring, followed by voices at the front door. Judy inched the door open and waited. After a minute, she opened it all the way and crawled out on all fours to the windows. There were two police vehicles. She saw several neighbors on their front steps looking at Simpson's house.

"I'm going to the front door," Judy whispered.

"I'll tell them you're coming," the dispatcher said.

"Too late. I'll be there in five seconds. Thanks for your help." Judy hung up, put the phone in her back pocket and bolted into the kitchen. She saw Daria's back as she stood facing the front door. She heard, but could not see, Simpson talking loudly.

Judy ran up behind Daria and shoved her aside, pushing herself past Simpson. He grabbed her arm.

"Judy, did you call 911 again? Oh heavens. I wish you wouldn't do that. I bet you stopped taking your medications, didn't you?"

There were two uniformed Fairfax County policemen standing side by side on the front step; one was older, tall and black, the other was white and short. The flashing blue lights created a strobe effect on everyone's faces.

"Sir," the black officer said to Simpson, "please don't touch that woman. Hands off please."

"She's capable of hurting someone," Simpson said. "You really don't know the whole story here. She came home after being released from the psychiatric hospital. She had a break. I know you're just trying to help, but we need to take her back to the hospital. I had no idea she was off her meds, did you, Daria?"

"No," she said.

"Sir, I'm going to ask you again to release her arm. We can talk all we want, but you cannot touch her or anyone else. Do you understand?"

Simpson refused to release her.

Judy turned to see that Karl had nonchalantly moved from the doorway to the street, where he chatted with another uniformed policeman.

"Officer, that man has a gun," Judy yelled.

The mention of a gun, as Judy predicted, changed the tenor of the meeting dramatically.

The two officers at the door turned quickly to look back at Karl, and the policeman next to Karl reached for his own handgun.

"I have a license to carry!" Karl said raising his hands.

The officer at the street spoke to Karl, turned him around, removed a pistol from Karl's pocket, and took several steps away from him.

"Put your hands on the hood of the car, please," the policeman told Karl.

"Sure," Karl said, smiling. "No problem."

The two policemen turned again to face Simpson, who still had a firm grip on Judy's forearm.

"Sir," the black policeman said to Simpson, "I'm going to ask you one more time to release that woman. We had a call that a woman was being held against her will. Until we clear up what's happening here, we need everyone to keep calm and refrain from any physical confrontation. Do you understand?"

Judy was frightened that Simpson was going to talk himself out of the situation, and she felt a rush of anger.

"He tried to suffocate me," Judy said as Simpson finally released her arm.

"Oh, Judy," he said with unctuous familiarity. "Each time you do this, you have to stay longer in the hospital. You must take your medication. Daria, dear, could you get Judy's meds please?"

"No ma'am," the black officer said. "You don't need to do that. Everyone should stay right here. Sir," he said looking at Simpson, "is there anyone else in the house?"

"No."

Turning to Judy, he said, "Are you the person that called 911 saying you were being held against your will?"

"Yes, I am. This man"—Judy decided to keep Daria out of it for the moment—"tried to kill me, and I hid and called 911. He's very dangerous. I'm an Australian police officer. I'll show you." Judy dug her right hand into her front pocket.

"Hey," the white police officer said. "Slow, please."

Judy pulled out the two items wrapped in the rubber band.

"Those are fake," Simpson said. "Judy, you need help. Please stop concocting these wild stories. Daria and I are exhausted. And you fellows. I want to save you a lot of embarrassment and trouble back at the station. I hate to pull rank here, but I'm the deputy director of operations for the Central Intelligence Agency. This neighborhood, as you know, has many important people residing here. Senator Johnson from Kansas lives across the street. Yes, that's him at the front door watching us. Congressman Salucci from Delaware lives behind us, and the list goes on. We have a sad family situation here. Mental illness is hard to comprehend at times, and I'm sure you've seen plenty of it. But you'd better check with the station before you do something that will get you and your chief in serious trouble. *The Washington Post* loves stories like this—police mistakes leading to lawsuits and ruined careers. Think of it, men. Just call the station. Talk with Colonel Francis. He's a friend of mine."

Judy was stunned at how manipulative and commanding Simpson was; did he really know the Fairfax County chief of police?!

"Please, Judy," Simpson said, again taking Judy's forearm. "Come inside and take your meds. Thank you, officers."

There was a surreal moment of silence as Simpson's bluff appeared to freeze everyone in their tracks.

"Why don't you take me to the station?" Judy asked the black officer. "It would be safer for everyone."

Simpson tugged Judy and she resisted.

"Sir, I've asked you repeatedly to stop grabbing this woman," the black officer said. "We can talk here without resorting to touching people. I will call back to the station, but this woman will sit in our squad car until I can get some guidance. Please wait here. Jim, stay here," he said to his partner.

Judy turned to follow the officer to the car, but Simpson said, "I can't let her do that. She's escaped from the hospital three times, and if you take her down to the station I guarantee she'll figure out how to get away."

With her free hand, Judy ripped Simpson's hand off her.

"Oh," Judy said digging her hand into the left front pocket, "I have Louise's earring right here. You should have paid more attention." She pulled the delicate piece of jewelry out and held it between her thumb and forefinger.

The two officers looked confused and leaned in to look at what she held. They were unprepared for Simpson, who grabbed Judy's closed hand with his two hands and started to pry it open.

"That's private property! You little goddamned thief!"

"Hey," the black officer said grabbing Simpson around the shoulders. "Hold on there."

Simpson shoved the officer away and again tried to pry her fingers apart.

Judy furiously held on, as Simpson pried a finger free.

"You filthy, sick bastard," she yelled. "Sicko!"

"I'm not sick," he yelled, as the scrum of four grappled on the front steps. Simpson kept trying to pry Judy's hand open, while both police officers tried to restrain Simpson. Daria watched dispassionately from inside the hallway.

"Sicko!" Judy kept yelling. "Sick, pathetic bastard."

Suddenly, Simpson slammed an elbow into the black officer's chin, stunning him. The white officer tried to shove Simpson back into his hallway.

"Weak, pathetic sicko!" Judy yelled into Simpson's face.

He reared back with his right arm, and even though the black officer had recovered enough to grab Simpson's chest, the deputy director of operations threw a devastating right cross and hit Judy square on the chin.

And just like in a cartoon, she saw a rainbow of yellow stars silhouetted against a jet-black galaxy.

She woke in the back of an ambulance, its red lights reflecting through the front windshield.

"Where am I?" she said to the EMT on her left.

"Ma'am, you're in an ambulance being taken to a hospital. This is just a precaution. You were knocked unconscious. Everything is going to be fine."

"My head hurts."

"I bet it does," he said. "Just relax. You probably have a concussion."

"Hey!" she yelled, looking at her empty left hand, "the earring! What happened to the earring? I had it in my hand."

"We found it," came a voice from the other side. "Judy turned to see the face of the white police officer who was at the front door. "Took us a while, but we found it. We have it. Take it easy. You've been through a lot."

"What about the man? Simpson?"

"At this particular moment he's being booked on an assault charge," the officer said.

"Are they going to release him on bond?"

"Well, given his government position, and no apparent prior record, I'm sure they will."

"No! Don't release him. He'll hide the evidence! Take me back there now. It's important!"

She saw the men look at each other from their opposite benches.

"Ma'am," the EMT said, "Please try to calm down."

"We need the box! Please, let's go back for the box."

"What's the big deal about that box?" the policeman said. "Strange, but that guy's wife came out when her husband was being taken away, and she gave Sgt. Thompson a wood box."

"She did?" Judy said, turning her head.

"Yeah. The sergeant didn't know what to do with it, but the woman said we will need it. So, he asked her again whether she was giving it to him of her free will. She said yes."

"Oh, my god," Judy said, leaning back onto the stretcher. "I can't believe it."

"Ma'am," the policeman said, "did you happen to see how that woman got the bruise on her face? Sergeant asked whether she had been beaten, but she denied it."

"He hit her."

"You sure about that?"

"Yeah, I'll testify, if it gets that far."

"Oh, it'll get far, believe me. That guy is easily up on assault and re-sisting arrest."

"Don't count on it, officer. It's a different world over there."

"Where's 'there'?" he said.

"Langley. The land of make believe."

⊙

Seven weeks later

Dennis stared down at the little dimpled ball as it sat nestled on a thin wood tee. After a second's delay, he swung viciously, smacking the ball high into the air and down the fairway.

"Hell of a drive there, Dennis," Joe Parsons said leaning on his golf club.

"How can you just disappear for a couple of months, come back slimmer and a much better golfer?" said Fergus McMaster, climbing into his golf cart.

"I was able to clear my head," Dennis said walking around the back of the cart and pushing his golf club into his bag. "Like, completely clear my head."

"Was it a yoga retreat? Something like that? Here in Australia?" Norman Cower said.

"No. Las Vegas."

The three men laughed.

"You didn't say that!" Parson's said. "Was Judy there too?"

"Oh yeah. Wouldn't dare go to sin city without her along for the ride."

"Well, congrats again on the engagement," Cower said. "You and Judy make a bonza couple."

"Thanks," Dennis said. "I couldn't imagine being without that woman. She is one tough, extraordinary cookie."

"If you don't mind me saying, mate, she's one very attractive cookie," Cower said.

"That too," Dennis said. "Every man needs a Judy."

⊙

She sat at the bar with both hands curled around the wine-glass stem and stared at Dennis.

"How was golf today?"

"Better than golf the day before," he laughed.

"Are you sure you don't mind a small ceremony?" she said.

"I could care less if was in St. Peter's Basilica. I just want whatever you want."

"You're so compliant."

"Well, when you get to spend some time with Chili in the Clark County House of Detention, your world view changes."

"If it means anything, you seem like a different person."

"I am a different person. I've come to the realization that my world was upside down. The people I believed in—like Peter Harbaugh—were bums. And people I distrusted—like Louise—were on the up and up."

"I feel bad for what happened to her," Judy said, taking a sip of wine. "What an awful way to go."

"She was something else," he said. "The agency is much worse off not having her around."

"Can I ask you something?"

"Sure."

"Did you have a thing for Louise? She was quite pretty."

"Did I have a thing for Louise?" he repeated. "Mmm. Well, I admit that I decided late in the game that I liked her if that's what you mean."

"No, did you have a *thing* for Louise?"

"By 'thing,' do you mean was I attracted to her?"

"Yes. That kind of 'thing.'"

"I'll admit to being a little attracted to her, but she was not my type. You're my type. Why do you ask about Louise? What's she got to do with us?"

"I don't know. Sometimes I got the feeling that you had a thing for her."

"You're not allowed to drink any more wine until you stop with this nonsense," he laughed, pushing her glass away.

"Do you think you'll be bored with me?" she said.

"Yipes! What happened to you? What did I say to bring this on?"

"I just wonder sometimes whether you'll be satisfied in Perth. And with me."

He swiveled to look at her.

"Judy, please stop this." He leaned over and kissed her gently on the lips.

"I suppose I'm just insecure," she said.

"I'm sorry, but a woman who walked alone into Simpson's house and came out in one piece is not insecure. I feel sick when I think of him and that woman trying to suffocate you. And to think that I wasn't able to warn you about Harbaugh. God. As soon as Chili said the words 'hard-ass' in that damn jail cell, I remembered that's how Harbaugh described his good friend Simpson."

"But in the end, it worked out, didn't it?" Judy said. "If I had suspected Harbaugh tipped Simpson off, I wouldn't have gone through with it. And if I hadn't gone through with it, we wouldn't have the garbled confession recorded on my phone. And we wouldn't have the box of ghastly souvenirs he kept, thanks to a tormented Broom-Hilda. And you might still be in jail with your friend Chili."

"Ah yes, Chili. I kinda miss the old guy."

"You do?"

"Yeah. He had only two things on his mind: cigarettes and Big Macs. Can you imagine that? Just two things. What a perfectly simple and unified theory to life, cigarettes and Big Macs."

"You'll never be a simple man," she said, taking a sip of wine. "But I like that about you. Simple is boring. You'll never be boring. Ever."

"Is that a good thing or a bad thing?"

"A bloody good thing."

ACKNOWLEDGMENTS

While *writing* is a solitary task, *publishing* requires cooperation. This novel would not have been completed without the aid of several individuals, foremost my wife Denise. Her reading of earlier drafts was instrumental in identifying inconsistencies and plotting issues. As a licensed psychologist, Denise and my sister Kolleen Martin—also a licensed psychologist—provided background on HIPPA rules regarding patient notes, as well as other aspects of clinical outpatient and inpatient treatment. Lynne Gaines continues to be a strong proofreader and did an excellent job whipping the manuscript into *Chicago Manual of Style* shape. She pointed out, rightly so, that I have a "semi-colon problem," and I have started treatment for this malady. Lastly, I'd like to thank retired Detective Phil Ramos of the Las Vegas Metropolitan Police Department. Ramos, a 33-year veteran of the LVMPD, was extremely helpful in detailing homicide investigatory procedures and other law enforcement practices in that unusual city in the desert.

MORE FROM KEITH YOCUM

Color of Blood

(BOOK 1 OF THE DENNIS CUNNINGHAM SERIES)

Dennis is glad to be back at work. His wife's death left him devastated but he'll do anything to lose himself into work at the Inspector General's office of the CIA. A brilliant, if prickly investigator, he's spent his career chasing down the Agency's thieves and liars. When his boss forces him to take a low-level assignment to investigate a missing employee in Australia, he soon finds that even in the red dust of the Outback, there is romance – and death – just a sweltering heartbeat away.

A Dark Place

(BOOK 2 OF THE DENNIS CUNNINGHAM SERIES)

An old case spills new blood. Dennis loves policing the CIA's network of spies for liars and thieves. But each time he plows into a case, it's harder for him to keep alive his relationship with Judy, an Aussie cop and the only woman who understands his passions and quirks. When Dennis and Judy meet in London to rekindle their relationship, they are sucked into the city's dark underworld. To save Judy's life Dennis must solve two cases simultaneously. If you like non-stop action, dark humor and complicated heroes, then you'll love *A Dark Place*.

Daniel

STRANGE THINGS HAPPEN IN WAR –
BUT THEN VIETNAM WAS ALWAYS DIFFERENT

In January 1972, during the waning days of that sad war, a lone soldier crawled through the barbed wire and entered an isolated American firebase. He said his name was Daniel Carson, but a quick check found that a soldier with the same name and physical description was already buried at Arlington National Cemetery. Who was this new soldier named Daniel? Was he a crazy man, a common deserter or something else entirely? And why did he have such a profound effect on the unlucky company of grunts trying to survive the last days of the war? As a fierce regiment of North Vietnamese regulars prepares to destroy the forgotten hilltop firebase, the odd little soldier named Daniel seems to have all the answers to their survival. Several years after the war, three survivors of the firebase meet in Washington, D.C. and, almost by accident, discover the shocking truth about Daniel.

Titus

IN THE MIDST OF CARNAGE IN THE CIVIL WAR,
IS THERE A SERIAL MURDERER AT WORK?

A Union soldier is found dead on the outskirts of camp, his neck sliced open from ear to ear. But when more soldiers are found with their throats slit, an uneasy mood falls over the Union regiment.

Who is killing these soldiers, and what does the strange mark on the dead men's foreheads mean? A young Union lieutenant and an eccentric field surgeon are ordered to get to the bottom of the killings. Can the two officers unmask the killer and motive before the fog of battle hides his identity forever?

KEITH YOCUM is a novelist living on Cape Cod. His career has oriented around publications and digital businesses. He has worked for *The Boston Globe* and *The New England Journal of Medicine*. He was also the founder of *NewsWest*, a chain of local newspapers in the Boston area that was sold to a competitor in the late 1980s. He is the author of five novels and welcomes feedback at www.keithyocum.com.

CPSIA information can be obtained
at www.ICGtesting.com
Printed in the USA
BVHW031836070521
606800BV00012B/60

9 780997 870831